KALLY HALLETT

Should I be Worried?

To those of us who don't believe people or actions or choices or relationships are either simply black, or white. To everyone who sees a multitude of shades in between. May we always try to see life from more than one point of view. Always fly above to gain a new perspective.

Acknowledgement

Writing a book has always been a goal I thought I'd never accomplish, and now I find myself itching with ideas for the next one... and the next one after that!

I owe this tingling of eagerness and excitement to everyone who has supported me along this journey, starting with my mom. You may not know my mother, but she is *very* opinionated, making her my toughest critic. The thing about people who will tell you when they're unimpressed is, when they *are* impressed, you really believe their praise and feel entirely confident in what you've accomplished. Thank you, mom, for convincing me my work had potential, and for listening as I read my chapters aloud and we enthusiastically raved about the characters and future ideas. You lit the flames beneath my fire.

Then there are the people who fueled that fire up to the clouds: my readers.

Bella, you were the first person to read my story all the way through from beginning to end, and the first person to make me cry... in the best way! I didn't know exactly what to expect from my beta team, but the few expectations I *did* conjure up in my head, you completely shattered. You were beyond helpful, professional, organized, and, most of all, supportive. The giddiness in the notes of your favorite chapters will forever bring a smile to my face.

Kyra, we learned so much together on this journey! You

showed me how vital it is to slow down and take the time to pour our entire hearts into editing. At first I dreaded the process, but you taught me heaps about what an opportunity for growth it can really be. From medical slang to punctuation to the proper way to write SpaghettiOs, we discovered more than we anticipated, and I cannot thank you enough for taking my hand and growing alongside me.

Cathy, you are so accomplished in your career, and yet you selflessly gave me huge amounts of your time and dedication. Thank you. Your advice helped me shape the story into what it needed to be, and your "hype girl" mentality was the cherry on top!

Amber, the speed at which you devoured the story convinced me that some people really do love these characters as much as I do. Your sharp editing eye saved me, and I hope many more authors are smart enough to utilize you for their future books.

Kenny, the book trailer was one of the ultimate highlights of this experience. You brought this book to a whole new level. You're professional and hard-working, and I looked forward to the times we would discuss any details during the filming process. The final result is absolutely incredible, and I still get goosebumps every time I watch it... and it's not just me! From friends and family to online viewers, no one seems to be able to get over just how chilling your work is.

Kelsey, I don't know how you do it. Your art always completely blows my mind, even when you just make a quick doodle in a notebook. Thank you for seeing my vision, and then making it ten times better! I don't care what people say, they *do* judge books by their covers, and you made this one fantastic.

I've been looking forward to this since before I even started writing: I want to thank our TikTok community! Social media has been one of the most fun and rewarding aspects of this experience. You've all been on this journey with me, through every twist and turn and fork in the road. When I didn't know which direction to turn, you all engaged with me and commented and shared your thoughts and opinions and pointed the way for me. You made me feel relatable and interesting and like I wasn't alone. Because I wasn't. So thank you for being my guiding lights, my book recommenders, my idea generators, my cheerleaders, and, above all, my friends.

And finally, Will. Fine, you called it: you're last and have the sappiest message out of everyone. Happy? In all seriousness, of course you do. You've been my number one fan since this story was just a series of excited, flurried ideas which I hurled at you faster than you could catch them. I love that you've always believed in this book, but even more than that, you've always believed in *me*. We've discussed many times how authors write what they know, and all the best parts of these characters were drawn from you. Whenever they bare their flaws - and I know they're *very* flawed, I had to rely on the past, or pull from my imagination. But when these characters love hard, when they show compassion, when they are being the very best versions of themselves... that's all you. Thank you for being the most beautiful muse. I love you.

1

Alyssa

Alyssa Hart chewed on the end of her pen. It was a bad habit, she knew, but one she could never seem to control when her nerves were taking over - and her nerves were at an all time high today.

She sat anxiously in the examination room. She'd figured the room would be at full capacity, but of the twenty-six tables and two hundred eight chairs, only seventy-four seats were filled. She thought back to her first day of classes.

"Look to your left," her professor had stated seriously. "Now to your right."

Everyone's heads had swiveled, excited new med students eager to follow instructions.

"Did you get a good look at your peers?" Confused nods. "Good. You may as well notice them now, because, statistically, at least one of those two will be gone by the end of this journey. And if you really want this, you're gonna have to work hard every moment of every day from here on out to make sure that person isn't you."

Alyssa's eyes darted around the room, as she realized just how right he had been. Makaelyn Crane, the "girl to her left," left the program two years ago after miscalculating an IV percentage, causing her patient to overdose. Austin Broker, the "boy to her right," had quit just last month because he was assigned to the ER the day after a massive train crash and couldn't stop having nightmares ever since.

As much as she felt for her peers, she stood apart from them because she didn't let the negative consume her. She loved working, sort of in the same way a soldier "loves" war: It was brutal, with endless hours and psychological strain. She was always tired, and never smelled quite the way she would have liked. She saw terrible things. She had immense pride in what she did. She knew her position was important, and she knew she was making a difference. Her duty brought her purpose - a purpose she didn't think she could live without.

And then of course, there was the adrenaline, that rush she received that she never quite knew if it was good, if it was healthy, but she never let herself slow down enough to find out.

Here, in this examination room, she'd reached her final step to becoming a surgeon. To be able to do this work that she loved, that she needed, every day. As soon as the professor called "time," she would begin taking the last test of the United States Medical Licensing Exam. The USMLE. The residents always mocked the name, since no one ever "smiled" while taking it.

She took another quick glance around, reminding herself that her peers looked nervous, too. After all, their futures were dependent upon this exam. They'd been working towards this moment for nearly thirteen years, and this was the last obstacle before freedom... If you could call being on call twenty-four/seven and working thirty hour shifts "freedom."

However, unlike the other students, this examination was

not the event that was making Alyssa nervous today. She was possibly the most gifted intern in her residency. Everyone knew this, including Alyssa. She wasn't conceited, but she *was* confident. She had a gift, not only with the scalpel but with all aspects of medicine, including the schooling portion.

No, Alyssa was not nervous about how she would score on this test - if she would pass or what it would mean for her if she didn't. What she was nervous about was something very different, at least, it was very different for *her*:

She had a date tonight.

It had been years since Alyssa had given her attention to anything other than medicine. Boyfriends had been completely out of the question, and even her friendships had slowly fizzled out over the last several years. She threw herself into residency, and it had taken a toll on her. She hadn't been herself for a long time.

When she was fully committed, and not so worn down, she never had a problem gaining interest from anyone, romantic or otherwise. She was kind and selfless, always wanting to hear about everyone else before ever talking about herself, and when it *was* her turn to talk, she was animated and entertaining. She always had a story to tell. She cared intensely about the people she loved, and she would drop everything to be there for them, even if she was tired or covered in stains or if she had to be back at the hospital in six hours after working for twenty-six... it never mattered.

And she was beautiful. She had heaps of thick, blonde hair, naturally highlighted even though she hardly spent any time out in the sun anymore, and it was often hidden, tucked away under a scrub cap. Most of the girls' beauty lessened when they had all their hair stuffed inside those caps and no makeup on, but not Alyssa.

Probably because her eyes were so bright and round that she never looked tired even though she always was. They were pear green, with rays of brown on the insides. Her old boyfriends swore the green was more vibrant whenever she was excited about something. She wondered how green they'd looked at the campus store a couple weeks ago... That conversation had definitely excited her. She smiled just thinking about it.

There were a few different smiles Alyssa wore - all beautiful in their own way, though arguably the most stunning was the one she gave when she was impressed by someone. Nearly everyone who knew her aspired to get *that* smile out of her. Earning that smile of approval and acknowledgment from Alyssa Hart was enough to make anyone feel validated.

She used to dream about her mother's face lighting up with that type of smile. Flashbacks of prom season streaked through her memories - she'd watched other girls' parents hand out a hundred of those smiles as if lifted cheeks and bright eyes were nickels and dimes and the parents were millionaires. Gushing about how stunning their daughters were, while Alyssa set up balloons for volunteer hours, then promptly rushed home for a study session with her mom. "It's almost the end of the year, which means your grades are more important now than ever." Never mind the fact that her GPA at that point had been a 4.7. The school had to get special permission to go above the original maximum.

Growing up with a mother who valued achievements over everything else had its perks. She'd learned to be confident in her abilities.

Usually. She was *usually* confident.

Once again, her thoughts drifted back to the playful boy who'd made her blush and she found herself as nervous as she had been two weeks ago, the day she'd run into *him*.

2

Jackson

Jackson Halloway lay sprawled out on his twin-sized mattress in the Loft. The Loft was what he called the attic in his parents' house ever since he had remodeled it and claimed it as his own.

Initially, he'd stayed at home so he wouldn't accumulate college debt. Though his online school was comparatively affordable, he wasn't interested in working more than he had to. Living in the Loft allowed him the freedom to work part time, and still build a bit of a cushion in his savings account. Hence, he decided to continue living in the Loft rent-free until he had a reason to move out.

For now, his mom made him and his father delicious meals three times a day, as well as provided him with clean sheets and a bed to sleep on, and what more did he really need?

He had an assortment of plain t-shirts and jackets that served him just fine, and a few Christmases ago he had gotten a pair of Nike sneakers that were still in decent condition considering he didn't go out much.

The one area where he would always splurge was electronics,

mainly computer software.

He had received his degree online in Information Technology - a degree perfectly suited for someone like Jackson, who was fluent in the ever-changing and complex language of the internet.

Working in IT was his chance to show off his skills. He'd been coding and working computers since before he'd even reached middle school.

Having a job in the technological field also meant that his parents and relatives would often spoil him with expensive gaming computers and programs, making exclamations like, "Anything to help you with school, Jackie, we're just so proud of you!" and, "It's an investment in your future, Jackie, you're gonna be a huge success one day, you mark my words!"

Though he didn't necessarily need the newest gaming model computer for his casual job at the University, they didn't need to know that, right? After all, they had offered to get him a computer, so why not ask for the one he really wanted? *They have the money to spend, and they wouldn't know the difference, anyway.* Who was he hurting?

The online world was his comfort zone. Where he felt most confident.

A lot of people unfairly assumed Jackson was introverted and antisocial because he spent most of his hours in front of a computer screen, but they'd never tried to get to know him. If they had, they would've discovered he was interesting and charismatic, and could be surprisingly charming. The online community had given him the opportunity to practice chatting and bantering with strangers, and he found joy in entertaining people.

He wasn't necessarily conventionally good-looking, mainly

because he didn't know how to put himself together like most men figure out well before they're twenty-six, but his extensive internet socialization had built up his confidence over the years. In the virtual world, with his smooth, captivating voice and impressive computer skills, he felt accomplished and desirable - feelings that he hadn't experienced much in his brief life before the internet.

Jackson's headphones sat on the floor beside his bed amongst a half-eaten bag of potato chips, an empty can of soda, and a wireless Xbox controller. They had fallen there sometime after he'd drifted into sleep last night, or rather, this morning, during a livestream he had been swept up in. Though they were off his head and nearly four feet away, Jackson jumped awake when a loud, overly-excited voice screamed through them, urging him to "SUBSCRIBE FOR MORE CONTENT LIKE THIS!"

He groaned and fumbled to turn the volume down, and eventually stretched and shoved the blankets off so he could make his way to the bathroom. He ran the water and placed his toothbrush underneath, still trying to blink the sleep from his eyes.

He inspected himself in the mirror, criticizing his face as he did so. His eyes were sunken in - it was obvious he had stayed up too late, for too many nights in a row. His skin was dry, and he couldn't remember the last time he had been out in the sun for any longer than ten or fifteen minutes, or with any less clothes on than a t-shirt and sweatpants. His facial hair was patchy and multi-textured, since he never could get the hang of shaving, and he hadn't adopted a schedule where he shaved often enough for the clean-cut look he envied on other men. His hair had begun to produce enough oil where it was clear he was due for a shower at least the day before, and the oil appeared in the pores of his nose, too.

Some days, he would push it another day or two before finally giving in to take a shower. After all, he worked part-time as an IT Specialist at the University of Michigan - a job where he never had to show his face in person, or even on the screen.

Aside from work, the majority of his personal life was spent online as well. Other than seeing his family and the occasional errand or special trip, he stayed in the Loft most of the time. But today was one of those "errand" days, so he bit the bullet and jumped in the shower.

Underneath the awkward paleness and inexperienced self-care, he really did have the structure to be an attractive man. The water helped wash away the evidence of his lacking hygienics, and he came out looking almost handsome with his wet hair and fresh skin. A person who had a slightly higher understanding of social customs than Jackson would realize that, with an overly-expensive haircut and an elevated outfit, along with a few other simple "fixes," Jackson Halloway could be almost head-turning.

But his mother, doting as she was, always felt uncomfortable having "those talks" with her son. She avoided teaching him about proper showering techniques for fear of having to discuss things like which "personal" areas to scrub and how to scrub them. She conveniently never got around to showing him how to shave because she didn't want to admit he was becoming a man. And she was absolutely horrified at the thought of talking about anything remotely related to "the birds and the bees," so needless to say, that information was never passed on to him either.

His father was no better. He wasn't a big talker, and besides, he'd never understood Jackson.

Jonathan Halloway was a man of a different generation, one where men "took charge" and "figured shit out on their own." They didn't talk to each other about their feelings, they didn't continue living at home after the age of eighteen, and they certainly didn't spend hours a day online. "Online" hadn't even existed when Jonathan was a boy.

He told Jackson it was unnatural to be so involved with technology. He'd prefer if his son got up, cleaned himself up, put on a business suit, and went out into the world with a briefcase and a high work ethic and didn't ask any questions.

Jackson wiped himself down with his towel, and for the first time in nearly three days, he ran a comb through his hair. He usually kept a short hairstyle because it was easier to manage, but he was about three inches overdue for a haircut, and the sparseness and slightly-receding hairline never allowed it to look fully "managed" anyway.

Sliding on the glasses he donned when he didn't feel like putting in his contacts, he reached into the closet and grabbed at his pile of t-shirts. He didn't particularly care which one he reached first; they were basically all the same. He slid on his boxers that had been too loose for a few months now, and then pulled up his sweats and tightened the elastic enough so that everything stayed in place. Plucking his wallet from atop the dresser, he headed downstairs.

"Good morning, Sleeping Beauty," his father mocked from behind his newspaper.

"Ha. Ha." Jackson wasn't amused. He heard this nearly every morning, well, afternoon, when he finally came down to greet the family and have his "breakfast" for the day.

Even though it was usually around 12:30 or 1:00 by the time Jackson came downstairs, his mother had breakfast hot and ready for him. A lot of the time, she was prepping her husband's lunch at the same time as her son's breakfast.

Where Jackson found joy in entertaining people, his mother, Cathy, found it in serving others. She made "her boys" breakfast, lunch, and dinner every day (though Jackson usually saved his dinner and heated it up in the early morning hours while engulfed in his computer screen). And food was just the beginning.

They were never without fresh sheets and pillowcases, as well as newly laundered and ironed clothes.

On top of taking care of her family, Jackson's mother often baked pies for the neighbors or provided casseroles for church functions. If someone in their community created a post saying they needed anything, Cathy was always the first one to help. Given that his mother had always been this way, Jackson knew nothing different, and therefore came to simply expect to be taken care of in this manner.

"Jaaack-ieee," his mother sang, "I made your favorite: bacon and eggs with buttered toast!"

"Thanks Mom, it looks perfect." He kissed her on the cheek.

"Oh, and don't forget your coffee!"

"I don't drink... coffee," Jackson mimicked in his very best Gerard Butler impression, which was actually pretty convincing. He'd always had a knack for impersonating accents and voices.

This was a regular routine for them. Jackson, with his witticism, would cleverly quip a movie quote with quick timing in the perfectly appropriate moment in conversation, and his mother would make her best guess at where the reference came from.

"*Dracula!*" his mother exulted gleefully, proud that she had

11

known straight away.

"Ah, you're getting good at this. Pretty soon you'll be giving me a run for my money! What's next mom, are you gonna start coding, too?" He gave her a little wink. Being around his mother always brought out the more playful side of him.

"You never know, by tomorrow I'll be 'riding the websites' even better than you, Jackie."

Jackson spit out the bite of toast he had just taken and his shoulders shook up and down in sudden laughter.

She looked at him, knowing her attempt at being "cool" had obviously failed. She couldn't help but let out a giggle herself. "What?"

He picked up his toast, exhaling after his bout of laughter. "It's *surfing the web*,' but I think I might like your version more."

He finished the toast, and his mother instinctively went to grab him another piece, but he was already standing up and setting his plate in the sink for her to wash. "I'm going out for a bit, I have some errands to run. Work stuff."

"I thought you worked from your computer?" *Cheeky.*

"Exactly, and do you know how you can tell I've been doing lots of good work on my computer?"

She shrugged, giving him an "I-don't-know" look.

"When it's time to shop for a new battery." He pointed his finger at her, conclusively.

"Oh I'm not surprised, Jackie, you have been working *so* hard, staying up all hours of the night on your machines. At this point you might as well just plug yourself straight into the computer, it'd probably be easier."

Jackson chuckled, amused by the thought.

His smile faded for a brief second when he fully took in what she'd said. She was so proud of him, his parents both were. For the first time in what seemed like forever, they respected him.

If only I was being honest with them.

Jackson had gotten a job as an IT Specialist, that much was true, but he'd omitted the detail of the job being part time.

At first, he hadn't been deceitful on purpose. He'd simply told them he'd been hired and they'd all celebrated. Talented as Jackson was, coding had gotten him into some trouble in the past. He'd been turned down by several potential employers because of it, so finding a decent job with his track record was an accomplishment.

His parents had been elated by the news. *A college position?* In all the excitement, they'd immediately gone out to dinner to congratulate him, and they hadn't thought to ask about the specifics of his hours.

Then, a week later, his mother had walked in on him gaming (at 10:00 p.m., she'd come in to see if he wanted a late night cup of hot cocoa) and just assumed he was working. She knew his position was on the computer, and he had just gotten the new gaming computer he'd asked for, the one he'd *said* he needed for his job.

She'd thrown her hands up to her cheeks and practically squealed with delight. "Look at my hard-working son! They ought to know how lucky they are to have you. Only been working there a week and you're already working all hours into the night. You're such a great boy, you know that?"

Jackson had smiled, lowered his voice to the grizzliest tone, and half-whispered "Great men are not born great, they grow great."

His mother hadn't gotten *The Godfather* reference. Instead, she had mistakenly guessed *Rocky* and he'd teased her and they'd laughed and they'd both been so happy and distracted that he'd somehow forgotten to tell her that he hadn't actually been working.

From then on, it'd become all too advantageous to allow his parents to continue to believe all his time in front of a screen was spent productively. "Working."

His mother was so chipper lately, and even more pleased with him than usual. In fact, she'd begun making him more elaborate meals, since he "must be so hungry from all that hard work," as well as taking over the very few chores he'd been expected to complete before, so he could focus all his energy into his "new career." And his father's judgmental glances into the Loft had been replaced with approving nods.

Jackson felt the weight of his fathers' expectations lift a bit off his shoulders for the first time in he-couldn't-even-remember-when, and he was in no hurry to let that weight begin crushing him again.

Jackson shook himself back into the moment. *What were we talking about? Oh right, that I should just plug myself into the computer at this point.* "I could do that," he pretended to consider, "but then who would help you eat Thanksgiving dinner in a couple weeks?"

Cathy chuckled, and told him she was touched that he was already thinking about their holiday time together. She'd always said she was lucky to have a son who spent so much time with his parents.

"You're right, Jackie, what was I thinking? That is a special talent of yours, and we can't let it go to waste now, can we?" She returned his wink from earlier.

He checked his watch. He hoped to be back home by 3:00 to join some buddies in a game of *Call of Duty*, which meant he ought to be out the door by now. "Alright I gotta go mom, but 'in case I don't see ya, good afternoon, good evening, and good night!'" He knew she'd get this reference; he loved this film and made her watch it with him at least once a year.

He heard her yell the correct answer, *"The Truman Show!"* just as he was closing the door behind him.

3

Alyssa

"Nooo, come on, come on, *come on!*"

Alyssa was furiously wiggling the charging cable to her computer, hoping that if she placed it in just the right spot it would start working, but her screen stayed dark. Her roommate, Bella, popped her head out from the bathroom to check in.

"What happened?"

Alyssa was shaking her computer defeatedly, trying to bring it back to life even though her gut assured her it was lifeless.

"My computer died, and I was almost done with that final!" She dramatically flopped face first into her pillow. Bella giggled at her acting, but still offered her sympathy.

"That sucks." Then she started to panic, "Wait, which final? I thought I wrote down everything…" She pulled out her planner and furiously flipped through the pages. "Yeah, that's what I thought, I don't have anything due before the twenty-fifth, did I miss something? I'm freaking out!"

Bella was very serious about school, which was one of the many reasons her and Alyssa got along so well.

"Bella, breathe," Alyssa exaggerated her breathing, taking a deep breath in and a slow breath out to jokingly help her friend calm down. "You didn't miss anything, I was just ahead of the game. This one isn't due until that Tuesday, the twenty-sixth. I just wanted to finish early so I'd have more time to study for the USMLE."

Alyssa was much calmer now herself, after taking on the soothing role to placate her roommate. Bella sighed in relief and relaxed, but she didn't stay still for long. After the fear left her body, she slapped Alyssa on the shoulder and then crossed her own arms in front of her chest. "Girl you *scared* me!"

In all the commotion, Alyssa had almost forgotten that all her hours of work on that final paper may be lost.

"What am I gonna do? I am *not* going to do that all over again; I refuse!"

Even though Alyssa said this firmly, both her and Bella knew that she would absolutely write it all over again if she really had to, but both girls were hoping that wouldn't be the case.

"Didn't you write it on Google Docs? You write everything on there."

"Yeah, but my computer has never done this before! What if it wiped out everything?"

"Let me see," Bella snatched the computer off the mattress to examine it. She felt the heat coming from the side where the fan was. "Oh, yep," she declared confidently, "you killed the battery. Probably from having a million tabs open and being on it for a zillion hours, that's the end-of-semester curse. Happened to me a couple years ago."

"All my work is on this computer!" Alyssa was breathing hard. "And I don't know if I can afford to get a new one. I'm simply going to pass away." She fell into her pillows for a second time.

Even in her distress, she was nothing short of entertaining.

Now it was Bella's turn to pacify. "Chill out, you just need a new battery." She flipped up her watch, which matched with Alyssa's. "But the campus store is only open 'til two I think. They have weird hours. So if you're gonna go, you better run over, like, right now."

"Ugh, my savior!" Alyssa jumped up and kissed Bella on both cheeks, overexaggerating the "muah, muah" of the kisses, and then scooped up her keys and ran for the door.

She contemplated driving, but the roads were newly icy and the store was so close anyway that she ultimately decided it would be quicker to try to jog over.

She shivered as she ran. The Michigan air was already frosty, and it whipped at her exposed face. "Why is this state so dang cold?" she groaned to no one in particular.

There are some rare girls who can somehow complain without actually being negative, and Alyssa was one of them. Instead of being annoying or sounding like a "Debbie Downer," she was relatable. Comforting.

She chose difficult paths in life, like going to medical school, or living in a college town that has brutally chilling winters, and people on similar paths tend to bond by grumbling about their situations. Alyssa knew this, and being the social butterfly that she was, she subconsciously used complaining as an engagement tactic.

The word "complaining" doesn't accurately encapsulate the way she would go on and on about her life every day. It was more like acting. Just like proclaiming death and falling onto a pillow, it was simply part of her incredibly enticing personality. Her peers found Alyssa refreshing for being so real, especially in the world of social media where girls as gorgeous and bubbly

18

as Alyssa typically put on the facade of a perfect, positive life where nothing goes wrong.

Not Alyssa. She would burst into the hospital telling stories starting with, "You'll never believe the morning I just had!" or "Oh my gosh I just had the *worst* appendectomy, every single thing went wrong, listen to this!" and everyone wanted to hear her story. She never had legitimate complaints, she just used the negatives as guises to tell tales to amuse and enthrall those around her.

So, when she was finished trudging through the cold and finally huffed and puffed her way to the battery aisle at the campus store, she proceeded to do just that.

"You... will... *never*... guess why I'm here!" She dramatically panted to the only other person in the aisle - a young man with still-damp hair and a captivated look on his face who was also in need of a new computer battery.

Jackson effortlessly matched her energy. "Hmmm," he fake pondered, "You wanted an iced coffee?"

Alyssa laughed, looking at this boy for the first time. He seemed younger than her, but the bags under his eyes matched hers.

"Yep, that's it!" It had been a while since she had engaged in this sort of back and forth exchange, and she was enjoying herself. "I'll take a very large cappuccino, and add some espresso in there, I'm gonna need it. Double shots."

The topic of coffee was silly, but Jackson was seriously drinking in every word. "Well, first of all, I don't know what a 'large' is, did you mean a 'trenta?'" Alyssa rolled her eyes but stifled a smile.

"And secondly, what happened to you that you need 'double shots' of espresso? That's hardcore... I bet there's a story there."

19

"Oh no, I wouldn't want to burden you with my story," Alyssa sighed playfully, even though she could tell full well that this boy was in no rush to end the conversation.

"But miss, I'm just a humble barista, it's part of my job to listen to the woeful tales of my customers while I mix their caffeinated beverages."

Alyssa's lips formed a full smile this time, unable to hide how smitten she was.

"Well, if you insist," she turned fully towards him, and an emotion spilled onto his face that she couldn't quite read. She'd seen similar looks on her patients. Typically, that slight gasp and stumble backwards meant they were nervous. *But is he nervous* good, *or nervous* bad? He blinked and looked away, and she kept talking.

"So I'm in my last semester of med school at UMich," Jackson's eyebrows rose in the same way most people's did when she divulged her career choice, *he's impressed*, "and I thought I'd be *sooo* good and try to finish one of my finals early, but my computer died. Dead. Stopped breathing right in front of my eyes. I tried to resuscitate her but it was no use. So now I'm shopping for a new battery in the desperate hope that my work is saved because I think I will completely lose the very little sanity I still have left if I find out my entire paper has been obliterated and lost to the void forever."

Alyssa found she was speaking so fast by the end of the story that she had to stop to catch her breath. Jackson looked like he was about to ask a question, but it took him a beat too long to form the words and more came tumbling out of Alyssa's mouth without her consent. Something about him made her want to keep talking.

"Sorry, I'm just really anxious and I was on a mission to get this battery before the store closes in," she glanced at the lit-up watch on her left wrist, "eight minutes! And somehow I let myself get distracted by a cute boy and now, since I have no idea what I'm looking for, I don't think there's any way I'll be able to find what I need before they kick me out of here and tell me I'll have to come back tomorrow."

Though she had continued on as if she hadn't said anything significant, they both still felt the words "cute boy" hanging in the air between them. Alyssa hadn't said that by accident, but she put on an innocent expression to make it appear as if she was oblivious to the weight of her words.

Jackson was frozen, probably taken aback by her inconspicuous compliment. She'd said that so boldly. Unabashedly.

Again, she had trouble reading him. Strange, since it was part of her job to read between the lines of patients' stories. But he was no patient. He was like a complicated recipe that doesn't seem to make sense on the page. Like, how can you put something savory in with all these sweet ingredients, and then a little hint of sour... they shouldn't go together. Somehow, though, when they're all mixed up, they make the most delicious treat that you can't get enough of.

There was a silence, and Jackson looked down. His eyes landed on the computer battery in front of him and finally he swallowed. She'd noticed he was holding his breath before. Had he even been aware of that? She had to wonder again: *nervous good or nervous bad?*

"What kind of computer do you have?"

"Ummm, a Chromebook. 2013, I think."

"2013?" He drew in a sharp breath, matching her dramatic anecdotes by placing his hand over his heart. "No wonder it died! Without a new battery, a chromebook only lasts somewhere between five and eight years. You're at six, and if you've been using it for med school work that entire time, I can't believe it didn't go dark until after year four."

Now it was Alyssa's turn to be impressed. "How do you know all that?"

"Even though I'm a barista by day, I'm kind of a computer expert by night." He'd regained his composure, accompanied by the banter.

Alyssa was too curious to joke. "No seriously, what do you do?"

She watched Jackson contemplate for a moment, likely wondering if he should continue joking or match her energy and be serious. There was a hint of a smile in the very corner of his mouth, like he thought of something shameless to say, but then it disappeared as he thought better of it. "I'm a computer programmer. I code, I do IT work, and, luckily for you, the main part of my job is problem solving."

"Oh, so I'm a problem, am I?" Flirting with him was an adrenaline completely separate from the rush of surgery. It was a high without consequences. No one's life was at stake. She didn't need to be "oh so careful," or move slowly and cautiously. She could run, full speed ahead, hair flying out of her cap, free in the wind.

Jackson choked, and Alyssa had to stop herself from letting her emotions pour out all over her face because he'd just made it obvious: He was nervous *good*. Really good.

Alyssa saw she needed to take control. "Well, for *this* problem, which battery would you recommend, Mr. Computer Expert?" The space between them had somehow gotten a lot smaller.

Jackson, still silent, fumbled for the correct battery and handed it to her.

"Thanks!" she chirped. "And for any future problems…" she continued, slowly, "how would I get in contact with you for that?"

Realization dawned on Jackson's face as he understood what she was asking. It looked like he had to force himself to speak, like his body was frozen in disbelief, and instead of dumping hot water on it, he was whacking himself with an ice pick, freeing the words with a great amount of effort.

"You'll just have to call me," he tried to feign confidence, although his hands were shaking as he reached for her phone, "I'll put my number in here."

After an awkward moment of silence and typing that made Alyssa feel like a teenager again, her phone was placed back in the palm of her hand.

"Mr. Computer Expert," Alyssa read, and caught herself smiling again as she noticed the robot emoji next to his alias. She opened her mouth to ask him what his actual name was, but when she looked up, he was already gone.

While she was waiting in the check-out line, some boxes of M&Ms lined up on the adjacent shelf caught her attention. She bought the entire row, figuring she owed Bella a very chocolate-y "thank you."

4

Clayton

"Mr. Reynolds isn't doing well," Jeremy Barnes whispered into his headset. "He's developed a blood clot in his left leg, and one of his bed sores has become infected."

Even through an earpiece, Clayton could tell Dr. Barnes was worried, but he didn't reciprocate the concern. "We knew there would be side effects, Jeremy. Every medical solution comes with a whole list of them, don't they?"

"This is different," Dr. Barnes urged, sounding panicked. "It's not just this patient; urinary tract infections are up sixty-four percent among users, and—"

"Chest pain, difficulty breathing," Clayton listed slowly, cutting him off. "Abdominal cramps, severe convulsions, even blood in the urine. Do you know what those are the side effects of, Jeremy?"

Dr. Barnes stuttered, "N...no, but Clayton—"

"Aspirin," Clayton interrupted him a second time, laughing slightly. "Simple, run-of-the-mill, over the counter Aspirin. People aren't going to stop taking Aspirin just because the side effects sound scary, now are they?"

"This is different, we can control these outcomes, we can limit the amount of time people can be logged into the system, we—"

"Back pain, loss of hearing, sudden blindness," Clayton went on calmly, acting as though he hadn't heard the doctor. "Seizures, memory problems, and even the inability to differentiate between the colors red and blue." He laughed again, accentuating the ridiculousness of this list. "Take a guess, what horrible pill could those possibilities belong to?"

Dr. Barnes seemed to have realized he needed to play along. "Um… memory loss is often associated with prescription anxiety medication, like Xanax or—"

"EHHH!" Clayton made a loud "buzzer" noise. "Wrong! It's Viagra. You don't suppose all the old men using Viagra are suddenly going to stop enhancing their lives just because they read the bottle, do you? They put it right on the bottle, Jeremy, right in front of their faces. They. Don't. Care."

"I understand that. But *you* need to understand, these are unnecessary risks. If we simply made some alterations… Mr. Reynolds still needs to complete his physical therapy. We need to be very clear that this technology is not a cure, patients need—"

"Patients need…." Clayton lowered his tone. He'd learned how to cater to his audience. He knew how to get people to listen, how to tell them what they wanted to hear.

To his investors he might have screamed about money, and how the more patients logged into his Program, the more cash went into their pockets. But to Dr. Barnes he said:

"Patients need a break from their pain. And that's what we're giving them. The mission we've had from the very beginning…

we're accomplishing that. And guess what? They're happy. Isn't that what we really want: to give people who are suffering the type of life they deserve?"

"Of course," the doctor conceded, "but it's making their *real* lives worse. It was different when it was only patients in critical conditions, ones we knew were never going to improve physically, but people like Herold Reynolds actually have a chance of recovery in the real world. In his case, the Program could actually be making his condition *worse*."

"And when he logs into Salvation, he doesn't have to deal with any of that. He can be free. Perfect."

"I'm afraid that's part of the problem," Dr. Barnes admitted, gravely. "He's gotten used to how he feels inside Salvation. He doesn't want to log out. Ever. Sure he can run and jump in the game, but in reality his body is deteriorating. And this is going to become a cycle if we don't do something," he insisted, speaking more and more direly as he went on.

"The worse his body feels in the real world, the more he'll want to log in. And the more he's in, the more he's ignoring his body's physical needs, and therefore depleting, or ruining altogether, his chance of healing."

To Clayton, this was incredible news. It's what he'd been hoping for since designing the Program. They'd decided part of their business model would be offering a "pay-as-you-go" system, where users pay per minute used. He'd gotten the idea from his first prepaid cell phone.

He'd gotten a prepaid phone when he'd graduated college, right as they were beginning to become popular. At first, he remembered, almost every phone was "pay-by-the-minute," and this was because people didn't use them very much. Why pay a monthly or yearly subscription price for unlimited minutes when you know you won't use very many anyway?

However today, in this new age of modern technology, society is full of people glued to their phone screens. In their minds, they're saving a fortune with their phone plan because if they paid by the minute, their bill would be astronomical. People first needed to dip their toe in with the cell phone, discover they can't live without it, and then hand all their money over to their provider.

And then they're hooked. Once someone buys a year-long phone plan, what are the odds they'll ever cancel it?

They become dependent on their brainwashing, plastic devices. Then, the device adapts to make people need it even more: maps, calendar, contacts, calculator, flashlight, timer, camera… how would a person live anymore without it? They'd be like a helpless, newborn baby, attempting to survive without their mother there to nurse them.

This was Clayton's goal for his Program. And it was working, thanks to his innovative technology and his practices in persuasion. Clayton knew he was gifted in getting people to listen to him, he always had been. He'd been able to recruit all of his investors single handedly, thanks to his pitching skills. He could sell anything, even a bad idea (and he'd had many of those). But for once, this time, he actually had a good one.

He hadn't been able to do everything alone, he had to admit. That's why he'd found Dr. Barnes.

It was all too easy to talk the doctor into teaming up with him. Clayton had done his research. He'd found someone respected enough to be taken seriously by the medical community, but gullible enough to be convinced Clayton's intentions were pure. Oh, and desperate enough to stay with the Program even when he inevitably started to discover the "downsides." Clayton had made sure of that.

He'd been trying to appease Dr. Barnes by appealing to his weakness: his desire to help people. But clearly, he needed to take a different approach.

"We *are* helping people, Jeremy. That I can assure you. But," he inhaled deeply, "if you're having doubts about your loyalty to Salvation, need I remind you of my knowledge of Brazil?" Clayton's room went eerily quiet then, with only the humming of his ear piece reliably continuing.

"My loyalties are not in question, Clayton," Dr. Barnes managed to say after their moment of silence. "I'm your partner. And I believe in the Program. I really do."

Clayton was comfortable again, not that he would've admitted that, for a few seconds, he wasn't. The conversation was over. He was about to bid Dr. Barnes goodbye, when he heard the doctor's next message in his ear.

"It's not just Mr. Reynolds who's logging excess hours. Your mother," Clayton winced, "has been logging no less than ten hours a day. I'm telling you this as your friend. Even if you choose to ignore the others for now, you need to talk to your mom. If you want her to be around longer, you—"

"My mother hasn't been this happy in twenty years," he made sure to sound collected. "But I appreciate all your advice Jeremy, I always do. I'll see you at eight, as usual. Bye now."

Clayton hung up the phone, then grabbed his keys and headed to BrightView, where he could check on his mother himself.

5

Jackson

"My goodness, you've been gone all day! Did you find your battery okay?"

Suddenly, it dawned on Jackson that he was empty handed. His mother spotted the amused look on his face, and her nosiness got the best of her. "What happened, were they out?"

He grinned, mostly to himself. "I don't know, actually, I got distracted at the store. I ran all these other errands first, so by the time I got to the store it was already about to close, and then this girl started talking to me, and... I don't know, I guess I forgot to grab it." He instantly regretted giving away that information as he watched his mother's face light up.

"A *girl*? A girl distracting enough to make you forget about your computers? That must have been some girl!"

Understatement of the century. "Well, I was already in a rush with the store closing, I wasn't really focused, it's not that big of a deal."

"Did you talk to her?" His mother was relentless, and Jackson crinkled his face to make it seem as though he was annoyed by this line of questioning. "Did you find out where she lives or works so you can talk to her again?" Why had he even tried with the face? She was never going to let this go. Jackson wouldn't be surprised if his mom was already designing a nursery for her future grandchildren in her head.

"I'm not a stalker, Mom, I don't even know her name." Saying this out loud was the first time the absence of her name dawned on him. He'd just had the most exhilarating interaction with the most intriguing girl who he couldn't manage to get out of his head, and he didn't even know what to call her.

He guessed at her name, excited about the prospect of having more information about this girl, even if it was just in his imagination. *Belle, maybe?* It would make sense; she was breathtakingly beautiful… even while having a nervous breakdown about her paper in sweats in the middle of the day. Jackson smiled to himself again, remembering how adorable she had been, all flustered about her final. His mother noticed, of course, and snapped him out of his guessing game.

"Look at you, you can't stop smiling, Jackie! How could you not have asked her name? Well, she must go to the University, right, if you met her at the computer store? So maybe you will see her again, if you get out more. You can start going to the campus like we talked about. You have access, right, through your job? It would be so good for you to socialize with the other kids! Take a book, lay on the grass, or even just go for a stroll. And who knows, maybe you'll run into her eventually."

Jackson was about to argue that he gets out plenty, even though they both knew that wasn't the case, but he flashed back to his interaction with the mystery girl and typing his name, or rather, nickname, into her cell phone. His mother was going to love this.

30

"I won't have to do all that," he hinted as casually as possible. "She'll probably just text me."

He began walking away, purely for the dramatics, knowing his mother would never allow him to leave after dropping that bomb of information.

As predicted, her mouth fell open. "You gave her your number?" Cathy shrieked, so loudly that his father came into the room to see what the commotion was about. Jackson nodded at his mother. "Jon, Jackie met a girl today and gave her his phone number!" She was jumping up and down. Jackson's face was flushing red.

"Geez I thought somebody was hurt the way you were yelling." Then he let the information settle and looked to his son. "You made a move like that?" Jackson nodded, and Jonathan raised his eyebrows and lifted his head slowly in surprised approval.

"'Atta boy, nicely done," and he went back to his office.

"I don't know why I'm telling you all of this, she probably won't even end up texting."

"I know exactly why you're telling me this." Cathy cleared her throat, and Jackson had no idea what was coming. "Because, a... a boy's best friend is his mother."

He let out a surprised laugh. She may be nosey, but he wouldn't trade her for anything. Her goofy bits, her sad attempts at slang. Even her prying; he knew it meant she was invested in him and his life. Plus, he didn't totally hate talking about the mystery girl from the computer store, even if his nervous posture suggested otherwise.

"I don't know if Norman Bates is who I want to be compared to, but I appreciate the sentiment." Seizing the opportunity to escape, he meandered back towards the Loft.

His mom called after him, "Okay, goodnight Jackie, I hope

she texts you soon!"

Even though he didn't respond, the next few hours of gaming in the Loft were filled with many instances of his character dying as he eagerly glimpsed at his phone screen, only to be disappointed when it remained dark.

6

Clayton

"Your mother's been awfully smiley lately," the usual receptionist, Amber, informed Clayton. "I think that experimental treatment you've got her on in there must be working wonders!"

"That's what we're hoping for," he enthused, "Is she in her room now?"

Amber nodded. "Yep, here's your visitor's pass, and your," she paused, and whispered, "special access key." Then, she spoke at a normal volume, "Tell her I said hi!"

"Will do," Clayton waved at her and threw the lanyard over his neck, the key clanging against the plastic guest tag. He was the only person who had the authority to be given the key without showing his ID, and one of only four people who were allowed to use it at all. Even Dr. Barnes, his co-founder, needed to be screened and checked before obtaining entry.

Besides himself and Dr. Barnes, only a security guard and a medical professional at BrightView Assisted Living were allowed access. Even then, he'd instructed Amber not to give them a key unless there was a dire emergency.

Clayton hadn't wanted to permit even this small number of people access to his hidden room, but BrightView had refused to try the Program under any other circumstances. They'd argued that Clayton was not a doctor, and while they respected Dr. Barnes, he wasn't at the hospital that often. "What if something goes wrong and no one is allowed in to help?"

Since Clayton couldn't exactly say, "That's a risk we're all willing to take and it's our business," he'd reluctantly agreed. Besides, no other assisted living facilities were willing to try his "experimental treatment" yet, so he didn't see another option. Still, he'd insisted that these two employees could only enter the room during a worst case scenario, and even then they needed to call him first and alert him that they'd be entering.

He knew he'd never miss a call; he wore his earpiece at all times. He couldn't risk disconnecting even for a moment, there was too much at stake. He insisted on knowing absolutely anything and everything happening inside the Program, and he'd threatened to fire any person who withheld even the smallest piece of information from him.

They'll be honest. At least, they will if they know what's good for them. The Salvation founder had made it painstakingly clear that he'd done enough homework to be able to blackmail and ruin any one of them with just the click of the "send" button on his email account if he wanted to.

This extortion made him confident, but smart men don't simply *trust*. They always have a back up plan. Unbeknownst to anyone involved with Salvation, Clayton had complete video surveillance of every inch of their simulated town.

Salvation could, when simplified, be compared to a virtual reality gaming system. Users put on their patented Ocular Exposers (Oc X's, for short), similar to VR goggles, in order to shut out the "real world" and immerse themselves in the imaginary town of Salvation.

In one of his psychology classes, Clayton's professor had made them watch and analyze the 1972 film *Clockwork Orange*, wherein aversion therapy is attempted by holding a patient's eyes open to force him to watch violent clips and pumping him with drugs in order to rewire his brain.

While Clayton found the movie to be severely flawed in its logic, he agreed with one thing: The eyes are the key to the brain. The Egyptians studied eyes with the Eye of Horus, Christians guard their mind by guarding their eyes and ears... Americans even have the Eye of Providence on what is arguably our most valued possession: the dollar bill.

Eyes and ears, Clayton discovered, were also the key to hypnosis - a vital part of the Salvation Program. The Oc X's were invented to hold a user's eyes open while they stared at the swaying image of a metronome and listened to Clayton's voice until they are lured into a trance deep enough to enter the virtual world.

Virtual, yes, but Salvation was no ordinary "VR." It was technology far more advanced than anyone else had ever come close to developing.

In VR, if a user wants to, let's say, jump over an obstacle, they have to physically jump. Of course, much of the world is "pretend," - the gamer isn't really in any danger, and they don't need to make a massive eight-foot leap - but what's *real* is that they do need to perform a physical motion. It could be a small jump, or depending on the technology, a user may only need to shake a controller and "imitate" a jumping motion. Either way, the user *must* be able to move.

Clayton knew his world was different. It was extraordinary.

And, more importantly, it was valuable. As an entrepreneur, he was familiar with supply and demand. Unfortunately, every other hospital and convalescent home in Chicago seemed to be grossly unaware of this concept.

He took a deep breath as he thought about the rejections. *Give it time. They'll come crawling back.* Once they saw his vision and understood the significance of what he'd created, yeah, they'd be back.

Because in Clayton's world, no movement was required at all.

That's where the hypnosis came in. In order for users to surpass the typical VR experience and become completely submerged in Salvation, more than a controller was needed.

Clayton's world involved technology, but more importantly, it utilized *psychology*. Both of his strengths, working together.

Clayton was a trained psychologist, among other things, and this is what allowed him to create such an immersive experience. His voice was the key. He could lure patients into the world using hypnotic suggestion. He'd always been persuasive, and now he was on the verge of making a fortune from it.

Salvation was a world created for the disabled. A miracle, designed to give them the movement they'd lost.

Every user had some sort of physical restriction. Paralyzed. Incapacitated. Bedridden. Miserable.

Clayton had designed a "Set-up" for users including everything they needed to enter Salvation. For now, only a few had been made for BrightView, but once the company took off, the goal was to have every user purchase a custom Set-up for their own home.

The Set-up consists of an all white, sheet-like tent that is draped over the user's bed. A small projector is included, used

36

to shine a video of a metronome onto the roof of the tent. The user then lays down comfortably on their bed, inside the tent. Restraints around the wrists and ankles are optional, if the user is particularly worried about rubbing their eyes or falling off the bed.

Prepped and relaxed, the user then says aloud "Join user 1," and the system boots up.

Clayton stands beside the user's bed and talks them into their trance. His guiding words, combined with the patented Salvation technology, place the user into a comatose state. The patients are hypnotized not only by Clayton's voice, but by the image of the metronome on the ceiling ticking back, and forth, and back, and forth. Their eyes held open, unable to look away.

Like any new invention, the Program had its roadblocks. *How the hell am I going to grow this company if I have to personally guide each user into Salvation?* Even if he hired more psychologists, he'd still need to have a one to one ratio of employees to clients. It wasn't fathomable. Unless... maybe there was a way he could record his voice and have users play it on a loop. *No, that wouldn't be strong enough.*

He would find a way. He'd already overcome every issue that had occurred so far. Okay, *most* issues.

The first big problem had been getting test subjects into that nearly-comatose state safely. The definition of a comatose state, Clayton discovered, is: "a profound or deep state of unconsciousness. Persistent vegetative state is not brain-death. An individual in a state of coma is alive but unable to move or respond to his or her environment."

After much trial and error, Clayton accepted he would never be able to harmlessly achieve such a phenomenon all on his own. That's when he'd decided to recruit a doctor as his partner.

While he was a technological genius in many ways, he had very little medical training and knew it was impossible for him to efficiently recreate a state similar enough to a coma without help. He needed someone to teach him how to monitor blood pressure and oxygen levels, how long a user could be under the hypnotic influence before it became dangerous, and any other medical questions he would undoubtedly encounter.

And, unfortunately, he couldn't hypnotize himself. He'd accepted that if he wanted to enter Salvation, and he did very much want to, he'd need a "dummy" to practice on. That's when he'd found Dr. Jeremy Barnes.

7

Derek

"911 where is your emergency?"

"MY WIFE! She.. She's bleeding, she's not okay, we need help!"

"Okay sir, calm down. I understand your wife is in need of medical assistance, is that correct?"

"YES! PLEASE! Hurry, I don't know what to do, she's screaming, she's hurt real bad, and I... I don't... I can't..."

"I know this is scary, but I need you to speak clearly so I can get you some help, okay? Can you tell me your name and address?"

"Derek Thomas. 423 Westbrooke Avenue, it's the white house on the corner, and we have a white fence... Oh, and there's black mailbox with a red flag... and..."

"423 Westbrooke Ave, got it. And what is your wife's name?"

"Are you coming? We need help! She's bleeding!"

"Yes sir an ambulance is en route, and I'm going to stay on the phone with you until they get there, okay? I'm gonna get some information that will help us get her the best help we can. Can you tell me her name?"

"Bianca. Bianca Thomas. Well, her maiden name is Sanderson."

"Bianca Thomas, perfect. And where is she injured?"

"Her... Well, she's pregnant, and I think something happened, there's blood running down her legs and she's in a lot of pain..."

For the first time since dialing, Derek forgot about the call and zoned in on his wife.

About three years ago, she'd twisted her ankle, and it was the first time he'd seen her actually *sob* from pain. When they'd made it to the hospital and it was all over, he'd begun crying himself, out of relief. It was over. He'd never have to see her hurt that badly again.

Watching her now, it was clear he'd been wrong.

Her usually pretty face was twisted up in excruciation, her body bent into an unnatural position. She almost didn't look human.

Derek tightened his grip on the receiver; this woman on the phone needed to tell the ambulance to drive faster. *What are they doing? Why are they taking so long?*

"You need to hurry! She needs help, right now!" His voice was shaking. He was trying to sound angry; angry people tend to get what they want, to get things done faster. All he sounded was scared. He was too honest, almost to a fault. And good. So good that he felt bad, even in this moment of his deepest panic, for attempting to intimidate the woman on the other end of the phone.

"I understand that, sir, the EMTs are en route and about seven minutes away. Is your wife breathing?"

Bianca wailed in agony, more than loud enough to prove her lungs were undeniably filled with oxygen. "Yes, she's breathing." Derek's fingers trembled around the receiver, and he hesitantly asked the question that wouldn't leave his mind. "Is she... is she going to be okay?"

"I'm going to stay on the phone with you until the paramedics arrive, they'll be able to better answer any questions you may have once they can assess your wife."

Why can't she just tell me right now? It must be bad. If everything was fine, there would be no reason for this woman not to answer my question. "Yes sir, she'll heal right up!" How hard was that? Bile burned in his throat.

"What if she's dying? That happens sometimes, doesn't it? Oh god. It does, doesn't it? I think I read about that in a book once, or maybe it was a mov—"

A calm voice stopped his spiral. "Derek, I need you to breathe in and out for me, okay? One big deep breath on the count of three. One..."

Had he said all that out loud? The anxiety-toting train burning circles in his mind must have run off its tracks and steamrolled right out of his mouth.

"Two..."

She still wasn't answering his question, but something in her cadence soothed him, pulled an emergency brake on his escaped locomotive.

"Three."

Without thinking, Derek sucked in a gulp of air. He was amazed when he didn't vomit it back out. Beside him, Bianca was quiet. Her face was pinched, but she was no longer hollering.

"Derek?" His attention snapped back to the phone. "Your breathing sounds much better. You're going to need to stay calm for me, okay?"

How am I supposed to relax when you still haven't answered the only question that matters right now?

It was as if she'd read his mind. "Now, I'm not there, so I'm not able to make any promises. But,"

He clung to that word, "but." Held on to it for dear life.

"But I also can't let you have a panic attack on me. So just know, if this *is* a miscarriage..." He shuddered at the word. "...she's still in her first trimester - I have her medical records pulled up right here - and a loss of child this early is relatively uncomplicated, medically speaking." *This* was uncomplicated? Silently, Derek prayed he would never have to face something this woman considered complicated. Still, her words made him feel better.

"Thank you." It was all he could muster.

There were a few seconds of silence that he could tell the operator wanted to fill. It was probably part of her job to keep him on the phone until the ambulance arrived. He was keeping track of the time; it had been six minutes and twenty-two seconds so far. The worst six minutes and twenty-two seconds of his life.

"You're doing great," the woman put an end to their pause, "You're being strong for her and that's what she needs right now. You'll have to keep being strong for her, okay? Even once help gets there, and even after you find out what's going on. Her body will heal, but the mind is much more stubborn. You'll need to be patient, and help her recover mentally. Do you think you can do that for me?"

Derek nodded, then, remembering he was on the phone, uttered a quiet "Yes ma'am," as the faint blare of sirens could finally be made out in the distance.

8

Clayton

D r. Barnes and Clayton had worked out of basements and abandoned buildings together, testing their hypotheses. Dr. Barnes would lay inside the Set-up, listening to Clayton's propaganda, absorbing the words into his half-conscious brain. Through what seemed like endless tests and combinations, Clayton had finally been able to transport Dr. Barnes into a dream-like state where he could enter the world of Salvation.

They'd discovered Dr. Barnes could enter, but he didn't have total control over his actions within the "game." He struggled to think on his own. Clayton's voice was so much a part of him that he often found he couldn't make his own choices or decisions. He would want to swim, for example, but found himself sinking until Clayton's voice-of-God would bellow, "Stop holding yourself back, and allow yourself to be the person you deserve to be. You are capable of greatness. You are powerful. The only person standing in your way is you. When we sink in life, it is because we have given up. Are you a quitter? Will you let this be the end for you? Sure, you can take a moment to pout and feel sorry for yourself, but then you must stand up and take charge. Reach your arms out and grasp what is rightfully yours! Take it!"

Only after this speech was Dr. Barnes able to extend his arms and swim to the surface.

He'd become scared to enter the game. "I feel helpless in there," he'd told Clayton. "I freeze up… it's like I cannot move until you give me permission. My brain is so reliant on you to tell me what to do; I can't do anything for myself."

This is exactly what Clayton wanted. To have control over everyone in the game, even on a subconscious level. He wanted his voice inside all of their heads.

"I'm watching you the entire time," Clayton had pointed to the screen. "You're safe with me. I only send you to the common areas where I can see you," Clayton assured him, omitting the fact that he had cameras everywhere, not just in the central hubs. "And if you are in any danger, I will direct you to safety. You can trust me."

He'd shown Dr. Barnes a smile while putting his hand on the doctor's shoulder. "Besides," he slapped the doctor on the back, "the psychosis isn't strong enough to actually allow you to die in the real world. You'd wake up before that could happen. You said so yourself; the data doesn't lie."

"That's just a hypothesis, we don't know for sure what could happen, just—"

"Haven't all of our theories been proven right thus far?" Clayton had cut him off. "We are onto something huge. We're going to be so…" he remembered who he was talking to. "…We are going to *help* so many people! We're going to better the world, Jeremy!"

"O…Okay," Dr. Barnes had agreed, reluctantly, "but we have

to figure out how to give users more control. No one will want to log in if they can't move around freely. Plus, you can sit here now and watch me and help me navigate the world, but if we get to a point where we have hundreds, maybe even thousands of users, you won't be able to speak individually with each of them. You can't be everywhere."

Clayton had known Dr. Barnes had a point, as much as he didn't want to relinquish control. If he wanted to make real money, he'd have to give up some of his power. "I do have an idea I've been wanting to run by you."

"I'm all ears."

"Well," Clayton had started, "Imagine I created pre-recorded audio tapes, and played those for the users instead of having to be present in person each time someone wanted to enter."

Jeremy seemed to ponder the idea, which meant there might actually be some merit behind it.

"I just don't know exactly how that will work… in order to achieve the level of hypnosis we've been able to reach, it seems I have to speak directly to you. Audio tapes would be too vague, not strong enough to alter your psychosis to the extent needed for this experiment."

Dr. Barnes had looked at Clayton, as if contemplating giving up the information in his head. Clayton had instantly figured out the doctor had information he wanted. "What do you know that I don't?"

"Technically," Dr. Barnes had stuttered, hesitantly, "there is a way to lower inhibition, which could potentially allow the hypnosis to sink in even easier. It wouldn't have to be quite as targeted, theoretically, that is. And you'd still have to constantly re-record the tapes so the brain doesn't adjust. But…"

"NO BUTS," Clayton had burst, "That's exactly what we need!

Let's do it!"

Dr. Barnes typically warned Clayton and fought with him about every medical decision, but this had been the first time he hadn't seemed to be able to come up with an argument. "I guess... I mean, technically..."

"What?"

"Technically, that problem is already solved." Clayton had raised his eyebrows, his interest piqued. Dr. Barnes had continued slowly, almost as if he'd been thinking out loud. "The best way to lower inhibitions is through drugs. Injecting substances into a person, my thought would be through an IV... which, of course, normally, I would never recommend, but,"

"But?" Clayton had urged.

"But, the patients we are aiming to work with would theoretically already have substances coming through their IV's that would do just that... I mean, think of the target demographic, who are they?"

Clayton had started to catch on. "People who have been severely injured," he'd realized out loud, "or who are too ill to get out of bed, or who—"

"Exactly," Dr. Barnes had been the one to cut Clayton off, this time. "And the list goes on. All people who would be on pain medications; medications intended to relax them and—"

"And lower their inhibitions!" Clayton had finished for him. "You're right! So what you're saying is, when a person is pumped up with certain drugs, I should be able to persuade them more easily. A recording of my voice would be enough?"

"Yes," Dr. Barnes had encouraged him, "so, in theory, your idea of pre-recorded messages might actually work, with your rhetoric."

Clayton had understood what needed to be done. "There's only one way to test our hypothesis," he'd said, forcing a smile. Since they hadn't had any licensing or investors yet, they'd known one of them would have to be the guinea pig. Since it was a physical, medical test, Dr. Barnes had to be the one to administer the drugs, leaving Clayton to be the one receiving them.

"We're not ready, yet," Dr. Barnes had reminded them, "but I'll work on getting the supplies we'll need if you create a tape to listen to."

"The problem is," Clayton had declared, pointedly, "my own voice doesn't work on me. Which brings me to the second idea I was thinking of: I'm going to need a partner."

Dr. Barnes had appeared offended. "I thought *I* was your partner."

"Of course, of course," Clayton had internally rolled his eyes, but externally he'd said, "You and I are the partners, the initial founders... What I mean is, I'm going to need someone to share the psychological duties with me. As you've previously mentioned, I can't be everywhere. And more importantly, I can't put myself into the simulation. I'm going to need to recruit more help."

Dr. Barnes had then grabbed his notepad and madly scribbled a to-do list.

"Get the suppressants, the needles, IV bag, tubes... that's my job. Find another motivational speaker—"

Clayton had ground his teeth at that comment. "Psychologist," he'd corrected.

"Right, sorry. Find another psychologist... glad that's your job and not mine."

That'd made Clayton snigger, though he hadn't disagreed that

47

his task was an extremely difficult one. Finding someone not only as skilled as himself, but an individual who was willing to join such a... *controversial* project. And they wouldn't be as easy to fool as Dr. Barnes. Clayton knew their true intentions would have to align with his.

It couldn't be someone weak, or morally righteous, or someone who would go running to the police when they discovered the intricacies of the Program. At the time, he hadn't known how he could possibly find the right man for the job.

"That's a pretty big to-do list," he'd told Dr. Barnes. Anything else we need to add?"

"Yeah, we've got to get some eye drops. Those Oc X's are killing me."

9

Alyssa

Alyssa never looked at her phone in class, especially this close to finals week, but she also never met people who piqued her curiosity this much, so today was the exception.

Even though she knew her watch would alert her of any messages, she found herself so anxious for a text that she didn't want to fully trust the black screen of her watch. *Maybe I missed it, or it's just glitching.* She couldn't shake the constant desire to tap on her phone screen every so often just to make sure.

But there was no glitch; the enthralling Computer Boy really hadn't responded yet. Alyssa wasn't used to this, and his absence made him even more interesting to her.

She had texted him at 6:23 a.m., right before walking to class. It was currently 11:15 a.m., and still no response. Everyone was usually so eager with Alyssa, and she admired that this boy seemed to have a life of his own. At least, she was trying to admire that, but she was also nervous. *Maybe he isn't going to text me back.*

She had been the one who had been forward. Hadn't *she*

suggested that he give her his number? *She* was the one who said *he* was cute... maybe he was just being friendly in return. Or maybe he was just a flirt; he definitely seemed younger - maybe twenty-five or so - and very good with his wit. She thought his charismatic voice had sounded natural, like he entertained all the time, so perhaps their meeting was not as special to him as it had been to her.

"Alyssa, did you forget your book?" Oops. Her professor must have asked them to pull out their text.

"No, sorry, I have it!" She dug into her bag. *Snap out of it.* This wasn't like her. Since when was she self-conscious about how she came across? Being bold and speaking her mind were her calling cards. Significant parts of her, and not accidental.

I'm glad I was so forward. This way I don't have any regrets. He knows I like him, and now the ball's in his court.

With that little bit of reassurance, she tried her best to turn her attention back to the lecture. Even though her mind still wandered back to the-boy-from-the-battery-aisle, she knew Bella would fill her in on what she'd missed when they were back in the apartment.

***

"ALYSSA HART ASKED A GUY FOR HIS NUMBER?" Bella practically shouted as Alyssa filled her in on the events of the night before.

"Technically, he gave me his," she corrected, "... buuut I guess I may have initiated it."

"MAY HAVE?" This time it was definitely shouting. "Girl, you totally initiated it, and I'm so proud!" Alyssa placed her hands under her chin and beamed, acting angelic.

"But I'm also so confused, I've never heard you talk like that. And I've *seen* the way guys throw themselves at you." Alyssa shrugged off her comment.

"No I'm serious, and you know it's true Alyssa, *everybody* drools over you, and you *never* flirt back. EVER. I mean, it's kinda sad, honestly. No guys even have a chance. Immediately to the friend zone."

"I'm focused on school," Alyssa interjected, "and friends." She gave Bella a big squeeze as she said this.

"Sooo then what is it about battery-boy that's made you change your tune?"

Alyssa blushed, making her already pink cheeks even rosier. "I don't know!" she exclaimed, falling backwards onto the bed, her head landing in Bella's lap. "He's fun. He's young, and he makes jokes, and he's... captivating, and..."

"Captivating?" Bella was grinning, fully invested and clinging to every word of Alyssa's account. "You make him sound like the main character of a movie or something."

Alyssa giggled, though Bella wasn't far off. "Honestly, he could be. I can't really describe it. He sounds like someone who would host a podcast or something... like, he just has a voice that you want to keep listening to."

"Ooh, maybe he's one of those people who narrate audio books!" Bella piped in, still trying to form a picture in her mind. "They're always so cute. It's funny, because you don't see their faces, so they really could be ugly and you'd never know. But somehow, they're always super hot."

The girls were having a lot of fun with this, enjoying the "girl talk" they'd both been deprived of as they had been getting older and busier. They felt like high-schoolers again, and until her recent encounter, Alyssa hadn't been aware just how much she missed it.

Alyssa was privileged: unlike many people, high school wasn't her "peak." While she'd been popular and talented all throughout school, she was one of those rare girls who managed to become even more attractive and well-liked as she got older. She grew into herself, in every way possible. She liked who she was, and who she was was intentional.

As young girls age, they often gain insecurities along with the weight that comes with evolving into womanhood, but not Alyssa. She loved her new lines and shapes, preferred them over her jutting bones provided by youth's fast metabolism and year-round sports. She was the epitome of the cliche of not caring what people thought of her, especially boys. Even if several of them might have been partial to a teenage body of knobs and muscles, believing the mantra of smaller always being better, Alyssa truly didn't give their thoughts an ounce of her attention.

This only made most men desire her more, though this was never her intention. People of all sexes and figures were drawn to her, in every sort of way. They wanted her, they wanted to be her, they wanted to be liked by her. She was sweet but not cheesy, loud but not attention-seeking, bold but not arrogant. The word someone would be most likely to use would be "effortless," because that's how she made it all look. She didn't spend time or money on her appearance, she was just natural and beautiful.

And even if she had a spot of acne, or a bad hair day, or she had to borrow Bella's scrubs that were completely the wrong size for her, she never acknowledged it. She spoke just as brazenly and just as often, instead of hiding in shame like many of her peers. She did her job just as well, she was just as kind to others.

All of these qualities worked together to create a combination that would be alluring to anyone. So Alyssa was loved. She was confident. She didn't daydream about the "old days," and she didn't wish to be younger. But something about this boy took her back in time, and she loved it. He had a Peter Pan-like quality about him, endearing in his immaturity. As she'd initially described him: fun. And she'd been missing his kind of fun, without knowing it. Until now.

"Actually he's in IT," Alyssa remembered. "... I think," she added, not wanting to sound like she'd been replaying their conversation over in her mind during her transaction at the store... and the whole walk home.

Bella's face changed drastically as she scrunched her nose and frowned. "Ew."

"What?"

"Girl, I've never seen a cute IT guy. Isn't that, like, the main reason they go into IT?"

"You just went on that whole spiel about audio book narrators being totally hot! Isn't that like the same thing?"

"No! Not even close!"

Alyssa gave her a confused look, reminded that the two girls, despite how well they got along, had a lot of differences. "Well, regardless, he is very cute. Maybe a little nerdy, but in a good way. I like that." She smiled at the floor.

"Ooohhh Alyss-aaa, I never knew you had a thing for hot nerds!"

Alyssa threw a pillow at her, and they both laughed. Bella still wasn't satisfied though.

"I'm still dying to see him though; let's look him up! Do you have his Insta yet?"

No. Wow, I really don't know anything about him, do I? "I don't even know his name!" She showed Bella the pseudonym he had typed into her cell.

"Okay that's hot." Bella seemed to love the mystery of it all, even if it probably drove her crazy not knowing everything about the first guy to capture her roommate's attention in the entirety of the three years they'd lived together. "I'm gonna need you to text him and get more info. Like, STAT."

Alyssa peeked at her phone, then took a dramatically deep breath and turned to Bella, knowing her friend would have quite the reaction to what she was about to say next. "Actually, I texted him this morning, but..."

"BUT?"

"But he hasn't texted back yet."

Bella looked shocked, and quickly tried to change her face to "casual" so Alyssa wouldn't feel bad. But Alyssa didn't. She was thrilled he was someone who seemed to have his own life. It made her curious to know more about him; she wondered what he was doing, who he was with, what he was saying... and not in a jealous way at all. Even if she'd known him better, Alyssa wasn't the jealous type, and certainly not after just meeting someone. She wondered more out of genuine interest.

Bella tried to sound chill. "Well, you know, it's only 11:15, he's probably just busy." Alyssa knew her best friend, which means she knew her roommate was secretly wondering if any boy in his right mind would be "too busy" to text back a "beautiful, hilarious, almost-surgeon," as Bella often called her. "Maybe he's in school too; you said he was younger. Did he mention going to UMich? Maybe we'll run into him!"

"No," Alyssa recalled, "but our conversation wasn't that long, and it was mostly about computers, anyway."

"Okay, that's it!" Bella's short fuse of patience had reached its end. "I'm going into super-sleuth mode."

Alyssa knew what this meant. Bella had an unusual talent for finding people based off of very little information. Bella pulled her hood over her head, put on some sunglasses for the sake of the bit, and hunched over her laptop.

After just twelve minutes, and only knowing that this boy worked IT and assuming he lived somewhere in the area, Bella had a profile to show to Alyssa for verification. "Is this him?"

Alyssa was amazed. Her face was all the confirmation Bella needed. "How did you..."

"Girl, don't question my gift!" Bella joked.

"Okay okay, I'll admit it, you're *very* impressive. All hail the all-powerful Bella!" She got on her knees on the bed, bending forward with her hands up in a bowing motion. Both girls chuckled. "But in all seriousness, shouldn't we just wait? He'll probably text soon, and if he doesn't, then why go through this trouble, you know?"

"Screw that, I want to see this guy! If you don't want to look, that's your prerogative." Bella pulled the laptop in closer, clearly continuing her work whether her friend joined her or not.

"Well I meeean..." Alyssa responded coyly, "if you're going to look, it's only right that I look too. I can't have you knowing more about Computer Boy than I do. That's more weird than *not* looking, right?"

Bella laughed, "Totally. It'd be super weird. So come here!"

Alyssa cozied up closer to Bella to share her view of the screen.

"Jackson Halloway," Bella read. Alyssa said the name in her head. "Jackson." She smiled, thinking it suited him.

The first thing Bella wanted to do was enlarge his profile picture so she could get a good look at him. "Hmm.." was all she had to say.

"'Hmm?' What's 'hmm' mean?" Seeing Bella at a loss for words was more than uncommon. "You're never this quiet. Spill it!"

"It's just... he's not what I would have pictured. Alyssa, he's not that hot. I mean, he's cute, I guess, in a 'I'm a twenty-two-year-old gamer boy who still lives at home' kind of way."

Alyssa felt defensive for some reason. "Come on, he's not twenty-two." Looking at his blown up face in front of her, she was *almost* positive he was older than that. The "almost" gnawed at her, and prompted her to add, "I don't think."

Bella gave an "are you sure about that?" look, her eyebrows high on her forehead.

Alyssa stood firm, mostly out of hope. She couldn't imagine telling her mom she was dating someone that young.

Dating? Where had that thought come from? She was so glad she hadn't said that out loud; Bella would have likely fallen straight off the bed. "No, he's definitely older. But... still younger than us I think."

"You *think*?" Bella exclaimed, "look at that baby face! He's crazy young."

Even if her friend was right, maybe "young" wasn't so bad - aside from the fact that her mother would have a hay day. "I think that's part of what I liked about him though."

"Ooh, you cougar!"

Alyssa threw another pillow at her. "No!" she half yelled, half laughed. "I'm serious though, joking around with him was refreshing. I'm so used to all of these medical guys being so serious. And I love them, you know I do, but it was just... nice."

Bella seemed to mull this information over for a few seconds. "Okay, if he's really that cool, I get it. Demeanor can take a guy from a seven to a nine real quick. And if he makes you laugh, he could be a straight ten." She looked at her friend with tender eyes. "Just as long as he doesn't make you laugh as much as I do. That's not allowed."

"Never," Alyssa giggled, "come on now!"

"Alright alright, I want to see more!"

10

Clayton

BrightView always stirred up memories of Clayton's early days with the Program. This facility is where it had all started.

For the first few years after his mother's accident, Clayton had felt hopeless. He remembered sitting by her bedside day in and day out, feeling as though she could never experience happiness again. He blamed himself. The guilt was like a Chinese finger trap; the more he struggled against it, tried to pull himself free, the tighter it gripped onto him. Even as she began to slowly improve, it'd been clear she would never be the same... unless he took matters into his own hands.

Eventually, Clayton had started using all his hours at BrightView to begin developing a way for his mother to once again do everything she'd been able to before the accident.

He'd drawn up blueprints for at least a dozen different inventions, but every nurse or doctor he showed them to looked at him with pity in their eyes, pushing him to start accepting the fact that she would never be able to do those things. She could never run, or jump, or dance... she couldn't even feed herself.

The countless rejections had been taking their toll on him, until one day, the hospital had a woman come in to do a VR demonstration for the patients as part of a community outreach. The game was a flight simulation, where players attempted to take off, fly, and then land a plane without crashing. They'd wanted to skip his mother's room, and Clayton had been furious.

"Hasn't she had enough opportunities taken away from her?" he'd shouted. "Now you can't even bother to include her in activities *meant* for patients? What kind of facility are you running here? I'm trying to push her forward, and you're pulling her back!"

A shaky nurse had profusely apologized. "We're so sorry, Mr. Reeves… it's just, with her paralysis, she won't be able to… that is to say, we weren't sure if she… well, she won't be able to use it."

"That's ridiculous!" He'd insisted. "Her eyes still work, don't they? She can put on the goggles. She can tell me what to do, and I'll use the controller."

His mother had loved the whole experience, and the idea for Salvation was born.

That little blue plane was her salvation. Her saving grace. They'd finally been able to laugh together, to work as a team. It seemed to cure some of her seemingly endless boredom, and most importantly, she couldn't stop smiling throughout the whole game.

Of course, Clayton had known there was a lot to be done. He sought to create an experience that his mother could use all on her own, even when he wasn't there to help her.

Though he'd still felt guilt, the finger trap wasn't too tight anymore. He'd stopped struggling, stopped fighting it. When the grip loosened, he felt a new kind of shackle. This time placed around his ankles, a ball and chain weighing him down. He began to see his mother as a burden.

He'd assumed responsibility for her happiness. Her entertainment. Her reason to continue living.

So he'd spent years developing the Program, and over that time, he'd discovered just how capable he truly was of making something extraordinary. He'd continued to raise his own expectations of himself and his project even more, lifting the bar higher and higher for what he knew the experience could be.

How much was he capable of? Could he truly design a system where people like his mom would be able to *feel* like they were moving their limbs? Where they could *feel* strong and capable and independent? Where she wouldn't need him anymore... wouldn't blame him anymore, but *thank* him instead for giving her her life back?

As he stared incredulously at her now, despite knowing he *had* achieved those goals, it was difficult for him to feel like he'd given her a miracle. She looked, for lack of a better term, horrible. The first and most obvious thing he noticed when he entered her tent to examine her were the Oc X's - round, metal claws forcing her eyes open.

He quickly grabbed the eyedrops off the bedside table and squeezed a few drops into each eye. It didn't make much of a difference. While they no longer looked dried out, they were so glazed over that a stranger walking into the room might not know if she were dead or alive.

And the smell was nauseating, though Clayton had grown used to it over time. She'd had a catheter ever since her accident.

It was usually quite manageable, but she was spending so much time in Salvation lately, and the nurses knew they weren't allowed to enter any of the rooms that were test running the Program unless Clayton granted them access. The test patients had all agreed to this; there was a contract to prove it.

Since the nurses were unable to tend to her as often as they needed, she was missing out on some basic hygienic practices. He didn't want her odor to become strong enough to alert workers outside of the door and prompt them to come in.

What *was* that smell? She'd had no one to help her go to the bathroom today, and her teeth needed a good brushing... but there was something even more than that... Clayton couldn't quite place what it was.

He didn't like seeing her like this. He wanted to log in and join her, but he knew Dr. Barnes was right about her needing to take better care of herself in the real world. It was only 6:00; he had plenty of time. He would talk to her about logging less hours later, when he saw her awake inside Salvation, but for now, he couldn't let the nurses see her in this condition, so he had no other choice but to help her himself.

He emptied her catheter, and filled a sponge to drip some water into her mouth. *When was the last time she had any water?* He wrung out a new sponge and moved to his least favorite task: cleaning her up.

Just as he finished her front and was about to move on to her back, his microphone started buzzing in his ear. He touched the piece to answer the call, but didn't speak. Anyone who had his number knew they were expected to talk first and identify themselves.

"Hey babe, it's me, Courtney," sang a bubbly voice over the phone.

He breathed a sigh of relief. He hadn't felt like talking to Dr. Barnes right now. Or his brand new partner, Gordon Avery - though Clayton actually liked the new psychologist. Well... liked that the newly hired man could potentially put him into Salvation. He liked that very much.

"Is there a reason you're calling me so close to 8:00?"

"Geez, someone's extra serious today." Though the words were accusative, she didn't sound annoyed - one of the many reasons they worked well together. She understood that a man needs to work, and she didn't get upset when he was short with her, or had limited time to speak with her, or was rushing out the door. "That's exactly why I was calling: because it's so close to 8:00. I wanted to catch you before you go into the office. I miss you!"

Another reason they worked. She was sweet. Carefree. He felt good when he was around her. Not so alone. She reminded him that there was a life for him outside of Salvation. The woman who used to remind him of that fact was lying in a hospital bed next to him, abandoning this life more and more with each passing day.

"I miss you too." He meant that. Even if she wasn't the prettiest girl in the world. She was smart. Challenging. And, she liked him, unlike most of the bitches in Chicago. She actually gave him a chance. Didn't mock him straight to his face. "But we are onto something here; we're making major breakthroughs... I mean, within the next few months our investors are going to visit, and when they see what we've accomplished... well, let's just say it's going to be life-changing." Clayton was breathing hard with excitement just thinking about it.

"That's amazing, babe, I'm proud of you!" Her joy was far from shocking. She would reap the benefits of his success, too.

"But you realize what this means, right?" *No.* "You have to bring me to see it now!"

He'd pondered the idea before, but had ultimately come to the conclusion it wouldn't work. "I told you, I don't think it's a good idea.You... you wouldn't like it."

She let out an exaggerated sigh of frustration. "Baaa-abe," she whined, "You've been working on this thing ever since I've known you, and you've *never* let me see what you're working on. You barely even give me any details at all! There's this huge, gigantic part of you that I don't know, and that I want to get to know."

As usual, he was touched that she cared so much; he hadn't yet gotten used to the feeling. "That's considerate of you, but it's just..."

"Just what?" Even while she was questioning him, there was a kindness to her voice that assured him she wasn't angry. "I'd be bored? I'd think it's dumb? I won't. It's important to you, which means it's important to me. And so what if I have a 'bad reaction?' If the worst case scenario is that I'm a little bored, well then—"

"That's not the worst case scenario," Clayton muttered, more to himself than to her. "I've got some work I have to finish up before I go into the office. I have to go." He hung up on her, an occurrence not uncommon for him. He shook off the conversation, turning his attention back to his mother.

As he gently rolled her over, he discovered the source of the previously unidentifiable stink: bedsores.

He tried not to blame himself, to pull again at his finger traps. *It's not that big of a deal, is it?* She was paralyzed; hours in bed without moving were inevitable. She wasn't like the other patients, where the Program was keeping her from physical therapy or going on walks.

The excuses weren't working. She needed more time with her nurses. They were supposed to be flipping her over regularly. Moving her limbs. Bathing her - his sad attempt at a spongebath wasn't cutting it.. *He* was the thing preventing them from caring for her.

"Snap out of it," he said aloud, to only himself. "This is what keeps the Program going. Lack of improving physical health forces users to continue renewing their membership, continue pledging their loyalty to the Program. Soon, our physical bodies will be obsolete. What good is this body even doing for her anyway?" He looked at it in disgust. "Nothing! Her life isn't here anymore, it's in Salvation. And that's *good*. She's perfect there. Except..." He squinted at the blemishes and her pale, veiny skin. He wished he didn't have to look at them. When he did, it was more difficult to convince himself she would be okay. That he was doing more good than harm.

Saved by the bell. His watch was beeping loudly to remind him of the time. 8:00. Time to log in.

11

Derek

The dispatcher had been right about Bianca. Her body had healed almost instantly, making a full recovery in just over a week, but the miscarriage had occurred six weeks ago and Derek's wife lay curled up on the couch in a tear-stained blanket looking as though she were in as much pain as she had been on the day she'd lost her baby.

She wasn't the only one who was suffering. Derek was battling his own world of pain. They were alike in that way. Each hurt, and each feeling alone in their journey of grief. Like two parallel lines. Both heading in the same direction. Both starting their path from the same X coordinate. Both close enough that they nearly touched, but neither one able to initiate getting closer to the other.

It wasn't the loss that upset him the most. Early miscarriages are fairly common, or so he'd been told a dozen times by a dozen different people. He and Bianca were still young, and the doctor had reassured them they could try again with a large probability of success. He could get over the loss. It was seeing his wife broken that he could hardly bare.

This was the human he adored more than anything and anyone, and to watch helplessly as she was snapped in half was slowly tearing him apart. But he couldn't show it.

He remembered the words on the phone urging him to be strong for her, and shielded his inner torment.

He peered into the living room, eyeing Bianca before going in to talk to her. He was stalling, praying some miraculous plan of what to say or how to "cure" her would pop into his head if he just waited another second more. His heart panged as he saw her hollow eyes, empty, staring at nothing, the same way they had been for what seemed like an eternity.

He didn't recognize this woman, the woman he had vowed to love in sickness and in health. He remembered the vow, but somehow he never thought sickness would turn her into someone he didn't know. This woman who was once so full of life and humor, now devoid of all emotion and movement. There had to be a way to get her back to herself. For him, but even more importantly, for her.

The tear he thought he'd made a deal with betrayed him, slipping out as he thought about Bianca not existing anymore - at least the Bianca he knew. *Could the world really be so cruel to allow someone as vibrant and beautiful as her to stay so dark and cold forever?*

Derek was angry at the tear, disappointed in himself for allowing it to fall. For a second, he was thankful for Bianca's absence of attention, because it meant that she didn't catch his slip-up. He swiped at his cheek, wiping the moisture away, and turned to the hall mirror to practice his smile.

Forced. But it was the best he could do, so he combed his hair back with his fingers and turned to walk into the room.

"Daaar-liiing," he sung, as he headed over to the couch and

66

plopped down at Bianca's side, "I was thinking we could go out for breakfast today. Mr. Mooney's, my treat!"

Bianca was silent, though her eyes did roll sideways and upward in his direction. Derek's smile turned a bit more genuine. Hopeful. This was more than he typically got out of her, and he had to run with it.

"That's right, baby: you, me, and a steaming pile of chocolate chip waffles. Maybe I'll even get you a hot chocolate... If you sweet talk me enough, I just may be able to be persuaded."

She didn't even crack a smile. Then again, he hadn't expected her to. He didn't lose faith, especially as he caught the tiniest shift in her body language. He could run with this momentum.

Over the last couple of days, Bianca had gotten worse, worse than the day of the 911 call, which was something Derek hadn't thought was possible. Since Wednesday, she hadn't moved at all, even to eat or drink. He'd been so worried he'd finally caved and called in her sister, who had left work immediately and practically force-fed Bianca.

Together, they'd talked to a doctor who'd told them Bianca was suffering from a severe case of postpartum depression. She'd suggested some pills that she highly recommended the two of them convince Bianca to take, as well as a second task: to get Bianca moving in any way possible.

"Whatever that may look like," she'd ordered. "A walk outside, going out to lunch, picking up groceries... even something as simple as cleaning around the house. She needs endorphins. She needs change. I mean, at the very least, she needs to get off the couch." Derek and Rin nodded. "A body at rest stays at rest," Dr. Andrews instructed, "and a body in motion stays in motion. Once you get her up, even for something small, that might be the small spark she needs to gradually keep improving." Derek had liked the sound of that. He was desperate to get her moving, to help her return to her old self again.

With his newfound encouragement from the small shifts in her eyes and body at his proposal of breakfast, Derek was determined. A window of opportunity. *Possibly my only window.* He ran to grab her boots and barreled back towards the couch. Flinging the blanket off of her, he sang, "These boots are made for walkin', and that's just what they'll do!" as he slid them onto her feet without asking or waiting for permission.

"No," Bianca's voice was barely above a whisper, but Derek was startled nonetheless. She hadn't said a word to anyone, including him, in these past six weeks.

Derek hadn't thought something like a miscarriage could be this serious, serious enough to send someone into a debilitating depression, but he'd quickly learned that he was wrong. The doctors told him all the medical causes - mostly messed up hormone levels and bodily trauma, from what he'd been able to understand - but Derek had trouble believing even those catalysts could cause *this much* damage, until one doctor pulled him aside and explained how the more a woman desires a child often directly correlates with how intense the depression that follows can be. *That explains a lot.* He thought about how much of Bianca's identity was tied up in being a mother.

It might sound strange to some, a young woman who has yet to have had any children being so wrapped up with desire to have and nurture some of her own, but to Derek, it had always made perfect sense.

Bianca had talked about kids from their very first date.

"How are you so gorgeous and yet *hilarious* at the same time?" Derek had sputtered between snorts of laughter.

Bianca was modest. "Oh stop! You're handsome, and funny to

68

boot, so don't go acting like I'm something special." Derek had been overjoyed that she'd said he was handsome, but anyone could see she was way out of his league, he was sure. He looked like a comedian, she looked like an old Hollywood actress. Or a model for the Parisian runway. He'd wondered if it was too soon to play the "architect" card. Ultimately, he'd waited to tell her his job title, opting to continue asking about her.

"No seriously, you have been lighting up this room all night; you've had a clever reply to everyone, even the wait staff. Do you do stand-up on the side?" he'd teased.

"Well, I'll tell you my secret... I coach soccer over at Eris Middle. Those little buggers will keep you on your toes. I swear my personality has changed so much since I started working with them. You have to be extremely sarcastic to keep up with them, or they'll eat you alive!"

Immensely excited by her, Derek was determined to find out more. Where did she grow up? What was her favorite hobby? Where did she learn to banter so well? He'd wanted to keep up. To match her energy. To prove *he* had a personality worth investing in, too.

Her looks had thrown him off his game, though. Scrambled his thoughts. She really was breathtaking, and in much better shape than he was. Hearing about the soccer had explained those muscular legs, discernible even through her jeans.

"That's sooo weird that you think you're sarcastic, I hadn't noticed at all." Bianca had rolled her eyes at his clearly sarcastic tone, but she'd been masking a smile and it'd been all the encouragement he needed.

Eager to learn more, he'd commented that she must love kids to have a job like that, and the way she'd lit up while talking about them made it more than obvious that children

69

were the highlight of who she was. The conversation veered to her babysitting days, her summers as a camp counselor, and even her experiences face painting during charity drives in her hometown. She claimed she was "absolutely dreadful at art," so she'd had no idea why they'd asked her to help with such occasions, but Derek could already hypothesize that her radiant spirit and intoxicating personality were just a couple of the reasons behind that choice.

Over the years, Derek grew to see with his own eyes what she'd been trying to express on that first date - an outing that had led to a second, and a third, and eventually a wonderful marriage. He watched her coo over the babies at church, and saw the joy bubble up from the tips of her dancing toes to the sparkle in her shining eyes. He cheered on the sidelines as she coached probably a hundred soccer games, laughing with the kids as much as she motivated them. They loved her possibly just as much as she loved them.

He helped her make costumes for the elementary schoolers when she volunteered to assist with their play, and he didn't know who seemed more proud, since her smile was as big as the little girl who'd had a solo of "Twinkle Twinkle Little Star."

Derek was there through bake sales and dance recitals and spelling bees... They'd become second parents to the children of their small town. Derek attended happily; he would do anything for Bianca, this shimmering jewel of a woman who made every aspect of life more exciting. More vibrant. More fun.

And as bright as Bianca was normally, nothing could hold a candle to the way she glowed when she was with children. Derek knew they gave her not just joy, but purpose. Filled with that purpose, she became a shooting star that never stopped hurtling through space. Not just ignited for a short time, but burning forever, where everyone could marvel at the light as they watched her soar past.

And so, it was no surprise when Bianca had immediately wanted to try for a family upon getting married. It wasn't coincidental that she'd planned their honeymoon in a fire-warmed cabin in Vermont during the heart of the snowiest winter month of the year. They'd had a week of romantic nights while the fire roared beneath the mantle, and a few weeks later Bianca had thrown up her breakfast and Derek was sprinting to the corner store for a test.

Bianca was always vivacious, she was always sparkling, and still Derek felt like he'd never truly known her, never saw the most beautiful parts of her, until she was pregnant. She'd gone through a metamorphosis, like a caterpillar changing into a butterfly - though she'd really never been a caterpillar in her life.

Jubilation radiated through her whole existence. And while a smile never seemed to leave her face, she still had that bite to her that Derek had fallen in love with. She had this sense of humor where she acted as though she could care less about things, but everyone knew she cared. She cared, and she was more passionate about people and about life than Derek had ever known a person could be. If someone would have asked her if she was happy, if she was in love with her life, there was no more obvious answer than "Yes!"

And now she was telling him "no." Not just in this moment, not just with this spoken "no" to the proposal of breakfast, but with every dead-eyed stare she was saying "no." "I don't care." "I don't want to be here." Each day she lay, only moving to achieve the bare minimum, she was saying "no." In continuously ignoring his desperate efforts to help her, she was saying "no."

And in Derek's head, to all his internal questions wondering if she still loved him, if she was going to be okay, if she wanted to fight to get their life back, their relationship back, she was saying "no." Which is why the next words out of her mouth shocked him.

"I'm sorry baby." She grabbed his hand. He couldn't process this gesture, she'd hardly been responding to his touches, let alone initiated one herself, since the hospital visit. And the term of endearment? He was confused. "I didn't mean to just blurt out 'no' to your fun idea."

This was the first time she seemed to be trying to manipulate her face to appear happy, and it was unnatural. The effort looked draining. "It's just that," she sat up, inching her face close to his, "I have another fun idea of something we can do."

Derek was still perplexed, until he saw the seduction in her eyes and felt her pulling him in by the neck of his shirt.

Instinctively, he jerked his face back, avoiding her contact. Her face dropped, and he instantly regretted how quickly he'd wrenched his neck, but not the action itself. He couldn't kiss her in this state, could he? *No. She isn't herself.* But the doctor *had* said to get her moving…

He was confused. Her sudden flirtation had come out of nowhere. Completely unexpected. He was a kid who'd just been given a pop quiz: completely unprepared, with no idea what he should say, or think, or do.

When Derek first dodged her pass, Bianca's nose had reddened with embarrassment, but she'd shaken it off and was back in seduction mode.

"Come on baby," She inched closer and softened her voice with each word, "It's been too long, don't tell me you don't want this." The warmth of her breath on the side of his neck almost made him believe that he did want this, that he wanted her. And the truth was, he *did* want her. But he wanted *her* - he wanted his Bianca back. Not whoever this false version of herself was. This fake lust. This half-attempt at intimacy.

It took more restraint than he knew he had to tell her no. That he didn't want her this way.

Not used to being turned down, especially by her husband, insecurity flooded her eyes. *Finally, an honest emotion.*

"I know I'm a mess, I know. And I'm so sorry, but I just need you so badly. I need you to come to me and love me and kiss me and tell me everything is going to be okay."

A glimmer of hope. They were actually talking; she was being vulnerable and real. Maybe everything really could be okay. He would give anything for everything to be okay. With a fistfull of her t-shirt, he pulled her in and kissed her. It was tender and intimate, hope emanating through his touch.

This kiss that felt like a first kiss happened in slow motion, and Derek's head should probably still be torn but he was getting what he'd been praying for through all these weeks and the culmination of his happiness and relief made his mind blank of everything except for how good it felt to have her back.

She broke the comfortable silence. "I love you; I'm so sorry." Another passion-filled kiss. "I know I haven't been here, but I'm here now. I want to be here. With you." Her eyes pierced his. "I want to give you all of me. I'm yours. All yours." She started at his lips, then his neck, nuzzling into him. Exploring him with her tongue like she was a pirate who'd been sailing for months, clutching her map, and she'd finally hit the island where the "X" was supposed to be.

Derek gently stopped her, picking her chin up with his hand so he could look into her eyes while explaining himself. "I want you so badly," he breathed, "but you don't need to do that."

Her eyebrows furrowed, but he wasn't done. "You don't need to do this to apologize; you haven't done anything wrong. You don't need to make me feel better. You don't need to go from zero to one hundred for me."

He brushed away the hairs that had messily fallen onto her face. "To me, this is one hundred. This is one thousand, one million, just seeing you feeling better. Talking with you. Getting any of you - your mind, your words, your company - makes me unbelievably happy. Let's go out to breakfast. Or stay here and talk. Or go for a walk... That would be more than enough for me."

His speech was intended to be sweet, to make Bianca feel at ease, but she looked *annoyed*.

"No, baby. It's alright; I want to. Listen, I'm not doing this just to please you. I *want* to. It's been six weeks, and the doctor said we could try again after six weeks. She said it's okay. We can try. We can make a baby."

And there it was.

The hope Derek had been naively digging his nails into was yanked away. She wasn't breaking her silence because she loved him. She was throwing herself at him because she wanted a baby. Yesterday she could barely manage to get dressed, and suddenly today she was fully capable of throwing herself at him? Of manipulation?

For the first time since the phone call, he decided to ignore the advice of the 911 operator. He couldn't stay by her side, or support her. Not when she was lying. To both of them. He grabbed his keys and walked out the door, leaving Bianca alone.

12

Alyssa

Together, the girls scrolled through Jackson's pictures, discovering his extremely awkward phase - and by phase, it was really his entire childhood until fairly recently when he'd finally cut his hair, started wearing contact lenses, lost most of the baby weight that had still been lingering in his cheeks, and cleared up his acne-prone skin.

Their research told them he'd been the salutatorian of his high school class, and seeing that he'd graduated in June of 2011, they estimated he'd be about twenty-six now - approximately four years younger than Alyssa.

They found he'd won an array of awards from all sorts of "nerdy, science-y competitions," as Bella called them, and that he'd been accepted into DeVry University in 2011, and graduated about three years ago, in 2016. Alyssa thought it strange that it took him longer than average to graduate, given all the evidence that he was extremely smart. But this puzzling information only fascinated her more. There was a story there, and she wanted to hear it.

Of course, Bella was most interested in finding his exes. There seemed to be only two from what they could find, which pleased Alyssa. *That must mean he's committed, and not dating around just to date around.* Bella argued that he really didn't have much of a chance of catching a girl's eye until about 2015, so it wasn't *that* telling.

The first girlfriend they found was Kenzie. The two had dated for several months, but there wasn't much evidence of them on the internet. Aside from the occasional updated profile picture or significant announcement, Jackson was very private online.

Thinking of the awkward features he sported when he was younger and imagining how he'd likely been treated, Alyssa wondered if he was simply insecure and didn't like posting pictures of himself. She found herself sympathizing with this boy that she hardly knew, resenting the idea that anyone may have hurt him in the past.

This certainly seemed to be the case with his next girlfriend, Kyra. Upon a basic investigation, anyone could see Jackson was infatuated with her. That relationship was the first and only time the girls could find evidence of Jackson consistently posting pictures.

The captions were sweet, and he was unashamed to outwardly express his admiration of her. He was the one to pen a loving caption on their anniversary, and he was the first to share pictures from their trip to Alaska. He wanted to show her off, and she...

"Oof," Bella breathed in through clenched teeth, "She didn't even *'like'* this post." Another mystery. But their break up was not one.

Upon a more intense examination - the search *was* being led by Bella after all - the two found Kyra's page. They scrolled back to the general timeline of when Jackson had stopped posting about her, and the first pages that popped up were several rants from the bitter ex. She never named him, but a person would have to be blind to not see she was talking about Jackson.

They were mostly complaints about how "guys suck," and that she was "looking for a man, not a boy" and her inquiring if anyone knew where she could find one.

To Alyssa, publicly slandering an ex was unbecoming. *Relationships are never black and white.* She thought back to past experiences where she'd tell her friends one or two qualities that annoyed her about whoever she was dating at the time, and they'd immediately jump to, "Yeah, maybe you need to dump him." This conclusion baffled Alyssa. The intricacies of her relationships were so much greater than one or two habits of her partner. There was always more to consider. She would think, "This person is *more* than 'not buying me gifts,' or, 'hating talking on the phone.'"

The boyfriend who didn't express love monetarily or disliked communicating through a cell phone was often the same boy who wrote her handwritten notes, and would drive over at 2:00 in the morning if she'd texted, and was sweet to her parents, and showered her with compliments, and helped her study, and put up with her long hours without complaints. An abundance of colors between black and white.

She imagined their mutual friends seeing Kyra's posts and judging Jackson, and she had to stop herself from digging her nails into her palms. If anything, Jackson should be commended for being the bigger person, and keeping any cruel words she was sure *he* could conjure up about his ex-girlfriend to himself.

But people don't tend to work that way. Considering the friends that used to be mutual online were now only friends with Kyra, her belief was solidified.

Bella must've caught Alyssa's expression as they were looking through Kyra's page. "I know, maybe he's not as great as you thought after all." Alyssa was shocked that this was the conclusion Bella had drawn from all they'd seen.

"Come on, we can't go off the word of an angry ex now, can we?"

"Good point… I guess you'll have to go out on a date with him so you can find out for yourself!" Bella playfully shook her friend's shoulders.

Alyssa suddenly remembered her phone, and felt under the pillows to feel where it had slid to. When her fingers brushed against metal, she pulled the device out and tapped the screen to check her notifications.

There it was: the name "Mr. Computer Expert" was written next to the little green text bubble symbol.

Bella screamed with glee. "SHUT UP!" She leaned her face as close to Alyssa's as possible so she could read along with her. What's it say?"

Alyssa thought for a second about privacy, but figured Jackson's privacy had already been thrown out the window when Bella decided to search up his entire life history online, so what difference would it make if she read the text? Besides, she shared everything with Bella.

She just didn't want to be like Kyra, who seemed to have no respect for her previous relationship with Jackson. Alyssa wanted *their* relationship to be different.

Wow. Alyssa's mind was spiraling; why was she jumping ahead and thinking about terms like "relationship" already? Perhaps she was getting a little too caught up in the teenage-like feeling of it all.

She swiped up and checked the text. "**Ahh that makes**

sense, even though I doubt your last name is Milano, I was definitely Charmed."

"Oh my GOSH! Bella swooned, "he is SO flirting with you! What did you say to him?"

"I just said he was such a lifesaver for saving my paper," Alyssa recalled, "and then I said something like, 'Oh, this is Alyssa, by the way.'"

Her phone lit up again.

"So much so that I actually walked out of the store without the battery I needed for myself... oops."

Alyssa chuckled to herself, gratified she'd had such a powerful effect on him already. Bella, as though reading her mind, chimed in with, "You have that effect on *everyone*, Alyssa. Remember when Cameron missed that final because he was hanging out in the OR observatory talking to you?" Bella laughed as she remembered that day, and how frantic he'd been when he'd finally glanced at his watch and saw that he'd talked through half of his exam.

"Professor Jones let him take it during the next hour; it was totally fine!" Alyssa corrected her friend, defensively.

Bella's hands were on her hips. "That's not the point, the point is..."

Another text. Both girls stopped and turned their attention to read.

"Oh, this is Jackson, by the way."

"You're blushing!" Bella pointed at Alyssa. There was no denying it; her face was the color of a Rainier cherry.

"I just feel bad!" Alyssa partially lied, "we already know his name is Jackson because we're horrible stalkers!" She stood up to glance at the wall mirror as part of the gag. "I can't even look at myself!" She turned away, feigning self-loathing.

The reason this was all a partial lie was because she really did feel bad, but that wasn't the full reason she was blushing. She liked this text exchange, just as she'd liked their first meeting in person. These back and forths with Jackson were invigorating, and she was hoping for more.

"You're right," Bella sighed. "I feel just awful. Christmas is so close and now we're probably going to be on the 'Naughty List.'" Alyssa snorted. "But I mean, if we are already on that list, we might as well keep going..."

"Bella!"

"What?" Bella was not letting up. "Come on, we've already seen this much, will it really make a difference if we look at more? Besides, he doesn't post much anyway, it's basically all from his mom." Bella half-laughed, undoubtedly believing this was embarrassing for Jackson.

It was true though; almost everything the girls learned about this boy came from his mother posting on his timeline.

She boasted about how proud she was of his Computer Science award from the Imagine Cup, how handsome she thought he looked for the Christmas Eve church service, how wonderful she thought the bouquet of flowers was that he bought for Kyra one day... Anything and everything Jackson did got the stamp of approval from his mom, apparently. No matter how significant or how small, Cathy Halloway was constantly bragging about her son for all of the internet to see.

Alyssa was aware that life online was often just a "highlight reel." People often like to show off the good parts, and keep the bad parts hidden. But she had a feeling Jackson's mom legitimately thought everything her son did was good, and none of it bad. Alyssa had no way of knowing for sure - Cathy wasn't likely to post if she was angry with him or disappointed - but the way she rambled on about her son made it pretty clear she held the highest opinion of him.

This is a good sign. They always say you can tell how a boy will treat you by how he treats his mother, right? Clearly he was doing something right to gain so much approval from her, and their relationship appeared to be an extremely loving one.

Bella clearly didn't share the same perception of their findings. "Ugh, I can't stand a mama's boy."

"That's just because Clark's mom babied him and now you're paranoid whenever a guy even slightly gets along with his mom."

"Am I paranoid, or am I just enlightened?" Bella started. "I've seen what happens when a woman thinks her son is God's gift to this earth." She was getting heated now. "He becomes spoiled, Alyssa, spo-*iled*. And he can't take any criticism. I mean, when you tell him one thing you want him to work on, *one* thing, he gets so defensive and thinks *you're* the problem because you won't just tell him how perfect he is. And before you know it, you'll be cooking for him and cleaning and packing his lunch and folding his clothes because that's what his mommy did and he just expects..."

"Whoa, okay, slow down Bella," Alyssa put a palm on her impassioned friend's knee. "I'm sorry Clark was such a jerk. You deserve better. Not just better, the best. But," she gently argued, "not every guy is like Clark. What do you want me to do, date a guy who's mom hates him? That can't be a good sign, can it?"

Bella tilted her head in thoughtful agreement. "Besides, I just learned Jackson's name half an hour ago. I don't know him at all... *We* don't know him. If we get to know him and we don't like him, I'll totally kick him to the curb, okay? Promise."

Alyssa held out her pinky finger, keeping with the spirit of young girlhood. Bella extended her hand and locked pinkies with her best friend, praying that this type of promise was just as binding as if Alyssa would have signed her name on a contract in ink.

13

Clayton

Rifling through his briefcase, Clayton pulled out his pair of Oc X's. He'd tried them on before, in anticipation, imagining what it would be like to join Salvation himself, but never getting to enter. Until today. If the new psychologist's voice worked for him, that is.

His mother was currently logged in, the projector already on, so he went ahead and crawled onto his cot inside the Set-up. The white tent draped over both he and his mother as she lay mouth open, unblinking, in her BrightView bed beside him.

He inserted a long needle into his vein so the drugs in the IV could "calm his mind." The cold liquid entered his bloodstream. He laid his head down and placed the metal rings around his eyes, expanding their circumference, and pushing them tightly into place.

Oc X's secured, he laid his hands onto the restraint pads, and they tightened around his wrists and ankles. "Join user 2." Seconds after the words barrelled out, he became less and less conscious of the feeling in his real body as he watched the metronome tick tick tick above him. The system warned,

"Logging in in five, four, three, two..."

His new partner Gordon's voice was smooth as butter on the audio tape. *Holy shit. This is going to work.* He watched the swinging pendulum and, to his astonishment, faded into Salvation.

Immediately, he felt relief. His body mass no longer weighed on his joints, and his knee and back pain disappeared. He ran a quick lap around headquarters, just because he could. Then, he went off to search for his mother.

The word "search" was applied loosely, since he checked his cameras constantly and knew exactly where all six users were at all times. He knew when they were logged in, and when they exited the Program. He knew what they did while inside the Program. He left no stone unturned.

He was aware of who each user interacted with, and often checked in to hear what they were talking about. Right before he'd entered, he'd heard his mother tell Jim - another patient - that she was heading over to Dr. Barnes' office to see if he had joined yet.

His earpiece had kept him up to date, but now that he was inside the simulation, he could walk into his Salvation office and monitor from his security camera there. He'd thought it would be convenient to have a way to monitor from headquarters, but he had several other surveillance rooms as well. Some, like the windowless room he entered now, were secret, and he was the only person who had the key.

These secret rooms were marked as "full access" in his private notes, meaning they showed every inch of the Program's layout. His personal bedroom was "full access" as well, but the rest of them were what Clayton considered decoys.

The decoy surveillance cameras only showed public areas

so the other founders would assume they could see as much as Clayton could. He wanted Dr. Barnes and Gordon and the other members of their hopefully soon-to-be-growing team to be under the illusion that they held just as much power as he did. That he had nothing to hide from them.

Through the screen in his private viewing room inside headquarters, he clicked on the square that showed Dr. Barnes' office, enhancing the video. Sure enough, he saw his mother walking up and knocking on the door.

"Georgie, please, come in." Clayton watched as the two made themselves comfortable on the long, brown leather couch. "Has Clayton spoken with you today?"

"No, I... I haven't seen him." The question mark in her voice told him she was realizing this now for the first time.

"Wait, he hasn't been to see you yet today? He hasn't stopped by BrightView at all?"

"I guess I... I'm not so sure."

"You're not sure?" Dr. Barnes tilted his head, "are you feeling okay?"

"Oh, I feel fantastic!" she gushed. "It's not that I don't remember, it's just that, well, I think I must've lost track of time again. I haven't been to BrightView since this morning."

"*Been to* BrightView?" Dr. Barnes' mouth gaped in astonishment. "You're talking as though that facility is a place you go visit... Like this is the real world, here. It's not, Georgie. Chicago, BrightView, *that's* what's real. And you *have* been there today. All day, laying in your bed, not getting any proper care because you've been—"

"You're wrong," Clayton's mother picked at her fingernail, completely calm. "Maybe what you're saying is technically correct, but I don't care about technicalities. I don't care how

I'm here, I just care that I'm here. This is real to me. What does anything else matter?"

"Your body matters!"

"My body is doing amazing. Look." She sat on the ground and bent at the hips to easily touch her toes. Then she sprang back up, and spun in a circle, holding her arms out as if to curtsy and say, "See?"

Dr. Barnes wasn't impressed. "Look at yourself." He gestured to her wrists. "For starters, you're completely bruised from overuse of those restraints. They were never intended for the amount of wear you're putting them through. And I'm sure your ankles look the same way." Georgie looked down, sheepishly. They were covered by her hospital socks, but the bruises were, in fact, there. "Your skin is flakey and pale, which tells me you haven't been going outside, or implementing any kind of skin care routine—"

"I have been going outside. Every day, Dr. Barnes. I can walk outside right now—"

The doctor wasn't getting through to her, and the sweat above his brow gave away his growing frustration. "You are not outside, you are lying in a bed at BrightView Assisted Living."

"I'm not there; I'm here. Look at me. I'm right here."

"Then what are these?" Dr. Barnes shifted her gown to reveal her bed sores.

She looked at them, Clayton could tell, for the first time. He thought he saw tears welling up in her eyes as she stared, but he couldn't tell if he imagined it because within milliseconds she yanked her gown back into place and insisted, "Clayton can get rid of those! Just you watch. Look at everything he's done so far. Look at what he's created. I remember when we used to spend hours playing that virtual reality game." After the accident. Clayton remembered too, fondly. "We could change our outfits, our hair, our skin color, our weight," this aroused Clayton's attention, "and that game was child's play compared to what my son has created. He can get rid of everything you're pointing out. I'm doing great physically, which is the most important thing, but if the looks are bothering you, he can just fix that. Will that make you happy?"

Clayton didn't bother listening to Dr. Barnes arguing with her any further. He'd deal with his "partner" later. What he was far more interested in at the moment was his mother's stroke of brilliance. It was so simple, so obvious, and yet it hadn't occurred to him until right now, in this instance. Of *course* he could change imperfections in appearances. How had he never thought of that?

The Program was designed to eliminate imperfections in bodily functions. His own campaign spoke of "having the life you deserve" and "being perfect inside of Salvation." But what could be more perfect than being healthy *and* beautiful?

If he really aimed to create a society of perfection, wouldn't that mean a world full of attractive, flawless-looking individuals? It was too easy, really. The simulation was rooted in psychology. If users simply chose how they wanted to look, he could adjust their audio to describe that version of them. Then, a simple update in the system and their "player" could appear to themselves and others however they desired. *He* could look however he desired.

The possibilities hit him like candy being thrown from a parade float. He could be taller. Thinner. More muscular. He could get rid of the gray in his hair that he so despised, maybe even try a new color and style. He'd always envied Leonardo DiCaprio, and he thought he'd like to give his hairstyle a whirl.

And a chiseled jawline; that was a must. It would always look sharp, and he wouldn't even have to shave. He could never shave quite right, anyway, always self-conscious of the cuts on his chin. And why stop there? He could have a whole new wardrobe, a luxury car... He'd never had a nice vehicle before.

He'd always driven what his mother called "rusty old pieces of junk," and Clayton had a hunch his old, crappy car was part of the reason his mom blamed him for the accident. "The steering wheel probably jammed on that deathtrap, or the tires were too flat, or the brakes weren't working right... You never got them checked when you were supposed to, and —"

His thoughts were abruptly slammed to a halt as the entire ground began shaking vigorously beneath him.

The force was so powerful that several trees were completely uprooted and fell to the ground, and the glass window next to him threatened to burst. Even though he was pretty sure getting injured inside the Program wouldn't affect his real body, he still ducked under his desk out of instinct.

These vibrations had similar effects to an earthquake, and they happened frequently, and seemingly randomly. At least, he hadn't been able to discover a pattern yet. As confident as Clayton was, his project still had some glitches that needed to be resolved.

Better add "somehow figure out how to stop the world from shaking every few days" to the to-do list. Though he told himself not to be, he was worried about these defects. He brushed them off while talking to Dr. Barnes, or other members of the staff, assuring them he "had everything under control." That he simply "hadn't gotten to it yet."

Those were lies. As adept as he was when it came to tech, he was in over his head with Salvation. If he really wanted to get this project off the ground, he'd need more help.

He was going to have to recruit some sort of master coder, that was inevitable. Someone who could help fix the glitches and who could also make room for the Program to continue expanding without crashing. A coder would be useful for keeping Salvation safe and protected - implementing an even stronger firewall that would be impossible to hack.

Clayton had done an impressive job, but for the size of the production he dreamed of growing into, one man, no matter how proficient, wouldn't suffice.

He'd also need an architect or engineer to construct a more monumental and tempting paradise, especially now that his mother had inspired new visions of cars and pools and everything glamorous.

A team to manufacture the Set-ups, creative designers, not to mention someone to handle legal... He couldn't continue doing it all. Salvation needed a voice to inspire - *that* was his job. While he wanted to have his hands in every department, he was stretching himself thin.

He watched the monitor as the users calmed down after the "earthquake," and decided to head over to Dr. Barnes' office. Just as he was easing his car into the parking lot, he saw his mother walking out the door.

"Clayton! Hi!" Her voice was an octave higher than normal; she was probably still a bit frazzled from her scuffle with Dr. Barnes. Clayton thought it unwise to upset her further, but after seeing how severely her body was degenerating lately, he decided he had to speak with her.

"Hi mom," he grinned and embraced her in a giant bear hug. She squeezed back, tightening her grip around his abdomen. A portion of his guilt subsided - how flawed could this place be if it allowed them to hug again? "Listen, Dr. Barnes thought I should talk to you. He's... We're worried about you."

"There's nothing to talk about. Your job is done, honey! Look at all you've done for me? You've attained the unattainable, achieved the unachievable. You're incredible. This place is incredible. Darling, do you even know how groundbreaking this place is? You don't have to worry about me; I'm doing better than anyone could've ever dreamed would be possible. You've done more than enough for me. You can finally stop worrying. You did it!"

He wished that were true. "I want to be completely and totally happy for you, I do, but mom, you can't be here all the time. Do you understand? Your body, your real body, the one at BrightView, *matters*. You have to take better care of it."

Her expression morphed into frustration, then anger. "What do you want me to do, take a walk? Huh? Stretch my legs? Is that what I need to do? So I can prevent them from becoming useless?" The originally bright color drained from Clayton's face. She hadn't spoken about her body like this in a long time. Her voice was filled with hatred. Bitterness.

"Or maybe I should go back so I can raise my arms up in the air, move them side to side, try a little yoga," she spat sharply. "No one is listening to me. My body there is useless. My life is here now. And that's okay! It's more than okay; it's wonderful."

"*You're* the one who's not listening," Clayton hissed back. "Seriously, you won't be able to log in if you're dead."

Regret more instant than ramen filled the space between them, both wishing they could start the conversation over.

"I'm sorry, mom. But, you didn't even drink water today. The line has to be drawn somewhere..."

"You're right; that was irresponsible of me. I'm sorry."

Clayton used this newfound truce to reason with her. "Look, it might not have seemed like it just now, but I'm on your side. I think people *should* be able to spend more time in Salvation. I'm about to make some changes, changes that I think will make people want to stay even more. We just have to be more responsible, okay?" She nodded. "Eventually, investors are going to want to talk to you, and the other test patients. In the real world. We need you to look halfway decent if we want to impress them."

"Fine," Georgie agreed. "And your town will have to have less earthquakes if we want to impress them. There was another one right before you got here. You'd think Dr. Barnes would be used to them by now, but I swear he looked like he was going to wet his pants."

They both had a good laugh at the doctor's expense, after which Clayton bid his mother goodbye and walked through the door to the doctor's office. He was ready to pitch his new idea to his partner.

14

Jackson

While Bella morphed into quite the sleuth when it came to finding information about people - namely boys - online, her detective skills were no match for "Mr. Computer Expert" Jackson Halloway's. He had Alyssa's smiling profile photo on his screen within seconds of entering the Loft, and spent any ounce of free time in the days that followed combing through every bit of her social media.

He found pictures of Alyssa Gloria Hart - as he'd discovered was her full name - laughing in scrubs, eating ice cream with Bella (strawberry, he noted), and opening gifts with her mom (Renee Hart) at Christmastime (no dad as far as he could see... Maybe he just didn't like photographs, though - Jackson could understand that).

He was entranced by the sight of her pretty face scrunched up in concentration while suturing a banana in what appeared to be the hospital break room, and he couldn't help but pause and zoom in on the image of her sleeping in that same room, covered by a big jacket. He zoomed closer. It was definitely a man's jacket.

He wondered who it belonged to, but pushed those thoughts aside. *She was the one who asked for my number. She must be single.* Or maybe she was the type of girl who flirted with guys all the time. *No.* Not this girl. He transferred his attention from the jacket back to her sleeping face. This girl was special. Different.

He was surprised to discover a girl as beautiful as Alyssa didn't post a lot of pictures. She was mostly tagged in photos by people at the hospital. He was also curious as to the small amount of friends she seemed to have. Not Facebook "Friends," she had a couple thousand of those, but real friends.

Other than Bella, and sometimes, rarely, her mother, she was only captured with people she worked and went to school with. And even then, the pictures were all taken at the hospital or in various classrooms. She was never captured out at a bar or hanging out with a large group of friends. *She's probably way too busy for that.* But most people he knew made time for those activities, regardless of their schedules.

He felt special, thinking about how many individuals he was sure wanted this remarkable girl's attention, and seeing how few she seemed to actually give it to. Yet, she'd been willing, if not eager, to give it to him.

Buzz-buzz. He grabbed his phone so quickly he almost felt embarrassed by it, even though no one had been there to witness the scene.

Darn. It was just his boss, Mr. Mejia. Initially he felt disappointed, a feeling that quickly evolved to concern as he wondered what the contents of the message could be.

Jackson had to admit he'd been exceptionally distracted these last few days, ever since meeting Alyssa. Plus he had an extensive history of getting into trouble at work. He wasn't a goody-two-shoes like everyone else; he would never be one of those guys who dedicated all his time to a job.

He slid his finger up his phone to open the message.

"Good afternoon, Jackson!" Was it only the afternoon? Yep, 2:17. He'd thought it was much later. He'd been waking up significantly earlier the last couple of days, which might have something to do with the fact that the more he adapted to Alyssa's schedule, the more they could talk. He'd cursed himself when he'd woken up past noon the day after their date to discover she'd texted him many hours earlier and he'd dozed right through the notification.

"I've been going through the data, and I noticed something about your performance."

Here it comes. It served him right; he really didn't log into work nearly as much as he should.

"Compared to the baseline, IT ticket speeds of our other branches and campuses, your tickets, on average, have been successfully resolved 15% quicker and 28% more efficiently than your counterparts."

Oh. He hadn't expected this.

Every technical issue he'd been assigned at the college had been simple so far. Problems uploading a lecture, glitches in videos, system crashes... They were all easy fixes, mostly from professors trying to upload too much data into an outdated system. Very basic override codes and storage hacks could solve any of those failures. At least, they were basic to him.

He read on, invested now that he knew it was positive feedback.

"That's very impressive work. That being said, we were wondering if you had any interest in applying for the Software Developer position. I know you were looking for part-time, so we understand that this full-time role

might not be the right fit for you. However, it would be a big promotion, and not to mention a substantial pay raise. We think your talents are above support work. If you are interested now, or become interested in the future, please fill out the transfer application online as a formality. Thank you, and keep up the good work!"

Jackson sat in this feeling for a moment. As he sat, his phone timed out and went dark, his reflection appearing on the screen. He was the same person he had been a week ago, so logically his image couldn't have changed... But he could swear something was different. He didn't immediately look away, or try his best to ignore what he saw. Instead, he examined himself with content approval. *Maybe I'm not so bad.*

He flicked the screen back on and began moving his thumbs furiously, typing a quick message before he lost the courage to do it. But it wasn't to Mr. Mejia.

"Let me take you out. This Friday. 7:00. You and me... No, Prue and Piper are not invited! What do you think?" He hit send before he had time to change his mind. He didn't want to overthink his choice, so he opened the text from his boss to respond to that.

"Thank you so much for the appreciation, sir, it feels incredible. Unfortunately, my schedule only allows me to work part time right now, but if that ever changes, I'll be sure to let you know. Thanks again."

This wasn't true, of course. Jackson could easily work full time. There was nothing holding him back; the job was online, and he had an abundance of free time at home with a perfect computer setup and a great internet connection. But he was spoiled when it came to working. Thirty hours a week with easy tasks was ideal to him, and he wasn't in a hurry to change that.

Right as he hit send, his phone vibrated in his hand. *Alyssa!* He opened it immediately, and felt sheepish again, thanking whatever lucky stars must be above him that his "read receipts" were not active.

The warm fuzzies swarming in his face stilled when he scanned her text. **"Ugh I'm sorry, I'm busy this Friday."**

Is this instant Karma? It sure felt like it. Maybe he should text Mr. Mejia back.

"What about next Friday? At 5? And my magical sisters are busy then so they won't be insulted by not being invited. But I can't guarantee Coop won't crash our party..."

"Ha!" Jackson let out involuntarily, smiling from ear to ear. Every time he got a response from Alyssa, he liked her more and more. She was cute. Witty. Sweet.

Buzz-buzz. Now this must be Mr. Mejia.

Nope! Alyssa again!

"Where are we going? Not to Billie Jean's house I hope..."

Clever girl. He played on her name, she played on his. He certainly didn't mind being compared to the King of Pop. She matched his energy, and he was loving it. There was only one problem; he had typed in the adrenaline of the moment and hadn't thought past hitting send. He had no absolutely no idea where they were going.

"I can't tell you, now, can I? That would ruin all the fun!"

Crap. He needed to figure out a plan.

He yelled down the stairs. "Mooommm!"

***

"Oh, how about mini-golf!" Cathy Halloway was over the moon.

Jackson's face was red. Yes, he'd asked for her help, but she was having way too much fun with this and it was getting cringey. Somehow, everything becomes mortifying when your parents are excited about it.

"Mom, she's potentially about to be a surgeon, she's way too sophisticated for mini-golf." He'd already explained to his mother that Alyssa was taking her final exam the same day they'd planned their date, but he could see her light up again as he mentioned it. Alyssa wasn't impressive only to Jackson.

"Come on Jackie, everyone loves putt-putt! Besides, I'll bet she'll be tuckered out after that whole test thing and a little fun might be just what she needs."

His mom actually had a good point, but he didn't want to risk looking any more juvenile in front of this girl. "She's really smart, mom, I don't want to make it so obvious that she's way out of my league. And I think she's a little bit older, too. I don't want to seem too immature for her."

"What's wrong with dinner and a movie?" His father chimed in. Jonathan had come looking for Cathy about five minutes into their conversation. After she'd told him where the remote was, he could've left, but curiosity had kept him around and now, to Jackson's dismay, it was a whole-family discussion.

"You can't talk at dinner and a movie!" Cathy argued.

Jonathan shrugged. "So?"

Cathy rolled her eyes.

"That was our first date, and it went just fine. That's what everyone used to do."

Cathy ignored him and turned her body and attention towards her son, circling back to his previous apprehensions. "You're smart too, Jackie. Wicked smart. She's not out of your league." He didn't know how to respond to that. Luckily, she

97

broke the silence. "But, if you really want to do something 'sophisticated,' why don't you take her to one of the university museums?" He pondered the suggestion. "Aren't there a few of them? I think there's an art museum. And the Museum of Natural History!"

"Yeah," Jackson thought out loud, "the University of Michigan Museum of Natural History. It's so close by, we could walk there."

Cathy beamed, thrilled by both her son accepting her advice, and the prospect of this soon-to-be date. "And I bet you both get in for free, or at least a discount, seeing that she attends the school and you work for them."

"Great idea mom." He squeezed her tight in a "thank you" hug, and then couldn't resist quoting DiCaprio. "An idea. Resilient. Highly contagious."

Cathy could tell by his tone of voice he was slipping into their routine. She listened closely to see if she'd recognize the film.

"Once an idea has taken hold of the brain it's almost impossible to eradicate."

It was clear his mother remembered the quote, but couldn't quite place it. She squeezed her eyes shut, trying to think. "Ugh, I know that one! Oh, that was a good movie, too! It was the guy from *Titanic*, I remember him saying that!"

Her descriptions always made Jackson chuckle. "The movie was called *Inception*," he picked up a couple empty water bottles and handed them to his mom. "Now if you'll excuse me, I have to do some research on the exhibits at the Museum. I want to be able to bring up facts about them as we go past."

Cathy giggled, but of course she couldn't let it go there. She just *had* to throw in a little advice. "Just be yourself, Jackie." She took the water bottles from his room to go refill. "You don't need to do all that. She's gonna love you just the way you are."

Jackson paused, unsure if he should ask his mom the question burning in his brain. Before he could fully decide, it just came out. "But… What if she doesn't? What if she sees the real me, and rejects it?"

His mom considered this for a good few seconds, fully forming her thoughts before sharing them in this delicate moment. She let out her breath, and spoke extra softly, "Then you let her go." She had to know Jackson didn't want to hear this, her tight face affirmed it, but she seemed determined to share her thoughts. "We don't force people to love us, honey." She put her hand on his shoulder. "You are a beautiful, talented, silly, wonderful human being. The right girl will love you for you. Without you trying to impress her, or pretending to be something that you're not."

They both jumped at a loud beep coming from the other side of the house. "That's the chicken I put in the oven; I'd better run and take it out. Your dad and I are eating in ten minutes, and we'll make you a plate that you can grab whenever you'd like. Where did he go, anyway? Jon, can you stop the timer?"

She scurried away to prepare their meal, and Jackson was left to mull over her words. Touching as they were, he still wanted to look up the museum. He would be himself with Alyssa, he really would be, just a slightly academically enhanced version of himself. What was the harm in that? He could be himself *and* woo her with his knowledge of - he looked at the screen - "the Ancient Egyptians and the Eye of Horus," right? Besides, it honestly looked pretty fascinating. He scrolled from article to article, fact to fact, readying himself for a night Alyssa wouldn't be able to reject.

15

Clayton

"Jeremy!" Clayton belted, overly joyous, "We've got a lot to talk about!"

Dr. Barnes didn't match his excited energy at all. "We certainly do. Like how you didn't speak with your mother yet?"

"Actually, I just did. We've come to an understanding."

"Good," Dr. Barnes acted as if he wasn't surprised. "You'd better have. Because the investors will be here before we know it and if they see everything in the condition it's in..." he trailed off, remembering, "did you know there was another earthquake earlier? Not long after 8:00. There are still some trees down."

Clayton wasn't in the mood to listen to the doctor continue going down this negative road when he was so positive right now, filled with the adrenaline of his new idea. "I'm working on that, it'll be taken care of. I need to get you onboard with this update I've been thinking about; it'll fix all of your concerns, and more." He wasn't sure this was true, but he was manifesting.

Dr. Barnes looked skeptical. "We don't need something new, we can't take on any more at this point, we are already in over our heads—"

"That's why we are going to look into finding more help." Dr. Barnes looked relieved. "Eventually." His face fell again. "But for now, I'll do the prototype myself. You just need to imagine it with a real architect, an engineer—"

The doctor had had enough. "I'm tired of imagining. We need more people now, people who are professionals in those fields. You're an incredibly smart man, Clayton, there's no denying that, but you can't keep doing this alone."

For once, Clayton was completely transparent. "I know." He wondered if Dr. Barnes could hear the sincerity in his voice. "You're right. The problem is," he hesitated to say, "we keep hitting the capacity of our funds every month. The money from my mother all goes towards equipment and programming, and the limited amount we've been getting from the investors isn't enough to cover salaries for more employees yet."

Dr. Barnes was listening intently, but his clenched jaw gave away his concern. "Then how are we going to expand?"

Clayton knew he had to take advantage of the doctor's attention. "Okay, so obviously we need more money, which requires our investors to increase their contributions generously. The way to do that is to impress them." Dr. Barnes nodded in agreement.

"Many of us believe the Program speaks for itself. That's why we're here. However, we know there are a few... Flaws. Flaws that could potentially distract investors from truly understanding the impressiveness of the world we've created." The doctor nodded again.

"So, my proposal is that we give them a world so flashy it would be impossible for them to become so easily distracted by those minor details we are still working on."

"Flashy?" Dr. Barnes questioned, intrigued.

"Precisely." Clayton felt his blood pumping. "As experts in our fields, we are aware of just how remarkable the Program truly is... without all of the 'glitz' and 'glamour.'" His fingers made air quotes as he spoke of the "two G's." "But people like our investors, they don't necessarily care as much about the science and the logic. They want a show. And we are going to give them one."

As much as Dr. Barnes was attempting to suppress his curiosity, Clayton could sense it, saw it buzzing all around the doctor's head like flies over roadkill. "How exactly would we do that? And, follow up question, how difficult would it be?"

"Not at all!" Clayton's voice was loud with exhilaration. "That's the thing, the basics of it are actually so simple!"

"Go on."

"What I'm suggesting is essentially giving Salvation a makeover. And before you laugh," he'd noticed the doctor's amused face, "just hear me out. We are advertising ourselves as the perfect world right?"

Dr. Barnes could do nothing but nod some more.

"Then let's make it perfect. In every. Single. Way."

"What do you mean?"

"Forget the medical stuff!" Clayton shouted. His brain stopped on its heels, turned around, and started over when he saw how immediate Dr. Barnes' curiosity flies darted away to find a fresh meal. "I mean, okay, we obviously don't forget it. Of course. But," he had to get the doctor back on his side, "But, just hear me out, we focus on showing the investors just how perfect this world is, even aside from that. Rather than having our bland, brown box houses, we give ourselves mansions in here." He gestured out the window to the undeniably boring-looking town. They hadn't put that much thought into the housing, after all, it wasn't what they'd believed was important.

"Instead of our little 'Toyota Camry' knock offs, why not have Lamborghinis? It's just a simple update in the software. I mean, eventually we'd need someone with some real experience to build this world, but for now, I can do my best to at least give them an idea of what it could look like."

As argumentative as Dr. Barnes often was, Clayton could tell he wanted to hear this plan out. The doctor was just as desperate as Clayton was to sweep the investors off their feet. If Salvation failed, he too would be left with nothing.

"And not only material items, but appearances, too. I can get rid of the sores on my mother's back..."

Dr. Barnes jumped a little as he said this, and Clayton remembered that the doctor was oblivious to his secret cameras.

"I, uh, I saw them earlier when I was tending to her at BrightView. And it got me thinking."

"That's funny." Was Dr. Barnes growing suspicious? "Your mother had a similar thought just before you arrived."

"See, it's a great idea," Clayton kept talking in hopes to distract the doctor from thinking too much about the "coincidence." "I can fix those up, and get her out of that hospital gown. We can give her a tan, add some color back into her cheeks... We could give this entire place a fresh new coat of paint."

"Just because you cover something broken with paint," Dr. Barnes replied, thoughtfully, "doesn't mean it's fixed."

Clayton wasn't willing to lose him now. "I know," he said, honestly. He'd never been so sincere with his colleague. It was a strange feeling, to be vulnerable. But he'd never be able to succeed on his own. "I know. We will still be working on all of that behind the scenes. But like I said, the underlying issues we are working on require more time, money, and people. Three things we don't yet have. Three things we won't be able to get if we can't knock the socks off of these investors in a few months.

Dr. Barnes pondered the promise for a minute, perhaps asking himself if he really believed the sugar-coated assurances coming from his leader. After a bit of internal debate, he finally landed on, "Okay… I guess it's worth a shot." Clayton patted him roughly on the back. "But you'll need to run it by Gordon."

"No problem," Clayton responded quickly, "He'll love the idea!"

And he did. Clayton had hired Gordon hastily, simply because he needed someone to help him get into the simulation. He'd listened to Gordon at a conference a few years back and had been intrigued by the way he spoke. The cadence of his voice. The conviction of his statements. Clayton agreed with a good portion of his values and teachings, and even kept up with his podcasts when he could find the time. He'd brought Gordon in for some initial questioning, and quickly recognized that he was a great fit for what Clayton needed.

A voice that could lull Clayton into a trance. Into a nearly comatose state. Into Salvation.

The irritating problem was, Clayton hadn't been able to dig up an ounce of dirt on this man. Gordon, or "Dr. Avery," was clean as glass, at least as far as the internet was concerned. He'd never cheated on his wife, made a racist comment, gotten a DUI… He'd never even skipped a class when he was in his college days at Northwestern University.

Clayton typically wouldn't hire someone who seemed so "holier than thou," but as far as he could tell, Gordon shared his goals. He was driven and ambitious, and, most importantly, he could transport Clayton into Salvation. That's what mattered for now.

Gordon loved Clayton's new idea for the Program. "Hey, our objective is to make people happy. To give them the lives we know they deserve. We are giving them physical relief, and more importantly, mental relief. If we have the tools to help our patients achieve greater confidence, then why not, right?"

Clayton beamed. "Precisely."

"I think it's great. Maybe we could even expand our audience. I mean, not everyone struggles physically, but I don't know a single person who couldn't stand to gain a little bit of confidence. Do you?"

"No," Clayton registered, the gears turning in his head, "No, I don't."

16

Alyssa

The snow was flurrying all around the couple as they strolled towards the museum, but even as the frozen flakes fell on Alyssa's cheeks and the tip of her nose, her face remained warm and rosy. She was filled with anticipation, unsure where this night would lead, and nervous to find out. But nervous in the fun way, where your stomach fills with butterflies and your heart fills with hope. Like the feeling right before you open a birthday present. You're pretty sure you're going to love it, but the uncertainty of what could be inside is half the fun. Shaking the box, trying to feel out what it might be.

She had an inkling that Jackson was feeling the same way. His cheeks were just as pink as hers, though that could be from the low temperatures and high winds. But if her hunch was correct, he wasn't even noticing the cold. She certainly wasn't.

He eyed her like she was his own personal Birthday present, wrapped in colorful paper, tied up with ribbons, and she was willing to bet he'd like to shake her to get a better estimate of what could be inside, just as much as she'd like to shake him.

Jackson's rattling of the box began with asking her about her exam. "I think it actually went really well!" She told him, cheerily. "I felt really confident about a lot of the questions. Most of them were exactly what I studied, and I mean, in theory, what we have been learning for the past, like, over ten years, so, it's one of those things where if you don't know it by now, you probably never will."

She was rambling. What was it about this boy that made her blather so much? And of course, her realization that she was already nervously rambling made her more nervous, and therefore ramble even more. "So, I think I did well, even though I couldn't concentrate for the life of me." She muttered to herself, and subsequently, to Jackson. "I kept getting distracted thinking about..."

Uh oh. Did she really just almost admit that a boy was taking away her focus *to* the very boy who was responsible for said lack of focus? She felt Jackson look at her - his eyes had previously been on the snow-covered sidewalk - and knew she had to dig herself out of this hole. "Thinking about, uh, my future, you know?" It wasn't technically a lie.

"Yeah, I mean, this test decides my fate pretty much, so yeah, obviously distracting." He was smiling to himself. She kept going. "And of course there's Thanksgiving in a couple days, and then break, and I've got to go see my mom so that's gonna be a whole thing..."

Jackson, who had been listening intently, letting her chatter on, finally spoke. "Why's that?" Alyssa contemplated how to answer, but it seemed it was Jackson's turn to nervously ramble. "I'm sorry, I didn't mean to pry, I'm just interested in learning more about you, and—"

"No, it's totally fine," she cut him off. The last thing she wanted was for him to think he was shaking the box too hard, and stop altogether. She wanted him to try and figure her out. She relished his interest. "I just don't see her all that much. So it'll be good, but I'm sure she'll have a lot of questions. At least now I can tell her I've been on a date." She elbowed Jackson playfully. "She'll love that."

Jackson's face flushed at the word "date," and Alyssa was giddy again. "Anyway, enough about me, I've been talking the entire walk, look, we're nearly there already and you haven't even had a chance to speak!"

"No, please," Jackson spoke up, sounding so earnest the drop of snow falling towards Alyssa's face liquefied instantaneously upon touching her hot skin. "I like listening to you talk." He looked at his shoes again. "You're so talented and hard working; I can't believe you even got to take that test, let alone if you pass or not."

Alyssa hadn't ever considered this. All throughout school, the emphasis had always been passing the USMLE. The end goal. Becoming a surgeon. No one in Alyssa's world gave students much credit or respect until they passed - *if* they passed. And even after, people were only ever focused solely on accomplishments. Data. Numbers. With this simple comment, Jackson had reminded Alyssa why she'd given him her number in the first place. Him, out of all the men who'd asked for it over the years.

Dates are always interviews. There's no getting around it. But Jackson's interview was nothing like the others she'd experienced. In the past, she'd felt like she was interviewing for jobs she wasn't qualified for. Jobs where the interviewers thought they were above her, and expected her to fail. When she told them her history, they checked a mark on their note pad and moved on, leaving her unsure of whether she'd passed or failed.

Jackson's interview felt like she had just won the Nobel Prize, and he was the lucky person whose microphone she chose to use to tell her story.

He wasn't checking off any list; he was drinking in her words like they were hot tea and honey for his sore throat.

"Thanks," was all she said, though that small word couldn't express the emotions swirling through her mind.

As they entered the museum, Alyssa couldn't help but marvel at the beautiful architecture and vastness of the building. "You know, in all the years I've lived right by this campus, I've never been here. Can you believe it?"

There was a skip in Jackson's step, his chest puffed, notifying Alyssa that he was proud of himself despite the absence of any boasting in his reply. "Well, sounds like you're usually too busy for things like this."

"That's an understatement. But now," she bent her neck back and stared up at the ceiling, pacing in a slow circle to admire the intricate designs, "now I really wish I'd made time for it."

"If it makes you feel any better, I've never been here either," Jackson admitted, "It's kinda cool seeing it for the first time together."

Alyssa appreciated that thought. "Yeah, it is. It'll be a great story for the grandkids, anyway!" she joked, well aware that Jackson would probably choke at her wisecrack. She watched him freeze for a second, but try to act like he didn't, and she giggled to herself, skipping off towards the dinosaurs.

Jackson ran after her and grabbed her arm. "Oh, actually, uh, I thought we'd go to the left first." Alyssa was puzzled, and her face showed it. "I... I think there's a bathroom over there."

"Oh, okay," Alyssa turned around, "Sounds good to me!" And they headed to the left, towards the Egyptians.

Jackson's eyes were scanning the room, searching. "Oh look, here!" he nearly shouted, his voice echoing loudly through the silent walls. Alyssa scooted closer to him to see. He tried to conceal a grin. "This is the Eye of Horus. It's really interesting, actually."

"I thought you'd never been here before?" Alyssa frowned, a little hurt.

"I haven't!" Jackson fidgeted, uncomfortable. "I just… I know a lot about it. I'm really into history, and, you know… knowledge."

It was an effort to keep her cheeks from drooping. Maybe he wasn't so different from the guys she knew. Always trying to show off, all studious and conceited.

Jackson didn't seem to notice her disappointment. He was concentrating hard on his "eye" story. "See, they call it the 'all seeing eye,' or 'the third eye.' Eyes are very important in Egyptian culture."

"Cool," Alyssa said, uninterested. It's not that she didn't enjoy history, she just thought they'd be bantering more and goofing off, like when she'd first met him.

"Yeah, they believed the eyes held the secret to enlightenment. To reach inner peace, and live a meaningful life. Almost like through the eyes, they could achieve an ideal world."

"How did they think they could do all that with just eyes?" Alyssa queried, careful not to let out a sigh.

Jackson perked up, like a kid in class who realized his studying was paying off when the teacher called on him and he knew the answer. "Well, they think the eye is not really an eye. It's actually a symbol for the limbic brain. Look at this, here."

He stepped over to the next display, and pointed out an eye carved into stone. Alyssa wasn't quite sure how this helped. Jackson had pulled out his phone and was searching something. "This is the limbic system of the brain. Notice anything?"

Alyssa didn't like being quizzed. She'd been tested enough today.

And she'd seen both pictures of brains and actual brains hundreds of times. She humored him and glanced over anyway, and was shocked at the resemblance. She'd never looked at the brain under this lens before.

"Wow!" as her head swiveled back and forth between the phone and the stone, she had to admit this was actually pretty cool. "They look just alike! Who knew the Egyptians were so medically advanced!"

"Exactly," Jackson beamed at her reaction to his expertise. "And the limbic system is responsible for—"

"Emotion and memory, mostly," Alyssa interjected. She wanted to banter with him again. If he was trying to show off, she could turn it into a fun little competition. A game.

"Nice!" He appeared to be having more fun now, too. "So in theory, if one can control the eyes, he can control someone's emotions and memory, too."

"Hey!" She teased him, with a note of seriousness, "Who's to say it's a 'he' who's controlling? All the best surgeons I've known have been women, sooo..."

"Very true, and girls *are* always trying to control guys anyway. The 'nagging girlfriend' is a stereotype for a reason, right?" He winked, his confidence was definitely coming out.

Alyssa's next comment came all too easily. "I'm not your girlfriend yet, so no need to worry. You can leave the toilet seat up all you want." The word "yet" made Jackson turn beet red, as she knew it would, and she laughed exuberantly.

Jackson clearly didn't know how to respond to that, so he reverted back to the original subject. "Anyways," he drawled out the word, and she was still chuckling, "I bet you didn't know that the ancient Egyptians also believed the eye was connected to all five senses."

Alyssa laughed even harder, and when she looked at Jackson she could tell he didn't understand why. "First you were Mr. Computer Expert, and now you're Mr. History Expert. But *I'm* Ms. Anatomy expert, and I bet I know something about the limbic system that you don't."

He stared at her blankly.

"It also primarily deals with sexual stimulation."

With that, they both giggled, and Jackson threw his hands up in innocence. "Whoa, hey you're right, I definitely did *not* know that." He was trying to play it cool, but his skin was turning the hue of a ripe tomato. "Maybe we should move on to the next exhibit."

"Are you sure? This one was just getting interesting," Alyssa kidded, as they headed towards the next display.

The room was filled with different forms of writing, from cave drawings to diaries. The evolution of documentation. Surrounded by stories, Jackson asked, "So, who's your favorite author?" Before she could answer, he intruded, "Mine is probably Hemingway. I like *The Old Man and the Sea*; it's a classic."

This comment confused Alyssa once again. She couldn't get a read on this boy. Was he trying to sound all "posh" because he liked her, or was he just another wannabe pompous snob?

Still, she answered honestly. "Sylvia Plath." Jackson squirmed a little, and Alyssa could tell he didn't know who the writer was. "She was this incredible American feminist poet in the 1950's. She wrote a lot, but her poems are my favorite. She was way ahead of her time, and her work is just beautiful." She was rambling again. "She married some British writer, but they had a lot of problems, and she killed herself when she was thirty by sticking her head in an oven. Very symbolic, really, considering she was fighting against sexism and gender roles like women doing all the cooking for their men."

Jackson's eyes were wide, and his mouth was even wider. "She stuck her head in an oven? That can't be real!"

"Well, technically she turned on the gas, sealed the room with towels, and then died of carbon monoxide poisoning."

"Ummm," Jackson backed away from her, "Should I be scared of you if that's the kind of person you look up to?" He was failing at hiding his sideways smile.

"She's a lot more than her death," Alyssa rebutted, "I admire her because she questioned societal standards and stood up for herself and the women of her generation by sharing her voice. I can't imagine how terrifying it must have been back then to be non-compliant. There was so much emphasis on just being a 'good girl' and 'serving' men, and she was a major part of shaking that whole belief system. Especially stereotypical norms like women being expected to get married and have kids, and being valued for that. Honestly, equality and feminism wouldn't be what they are today without her."

This was rambling she was happy to let slip out. If they were going to turn into anything, and that was a big *if* at this point, he needed to be aware of her core values. She wasn't sure if she'd ever get married. Surgery felt like her partner. All her attention went to the scalpel. She ate dinner across from the old surgical tables and showered next to the med student lockers.

And a family… That wasn't something she was sure she would ever want. Her own family history was complicated; she didn't want to put anyone else through what she'd had to endure. And besides, without children she could travel and save money, or even just relax after a long day at the hospital. Would it really be fair to a kid to only see them for an hour or two a day? She wasn't even sure that would be fair to someone like Jackson. But she was getting ahead of herself again.

Jackson hadn't spoken for a few seconds. Was he turned off by this conversation, or admiring her for it? She wasn't sure, until his eyes searched hers and he concluded, "I think you are the most… *interesting* person I've ever met."

The cadence in which he breathed this sentence stopped Alyssa in her tracks. The pause after, "most," as if he was in disbelief, and couldn't think of words accurate enough to come next. The pained emphasis on the word "interesting," convincing her that he was as sincere as he'd ever been, like if he'd ever said that to anyone before her, he didn't mean it. Or maybe he did at the time, but he was naive then, and wasn't able to comprehend what "interesting" really was, or that someone could interest him as much as she did.

Alyssa was frozen. This whole time, she'd been thinking *she* was the one holding all the cards on this date, pulling his strings gently and enjoying his infatuation. But now, *her* breath was the one taken away, *her* voice the one forgetting how to function. She swallowed hard.

This date was like buckling into a roller coaster that she'd mistaken for a kid's ride. She thought it'd be safe. That she wouldn't even need a lap bar. But as she sat in the padded seat, she took in her surroundings and noticed the track going up, up, up. Adrenaline punched her in the gut, and she buckled in for the ride. The lines on the sides of her mouth were like two parentheses, her smile the secret aside contained within. She loved a good rush.

17

Bianca

The sound of the slamming door still rang in Bianca's ears, even in the silence that now surrounded her. Every time she thought she couldn't possibly have any tears left to cry, she proved herself wrong. She pushed herself up to grab a tissue; her sleeve was already soaked through. .

Today, it felt like she had suddenly woken up out of a trance. Part of her was elated. Before, she wasn't sure she'd ever feel normal again, and now, finally, she did. This made no sense to her, because nothing was normal about today. Derek had never walked out on her; he'd always been the most attentive and devoted man she'd ever met.

But she couldn't blame him. She would have stormed out too if he'd acted half as terribly as she had over the last several weeks.

Something about being alone had snapped her awake. *Why did it take so long?* Maybe she'd grown to depend on Derek too much during this time. He had been doing everything for her, after all. *Was I taking advantage?*

She realized now she had been, but that had never been her

intention. She'd been overwhelmed by the grief. Her mind began to spiral, finally seeing how much she'd been asking of Derek. How could any person be expected to put up with so much, for so long? She was selfish, she thought. Only showing him any love when she wanted something? The shame was like a branding iron to both cheeks, burning in the words *"How could you?"*

How could she have done this? How had everything gone so wrong? Finally, her brain was allowing her to think and unnumb and process everything that had happened since that sudden burst of pain. She thought of Derek's panicked voice on the emergency call. She thought of the sound of him crying when he didn't think she could hear him. She thought of her sister scooping oatmeal into her mouth, and her hand flew up to cover her own, taken aback by everything she'd allowed to happen. She couldn't have lifted the spoon herself? She couldn't have spoken up?

And yet, moments ago, she'd talked to him so easily. Tried to *seduce* him, like it was nothing. Why had it been so hard before? She was awful, only speaking when she was being deceitful... Scheming to force her husband to try for a baby as soon as it was medically allowed, despite the fact that she'd given him no affection or even decency over all this time?

It hadn't felt like scheming when she'd done it... But then again, it hadn't felt like anything. She'd been frozen for so long. A therapist would have concluded that maybe the thought of a second chance at a child was the only thing her brain would allow her to think about after the trauma; it was the only thing getting her through, and it controlled her. But Bianca was no therapist; she wasn't willing to give herself grace.

She was angry at herself, especially for not being Derek's

equal partner through all of this. *In sickness and in health, right? For better, for worse, right?* It hadn't even been that long ago that she had spoken those words, *vowed* to keep those promises. She remembered their personal commitments to each other.

"I promise to always take care of you, even when you don't think you need to be taken care of." The audience had laughed along with her when Derek said that.

"I will be there for you, through everything. The ups, and the downs. I'll bring you soup when you're sick... Even though I'll probably be sick too since we'll be together all the time."

More laughter. "But seriously, I love you so much, and I know life won't always be perfect. But I promise I'll go to the ends of the earth to make the world perfect for *you*."

At that, everyone had let out a chorus of "Awws."

And she'd known he'd sincerely meant that. Derek worshiped her. He cared so little about his own happiness, but so much about hers. When it was his birthday, he worked. One year, he'd even picked up a co-worker's shift. When it was Bianca's birthday, he took two days off and took them on a surprise long weekend to Indianapolis. She'd confronted him about this the following year when he hadn't so much as thought about his own birthday until thanking her for cake and gifts the day of, yet he'd started gushing about hers more than three weeks in advance.

He'd shrugged her off, assured her he didn't care to make a big deal about birthdays.

"But you go *crazy* for my birthday... so you *do* make a big deal out of them!" She'd argued. "You're already telling everyone with ears how excited you are about all the little surprises you have planned, and my birthday is in, like, a month!"

"Yes, darling, that's because it's *your* birthday. It's the best day of the year; the day you were born is a day that deserves to be celebrated!"

. "Same with yours!" she'd retorted. "You're just as special as I am! If not more!"

He'd scoffed at that statement, but didn't fight it, probably because he'd known there was no point in arguing with her. He'd told Bianca before, though he found it very difficult to fathom, he believed somehow she loved him as much as he loved her.

So, it was only fitting when Bianca decided to retort his vow, reminding him that they were equal partners in love, and life.

"And I promise," she'd choked through the tears she'd been told to hold back on her wedding day, "that I will stop you from doing that." Laughter from their friends.

"No I'm serious," she'd insisted, solemnly, "Because I know you will if I let you. I know you'll push all of your own feelings aside just to make room for mine. I know you'll bring me soup when I get a cold... Even if you have pneumonia." She'd felt the approving eyes of their guests on both her and Derek.

"And I know," she was becoming even more teary as she continued, "that it would be French onion soup." Her voice broke a bit on the word "soup."

"Not chicken noodle," he smiled at her adoringly as she spoke, "because you know how I feel about it after I had that expired can that one day." Her sister Rin chuckled extra hard at that line, reliving the memory. "I mean, how does that even happen?" Bianca was smiling herself now. "Isn't soup supposed to last long enough to get us through an apocalypse or something?"

The mood was light in the room, but it was clear how serious Bianca was. "So, you'd bring me my favorite French onion soup. And you'd put round crackers on the side, because you know they help settle my stomach. Even if it meant you had to drive to three different stores to find them. That's how well you know me, and that's how much you care."

She'd grabbed his hands, and folded them inside hers. "But I promise not to let you do that. Because I love you just as much. And I'm not going to let you only think of me... Even though I do love it!" There were some soft chuckles. "If you're sick too, we can go to the store together. Or stay home and heat up leftovers together. Or order delivery together. We're in this *together*, Derek."

Her smile turned even softer. "And I won't let you go to the ends of the earth unless you let me tag along with you. You deserve the world, too, and I'm going to spend my life making sure you know that."

After she'd delivered that line, their friends and families had cheered and Derek had pulled her in for a hard kiss. She'd leaned into it for half a second, until her eyes had flown open and her head pulled back as she realized what he'd done.

"No, Derek!" She'd yelled and slapped him playfully on the shoulder, "It's not time yet!" Everyone had found that hilarious and sweet, and the flustered officiant wasn't sure where to go from there.

"Sorry, sorry," Derek held his hand out in apology, "How do people wait at these things?"

Though this was her happiest memory, Bianca didn't smile while she thought of it. She wasn't blind to the stark contrast between her current self and her past. She was completely disappointed with how quickly she'd already broken her vows. She thought of everything Derek had done for her over the last six weeks. She couldn't think of a word strong enough to describe her gratitude to him, or her love for him. Had she even told him that?

She thought back to every attempt made by her husband to help her... She'd said nothing. Shown nothing. Given him *nothing*. He probably thought she hated him.

She pictured her face, her body language, even the way she'd been dressing - if you could call it that. Every image made it look as though she'd given up. Is that what he thought? *How could it not be?*

While in her depressed, numb, trance-like state, she'd been unsure of everything. Except him. He had kept *his* vows. He'd been traveling to the ends of the earth for her, and she'd let him. She'd let him go all alone.

She'd been incredibly sick, and he'd been "bringing her soup" every day, regardless of himself, of his own needs. She thought of her vows again. For the first time, it hit her that he must be sick, too.

He wanted a family, too. She was dying to be a mother, but he also dreamt of parenthood and the beautiful, indestructible unit they could create together.

He'd been ecstatic when she'd told him she was pregnant, and he'd already begun collecting bibs and bottles, even though she'd told him it was way too early for all of that. He hadn't been able to wait. He'd put it all in the nursery, which was really just their old guest room that they'd already reassigned - partially because of their excitement, and partially because Derek kept coming home with little bits and bobs every time he'd gone to the store.

Bianca walked over to peek in the room. *I haven't been in here since...* She didn't want to think about it. She couldn't re-member everything they'd gathered, but she knew she'd begun painting the walls ("Yellow - it's what I've always imagined for a

121

nursery!"), Derek had started assembling a crib ("Someone was practically giving it away on Facebook marketplace!"), and, of course, there was the little stuffed bird.

18

Clayton

It was 1:46 a.m. when Clayton finally looked up at the clock. He'd stayed in his office much longer than he'd planned, and a very sleepy Courtney was probably waiting up for him. He debated whether or not to call her.

If she was awake, it'd be much better for him to reach out sooner, but he didn't want the ringing to startle her if she had fallen asleep. He decided to just get home quickly; he was already out later than expected and another half hour wouldn't change that. He was glad he'd stayed, though. The designs he'd drawn up were well worth a fight, if it came to that. Fights are temporary. *These plans are our future.*

He quickly collected the notes and drawings sprawled over every surface in his office. Salvation was about to be elevated to a whole new level.

The blueprints were just rough drafts, but soon his vision would be a reality. A casino, an Olympic-size pool, and a giant golden fountain in the middle of town were just the tip of the beautiful, glittering iceberg he'd designed.

He'd need to hire more men to truly complete his vision, but he could bullshit his way around the system enough to dazzle the investors. He didn't have the skill set to make Salvation fully functional on his own, but he could make it pretty. Maybe even pretty enough to finally show Courtney. *That'd be one hell of a way to make up for coming home late again.*

19

Bianca

"I love it!' Bianca'd cried when he'd walked through the door and pulled the plushy bird out from behind his back to present to her. It was the day after she'd shared the news of her pregnancy with him, and he'd run all around town after work to find her the perfect present.

"A little bird for my little bird," he'd whispered lovingly, planting a gentle kiss on her forehead. "I hope this baby will fly as high as their mama one day."

"Oh great, the hormones are starting already!" she'd re-remarked, shedding a new influx of tears as she thought of how long she'd dreamt of being able to use that phrase.

She'd stared at that sweet, soft toy every day since she'd received it - right up until the day of the miscarriage - welling up with emotion each time. It was a symbol to her. A symbol of how thoughtful Derek was, and what a great father he was going to be. A symbol of how much he loved her, and how he loved to watch her soar. A symbol of change, in the best possible way. It reminded her that there was a miracle inside her.

There was a tiny person who was going to be all theirs, to love and to cherish and, in her mind, to complete them. When she stared at the bird, she knew she had everything she'd ever wanted.

Now, in Bianca's mind, everything that toy represented had been lost. She wasn't completely sure she'd be able to handle seeing the nursery again, but she couldn't seem to stop herself from wandering over. The door slowly inched open and she peered inside.

Confusion pulled her up by the ankle like she'd stepped into the looped rope of a trap in the woods, hidden by leaves, then revealed all at once. It didn't look like the nursery at all. There was just the old guest pull-out couch, some packing boxes, and the plain, gray wall that had been there before.

How... What.... Where had everything gone? She distinctly remembered painting the walls yellow, or at least beginning to. They'd laid down newspapers, put up painters' tape... And where was the crib? They'd watched a YouTube tutorial on how to assemble it, she was sure. It'd taken them nearly three hours and Derek had sworn his back was "Never going to be the same after this!"

For that initial split second, she almost believed she had imagined it all. But she hadn't. Which meant...

Derek.

Derek, while she had been laying in her week-old pajamas on the couch, had been painting gray back over the yellow walls. Derek, while she had been staring at the wall, wallowing in self-pity, had packed up the crib and stashed the bottles and toys away. He'd erased all evidence of the pregnancy.

A chainsaw threatened to cut Bianca's heart in half when she saw the emptied room, but not for reasons of grief or loss. She didn't have room for those feelings anymore, because guilt had taken their place. Derek had been bringing her French onion soup by the bucket-fulls, but what had she done for him?

He was sick too, and she'd been doing nothing to help him. They were supposed to be in this together. She'd promised. Who was bringing him soup? Who was making sure *he* was okay? He was going through this alone.

They'd *both* endured a tragedy, but *she'd* had people by her side, checking on her through every waking moment. Every time she cried, someone was there gripping her in a tight embrace. Whenever she couldn't find energy, she had her partner there encouraging her, lifting her up, even helping her bathe. Today, finally, she recognized Derek hadn't had a partner to help him through his heartache, and that was her fault.

She was over feeling sorry for herself. Instead, she splashed some water on her face, took a hard look in the mirror, and asked herself what she was going to do about it.

20

Clayton

The new Salvation was truly amazing to see. Clayton and his team had spent the last couple of months upgrading the town to look like a prime vacation destination. There was a sparkling blue pool, and the default pine trees had all been replaced with clusters of bright green palms. The sun was shining bright, with not a cloud in the open, clear sky. The once brown, one-bedroom, square homes were now perfectly matching, pure white villas with green mowed lawns and surrounding plants and gardens.

Of course, the town wasn't reaching its full potential; they all knew that. With their combined talents, the team had been able to design the new Salvation on an "advanced beginner" level. Maybe "competent," if they were being generous.

None of the men had the background or expertise required to truly make the place incredible, or even fully reliable, but it was definitely a visual upgrade, and they were satisfied with it for now.

Users couldn't actually swim in the pool yet, or go into every room of the houses. The stoves didn't work, or the sinks, or the

---

lights. But the investors would be viewing Salvation during the day, so it was fine. They weren't worried... *Too* worried.

As aesthetic as the community was, the people were equally as attractive. No more pale, wrinkled, bruised or bandaged patrons. Instead, the Program was filled with beaming users in designer clothing and glowing skin. Some of them were just slightly filtered, but others were almost completely unrecognizable.

Reminders of the real world were virtually nonexistent now, and it was all too easy to forget who these users actually were. The patients who were attached to Salvation before were nearly inseparable now, often refusing to leave after their allotted time.

Clayton had been forcing them.

He knew their real bodies needed to be presentable for the investors. At first, he hadn't known how to get a person out if they were ignoring his orders to exit. That is, until the day Gordon fell off the roof.

A couple of weeks ago, Gordon had been up on top of one of the buildings attempting to fix some damage caused by another one of the earthquakes. He'd lost his balance, and before he could yell out for help, he'd tumbled off the edge and smashed into the ground.

Dr. Barnes rushed to help, but Clayton froze. He'd been running through ideas for cover-ups in his mind, planning exactly who he'd have to talk to and what would have to be done with the body, when suddenly, Gordon's body had disappeared.

No one had known what was happening, until five minutes later when Gordon had walked up behind them announcing, "Whoa, that was wild!" Apparently, when he had hit the ground and "died" in the simulation, he'd woken up in his bed inside the Set-up in reality. Basically, he'd been forcefully logged off.

129

He'd then been able to log in again, and resume as usual.

After that, getting people to log out had been much easier. Even though they didn't want to leave their utopia, Clayton's new threats to "force them" out scared them enough that they eventually willingly exited... at least for a little while. As long as they ate and drank, maybe bathed, they were fulfilling the bare minimum.

Clayton didn't push anyone to do more than that, because he understood them now.

He was gradually logging more and more hours each day. He loved how he felt in Salvation. He had total control; people respected him and practically bowed down to him here. Many of the test patients thought of Clayton as a god, granting them access to Heaven.

And here, he was handsome. Unlike in the real world, he actually went out of his way to catch a glimpse of his reflection smiling back at him in the mirror. A new confidence enveloped him, and he felt unstoppable. He loved being seen and admired in his finest form, and he wanted everyone to view him like this.

Why should the investors see an inferior version of him? He was the face of the company, the image of the brand. Maybe he could figure out a way to bypass them seeing his real body; maybe they could just meet him in Salvation?

Buzz-buzz, buzz-buzz. He clicked the button to answer.

"Babe. It's Courtney."

Clayton was going to say hello, but she was just getting started. "I'm trying to give you space, but seriously, I never see you anymore. Like, ever. And I try to be cool, I really do, but this is getting ridiculous. I swear, if this is what this relationship is going to be like then maybe we should just—"

"Do you want to come to work with me today?" He was aware this was a sentence she'd been waiting to hear for years; a sentence that would make her forget about his broken promises to work less and his lack of dedication to her lately.

"Uh... Yeah. I mean, of course. Yes. Wait, are you serious?" It was no surprise that she was taking a minute to process his question.

"Entirely," he said confidently. "You remember where BrightView is, right?"

"Um... Oh, the place your mother lives? Yeah, I know where it is."

Had it really been so long that she would have forgotten? He recounted the dates in his head. He'd signed the contract with BrightView only five months after meeting Courtney, and in those early days of dating, he'd taken her to visit his mom a handful of times.

After Georgie became a Salvation test subject, however, the visits obviously had to stop. Those days were so far in the past, he struggled to even picture that version of himself. No wonder Courtney had nearly forgotten."Good. Meet me in the parking lot in an hour." He clicked the microphone off. Nothing more needed to be said. She would be there.

***

A giddy Courtney jumped out of her car when she saw Clayton approaching her. Just before they embraced, Clayton noticed her bright expression dull for a second as her eyes scanned him. Suddenly, he was very aware that he hadn't looked into a mirror in the real world in... a while. Had he even brushed his teeth?

He thought about it for a moment, and was relieved to recall he'd at least done that much. But the neglect wasn't just today. He'd been avoiding Chicago since the Salvation renovations. He knew it would catch up with him sooner or later.

"Babe! I'm so happy to see you! You look…" She eyed him again. "Like you've been busy."

"That's an understatement." He grabbed her hand to pull her towards the door. "Come on, let me show you what all this work has been for."

She was bouncing with every step. "So, what are we doing at BrightView? Your office is here? I'm so confused."

Understandable. "And you'll continue to be at first, I'm sure. You may find some aspects of the process a little strange, and that's normal. But you need to trust me. It'll all be worth it when you see Salvation."

Her bounces slowed. "Babe you're kinda scaring me, what are you talking about?"

"No use explaining it now," he was firm with her. "Showing you is the only way."

He could tell she didn't know what to make of his cryptic message, but she followed him inside anyway. She watched quietly as Amber gave Clayton his access key. He'd hoped she'd be impressed by his authority, but she looked even more bewildered. It probably looked suspicious that his mother's room was so protected now when it never had been before.

Once the keys had been turned he paused, bracing himself for her reaction, then opened the door.

"What on earth…" She couldn't see his mother's condition yet, only the tent and equipment surrounding her.

He quickly and securely locked the door behind them, then took her hand again, peering intensely into her eyes. "No matter how scary this might seem, you have to trust me." She didn't respond, and her eyes didn't stay glued to his like he wanted. They darted towards the tent. No use delaying it. He gently pulled apart the curtains.

Courtney audibly gasped and her eyes widened, her jaw dropping and remaining agape. "Oh my god," she breathed, "What's wrong with her? What... What's on her *eyes*?"

Clayton gripped her hand tighter. "Nothing's wrong with her. She's great, actually. Let me show you." He grabbed a pair of the Oc X's off the side table.

Courtney ripped her hand out of his grasp and backed away, terrified. "Are you crazy?" she yelled, her voice cracking.

"Shhh!" Clayton eyed the door, not wanting anyone to hear Courtney's panic. "Please, let me take you to Salvation, and my mother can tell you herself how amazing she feels."

"Are you actually delusional right now? You think she's going to talk to me?" She gestured to Georgie's outwardly lifeless body. "You think this woman right here is just going to have a nice little chat with me and 'tell me how amazing she feels?'" Courtney's breathing was fast. Heavy.

"Yes, that's exactly what's going to happen. I know it sounds impossible—"

"You think?" She was backing away from him.

"Please, just calm down!" He glanced at the door again, questioning if his decision to bring her here was a good one.

She looked wild. Frantic. "Calm down?" She screamed, "Calm down? How can I calm down when your mother looks like a cadaver that's having scientific experiments done to it, and you're coming at me with some sort of torture device in your hands—"

"No, the Oc X's don't hurt!"

"You've *named* them?"

"If you'd like, I can put your IV in first so you can feel more relaxed. Here," he took a step towards her, now with the needle in hand.

If he'd thought she'd looked terrified before, it was nothing compared to this second wave of fright washing over her.

"Oh my god, get away from me!" She turned to open the door, but it wouldn't budge. Clayton was beginning to lose his cool.

Courtney was one of the only people he couldn't ever persuade or control; it was part of what drew him to her initially. She was a challenge. But now, it wasn't the fun kind of challenge, the kind that excited him. It was the kind of challenge that scared him, the kind he might lose.

Words failing, he turned to action. He lunged towards her, and firmly cupped his hand over her mouth, not hard enough to hurt her, but hard enough to stop the noises from escaping. He wasn't ready to give up yet. If he could just get her to Salvation, she'd understand.

He opened his mouth to tell her that they could take a step back, that he was sorry for approaching this all wrong, and that maybe he should have explained Salvation first before having a needle in his hand. He understood how that was alarming, and he hadn't meant for it to be. They could just start over. But as he was about to say those words, they were replaced by a howl of pain.

"Ugh!" She had bitten his fingers. Hard. His first reaction was to cradle his injured hand, but then she began shrieking.

"Help! Somebody help me! My boyfriend is—"

Thud.

Her body hit the floor.

Clayton had plunged the needle into her arm, pushing the back of the syringe with as much force as he could.

He hadn't known how much of a dose would knock her out, or if the drugs they'd been using to lower inhibitions even *could* knock a person out. He didn't even know what drugs were inside the needles and IVs... That was Dr. Barnes' job.

He hadn't expected her to fall so fast... *Shit, shit, shit! Did I use too much?* Could she die of an overdose?

"Okay, Clayton, breathe. Breathe," he attempted to self-soothe, "Check if she has a pulse." He reached two fingers towards her neck, and as he did, he could see her chest rising and falling steadily. "See, it's fine," he assured himself. "She's fine."

As he stared at her, wondering what he should do now, his eyes were drawn to the Oc X's that had been knocked to the ground when she fell, and were now laying beside her.

The opportunity was irresistible.

He picked up her body and slid her tenderly onto the cot, placing her arms in the restraint ports. He stroked her hair to feel better about himself, to fool himself into thinking he was doing this for her own good instead of his.

He secured the Oc X's into place, tight against the sockets of her eyes. His voice shook as he said for the first time, "Join user 3." He grabbed a random audio tape out of the pile he'd been working on and threw it in the player for her to listen to.

"Logging in in five, four, three, two..."

It worked. She was in.

Shit. He needed to get in there before anyone found her. "Join user 2!" He scrambled for his equipment.

He braced himself for whatever chaos was about to ensue, and then laid his head back, eyes held wide open, and let himself sink into his alternate world.

21

Alyssa

In all the time Alyssa was processing Jackson's claim of her being the most interesting person he'd ever met, his eyes were making small darts, as if looking into only one spot in one of her eyes wasn't enough, but staring into them nonetheless.

Suddenly, he seemed to become aware that she could see him. "S..Sorry," he stammered, "It's just, you're so smart, and—"

"Really?" Alyssa appealed, "Because from my point of view, you're the one talking about Egyptians and Hemingway, and I'm making sex jokes and talking about people sticking their heads in ovens." Her tone was playful, but she really did want him to arrive at the conclusion that "smart" wasn't what she most valued.

Hoping Jackson got her hint, she grabbed his hand and sang "Come on!" as she dragged him off towards the Greek statues. His hand tensed when her fingers held his, and she grinned confidently to herself.

The first marble god was standing with his finger to his temple. "What do you suppose he's thinking about?" she wondered aloud.

Jackson's face stiffened as he became noticeably serious. He bent his knees, hunched his back a bit, and lifted his own index finger to his head, perfectly replicating the statue. In a deep, gravelly voice, he croaked, "I wonder... Hmmm..."

Alyssa's eyes lit up, and she stifled a laugh, not wanting to miss whatever he was about to come up with.

"Did I... Did I remember to put pants on this morning?" He looked down at the zipper of his jeans. Though he was wearing bottoms, of course, the Greek man unmistakably was not. Jackson feigned horror and embarrassment, springing up and hastily covering his fly with his hands.

Alyssa burst into laughter, and immediately experienced a powerful sense of relief. She'd thought this was him. Wanted it to be so badly. The silly boy she remembered from their first encounter. Now that she had this version of him, the *real* him, it was clear how much she needed him. A splash of color in her world of black words in a white-paged textbook.

"Not again!" Jackson cried, still in character, "How does this keep happening?"

Alyssa snorted, placing her face in her palms and peeking at him through the gap in her fingers.

"They already had to talk with me about this the other day; they said I was a bad influence on the childr... Oh no..." He pretended to be appalled as he discovered the statue of the little boy across the room. Alyssa's laughter escalated as she got the joke, seeing that the smaller statue was, naturally, pantless as well.

"Not little Johnny!" Jackson was milking the bit, "What have I done?"

Her face still in her hands, Alyssa groaned. "So dumb!" she

137

called out, in the way girls do when they secretly find a boy's immature humor very amusing.

Jackson shrugged. "I mean, since you were feeling a little insecure about your sex jokes, I thought I'd make you feel a little better."

"Oh thank you, how kind of you," she joshed.

Jackson looked proud of himself. "I do what I can." He peered around the room. "And you know, I'm really proud of you."

"Why's that?"

"Because," he chuckled to himself, and Alyssa couldn't help but find him very attractive when he did so, "we're in a room full of naked dudes, and somehow you managed not to make another sexual comment. That's great progress!"

Her fist met his shoulder. "Oh shut up!"

And so their repartee continued over the next few hours as they toured the entirety of the museum. He copied more poses of Greek and Roman figures, "explained" what was happening in several paintings, and even demonstrated mating rituals of extinct creatures.

Neither of them wanted the date to end, but eventually they had seen - and split their sides in front of - every fossil, star, and microscope in the place. There was nothing left to do except leave.

They dragged their feet out the door, the sun setting in front of them. Alyssa hugged her shoulders as the warmth of the heater was replaced with the frosty winter evening air.

"Oh, we should probably get going—"

"I'm starving, do you wanna get—"

They spoke simultaneously over each other, and they each went to revise their statements now that they'd heard what the other had to say.

"Yes, I'd love to g—"

"No yeah we'd better head ho—"

They chuckled some more, though their cheeks were already hurting from their mirthful afternoon.

"Sorry, you go." Jackson's bashful grin was so wide it looked like one of the prehistoric birds had placed their fossilized feet on the outsides of his eyes.

Questions dripped into Alyssa's head like the sky had sprung a leak. He'd originally said they should go home… Was that what he wanted?

Or did he just see that she was cold and was trying to be polite? Maybe he was too shy to ask her to stay? What if he was having a bad time… Had she considered that possibility? Earlier he'd commented that she was smart, and that was the only adjective he'd used to describe her so far. It was plausible that she'd been in the tedious medical world far too long to meet his whimsical and exciting standards.

God must have hired a plumber, because the hole in the sky was patched and Alyssa could think clearly. The questions vanished. She didn't care what he may or may not be thinking. She wanted the date to continue, so she would suggest that it did. "If I didn't think, I'd be much happier," as Sylvia Plath once coined.

What was the use in worrying what other people thought? She'd undone those society standards and learned to be confident, go after what she wanted, and accept whatever reactions she received thereafter. The feminist in her slapped herself on the wrist for nearly stifling her feelings for fear of what a boy might be thinking.

"I'm really hungry! I'd love to go get dinner. There's this great place, Gianna's Diner on Fourth Street, have you ever tried it?

139

"No," the birds' footprints appeared again, "I haven't. Do they have burgers?"

"Only the best in Michigan!"

***

Alyssa had never been on a first date where the dress code was anything less than business casual, or the restaurant insisted upon by the man was three stars or lower. Why had she never done this? Tearing into a juicy, messy burger with Jackson was magical, and educational.

She learned that he despised tomatoes, and loved tuna but would never order it as a side at a restaurant because he used to eat it every day the one semester he'd actually attended college in person on campus.

And he learned that she liked extra, extra mayo on her burger, and don't forget the tomato! But if there was a pickle on the side, it couldn't even touch her other food or she wouldn't be able to eat it. She wasn't allergic, she just "suffered from an extreme hatred of all things pickled," as she so delicately informed him.

Jackson said he didn't mind tomato on his food, he could pick it off and be just fine, so he and Alyssa decided the next time they got burgers together (they'd both reddened at the prospect of a "next time"), he would order his with the tomato and give it to Alyssa so she could have two.

With the sky completely dark now and their plates empty, they again reached an impasse. Neither wanted the date to end, but neither had an excuse for it to continue. Until Jackson suggested ice cream.

The cold air actually felt pretty satisfying on their flushed faces, and they had to walk past two closed ice cream shops before they finally found one that was still open in November.

Jackson walked up to the counter, fishing in his pocket for his wallet. He had paid for everything on this date. Granted, it wasn't much, since the museum had hardly cost anything for them because of their connections to the school, and they'd only eaten burgers and fries up to this point.

Still, Alyssa added it to her list of things she'd been impressed with on this outing so far. She normally liked to split costs, but on a first date, it was definitely a nice gesture for him to pay. It felt like proof that he was investing in her.

Besides, he'd already brushed her off when she'd offered to pay her own way, insisting that he didn't have many expenses right now so it was no big deal. He admitted he lived with his parents, though she'd already guessed this from his profile, so he wasn't strapped for cash by any means.

Alyssa admired his financial stability, and appreciated that he wasn't too proud to live at home if it helped him save up, especially since she herself was in quite a bit of debt from med school. Not six digits deep like some people she knew, she'd gotten several scholarships, but still. Another difference in this sweet human that made him all the more intriguing to her. She found it fascinating how someone could have a mindset so opposite from everyone she'd been associated with before.

For instance, he hadn't talked about work all night. Alyssa didn't know a single person who wouldn't maunder on about surgery to anyone who would listen, herself included... normally.

But not tonight. Being around Jackson, her work somehow felt like the least interesting thing about her. And not because he didn't find her work riveting, but because he found *her* engrossing. Not her skills, or her knowledge, or her awards, or her milestones. Just her.

Her silly comments. Her hearty laughs. Her stolen glances into his eyes. It was that simple, yet her world was lit on fire. Like if she lost everything, it changed nothing. She could get her USMLE results in after Christmas and find out she failed it, that she got zero percent correct, and he'd still want to go grab pizza with her and stare at her face and laugh 'til his stomach ached.

She wondered if anyone else had ever felt such reassurance before. She figured some people had. She'd seen it in movies. The curly-haired lead in the romance film never seemed to get asked about her career.

But this was new to Alyssa, and for the first time all semester, she wasn't drowning in stress. She wasn't anticipating her results, or worrying where she'd get hired. She was simply enjoying where she was *right now*.

The teenage girl in front of them grabbed her sundae from the window, and then it was their turn. It'd happened so quickly that the two of them hadn't even discussed what they would order. Jackson stepped up to the counter. "Can I get one mint chocolate chip and one strawberry cone please?"

Alyssa's neck jerked left to look at him quicker than her thoughts formulated in her head. "How did you... Did I tell you I liked strawberry ice cream?"

She saw Jackson visibly swallow and shuffle his feet. "Uh, yeah... You... You said it was your favorite.... Don't you remember?"

She didn't remember, and she had an especially good memory.

"When we were at the burger place, talking about our favorite foods." He didn't miss a beat. "And speaking of, I know the perfect place we need to try next: Deli Square." He proceeded to yammer on about how good their subs were and how he bet Alyssa would love it because she could ask for all the mayonnaise and tomatoes she'd like.

She wasn't inexperienced; she knew exactly what he was doing. He must have found her online, just as she'd found him, and learned about her. Studied her like she and Bella had studied him.

He was trying to quickly move on to a new topic, and she decided to spare him and allow him to do so. She didn't mind that he'd looked her up; it was flattering and reassuring to know even all their texting hadn't been enough to satiate him. "It sounds amazing. I can't wait."

With their bellies completely full and the night growing later and later, both of them accepted that the date couldn't continue much longer. There was no excuse either of them could conjure up to stay together tonight, especially since the phone screens they'd nearly forgotten about showed it was past midnight.

Alyssa was glowing as they meandered towards her apartment, telling an animated story using her hands to emphasize the plot points. When she concluded, she rested her hands on her hips, and felt a tingling sensation jolt through her entire body when Jackson suddenly took advantage of the break and stole her hand from its weigh station, looping her fingers through his. She was reminded for the second time that she wasn't as in control as she thought.

She'd never been so aware of each nerve existing inside her hand. Sure, she knew the anatomy better than most. If shown an image, she could point out the synovial lining and the volar plates. She could label the blood vessels, the joints, and the tendons. And yes, she could draw the location and pathway of every single nerve. But to feel them was something different

143

entirely.

It was like there were wicks at the end of her fingers, and Jackson's were lighters.

With each tiny movement, even just the jostling as they strolled the sidewalk, she felt a shiver shoot up her arm and down her spine. And no matter where the conversation led for the rest of the walk, her consciousness of the feeling never lessened. She had to force herself not to acknowledge their wrapped fingers with every sentence she spoke, even as it was taking over and invading every thought.

They rounded the corner, and she saw her building.

"Well, looks like I'm home." She tried to sound chipper, though her insides squeezed with disappointment.

"A toast to the home." Jackson lifted his hand in the air. "One grander by far than a palace in Rome."

He knew *Sleeping Beauty*? This person in front of her watched Disney movies, and snorted when he laughed too hard. He danced in museums and offered to share his tomatoes.

"Oh, that's from *Sleeping Beauty*. Sorry, I really love movies and I quote them all the time. It's kind of this thing me and my—"

And then her lips were on his. She'd reached up, grabbed the back of his head, and pulled his mouth to hers. Her waist moved forward and her back gave in as he placed his hands on it gingerly, melting into the kiss. His hungry fingers grabbed at her fabric, squeezing it tightly and bunching up the soft cotton.

She pulled away after a minute? Ten minutes? It was hard to tell. It seemed to have happened in slow motion, yet was over far too soon.

Jackson's mouth was still partially open, almost as wide as his shocked eyes, but there was a glimmer of a smile in both of them.

"Wow," was all he could muster.

Yeah, Alyssa agreed in her mind. *Wow.*

Her lips curled up into a smile. *That* smile. The smile others constantly craved from her, but she seldom ever gave away. She rarely gave away her heart, either, but tonight felt like an exception.

22

Jackson

The "J" pendant Jackson had gifted Alyssa three months ago for Christmas swung back and forth as she pounded the buttons on his new Xbox controller. Christmas had felt early to give Alyssa such an intimate gift, but a lot of elements of their relationship seemed to come early. They'd exchanged numbers after only a few minutes of meeting, kissed after only one day together, and officially started dating after the three weeks following. And what a love-struck couple they'd become. Calls every night, dinners together throughout the week, movie nights… At least, whenever Alyssa had the time.

It came as no surprise to Jackson that Alyssa had aced the USMLE, and she'd been hired as a general surgeon immediately afterwards at her top choice hospital: St. Joseph Mercy Hospital Ann Arbor. What *did* surprise Jackson was that he was the first person she'd called when she'd gotten her results - Bella had been her second call, followed by her mother.

And here they were, up in the Loft playing Surgeon Simulator while his parents were out of town, surrounded by Chinese take-out containers and fortune cookies ready to be cracked open.

"The one who is your opposite will bring you your peace," Alyssa read aloud, "Aww, I'm gonna frame that!" she squealed, running over to jump lightly onto his lap and plant an obnoxiously loud smooch on his cheek.

I can't believe this is my life.

Their relationship worked out perfectly for both of them. Alyssa was busy most of the time, so Jackson could complete his small bits of work and then was free to hang out online for the majority of his day. He could continue to live his life as he pleased... with the added bonus of getting to talk to and hang out with and *kiss* this phenomenal woman on top of it all.

Since video games and podcasts kept Jackson up late anyway, he was always ready for Alyssa's call, no matter the time. She told him how lucky she was that he was willing to work around her schedule. For the first time, a girl appreciated him.

She gushed about how he was the best, most captive audience, always listening to her stories, no matter how long or "boring" she claimed they were. He theorized her adoration was due to her not having many people in her life who would listen to her about her surgeries, or the other various aspects of her day. From what he could gather, the people she knew were mostly in the same field, so something like an appendectomy was nothing special to them. And even when they were willing to talk about surgery, it sounded like they mostly managed to twist the conversation into bragging about their own exploits. In comparison, he was deemed the world's best listener.

Her co-workers and her best friend were all in the medical field, and from what Jackson could gather, her mother was much too proper to discuss people's insides. And besides, Alyssa didn't seem to talk to her mother often. She'd certainly never mentioned it to Jackson. He'd tried to bring up her family a couple of times, but he could tell Alyssa was very guarded about the subject. While she was totally open to discussing nearly anything else, almost to a fault, she'd admit, her parents seemed to be a delicate subject. She spoke of her mother little, but her father not at all. Jackson hypothesized that he'd hurt them in some way, maybe cheated on her mom, but he didn't know for sure.

In many ways, Alyssa had isolated herself.

She'd confided in Jackson that she'd inadvertently pushed people away over the years, majorly because she was so busy. She'd dedicated all of herself to school, and she'd had long, inconsistent hours for years now. Plus, she'd mentioned, her job was so mentally draining that when she did get home she just wanted to crash on the bed and do nothing. "But now, I want to do nothing with *you*."

And Jackson imagined that if anyone else in the world was speaking right now, all the words about to come out would hide in the caves of their owners' throats, knowing they could never be as comforting and cherished as the ones just spoken.

Still, it seemed odd, a girl so unbelievably social and bright and desirable could have so few people to talk to. Jackson had even visited her at the hospital once to bring her coffee - his mother's idea, and he'd witnessed her popularity. There was no shortage of individuals who would jump at the chance to be in Jackson's shoes, or even Bella's, but Alyssa was selective. Particular. How he'd made the cut he had no idea, but he was elated to be there.

Not only there, but at the top. Resting at the peak, taking in the view.

Alyssa told him all the time it was because he was "exactly what she needed." She said he was her "relief." Her "joy." "Do you know how good it feels to hear your voice after a day like today?" she'd purr. "I think my face has been in a permanent 'concentration frown' until now! Honestly, I should be mad at you; I'm gonna have so many wrinkles now that I have you around!"

Little did she know, she was exactly what Jackson needed, too. He could see now that he'd never really been in love before. Kenzie, his first girlfriend, was just that: First. That's all he could really say about her. He'd only dated her because she was the first person who seemed willing to date him. He didn't feel he could be picky, since he'd only had one option. There was never a special connection, and it naturally fizzled out.

Kyra, however, had been very special to him. She was gorgeous to start, and in high demand. Jackson felt like a different person when he was with her, and at first, he thought that was good. He felt cool and attractive walking beside a girl of her status. He felt wanted, with a girl so pretty fishing him out of her pool of options. They'd sat next to each other in his Introduction to Business class the semester he'd attended NMC. Jackson was there because it was required for his program, and Kyra took the course because she'd had a dream of opening her own clothing boutique. They'd flirted all during the first week of classes, and that ignited a flame that burned all the way through the following months.

Kyra's coldness, however, became a wind that flickered the light and eventually blew it out altogether. She would nag Jackson constantly, complaining that he didn't give her enough attention. *Alyssa* thought Jackson gave her more than enough of his time, and never said he should play his video games less.

She actually had a life, and didn't rely on Jackson to fulfill her. Kyra had ranted on and on about how Jackson was so immature, and how he was "lacking ambition." Alyssa praised Jackson for his playfulness and youthful energy. She said it was her favorite thing about him. And, for that matter, she admired that he wasn't caught up in the "hustle" of work. She said, "I wish more people had your mindset, the world would probably be a much calmer place." Alyssa said that to him, word for word.

How had he put up with girls of the past when Alyssa existed! God, she was unreal. Kyra insisted he was way too much of a "mama's boy," but Alyssa, Alyssa said it was sweet of him to hang out with his mom.

And Kyra, well, she'd also criticized his... *skills* in the bedroom. Made a fuss about how he "couldn't please her," and eventually decided she liked doing it better herself. And he'd been so willing to try, to learn. He'd wanted to improve, but she'd never given him the chance. He and Alyssa hadn't gotten that far yet, and he was a bit nervous for that day when it did come. That's why he never initiated anything, he supposed. He was procrastinating. Pushing it off because he was scared.

But why should I feel scared with Alyssa? She wasn't anything like those girls who made him feel unwanted. When he posted Alyssa, she "loved" the posts, and would add comments reciprocating his sappy emotions. When he wanted to download a video game, she challenged him and they played together. She said it was romantic that he bought Surgery Simulator to learn more about her world.

So, hypothetically, she would love the process of becoming more intimate with him... right? She would applaud him for caring about her needs, and she'd make him feel like the king he'd always wanted to be.

Until that moment arrived, his goal was to impress her as much as he could in other ways. And that meant meeting her friends - i.e., Bella.

The dreary weather of the February day when Jackson was finally allowed over while Bella was home reflected the atmosphere of the encounter. Bella was skeptical, to say the least. She had a million questions for Jackson. "Why are you always up so late at night? Alyssa says you ALWAYS pick up the phone, even if it's 2:00 in the morning."

"I'm a night owl. It comes with my job. I work IT for UMich, and a lot of it involves virtually controlling their systems after the staff and students are gone" *Not entirely truthful, but who is when they're trying to win over a girlfriend's annoying best friend?*

"How are you so okay with her long hours? She has no time for you. For 99% of your day, you don't even get to talk to her. Don't you miss her? What are you doing that so easily takes your mind off of her throughout the day? No other boyfriend has been this 'chill' about her lack of attention."

"Well I'm pretty busy with work too," *white lies*, "But really, it works out well for both of us, because I've been accused of lack of attention in other relationships myself" *See, I'm mostly being honest.* "Since I work remotely, my partners have felt neglected when I spend so much time online" *Listening to podcasts, gaming... But, still, based in truth.* "With Alyssa, we can both devote our attention to our passions during the long days, and it just makes us that much more grateful when we finally hear each other's voices and do get the chance to talk. Plus, we have way more to talk about since we have our own, separate lives."

"Okay, so if you're so busy, then how do you always have

time to talk to Alyssa? What, you don't have any other friends begging for your free time?"

"I'm kind of like Alyssa when it comes to people. Selective." *True again.* "And honestly, most of my friends are virtual. I talk to them throughout the day while I'm online." *Technically true.*

After what seemed like an eternal interrogation, Jackson paused, and tried to put himself in Bella's shoes. "You must really care about Alyssa."

Bella's pinched face relaxed a little in surprise.

"You've known her so much longer than I have, and gotten so much deeper with her, I'm sure. You want to make sure I'm not going to hurt her. That I really have her best interests in mind, and not my own selfish motivations." Bella nodded, giving in a smidge, waiting for him to continue.

"The truth is," he confessed, "I am selfish." Both girls looked at each other; that clearly wasn't what they were expecting him to say. "Everything I do *for* her or *with* her is completely selfish of me, because it's a privilege to get even one ounce of her attention."

Bella's eyes drifted to Alyssa for the first time. Alyssa was smiling at the ground, trying to conceal her rosiness but failing miserably. "Look, I'm not stupid. I know this woman is way out of my league."

"That is *not* true," Alyssa interjected, but he put his hand up to stop her.

"Oh yes, yes it is. I'm not stupid. I know it, Bella knows it, and every Tom, Dick, and Harry walking the campus watching you holding my hand knows it, too." Though he was "arguing" with her, his tone was warm, his eyes wet.

He turned back to Bella, as she was his real target audience today. "I am just as perplexed as you and them about why she seems to have chosen me, but as I said, I'm not stupid. I'm not about to lose the best thing that's come into my life."

While Alyssa and Jackson's conversation was always beautiful and flowing, he'd never said anything like this to her. Blunt. Vulnerable. He kept these thoughts to himself for many reasons, but the perturbation of rejection outweighed them all.

He didn't plan to spill his guts to her friend, but the words were forcing their way out, pleading for this person to understand how sincere he was, begging for approval. A bead of sweat made its way out of his hairline and onto his forehead, sweat of desperation. He *needed* Bella to understand. Part of him was doing it for the relief, to get these pent up emotions off his chest after all this time. The other part was doing it out of fear. Fear of Bella's influence. Fear of her whispering into Alyssa's ear and convincing her to walk away from him.

"So if I stay up late to talk to Alyssa, it's not because I'm sweet, it's because I'm selfish. Those thirty minutes of listening to her laugh and vent and worry and tease are the best thirty minutes of my entire day. The sound is like... It's like electrons moving from the cathode to the anode."

The girls' foreheads scrunched in unison. "You know, like in a battery?" Their faces didn't relax at all. "It increases the potential energy. It's like... It's like she's charging my battery." Finally, their shoulders dropped and their mouths softened as they understood his analogy.

"I have no problem giving her space and heading into the world of work and independence without her, even though that world drains my battery, because when I do see her again, she powers it back up to full charge. And of *course* I want more, but the way I see it, before Alyssa, I was running on a nearly dead battery all the time. Even if some of my passions charged me a little, they never brought me all the way up to the top. Those electrons were never moving fast enough or far enough."

Is... Is Bella starting to like me? He couldn't say for sure, but it looked like someone had taken a seam ripper to the middle of her eyebrows, where they'd appeared to have been stitched together before.

"So I'm selfish. I'm a computer who needs my charger. Of course I'm going to make time for her, of course I'm going to respect her and appreciate her, because without her, I'm nothing but a depleted battery."

A weight pushed him back abruptly and he nearly fell backwards as Alyssa jumped onto his lap and pressed her lips to the side of his head. "You're not nothing," she said firmly. Apparently this cross-examination by Bella drew previously unspoken words out of Alyssa's throat as well. "You're special. In fact," she placed her finger under his jaw and gently lifted it, "I feel the same way with you." If Bella's eyes were the hook of the Velcro, Jackson and Alyssa were the loop.

"I get drained too. Bella," she turned to her friend, as the sort of fourth wall was comfortably broken. "You know that better than anyone. You've seen how I've come home from the hospital. There were times when all I could manage was to get in the door and fall on the couch. I couldn't even make it ten more steps to my bed!"

Bella giggled for the first time all evening. "She's not wrong," she addressed Jackson with a smile, also for the first time all evening.

"And I haven't been that way in a while, have I?" It didn't sound like a question, more like a "checkmate."

"No," Bella had to admit, "You haven't."

Alyssa's fists punched her hips, victoriously, and Jackson

could see he had a teammate now. Before, it felt like it was him against Bella, and now, it was Alyssa and him working together to prove they were good for each other. And in doing so, they were revealing that truth to themselves, as well.

"That's because he moves my electrons, or whatever," she chuckled. "He charges my battery."

The sun seemed to stretch like vines through cracks in the ceiling to bathe Alyssa's face.

Then Bella interrupted, "Okay okay I get it, you guys are all goo-goo ga-ga for each other and it's adorable or whatever. So I'll give you my approval for now, Jackson Halloway. But just know, I've got my eye on you."

Bella's timbre was that of a jokester, sillily playing the role of the protective friend as she walked him to the door to show him out. But as she twisted the knob and let the cold air in, something far colder in her eyes told Jackson she hadn't been joking.

Bella's wintry stare had been like an ice pack disguised as a hot compress, which made the cold sting more than it normally would have. However, Alyssa called Jackson the next day to inform him that Bella did indeed approve of him... Mostly.

"We kind of made this pact," she mumbled, "A... pinky promise." She sounded like she expected Jackson to laugh, but he knew all too well the impact of those smallest fingers interlocking, so he didn't mock her.

"When I first met you, I told her that we'd get to know you, and if we decide we don't like you..." That pause was a little too long for Jackson's liking. "Well... It... It probably wouldn't work out between us."

Ouch. He knew Alyssa and Bella were close, but this surprised him. And he didn't like this whole "*we*" thing.

He pulled out the Plath card. "I thought you were a feminist, you know, that you made your own choices and didn't care about other people's opinions." What Bella had done yesterday to him, he now did to Alyssa - "joking" but concealing truth behind his words.

Even over the phone, he could hear her body language shift.

"First of all," she sounded half-cold, like she couldn't decide between being mad or being playful, "feminists trust the intuition of other girls. We stick together!"

Why couldn't I have kept my composure? This wasn't worth making her feel defensive over. Was this their first fight? It was hard to tell. *Stupid Bella.*

"And besides," she comforted, "I think she does like you. She's just protective, as you so cutely pointed out yesterday."

Phew. Not mad. We're still good.

"And…" He loved her "and's." She could talk and add and add and add and he'd never be tired of it. "If she keeps seeing how happy I am these days, she'll have no choice but to love you."

The humming of the phone was a lot louder now. Either that, or Jackson had become acutely aware of the sound. He hadn't noticed it before, but now, with the word "love" ringing in his ear, the humming seemed amplified. He knew she hadn't said that *she* loved him, but still, it felt big. Monumental, even.

"Speaking of people who love you," she trilled - Jackson's heart stopped in his chest. Where was she going with this? - "I think it's about time I meet your parents, don't you?"

156

23

Clayton

Clayton arrived at the Salvation headquarters, but he didn't immediately see Courtney. *Where was she?*

He ran through six rooms, until he suddenly spotted her walking into a conference area on the second floor. He was grateful no one else was in this building right now to see her; he had no idea how she was going to react and he was already in enough trouble in the real world.

He slowly approached her; she didn't seem to notice he was there. He touched her shoulder, hoping he wasn't poking a sleeping bear, and she turned around to look at him.

"Hi, beautiful man!" She sounded… Excited? But also a bit dopey, like she was on dru— *Oh.* That made sense.

He was cautious, not knowing where to start with her. "Hi… How are you feeling?"

Her airy aura changed to concern. "I need to find Clayton, he made this place, you know. And I need to go ask him what I should do next, to start living the life I deserve."

Did she not recognize him? "I'm Clayton, you know me, we—"

"Oh my god *shut up*! It's so good to meet you. You need to show me everything! Where is my house?"

He worked to process this whole interaction. He'd obviously overdone it on the drugs, but he'd had no choice. "You'll be living with me. Just like we do in Chicago."

She scrunched up her face real hard. "What's Chicago?"

"You don't remem—"

"Wait, living *with you*?"

"Yes, I mean we are together after all."

"We are?"

"Yes, we've been together for—"

"Clayton, there you are!" Dr. Barnes was red in the face, out of breath, bending over with his hands on his knees until he could catch it. Then he looked up, taking in the sight of Courtney standing in front of them. "What's she doing here?" He assessed her condition more closely, "What happened to her?"

Clayton hadn't had a chance to create her avatar yet. She wasn't an ugly woman, but she certainly didn't measure up to the newly beatified inhabitants of Salvation. Plus, in the struggle to get her here, she'd become quite disheveled. Her lipstick was completely smeared from where Clayton had been covering her mouth, her arm was bruising from hitting the floor after being injected, and her hair was tousled after being dragged onto the bed by Clayton.

He needed to come up with an answer, fast. "Well, Jeremy, the truth is, she wanted to see what we've been working on—"

"Oh, you mean this messed up world that's failing more and more each day?" He sounded furious, which took Clayton by surprise.

"It's not failing, we just—"

"I'm sorry," the doctor roared sarcastically, "you're right, the massive hole that just ripped through the ground is totally normal! My bad!"

He didn't know what Dr. Barnes was referring to. "I haven't seen any—" he stopped himself, as he peered out the windows for the first time since coming into Salvation with Courtney. He blinked hard, not sure if what he was seeing was real. The town looked like a tornado had gone through it. They'd had tremors before, but nothing that had caused this level of damage.

Dr. Barnes saw the expression on Clayton's face. "See, I told you. And let me guess, you just got here, right?" Clayton knew he looked "guilty as charged," because he was. "That's what I thought. See Gordon and I, we've been documenting all of the earthquakes." Clayton was shocked, but impressed. "And do you know what seems to be the constant variable? You."

Clayton considered this. Come to think of it, no one ever reported a rumbling when he wasn't there. Maybe his colleagues were onto something. Maybe he hadn't been giving them enough credit.

"That's pretty astute," he volunteered, "but earthquakes aren't the only problem we've been facing." He didn't know where he was going with this - pointing out more flaws probably wasn't the goal here. But he was curious if the doctor had formed any more explanations, explanations to events he hadn't been able to figure out himself.

"What about the glitches? Even when I'm home in Chicago, I've gotten wind of strange occurrences. Drinks being poured but missing the glass. Floorboards moving while people are standing on them—"

"Excuse me, do any of you know where I can find Clayton? I need him to show me where my car is, and my house." The two gentlemen had almost forgotten Courtney was in the room.

"And I ask you again," Dr. Barnes' face was a mix of fury and concern, "What is she doing here?"

"It was time to bring her here. She was asking questions."

"Do you think the people in my life haven't been asking questions? I'm getting them every single day. 'Why are you working so much? What are you working on? Why weren't you here for Henry's birthday? You don't even know if you'll be available for Christmas dinner? What on earth could you be doing that is so important?' I can't avoid these questions. No one understands what we're doing, or why we're working so hard." Clayton silently agreed. "But I wouldn't bring them here, especially when we're not ready."

Clayton couldn't argue with him. "Okay, Jeremy, I understand—"

"And you didn't even ask me, Clayton." Dr. Barnes wasn't done yet. "We're supposed to be partners. I've put up with a lot because I really do believe in this Program, you know I do. But we already have enough problems, and now you bring this girl—"

"Courtney," Clayton corrected.

"I'll worry about her name when I'm finished worrying about her condition." The doctor countered. "This is what I'm talking about, we need to be a team. You think you can do it all, but there's a reason I'm here. I'm the medical professional here. I'm supposed to assess any new applicant before they can even be considered for the Program. They need a psychological assessment, and a medical examination... I mean, maybe she's allergic to one of the drugs in the IV, that could be why she's so out of it."

To Clayton, this was an opportunity. If he was going to

continue injecting Courtney, and he figured now he was going to have to, he would need to learn about these drugs. And he couldn't have Dr. Barnes assess her now, it was too late for that. He would have to be able to do everything himself. Which meant he needed his colleague to teach him.

"You're completely right, Jeremy. I apologize." The doctor reluctantly pulled his distracted gaze from Courtney's rolling eyes and faced his boss. "You are so incredible at what you do. A medical genius, dare I say." Clayton was laying it on thick, but it appeared to be working.

"I mean, there were hundreds of candidates," a lie, "but you were, and still are, leagues above everyone else. I should be considering myself lucky to get to be your partner." He hated every minute of this, but he swallowed his pride like a child forcing down an adult-sized pill. "I want to learn from you. How about I get Courtney settled - again, I apologize for bringing her without speaking with you, but I'll be sure she adjusts quite nicely - and then I can come to your office and you can teach me all about the medical process of this whole thing. I'd really appreciate that."

The doctor would be an idiot to let Clayton off the hook so easily under normal circumstances, but their relationship was anything but normal. Clayton was extremely aware of the power he held over the doctor, meaning Jeremy would be wise to accept Clayton's offer, rather than continuing to argue with him. Dr. Barnes was like a vital piece of paper in Clayton's palm. Clayton needed the information, so he didn't squeeze his fist and crumple the paper into a useless, ruined ball... But he could. And they both knew it. .

"I guess that would be okay." The doctor was destroying the beds of his nails, digging into them so hard Clayton was surprised there was no blood being drawn. "But if she doesn't start improving soon, you need to let me know immediately. That's non negotiable. It'll be in both of our best interests."

"Deal." Clayton reached his hand. Dr. Barnes shook it, and Clayton grabbed Courtney's hand and whisked her away from headquarters before his colleague could change his mind.

Courtney was quiet the whole car ride to Clayton's house. His house in Salvation was so clean and organized compared to his place in Chicago - if Courtney was in her right mind, she'd probably really appreciate it. The drugs were having a different effect now, making her more sleepy and calm. Maybe they were wearing off.

He brought her inside, but once he sat her down on the living room sofa, he was at a loss, unsure of what to do next. He hadn't thought this far ahead, he'd just known he had to get her out of headquarters, away from Dr. Barnes and away from the portal back to Chicago. He didn't want her leaving Salvation, at least not until he could make sure she was okay, and prove to her his world was spectacular.

He decided he ought to find out what she did and did not remember.

"Can you tell me your name?"

She just stared at him.

"Who are you? What's your name?"

Completely zoned out.

"Okay... who am I?"

Nothing.

"Where are we right now?"

Silence.

He wasn't sure where to go from here... She was sitting nicely, for now, but he had no idea how long her compliance would last. Would she start revolting? Would she run and scare the others? Would she pass out from the effects of the IV?

He contemplated staying with her until she started talking, but not knowing how long that would take made him antsy. He was itching to talk to Dr. Barnes, alone, to figure out her correct dosage and combination of drugs so he could actually have a conversation with her here in Salvation.

For now, he couldn't risk the unknown, so he grabbed some duct tape and thought about securing her to the chair.

No, that's too extreme. But what else can I do?

Think, Clayton, think. What if I just asked her to take a nap? No, she could just fake it and try to escape. But what if I block the door? Just for a little while. That should work.

He asked her to follow him to the bedroom, and her only response was a confused, drowsy look, so he hoisted her over his shoulder and carried her through the doorway. He loved this strong, athletic version of himself.

He laid her down, told her he'd just be gone a short while and to get some rest, and then slowly shut the door. He quietly moved the couch in front, blocking her exit. There was no way she'd be strong enough to escape now. Hopefully the effect of the drugs would be much less prominent when he returned.

As he began walking away, he thought he heard pounding coming from behind him, but he didn't slow his pace.

24

Alyssa

By the time their evening with Jackson's parents reached dessert, opinions were swirling through Alyssa's head like chocolate syrup being stirred into a glass of milk. The most social, and newest of the group, she was the one leading most of the conversations, but that didn't stop her from carefully observing the interactions between the three Halloway family members.

It was a skill she'd picked up throughout her years of working in medicine. Every day was a tightrope walk of asking the patient questions, calming them down, addressing their loved ones' concerns, and listening to their stories... all while discerning their body language, their whispers, and often, their lies.

So, while she gushed over Cathy's cooking - and her son - she was simultaneously taking notes in the back of her mind, scribbling parts out and adjusting the bullet points as the evening went on.

At first, her list looked something like this:

- *Mom is super sweet, clearly loves Jackson.*
- *Dad is hard to read, but seems to like me.*
- *Jackson is different around them; hard to tell if that's good or bad.*
- *Mom really likes me, but honestly might just love that he has any girl, not specifically me.*
- *Cooking is phenomenal... I hope she passed that down to Jackson!*

As she dug into her red velvet cake, her list was revised to:

- *Mom might spoil Jackson a little... Should I bring that up to Bella and ask her how similar it is to her ex?*
- *Dad looks uncomfortable whenever Jackson brings up my "success," made a comment about how Jackson should be the "breadwinner." Still very nice, likely just a generational thing.*
- *I think the type of "different" Jackson is being tonight is actually not so much "different" as it is "comfortable." I really like who he is when he's completely himself, especially around his mom. I hope he feels like that around me some day.*
- *Mom appears almost relieved with us, like she sees me fit to "take over her role," in a way. Showing symptoms of trust and comfort.*

Alyssa let her brain take a break while she savored her final bites.

When everyone's last crumbs disappeared from their plates into their mouths, Cathy looked down at her cleaned dish and quoted, "Well, I had lunch, but... I seem to have missed dessert."

Delighted at the familiar reference, Alyssa yelled, "Oh my God! *The Spy Who Loved Me*! I love that movie!"

At her exclamation, Jackson and his mom shared a knowing glance, which Alyssa interpreted as, "Yep, she's 'the one.'"

Cathy clapped her hands together and marveled, "You've met your match, Jackie, she beat you at your own game!"

Jackson shuffled his feet under the table; Alyssa guessed he was embarrassed of his mother's affectionate nickname. He worked to mask his reddening cheeks by mirroring his mother's enthusiasm, moving on as if he hadn't even noticed the name. "Dang, girl! You fit right in with us."

The analyst in Alyssa noted his posture and expression: Genuine. Thrilled. Then, teasing.

"How'd you get that so fast? I think she's got note cards under the table. That's gotta be it!"

The group laughed, and Alyssa paused to appreciate Jackson's sparkle. This boy could work a crowd just as well as she could. He could hold his own. Because of his "gamer boy" look, people likely assumed he was quiet. Shy. But she'd seen past that from their very first encounter, and had been proven right ever since.

He had a presence about him, able to command attention, when he wanted to. She thought if he was blessed with clearer skin and a sharper jawline, he could have been a Hollywood actor in another life.

Jackson threw up the tablecloth in one quick motion, revealing Alyssa's jeans. No cheat sheet, of course.

She laughed along with them. "No, I just really love James Bond. I kinda always had a crush on him." Suddenly the pocket of Jackson's pants became very interesting to him, considering his eyes were fixed on it as his fingers traced the seam. *Is he...*

jealous? She kept going; a little healthy jealousy never hurt anyone.

"I mean, how can you not? He's strong, he's cool, and that British accent..." she sighed, overly acting out admiration, then muttered under her breath, but loud enough for them all to hear, "Of course, he's a total womanizer, so... there's that."

Jackson and Cathy chuckled, but Alyssa could've sworn she saw Jonathan scoff.

Add that to the mental list.

"But hey," she kept the tone lighthearted, ignoring his father's distaste, "I fell in love with him when I was like eight, okay? I didn't know any better at the time."

"You were watching James Bond when you were eight years old?" Jackson's mother didn't bother hiding her concern.

Alyssa shrugged, supposing it was a bit absurd. "They were my dad's favorite films." Her eyes landed on Jackson again. His ears were practically perked up at attention, like a dog hearing his master ask if he wants to go outside. He was curious about Alyssa's dad; she'd never mentioned him.

He really cares about me. He truly wants to learn about my family, my hobbies, my life... His interest in her father reaffirmed her fast-beating heart. He continued to prove how deep his feelings were, yet it was somehow still difficult for Alyssa to believe.

Guys were infatuated with her all the time, sure, but that's all it ever turned out to be: Infatuation. That's all it ever was with double–oh–seven, and that was all it ever had been for her father when it came to her mother.

Thinking of her father made her curl her hands into tight fists, her nails pressing painfully into her palms, but when she recounted their history to the Halloways, the memories came out sounding all blissful and nostalgic. Furious as she wanted to be, the little girl in her didn't have any hatred for that man. She remembered him as her hero, her guardian, her friend.

"He would make us popcorn, and roll out sleeping bags for us in the living room." The sides of her mouth involuntarily curled upwards as she thought of her giant father shoving his feet and shins into the child-sized Little Mermaid sleep sack.

"Oh how fun!" Cathy's chipper voice pulled Alyssa from her childhood living room back into the Halloway's dining room.

"Yeah," she reminisced, "It was." She blinked and inhaled deeply, convincing her body to change its tone. "God it's been forever though. Now I just go to the AMC when I wanna watch a film! Their recliner chairs are more comfortable than the floor anyway." She laughed it off, hoping the change of subject would prevent further conversation of the man.

And it did. Jonathan actually chimed in about how he and Jackson had the best time going to the premier of *Avengers: Infinity War*, and Jackson could geek out over Marvel forever, so she was in the clear.

While Jackson and his father were debating which movie was funnier, *Guardians of the Galaxy* or *Thor: Ragnarok*, Alyssa offered to help Cathy with the dishes. They shuffled around the chairs and into the kitchen, Cathy beaming the whole time. Once they were far enough away from the boys to have a bit of privacy, she surprised Alyssa by haphazardly dropping the dishes in the sink, then immediately whimpering.

Quickly but carefully, Alyssa laid down her stack of glasses and silverware and reached out a cautious hand to place on Cathy's arm. The movement was hesitant, unsure if Jackson's mother wanted her affection, or if she was the reason the woman was crying in the first place. "Oh... What is it?"

Cathy didn't answer. Alyssa nervously kept her hand in its

place. *What on earth could she be this upset about?*

"I think everything is going really well, the food was—"

"Yes, I think everything *is* going really well." Alyssa didn't understand, and nearly reached to rub her temples but remembered to keep that hand steady. "I'm so grateful Jackson has found someone like you."

Oh... She's just... happy? Happy enough to send wet droplets of proof to the floor.

The sweetness was overwhelming, but not in a bad way. There was a sense of power in Cathy's words, like they had more weight to them than she was letting on. "I care about him a lot."

Cathy swiped at her wet cheeks. "I can see that you do. I worry about him, I—"

Alyssa wondered why she'd stopped mid-sentence, then followed the woman's gaze right back to her own face. *Oops.* She'd forgotten to shield the confusion left carelessly for anyone to see. And now she was doing no better at concealing the pomegranate shade tinting her cheeks.

"Oh, not that he can't take care of himse— Well... I don't know. It just gives me solace to think that one day, if I'm not around, there will be someone there to look after him."

The list in Alyssa's head was updating rapidly:

- *Confirmed: mom REALLY loves me. I almost feel like I should be weirded out by the intensity of it, but I don't feel that way.*
- *Why is mom talking about not being around? She looked down and to the right, shifted her weight, and her voice rose at the end of the sentence when she spoke of this... All typical behaviors exhibited by patients experiencing acceptance of grief.*

- *Why doesn't mom trust that dad will take care of Jackson in such an event?*
- *Don't bring up him being spoiled by his mom to Bella anymore. Clearly this is different from Clark, and I don't need Bella to have any more reason to try to dislike my boyfriend.*

She heard the loud rubbing of chair legs on tiled floor; one of the guys was moving seats in their absence. Then there was the loud, unmistakable voice of Jonathan Halloway, and he didn't sound as happy about Alyssa as Cathy did.

She couldn't tell exactly what he was talking about, but she heard, "too independent they have no problem leaving, they don't need—"

She had to fight the urge to eavesdrop; Jackson's mom was the priority right now. "I don't think you have to worry about your son." She had plenty of practice consoling patients, but this was so much more complicated. She couldn't give her unbiased advice. Couldn't leave out her emotions.

"I haven't known him nearly as long as you, obviously, but in the time I have gotten to know him, I've seen that he's extremely smart - a lot smarter than he gives himself credit for. And caring, and funny, and… Well now I'm rambling, but… I know he's capable of a lot. I don't think you need to worry about him."

Arms were around her neck. *I'm in my boyfriend's kitchen, being crushed by his crying mother.* If you would have asked her a few hours earlier, she would not have anticipated the evening would turn out this way. In the few seconds they embraced, she could just barely make out Jackson's dad uttering, "What are you bringing to the table? You're certainly no James Bond."

Time to break up that conversation.

"Here, why don't I get Jackson to help me with the dishes, and you go to the bathroom and freshen up." Cathy agreed, and Alyssa called Jackson in to help her.

He made her laugh the entire time they scrubbed and dried, swinging the dish towel and pretending to *almost* drop the dishes as she handed them to him to dry.

Her thoughts skipped forward, as they often did when she thought of this sweet boy, and she imagined how fun her life could be with him. Washing dishes, packing lunches, grocery shopping... Every mundane task sounded like it wouldn't be so bad if they were doing it together.

With only a few cups left, Jackson's mom emerged from the bathroom, no signs of her emotional episode still apparent on her face. In fact, she looked overjoyed, watching the two of them laugh and work together, then a bit stunned.

"He must really like you; I can never get him to help *me* with the dishes!" Jackson sheepishly rubbed the cloth over the glass in his hand.

Cathy's sentiment sparked a memory alive, from Halloween a few years ago, and Alyssa seized the opportunity to get in on their little family tradition. The "flirtatious baby doll" voice was difficult to master, but she gave it her best shot. "A woman spends all day over a hot stove slaving away for her man. The least he can do is the dishes."

Jackson knew instantly, cracking up at her impression as he called out, "*Bride of Chucky!*" He lifted his hand to high five her, and she proudly obliged. "That voice was spot-on."

Even Jackson's dad let out a little wheeze, and Alyssa thought it was the perfect note to end the night on. She didn't want to be the one to dismiss herself, as the guest, but luckily Jackson must have had the same thought, because he placed his last glass down and held his palm to her shoulder blades.

He'd touched her before, many times, but something about learning who raised him and where he came from anchored her feelings further into the solid foundation - like spikes hammered into the soil of a forest to hold down a tent. If the spikes were pushed down with enough strength, the tent could weather any storm. So when he touched her this time, his hand was strong as a spike, holding her in place, keeping her safe.

"On that note, it's getting late and Alyssa has to be at the hospital early tomorrow, so I'd better walk her out." They exchanged friendly goodbyes and Alyssa hugged each of his parents, then Jackson put that strong spike on the small of her back and led her out the door.

Alyssa was prepared to dissect the evening with Jackson as couples typically did when meeting parents, analyzing their actions and deciding whether it went well or not, but before she could get a word out, just as the door snapped closed, Jackson's hands were in her hair and his lips were forceful on hers, impatient, but still careful. When their mouths parted, he breathed, "Hey, I know you've got a lot going on, but do you think you can come over again tomorrow night?"

"Another dinner?" she wondered, surprised. She thought it had gone well, but probably best to leave well enough alone for now.

"No," he was confident. Firm. Bold. "Just us. I want to... Well, you'll see. Can you come?" Both of his hands grabbed hers. He was looking down into her eyes, yet there was a sense of pleading innocence as if he'd been looking up. "Please?"

A begging Jackson was almost too much for Alyssa to handle. Perhaps it was because she was wondering what the rest of his sentence was going to be after "I want to," or the fact that she could still see the shine of her saliva on his lips as his sultry eyes waited for her answer, but she became distinctly aware of the fact that they hadn't been intimate yet.

And of the fact that she wanted to.

"Yes," she was glad she sounded more composed than she felt, that her voice wasn't as shaky as her wobbling knees, "I can come." The words were coated with sexuality... Or maybe that was just how Alyssa perceived them as her thoughts wandered to the possibilities of tomorrow night.

25

Bianca

She knew exactly where to find him. The soccer field. She'd taken him there shortly after they'd met so he could watch her coach. It had been her brilliant idea, because there, he could see how good she was with kids... Plus she could show off some of her soccer skills. *Sue me for wanting to impress him... He was cute!* And impressed he was.

Not only did he end up falling in love with Bianca, but with the field as well. Derek had just moved from St. Louis, and he'd never had so much open space where he could explore without the area being chained off or in use.

When his father passed, she'd been worried sick when she couldn't find him anywhere, and then she'd thought to check the field.

He'd said it gave him a sense of peace. It was his sanctuary. And that was even before he'd grown attached to the kids.

Her students loved him, and the two of them would go to every game, even the ones she wasn't coaching, just to socialize with the staff, the parents, and, most importantly, the children. To Bianca this was normal, living in a small town, making friends with everyone, but to Derek, it was completely foreign. He'd never talked to so many people, experienced so much community, or witnessed such a beautiful view. He told Bianca she was a bird, and that once he'd met her, he'd been able to fly with her above the world and look down at the life he didn't know he'd been missing.

Sure, he'd been exposed to large amounts of people, culture, and diversity in the city, but he told her he never really *saw* the beauty in any of it until she showed him how. Said she'd had a way of spreading her wings and flying over everything to gain a new perspective. Up close, he said, people had always been confusing and uninteresting to him, but she'd shown him how to see their full pictures. Like looking at a mosaic too close, then one day viewing it from a new, distanced angle.

Like when he'd nearly gotten into a fight with a thirteen-year-old because she'd yelled at Bianca during practice and called her a series of expletives. Derek was ready to get that little girl expelled, until Bianca took him by the arm and explained that there was more to her story. Showed him the bigger picture - another perspective. Informed him that the girl was raised by her grandfather who was "unfit," to say the least, and now the court was deciding on whether or not she should be placed into foster care. She told Derek the girl didn't have many positive female role models in her life, and hadn't ever been taught proper respect. Her grandfather hadn't even allowed her to go to school most of the time, and she was still in the learning stages. Learning how to socialize, learning how to function with healthy balances of power, learning how to accept Bianca's tough, but motherly, love.

Derek and that girl still kept in contact today, and she'd admiringly credited both of them in her high school graduation speech, since she'd become the salutatorian and class president. That was Derek's favorite story about how Bianca gave him perspective. Showed him people are always more complicated and more beautiful than they appear at first.

He'd always credited Bianca for the new person he'd become since they'd been together. For being part of her community. For wanting to become a father. And whenever he needed to breathe in some fresh air and remember to gain a new point of view, he'd come to the soccer field.

He was lying on the grass in front of one of the goal posts, looking up at the sky. When he heard her approaching, he sat up, and to her surprise, smiled at her despite the redness in his eyes. He'd been crying. Still, he looked happy to see her.

Her suspicions proved correct when he jumped up and, before saying a word, scooped her into a desperate embrace. His rough hands had her hair gripped inside their fists, and his chin was on top of her head, holding her there, not letting her go. She was perfectly alright with that. She didn't want to go. This was exactly where she belonged.

It was the most they'd ever said with silence. His hands on her were a form of sign language she understood completely. Her head on his chest was more eloquent an apology than she'd ever been able to convey with her voice. His tears falling onto her hair were screaming "I forgive you" with more conviction and passion than three measly words ever had.

Bianca felt more invigorated, more alive than she had even before the last six weeks. She felt sure. Sure of their love. Sure of him. Sure she'd be okay, even if they never conceived again, because *he* was her family, and he was already so much more than she could ever hope for.

And yet, six months later, without trying, and when she least expected it, Bianca got pregnant again.

26

Clayton

From his meeting with Dr. Barnes, Clayton had learned a lot about the medical side of the Program. Turns out the process was a lot more complicated than Clayton had always assumed.

As they'd discussed before, the test patients were each already on medications, so they didn't need much to dull their senses. Still, it was all an exact science.

Every individual patient was on different meds, and some needed slight doses of outside drugs for the Program, while others needed none at all. Mix the wrong kind of drug into a patient's pre-existing IV, and the effects could be severe.

Founders like Clayton, Gordon, and Dr. Barnes, who were entering Salvation without having any pre-existing medications, needed a specific combination of substances as well. In order for Dr. Barnes to determine which drugs everyone would need to take, and how much of each, he'd had to sample their DNA.

So that's why he had us pee in a cup. He was sure Dr. Barnes had, in fact, told him why he was donating, but he hadn't cared at that point. He'd been far too invested in his contributions to the Program to concern himself with whatever his colleague was doing.

So he'd need to get a urine sample from Courtney. That was his takeaway. He could bring it to Dr. Barnes, telling him it was for a hypothetical patient, and the doctor would be able to prescribe the right dosage for her IV.

He walked back into his house, eager to discover what Courtney had been doing while he'd been away. There was sobbing coming from the bedroom... That couldn't be good. He pulled the couch aside and opened the door. Courtney was sitting in the corner, with her knees up to her chest, holding them in her arms. There were tears running down both cheeks.

When she saw Clayton, she jumped to her feet. "Babe, what's going on?" She was scared, but looked relieved to see him. He took that as a good sign... She must not remember what had happened. What he'd done.

"Where are we? What is this... Wait..." Was she about to accuse him? He prepared himself. "Why do you look so... different?"

That wasn't the question he'd been expecting, but one he was happy to acknowledge. "Do I look good?"

She was clearly confused, not knowing which questions to focus her attention on first. "Yeah... You look... Well, you look really great, actually. Like, super handsome."

Clayton knew he should care about so many other things right now, but all he wanted to do was soak up this moment. "Yeah? Go on..."

She might have been about to indulge him, but then she blinked and shook herself back to thinking about the more pressing questions. "Where are we? And how did we get here?"

Suddenly, a light bulb went off above Clayton's head. All the patients had asked these questions, and how had he been giving the information to them? Through his curated audio tapes. While the generic audio could get most users immersed into Salvation when combined with the drugs and projections, it still left users a bit confused. Once Clayton had started making more *specific* tapes catering to each unique patient individually, that's when he began seeing booming success. Applying the same logic, if he could make Courtney her own recording, she wouldn't have all these questions.

There was only one problem: No one else in Salvation was there against their will. No one else was this disoriented - they knew exactly where they were; they'd prepared for it extensively and were well aware of what they were getting themselves into when signing up for the Program. So even with the tapes, Clayton wasn't necessarily sure an unwilling Courtney would be able to shake her grogginess and dementia. But he had to try.

"I promise you I will explain everything in just a little bit," he fibbed, "But for now, just know that everything is great, this place is good, and you are perfectly safe, okay? Just trust me."

He shouldn't have added that last part, because asking her to trust him was what he had done just before bringing her here, and repeating that phrase seemed to arouse part of her memory that had been lying dormant.

She held her head as if the memories trying to come back to her were physically hurting her. She squeezed her eyes closed. "You... What... What did you do to me?"

This was all wrong; she was supposed to love him in Salvation, not look at him with disgust. He thought when he showed her his world, she would be impressed with him, and when she saw

180

his newly improved self, she wouldn't be able to resist him. It wasn't supposed to go this way...

Her attention turned to her arm, noticing the bruising around the small puncture where he'd stuck her. "Clayton..." He'd never seen this look in her eyes. "What did you do to me?"

She was in a crouched stance, knees bent, one foot in front of the other, ready to run or attack at any given moment.

Her eyes shifted to the open bedroom door. *She's plotting her escape.* Before she could execute whatever plan was forming, he leaped out of the room and slammed the door shut in one swift motion. Then, he grabbed the already nearby couch and shoved it in front, blocking her only exit. The handle jiggled furiously, and Courtney screamed and clawed from the inside, and he ran.

He ran as fast as he could towards his car. He raced to headquarters, and noticed Gordon watch him zoom by, lips parting in confusion.

When he finally made it up the hill, he sprinted to the portal and leaped through without slowing. Instantly, he was back in the bed next to Courtney and his mother.

Georgie's glossed eyes were just one of many indications that she was clearly still inside Salvation. He hadn't expected any less, but... he'd hoped. Before taking care of business with Courtney, he wet a cloth and squeezed some water into his mother's mouth. He changed her catheter and applied lip balm to her cracked lips. She was supposed to be doing these things, entering the real world enough to get help from the nurses. They had a deal.

I need to address this with her later. He didn't, *couldn't*, blame her. This world was nothing but a mess. *Why? Why do I even bother? No one wants to be here in Chicago anymore, and why would they? I don't want to be here either.* He couldn't avoid his reflection in the mirror of the small, open bathroom. *I really don't want to be here.*

The only reason I've been nagging users about taking care of themselves in the real world is so they'll look halfway decent for the investors. But why do the investors need to even see them in the real world? Can't the investors just meet us in Salvation? He made a mental note to talk to Dr. Barnes and Gordon about that later, then refocused on his mission. *Okay,* he pulled himself together. *Where is my recorder?* And he got to work.

He explained everything to her, just like he'd promised earlier. The explanations were not complete truths, but the truth would only scare her. He spoke into his microphone, telling her what an amazing place Salvation is, and how she was lucky to be there. He described where she was allowed to go, and all the beautiful amenities they had to offer her.

"You'll live with Clayton. He is your boyfriend." He stopped, and a new thought registered for the first time: He could tell her anything he wanted to.

He rewound the tape, and began to re-record. "You'll live with Clayton. He is your husband. You love him. You met on a dating app in 201—" Rewind, re-record. "You met on a cruise… to Europe. It was actually extremely romantic. You dropped your scarf, and the wind blew it across the deck, but right before it went overboard, he snatched it up and saved it for you." Clayton smiled, blushing a bit as he reveled in the romance of that story. He'd always wanted to have a suave meet-cute like that, the type of story only a certain category of men got to have. He usually had to watch that type of chemistry from the sidelines. But he was writing his own story now.

Swept away by the power, Clayton created a whole new life for him and Courtney. "Your wedding was beautiful, and Clayton's mom walked him down the aisle." *If only.* "His vows were heartfelt, and you felt like the luckiest girl in the world." *This is fun.* "You honeymooned in the Bahamas. The sunset on the beach was unbelievable and you splashed around in the salty water… Whenever you actually left the hotel bed, that is." He went on and on. He created imaginary memories of their vacations and inside jokes, their talks of children and dinners with friends. And as he chattered away into the recording, he began to grieve over the life he didn't have. The mother who was happy, the wife who loved him, years of laughs and fun instead of computers and spreadsheets. *It doesn't matter,* he told himself. *I have it now.*

When he was satisfied with his work, he downloaded the file and synced it with the projection for "user 3" of his unit. Before pressing "start," he pumped a little more ketamine into Courtney's IV. It'd made total sense when Dr. Barnes had revealed this was one of the substances he'd chosen for the users. "Euphoria, relaxation, and anxiety relief" mixed together with "mental clouding" were his recipe for success. Clayton figured Courtney could use a little mental clouding after everything that had happened.

After he clicked "start," Clayton waited several minutes before entering Salvation himself. He wanted to give her some time to really let his messages, and the drugs, sink in. His mother, of course, still hadn't logged out of the Program. Her eyes continued staring at the projection on the ceiling, held open unnaturally wide by the Oc X's, the metronome swinging back and forth and back and forth as she stared. Unblinking.

Since Georgie was ignoring her needs, Clayton continued tending to them himself. He gave her a bit more water, brushed her hair, and moved her slightly, positioning her at a different angle to try and prevent more sores. He figured it was time he started taking care of Courtney, too. He became stressed again, wondering how he could "take care" of this mess that was only getting messier by the day. Surely Courtney wouldn't be able to log out... He couldn't let her. She would realize what he'd done to her and leave him, or report him to the police.

I'll have to become her full time caretaker. While it might seem like a huge task, he assumed soon everyone in the Salvation Program would need to be taken care of by someone in the outside world because, like his mother, they'd never want to leave. And once his Program was approved by the medical board, people would be able to talk about it and ask a friend to help take care of their real bodies while they were logged in. For now, though, with most people overreacting to his idea and deeming it unsafe, they had to be discreet.

He remembered one of the reasons he'd come here: He had to get a urine sample from Courtney. He needed something concrete for Dr. Barnes so he could tell him the proper IV doses needed to drug her safely. It looked like she'd already wet herself. He took care of it, and placed a bedpan under her for whenever she was ready to go again.

Buzz-buzz, buzz-buzz. Crap. Her phone was ringing. It was coming from inside her purse, which had also been knocked to the ground. He looked inside and found her cell, cracked, but still working. "No, no, nooo!" he screamed, slamming his fist into the wall. He was too weak to put a hole through it - his muscle mass was severely depleting from lack of use in the real world. Six missed calls from her sister. *Six.* And he knew they weren't going to stop. He looked at the clock; Courtney had been logged in for over twelve hours already. She lived with

184

her sister, and hadn't made it home for dinner.

Okay, think... Stall her until you figure out how to explain this.
He tried to open her phone. "Show face ID." He grimaced. Even
he was a bit disgusted by what he was about to do. He held
the phone up to Courtney's face, her wide eyes staring past the
camera. It unlocked.

Clayton went to her text messages. Her sister had been
hounding her phone.

Where are you?

I thought you were coming home for dinner?

Dude, seriously are you good?

**I've been trying to call you... You're scaring me, just let
me know you're breathing please!**

Okay, this is not funny, did your phone die?

Court! Call me!!!

Buzz-buzz, buzz-buzz. This time, the call was coming through
Clayton's earpiece. Courtney's sister despised Clayton, so he
knew she had run out of options when he saw her name on
the caller ID. She had no one else to reach out to but him. He
ignored the call for now. It would look too suspicious if *he*
answered but not Courtney, considering they were supposed
to be together.

Back to the text messages. He typed as Courtney:

**OMG I'm so sorry! Clayton and I were both on a plane
and couldn't use our phones. I cannot believe I didn't tell
you, but we decided to go on a vacation! I know, I know,
it's so crazy, but we decided to be super spontaneous and
it all just happened so fast! This insane deal popped up
through Clayton's work and we had to book it right away
and run to the airport! Also, I probably won't be on my
phone much here... trying to soak it all in, you know? But**

anyways, sorry I scared you!

Hopefully she'd buy that. He hit send, and turned the phone to airplane mode.

A sudden noise startled him, but he was happy to see that it was Courtney filling the bedpan. He collected the sample and disarmed all security so he could open the door and run the specimen to the receptionist to give to Dr. Barnes. He looked around the facility; everyone was operating as normal. *Good.* No one had noticed the commotion. He gave the collection cup to Amber, who gave him the concerned look he'd been getting a lot in the real world lately, since he'd stopped taking care of himself. He ignored her judgmental eyes scanning him and instructed her on what to do with the sample, then quickly headed back to the room.

By this point, a little bit of ketamine was starting to sound very appealing. He was ready to log back in, to reduce anxiety, and to relax. But there was one more thing he wanted to do first.

Courtney's bruising wasn't looking great, and in general, she was a mess. He didn't want her to stand out in Salvation, which meant he'd need to change her avatar. He stared at the screen, clicking through the options. What did he want his Salvation wife to look like? His final outcome ended up looking like a real-life Barbie doll. *Perfect.* He could log in.

27

Jackson

"Honey, the doorbell just rang, I think Alyssa is here!" She was early. Even though he'd assumed she would be, she always was, he still felt a rush of anxiety. Jackson eyeballed the room, checking off his list as he turned three hundred sixty degrees, ensuring everything in the Loft was looking just as he'd envisioned. *Sleeping bags? Check. Popcorn microwaved? Check.* From Russia with Love *set up on the TV? Check. The Loft cleaned spotless, for once? Check.* He pressed "play" on the remote control. When he was anxious, having a screen on with noise playing usually helped. Plus, this way, Alyssa would get the full picture when she walked in.

Then he went through his personal list. *Teeth brushed? Check. Contacts in? Check. Freshly showered? Check. Deodorant? Oops, I knew I was forgetting something.* "Coming!" he called out as he grabbed the stick and swiped under his arms on the way down the stairs. He was in such a rush that he still had his shirt part way up as he yanked open the door to reveal a stunning Alyssa. Her eyes flickered to his exposed skin, and he quickly smoothed the fabric down. He still had the tube of deodorant in his hand.

His face was burning, and Alyssa laughed that bubbly laugh of hers, the one that sounded like echos being played over a reel of happy memories.

Most girls Jackson knew, even the ones who he later found out had no real interest in him, would apologize when they met with him immediately after a full day of work. "Sorry I look awful, I just finished a long shift and came straight here." "Excuse the hair, it's been up in a bun for the past ten hours." "Don't look at my makeup, it's probably a mess, it's been quite the day and I didn't have time to touch it up." He'd heard these lines from partners and friends, but not from Alyssa.

Of course, she looked completely beautiful to him, as she always did and always was. Even so, he'd only known girls to pick themselves apart. To apologize. But Alyssa never did.

She didn't acknowledge all the loose hairs wildly escaping what was left of her once-tight braid. She didn't ask forgiveness for still being in the two-sizes-too-large t-shirt and gym shorts that he knew was the uniform she kept in her locker to change into after work at the hospital. She simply reached her arms out with a two-sizes-too-big smile on her face and wrapped him up in an it's-great-to-see-you-again hug. "So," her eyes twinkled like mirrors, "What was so important that you just had to have me over again?"

"Does there have to be a special occasion for me to want my very sweet and pretty girlfriend to come over and hang out with me?"

Alyssa crossed her arms. Her uncontained smile accepted the compliment, even if her body language didn't. "No, there doesn't *have* to be. But this time, there *is*. It's pretty obvious." Even with her arms over her chest, her voice was laced with delight.

"Am I that bad at hiding it?" He was just as delighted; her mere presence made him feel full. His battery was charging again.

"Terrible. Probably the worst I've ever seen." They were still in the doorway, so Jackson took her hand and led her towards the stairs. They passed his parents on the couch, and Jackson felt self-conscious. A boy. That's how his parents saw him. A boy next to a *woman*. A doctor.

Their age difference was often forgotten, pushed to the back of his brain, but in moments like this, holding hands with a medical professional after a day of surgeries, it forced its way straight to the front. They weren't many physical years apart, but anyone could see she was light-years ahead of him, regardless of age. She was a thirty-year-old surgeon. It didn't always feel like it when they were together, but he had to remind himself of this fact.

He didn't want to get trapped in a web of small talk with the family, and fortunately her hand was still in his, so he just kept pulling her past them and up the steps. He let her at least splutter out a greeting before whisking her completely away around the corner.

Nervously, he opened the Loft door, revealing the room, tuned in to Alyssa's face for her reaction. Since he knew very little about her father, he couldn't rule out the possibility of Alyssa being offended by his gesture. Would it stir up bad memories for her? He'd almost talked himself out of the idea earlier, but she'd seemed so euphoric talking about her childhood yesterday, and he'd already bought the sleeping bags.

He tracked her expression, initially perplexed, then turning into something else... droplets forming in the corners of her eyes. *I knew this was stupid. I should've returned the sleeping bags, cut my losses.'* Sean Connery's voice was drowned out by his own rushing thoughts. "I'm so sorry, I thought maybe you'd... I just, I thought I'd... But now I see that it was really—"

"Unbelievable," Alyssa finished for him.

"I know, I'm sorry, I—"

"Sorry?" She reluctantly peeled her eyes from the scene and focused them on his. "This is the most thoughtful thing anyone has ever done for me."

The silence was thick as a cake. It could be sliced with a knife, and the delicious, sugary residue would stick on the utensil, turning it just as sweet, tempting the cutter to lick the very thing that could carve them.

Jackson paused, stunned. He recollected his thoughts. *She loves it?* "Well, last night you were talking about how you used to do this with your dad. And I just thought—"

Alyssa cut him off with a kiss, which seemed to be becoming a habit of hers, and one Jackson was definitely on board with. The sleeping bags stayed zipped up, but they fell on top of them, intertwined, as the smell of popcorn drifted through the room. They kissed as Bond was informed Romanova had requested his help. They kissed during his arrival in Istanbul, and all throughout his meeting in Romanova's hotel suite. When Jackson finally forced himself to pull his lips from hers, Bond was on the train questioning everything around him.

As much as Jackson was enjoying this lapse in conversation, that wasn't why he did this. He wanted Alyssa to open up to him. To feel comfortable. To trust him.

"Alyssa," he started, still cradling the back of her head and her now completely ruffled braid.

Her eyes spoke for her, sending her message to his. "Yes?"

He forgot what he'd planned to say, forgot how to breathe. Her hazel irises - and hazel was a simplified definition, not managing to encapsulate the pure magic of the irish hill green contrasting with a brown the color of warm chocolate and old leather wrapped around first edition books - were enough to make any man lose his mind. There was no getting used to them. There never would be.

He willed his brain to start thinking, though it seemed dead set on transferring its job to other parts of his body. "Why was last night the only time I've heard you talk about your dad?"

Alyssa gulped down a short breath. It sounded like hesitation, and maybe Jackson should have felt like he'd pried too far, but he didn't. Somehow, he sensed Alyssa wanted to talk about it, even if every signal she'd given since he'd known her claimed that she didn't. He didn't say sorry this time, or change the subject. When her head began tilting downwards, he removed one hand from her loosely braided hair and blocked her like a football player making an interception. A successful one, as he stopped her head in its tracks and reclaimed the power.

Her mouth looked like it would have fallen open if his sturdy hand wasn't under her chin. Surprise splattered her face, a deer standing in the middle of an open field, not even attempting to run once seeing the hunter. She must've been able to tell he wasn't holding a gun.

His unwavering gaze sent his intended message: He was not backing down.

She quivered, barely louder than the wind, "He left us."

Jackson didn't speak. Though he'd anticipated this is what she might say, her cracking voice put a crack in him. He'd never felt a pain like this. Helplessness. She was a precious jewel, and someone had decided to discard her in the dirt. *How could they*

191

do that? How did they not know how lucky they were?

But it was more than her not being appreciated that tore him open. It was seeing how much it had hurt her, how much it *still* hurt her. He wished it was his father that had been so careless, his family that was separated, just so it wouldn't be hers, so he wouldn't have to see a jewel lose its shine. But even if he was willing to make that sacrifice, it was impossible. So all he could do was listen.

"My mom and I. He just… left." She was far away, even as their bodies were close enough to catch fire; he could practically see her watching her father pack a suitcase. "Well actually, he didn't *just* leave; he left and found himself a whole new family. I thought maybe he left because he didn't want a daughter, or maybe even a wife. But he has one of those now, a wife. And three daughters."

Now Jackson was the deer in the field, frozen in place, unable to camouflage his emotions.

"At least that's what I hear. We haven't heard from him since he left. And the worst part is," *Worse than him having three daughters after abandoning one?* "We have no idea why. He and my mom were both powerhouse surgeons. Yeah they worked all the time, but they loved it. Or at least she thought they did. She said there was never any indication that he was unhappy. One day he was just… not there anymore."

Jackson had learned by now that Alyssa rambled a lot. Sometimes she rambled to fill awkward silences, sometimes to entertain friends, sometimes to assure others she understood them, but he'd never seen her ramble like this. For herself. To say something out loud for the first time. To face it.

He didn't want to derail her train of thought, so he stayed silent, though he had what felt like an entire steam engine thundering through his head right now.

"And my mom hasn't been the same since. We used to be close, but..." she moved as she spoke, and he followed suit, first to their knees on the sleeping bags, then to their stomachs as she released her story like a kite - letting it drift into the sky and turn into something new, useful, but keeping it tethered to her still to carry home with her later. Bond and Romanova were deciding their escape plan in the background.

"I still love her, I just... I used to idolize her. She's the one who taught me, by example, that women can be strong. That we can have any career we want, that we can take care of ourselves, that we can be serious *and* fun. They always used to have fun with me..." She trailed off, but Jackson laid motionless beside her, unmoving, and she kept going. "She's so different now. She quit surgery. I mean, she could've been head of neuro at Sparrow, or Beaumont. They were competing for her attention." She shifted her weight onto her left elbow so she could look at him to her right. Up until that point, he wasn't even sure she even remembered he was there. "That never happens, ever. She was a legend."

She turned back towards the TV. "And she stopped. She always said you don't need a man. But then she crumbled when hers was gone. And he always said he loved us, but then he disappeared." She didn't sound sad anymore. Just factual. Empty. "And like it or not, I'm a smart girl. I always have been. I rely on evidence to form my knowledge. If you look at the cold hard facts, you can only arrive at one conclusion after all that: People are not honest, especially when it comes to love." She was so serious, like a mathematician explaining how to find "x."

She was studying her fingers, and he was studying her. "I

know I push people away." She laughed a little then, but it wasn't sunshine and light like it normally was. "Well at least, I try to. I'm nice and all, but I don't trust everyone like I did when I was a kid. I say 'no' a lot. People wanting to hang out, guys wanting to go on dates... I blame it on being tired or busy. 'I need to study,' 'I had a long surgery.'" She looked up then, still not at Jackson, but ahead at the television. For an eternal second they watched Bond in his great escape.

Then a smile blossomed on Alyssa's face, and this time it was genuine, both the flower and the sunbeams which enable life. "But some people make you reevaluate your analysis. I met Bella, and she was the only exception." Jackson smiled at her smile, not expecting her to look up at him, but she did. "She *was* the only exception. Until now." Jackson didn't know how he was able to hold her gaze then; her eyes were like two planets, bright as full moons but with more depth than planet Earth itself. Even so, he forced his eyes to stay open, to continue to stare into hers, feeling as though he may never experience a moment as serene and powerful as this again in his life, and refusing to throw away his opportunity. Refusing to be like her father.

After what was both an eternity and an instant, she set fire to every part of him with four extraordinary matches. "I love you, Jackson."

28

Clayton

Clayton joined the simulation, exited headquarters, slid into his car, and drove straight to his house. He was eager to see Courtney, but as he went to move the couch away from the door, his strength ran away from him, scared of what he might see.

What if the tapes didn't work? What if I gave her too many drugs... Dr. Barnes had made a point to mention how dangerous it could be to accidentally overdose, even by a small amount. Plus, he was only guessing on the quantities for now, until the doctor had a chance to analyze the contents of the cup.

Okay, I can stand here outside the door wondering what's going on in there, or I could go in and find out. Good or bad, I need to know. He pulled the couch aside, turned the handle of the door, and pulled it open.

"Darling, you're home!" An elated Courtney skipped over to him and planted a big kiss square on his lips. "How was your day? I want to hear all about it!"

Clayton was stunned. He knew he shouldn't be, he'd programmed this to happen. But still, to see it work so seamlessly...

He'd impressed even himself. He couldn't stop gawking at her - this impossibly gorgeous, sexy woman who was all his. Who didn't know any of the bad parts of him. Who had no idea what he'd done to her.

He pulled her in and kissed her again. "My day was busy," he thought back to all of the events - meeting with Courtney, bringing her here, locking her up, speaking with Dr. Barnes, going back to Chicago, making the tapes, taking care of her and his mother, the missed calls, texting her sister, dropping off the sample, coming back here - "And messy." He pictured the fight, the needle, the bedpan... "But it's phenomenal now." He drank in her white smile, her perfect body leaning in towards his.

"Aww aren't you the sweetest!" She was grinning from ear to ear. She'd never looked better, and even that was an understatement. "I'm so sorry I didn't make dinner, I couldn't open this silly door." She looked at it, perplexed for a moment, then dove into explaining what she was planning to make for them and seemed to forget all about it.

By the time they were done with their late dinner, Clayton was absolutely beat. Elated, but swaying from exhaustion. "I'm going to get ready for bed, my dear." He slid his chair out from underneath the table and stood up, ready to make his way to the bedroom.

"Aren't you going to help me with the dishes?" Courtney questioned. "I cooked everything, so I thought you'd offer to assist with the clean up."

Clayton sighed. "I'm so tired; I told you I had a busy day."

"It's nearly 2020, darling." She was still smiling, trying not to fight with him, but holding her ground. Typical Courtney. "We're in this marriage as equals, remember?" He opened his mouth to argue, only to be overstepped, "But I love you, my beautiful husband, and that's why I'm offering to share the dishes with you. You don't even need to do them all, just help me out a bit. Alright?"

He drank another glass of her stunning face. He didn't want to fight either. "Of course I'll help, I apologize, dear."

Though he sidled up beside her and ran the water over the first mashed potato-crusted dish, he made a mental note to edit her audio tape.

And so it went for the next week. "You love your husband, and you do everything together." Rewind. Re-record. "You love your husband, and so you love to serve him."

"You get to relax in Salvation while Clayton is away." Rewind. Re-record. "While Clayton works, you enjoy taking care of the house. Your job is very important." He thought for a moment, then added, "But after your work is done, you get to live your best life. It's a privilege to be here."

And he just kept adding, and adding. Courtney didn't feel like engaging in Clayton's desires one night, so the next day, he recorded: "When it comes to your incredible husband, you have no sexual limitations. You want it just as much as he does. Every time."

In another instance, she'd kept him home from going golfing with the boys. The next chance he'd gotten alone with the recorder, he'd explained, "You support Clayton with both his work, *and* his hobbies. You know how hard he works, and you want him to wind down in any way he sees fit."

And of course, there was the most common problem of all: her curiosity about the Salvation Program. She wanted to know what they were doing, why there were earthquakes (though there had been none for several days now), what was at headquarters, why she couldn't go there... Her questions were endless.

He had to keep going back to the tapes. "The Salvation Program is kept secret for your safety. You do not need to question what it is we are doing, just know that we are bettering the world. As long as you stay in your home, or the other parts of town that you've been told you are allowed to visit, you will be safe and happy. All you need to worry about is supporting your husband as he commits himself to this incredible opportunity. It is a privilege to be here.

And with that, Courtney was his perfect woman. She didn't question him. She catered to his every need. She gave in to his whims and desires, and she wanted him as much as he wanted her. He'd said "I love you" to her before out of necessity. It'd felt like time, she'd pressured him... But now, now he meant it. *Felt* it. He was repulsed by the imperfect version of her he saw when he visited Chicago. His life in Chicago was over.

He forced himself to set an alarm to leave Salvation at least once a day. He didn't want to leave for even five minutes, but he knew he had to take care of his mother, Courtney, and himself. He'd officially banned anyone else from coming into his mother's room at BrightView at all. And he limited access to the rooms of his other test subjects more and more as time went on. They all looked horrible, and Salvation would be over if the wrong person saw them in their condition. Plus, Dr. Barnes and Gordon were under the impression that Courtney was visiting of her own free will, and he didn't want them to look too closely at the scene of the crime and question anything.

But when Clayton wasn't in Chicago for his daily hour or so of chores, he was having the time of his life inside the Program. He was living every man's fantasy. He continued developing Salvation by day, preparing for the investors and solidifying his technology as best he could. But by night, and on the weekends, he experienced the lavish lifestyle he only ever dreamed of before. The kind he only thought existed for others, and never believed could be his.

They lived this way for a couple more weeks, Courtney loving him and tending to him while he was slaving the days away, until she started asking questions again. He saw her on the cameras, watching through the window as everyone else around her was thriving, probably not quite understanding how she fit in here. The others could drive in cars and go where they wanted, but she was stuck in the house. Alone.

"Something's not right, what's going on here, Clayton?" She'd ask, rubbing away at the migraine that never left her temples. "Why am I trapped here? What's out there? What is it you're building? Why can't I know what it is? Is it dangerous? I'm different from everyone else here... I can't explain it, I just am. It's like everybody knows a secret that I'm not allowed to know, and no one will tell me. I feel like I'm going crazy!"

"You've just been out in the sun too much," Clayton would try to calm her down, "All that time by the pool, you know? What a great problem to have, really! You should consider yourself fortunate."

She'd lost her mind at that. "No, you're not listening! Baby, I love you so much, but I'm trying to tell you something. I don't feel fortunate; I want to leave! Where did we live before this? I can't even remember... My head hurts when I try to think about it too much... Something is wrong!"

"I'll go talk to Dr. Barnes for you," he'd consoled. "Maybe he can help with all these headaches, and the anxiety. You're exhausted, and you're working yourself up. I'll see if he can give you something." This hadn't satisfied her, but he'd run out before she could argue.

He'd gone into the doctor's office, wanting to talk about more than just headaches. "Hey Jeremy, remember that test sample I gave you a few weeks back?"

"Well hello to you too." Dr. Barnes was clearly fed up with Clayton's demands, which were only multiplying as they prepared for the investors. When Clayton didn't apologize, he gave in and answered, "Yes, test sample K12. What about it?"

"What if a patient that size was taking the recommended dosage, but it still wasn't quite enough for some reason."

Dr. Barnes furrowed his brow. "That's highly unlikely, the dosages are assigned based on a thoroughly tested mathematical process. Based on the patient's body type and chemical makeup, the recommended dosage should always be able to lower inhibitions enough to allow a user to enter Salvation."

He wasn't understanding, but Clayton wasn't ready to tell him what he'd done yet. "You're right, of course. But, out of curiosity, what would happen if someone gave the patient *more*." The lines between Dr. Barnes' eyes deepened. "Accidentally, of course," Clayton threw in. "How much of an extra dosage would one have to give this patient before it became dangerous?"

"Well..." The doctor rubbed his head just like Courtney. *What a lovely effect I have on people.* "Technically, anything above the recommended dosage could be considered dangerous. But really, with the types of medicines we are using here, your test subject *could* accidentally receive a higher dose and most likely be fine, since what we prescribe is a relatively low amount. See, we prescribe just enough to calm the system a bit. But if the person were in pain, or if you needed to calm them down even more for some reason, you could give them, I'd say, almost double the amount. Theoretically it wouldn't be overtly harmful to them, but the effects would be much stronger."

Clayton wanted to hear more. "Which effects, exactly?"

"Oh you know, general grogginess. Our concoction makes us a little 'out of it,' in Layman's terms. So to give someone more than they are prescribed would cause them to feel extra dazed. Their memory would be pretty much useless under that kind of influence. There would really be no point, in our case."

Clayton grinned. "Yeah, I don't know why I even bothered asking."

He was pretty sure Dr. Barnes was oblivious to his motives, but the doctor had this annoying habit of always giving Clayton warnings. He looked Salvation's founder dead in the eyes - a look that went straight to Clayton's gut and gave him the strangest feeling that maybe his partner knew more than he was letting on.

"But overdosing is a very real threat." The eye contact didn't waver. Perhaps he wasn't the naive child Clayton had always assumed he was. "Drug overdoses, medical or otherwise, are extremely easy to achieve accidentally. If you push the limits too far, people could die."

Clayton was enjoying this staring competition. He felt he was supposed to be intimidated, but the reality was quite the contrary. He liked to be challenged. "Noted," he said with his mouth straight, but his eyes smiling.

Dr. Barnes was the first to break. *No surprise there.* But with his eyes on his hands, he added, unnervingly casually, "You should also note that giving someone extra doses consistently over the course of a long period of time *can* cause permanent damage. If you want your patient to maintain her current mental state, you should stop now."

Clayton's heart skipped, forgetting that when the brain

freezes, it's still supposed to keep beating. He hadn't told Dr. Barnes the test subject was female... *It's fine. He probably analyzed the urine sample for the sex. Be logical.*

"That is," the doctor continued, "*if* you'd been doing this. But not to worry," he looked in Clayton's pupils again. "This is all hypothetical, so we're good."

"Yup," Clayton muttered, taking in this new side of his old colleague. "We're good."

29

Jackson

His response came out immediately, sounding like shock but feeling like security. "You love me?" The words pushed all others out of their path to jump from his mouth as if they'd been caged there forever, and he could finally let them free. Unlike Alyssa's kite, kept in her hand, Jackson's words were released into the sky to float away, never to return.

"More than anything."

His heart slamming against his chest reminded him to say it back. He'd felt it since he'd met her, but now he could say the words. "I love you. I love you so much, you don't even understand."

The movie was still playing on the screen.

"I know all about you from your file," Tatiana informed Bond on the screen.

"I want to know all about you," Alyssa took inspiration from the script.

"You do?" Bond questioned, "Well, I hope you're not disappointed."

"I really hope you're not disappointed," Jackson echoed.

Tatiana replied, with a seduction so obvious a nun couldn't have misinterpreted it, "I will tell you... in the morning."

Jackson felt the room circling around him, wondering if Alyssa would repeat the dialogue, knowing what would happen if she did. He'd thought looking into those planets she called eyes would satisfy him forever, and he'd never ask or even hope for anything more ever again. He was wrong. His body was asking for more. Begging.

Alyssa's face inched forward, resting her forehead on his. Then she slid to the side of his face, her breath beneath his ear making the hairs on the back of his neck stick up, sending a shiver down his spine. "I'll tell you in the morning." Tatiana's words were practically monotonous compared to the way Alyssa exhaled them into Jackson's jawline.

And it was on. They both knew it. They reached and felt and touched and grabbed. They removed garments hastily and kissed slowly. They twisted and they pulled hair and they tasted... and then Jackson was between her thighs tasting. He wanted this to last, but more than that, he needed Alyssa to know he cared about her. He didn't want this for him, he wanted it for *them*. He had to make her see she was happy with him, happier than when she'd been with anyone else, that he would take care of her. He'd been waiting for this chance, this opportunity to prove to her she was making the right decision by choosing him.

Alyssa let him stay there for a minute, panting and lifting her hips, but then she was pulling him back up. He knew he hadn't accomplished his goal, so he fought her pulls, asking for more time.

Sex was his biggest insecurity. It was so far from his comfort

204

zone of screens and controllers. He couldn't keep practicing as much as he wanted, whenever he wanted, until he improved. He couldn't just fail and restart as if nothing happened. There were no cheat codes, no combination of buttons he could push in a specific order until he won the game.

Alyssa tugged at him again, silently telling him to bring his lips to hers - among other body parts. He wasn't going to argue with that. So he moved up, but in the back of his mind, as he heard Bond succeeding in all of his endeavors, he couldn't help feeling like he wasn't as similar to the British agent as Alyssa probably hoped he was.

***

Despite Jackson's fear of not being everything Alyssa was hoping for, the fire that spread from the match lit on that warm April night proved otherwise. While she still didn't seem to want him to make her satisfaction the center of their time in the bedroom, she *was* sliding under the covers with him any chance she got. She had limited free time, but Jackson was constantly waiting for her to get off work, volunteering as a very willing participant any day or time she may want to engage in his favorite activity. She said he was her stress relief, and he was honored to fulfill that role. They laughed and held each other and talked about their days and ate late night feasts - courtesy of Cathy Halloway - and Jackson felt something he'd never experienced before: He wanted to change.

Sure, he'd wanted to change many aspects of himself in the past. He'd wished he could change his hair, his body, his bad habits… But passively wanting to change and actively wanting to change are two very different wants, and he hadn't felt the latter until now.

He remembered his dad questioning him on the night they'd first had Alyssa over for dinner, asking what he brought to the table to offer a girl like that. His father had given versions of this same speech to Jackson ever since he could remember, asking him what he planned on doing with his life, pressuring him to gain some work ethic.

It pained Jackson to think that the side effect of becoming a man fit for Alyssa would coincidentally turn him into the type of guy his dad was always pestering him to be. Still, he was determined to become that man. *What can I say... I've been inspired.* Seeing the world through Alyssa's eyes gave him a new excitement for life. He wanted to be more like her, and he wanted to be better *for* her. And most importantly, he wanted to make absolutely, undoubtedly sure that he would never, ever, lose her.

So by the middle of May, he'd called up Mr. Mejia and told him he'd decided to apply for that promotion after all. And by August, he'd been able to add enough to his savings to do something else his dad often prodded him to do over the years: move out. Jackson did always say he just wanted to stay at home and save money until he had a reason to move, and now he had a beautiful, blonde reason.

Along with his new ambition came a new sense of pride. And freedom. It was amazing how free he felt when he was no longer tangled in his own web of lies. He thought there was no way he could be any happier... and then September came, and he and Alyssa were handed the key to 521 West Arbor Street, apartment C.

The day they moved in, Alyssa told him she'd forgotten one last thing in her car. She skipped down the stairs, and when she returned, she had her hands behind her back and a grin plastered on her face.

"Whatcha got there?" He widened his lips more than a Cheshire cat, swiping with his arm in one quick motion, pretending to grab at the gift.

"Ah ah ah," she scolded, "I have a whole speech first that goes along with it!"

Jackson's smile widened; knowing he held the power to scramble her brain. Reveling in it. "Oh, is that so?" He moved his mouth to her collarbone and began his trail of kisses. "I'm listening."

Her head rolled back and she sighed, clearly forgetting what she was going to say. He laughed at her and assumed his original position a foot away. Her eyes were still closed. He watched as she blinked slowly, noticed his smug face, and then stuck out her lower lip in a baby-ish pout. "Oh, now I don't even remember what I was going to say!"

Jackson tried to feign sympathy, but her cuteness was making it impossible for him to even pretend to be anything but content.

"And it was really good too!"

"Aw, I bet it was, baby." He knew he didn't look sorry, but neither did she. They were smitten.

"It really was. You would've cried at its beauty."

"I'm sure I would have." Their bodies drifted closer and closer with each word.

"And you would've loved it."

"Do you love me?"

"More than anything." She paused, perhaps basking in the feeling as much as he was, and then pulled the cylindrical package from behind her back. "Here, open it! I can't wait any longer, I might just die of impatience!"

There she was, overdramatic as always. Her knees sank towards the ground, as if she was becoming too weak to stand.

"Well we can't have that, now, can we?" He helped her up, and guided her to the couch where they could both sit as he undid the ribbon. The paper slid off easily after that, and he gently pulled out the poster that had been rolled up inside. It was a large print of *From Russia with Love*.

He didn't need what he was sure was a very sweet speech Alyssa had prepared. He understood what this symbolized for them. The first time they each said they loved each other. The first time they allowed their bodies to melt together, like how marshmallows bond with chocolate when building s'mores. The first time he'd felt complete.

He hung the poster up above his computer setup in his office, and every time he looked at it, he was reminded of that day and those feelings. It also reminded him of who he aspired to be. Someone successful. Someone cool. Someone worthy of Alyssa's love. And each day, he was feeling one step closer to that goal.

And whenever Alyssa came home to Jackson, in her typical extravagant fashion, she would vent about how cruel the hospital was for keeping her away from him all day and exclaim "I'd die to be always by your side!" as she collapsed onto his lap in his computer chair and fell asleep watching him play.

30

Clayton

With Courtney doubly sedated and no longer asking questions, Clayton was feeling good. Good enough to finally have the conversation he'd been avoiding since he started the Program.

Georgie was walking her brand new puppy down the streets of Salvation. Pets were one of the many upgrades Clayton was continuing to install. The residents of the Program looked like walking ads for Vogue magazine. A real gentlemen's club. They were dressed to the nines and had every accessory you could think of. Georgie's dog even had on a name-brand sweater, and a designer bag to ride around in when she got tired of walking.

Clayton had to do a double take when he spotted his mother. She was looking more and more filtered by the day. It seemed each morning her hair was a little longer and blonder, her waist was a little slimmer, and her lips a little pinker and plumper.

He jogged over to her, preparing his speech in his head. "So, I was thinking, with all these new changes with Salvation," he was going to say, "I've been running really low on cash…" No. That sounded like he was failing. "We could really use some more funds…" No. That was more like groveling. "We are just so excited, and we want to continue expansion! You think you love Salvation now, just wait 'til you see what we have in store! But with changes this big, we are going to need to increase our funding…" Too gimmicky? Still, it seemed like his best chance.

"Clayton! Darling! How is my beautiful baby boy doing today?" She'd been greeting him like this for weeks now - that bright smile, those complimentative remarks - but he still hadn't gotten used to it. Words of affection and approval he'd been wanting to hear for over 20 years now.

"I'm great!" He pasted a smile onto his face, hoping it would hide his nervousness. "Wonderful actually. And I wanted to talk to you about that… How wonderful things are, I mean." He was tripping over his words already. She gave him a knowing look, as if she'd been waiting for him to try to have this conversation with her. It wasn't a happy look, but he continued anyway. "We are just so excited about Salvation, and want to continue expansion!" She wasn't into it, but he kept going. "You think you love Salvation now, just wait 'til—"

"You want me to take an advance on my funds." She said flatly.

Clayton's shoulders dropped, defeated. He hadn't even gotten through his pitch. "Listen, Mom, I know you like taking it month by month—"

"It's the smart thing to do, Clayton, we've been over this."

"I know, but look at everything I've done, I'll put the money to good use! Don't you trust me?"

Her eyes made small movements towards the floor, then him, then her puppy. He could see she didn't know where to focus them… a sign of discomfort.

"Honey, what you've done here is truly miraculous." She was choosing her words carefully. "Lifesaving, really. For me, and

210

I'm sure for so many people in the future. It's just," her eyes shifted again, "It's reckless to take it all out at once. If something happens—"

"Nothing is going to happen! I've been working on this for years! I've put everything into Salvation! And I've taken every precaution to make sure it *can't* fail."

"I'm not so sure about that…"

Those words stabbed him, a dagger finding its mark. He was insulted. "After all I've done for you, you're questioning me?"

"The earthquakes, honey. Yes they're less frequent, but they're still happening. Dr. Avery has a theory, he says—"

"You've been speaking with Gordon about me?" He was insulted for a second time. "The earthquakes are under control; I'm taking care of it, these things just take time—"

"Dr. Avery thinks it has something to do with your brain. He says when you're stressed out, that's when they're the worst. When you're not doing well—"

"Gordon doesn't know what the hell he's talking about," Clayton sputtered, though his theory did make some sense. "I just hired him because I needed someone to put me into the simulation."

"Don't curse. And Barry has another idea."

Really? Saying "hell" is what she's concerned about right now?

"Mr. Whitmore?" Clayton was in disbelief… How had he missed all these conversations? He *had* been a bit distracted lately. Between having the time of his life in Salvation with his wife, working on the Program's augmentations, and taking care of their real bodies in BrightView, he hadn't had much time lately to monitor his cameras. "What does Mr. Whitmore know about any of this?" The man was just another resident of BrightView who'd agreed to the trial. He was about Clayton's age, and had cerebral palsy.

"He knows about computers, like you." Georgie answered. "He graduated top of his class at Brown. Like, *the* Brown University. He went for Computer Science, and he thinks your program may be overloaded."

"That's not even a real term, how do you know he's telling you the truth?" But Clayton knew he was. While Dr. Barnes performed many physical and mental examinations on each patient before they could enter Salvation, or even know what it was, Clayton had done his own research before bringing anyone into his world. Did they really think he only had blackmail-worthy dirt on his associates? No. He made sure he could take down anyone who had knowledge of Salvation if he needed to. Because of these investigations, he knew how incredibly brilliant Mr. Whitmore was with technology. The trophies alone spoke for themselves.

His mother interrupted his thoughts. "I don't know exactly what he said; I don't know computers like you two." Definitely not. She was barely able to change her email password, or switch to online banking. "But he was basically saying that you're exceeding the amount of data this world can hold. The software is malfunctioning because it's way too overstimulated. He described it to me as you basically having too many tabs open on a slow computer."

Slow computer? Was this "Let's Offend Clayton Day?" Her current criticism wasn't really what upset him, though. "Mom, why have you been talking to all these people about me? Do you not trust me?" He asked again, even though her avoidance of the question earlier had already answered that question for him.

"We're trying to help, honey." She sounded sincere. "Sometimes… Sometimes you get caught up in something and get way ahead of yourself before you really stop to think, that's all."

"All I've done is think about this! For years, every waking moment has been dedicated to me thinking about how to make Salvation a better place. How to make it succeed. And if you would just take the whole settlement instead of a monthly allowance, we'd have more than enough money to do that!"

The affection and approval from earlier had disappeared from her face. "It's my money, Clayton," she replied sternly. "I'm the one who got hurt, so I'm the one who gets to decide what to do with it. The state gave it to *me*." He thought he saw moisture appear in her eyes, but it vanished as quickly as it came. "And I've been smart my whole life. So I'm making the smart choice and taking the monthly payments. That's my final decision."

She didn't say that he'd been stupid his whole life. That he made stupid, reckless, irresponsible decisions. But she didn't have to. She'd always thought he was stupid, no matter how many competitions he won or inventions he designed. And when he'd let that cement truck slam into the passenger side of his car while they were driving to the courthouse all those years ago, "thought" turned into "knew." She knew it was his fault.

Never mind that it was undeniably the truck's fault - they didn't even have to sue, the state automatically offered up millions since it was obviously caused by a county driver - or that Clayton's attempt to swerve out of the way most likely saved her life - the doctors confirmed this - she had always and would always blame him.

He was the one driving. He was the reason they were in the car in the first place. He'd made a… questionable business deal and gotten caught. He'd had a plethora of technological inventions for sale before he'd created Salvation, each one just as seedy as the previous. He couldn't help that the type of clients who wanted to work with him didn't typically have the best moral compasses. Money is money, right?

Not right, as far as Georgie was concerned. He thought for once he was changing her opinion of him, but the past would always be there, creating a wall between them.

He didn't want to push any more, afraid of what she might say next. "Alright," he gave in, "I'll just have to 'wow' the investors when they arrive." She nodded her consensus. "It's only two weeks away now. I actually need to talk to Dr. Barnes about that..."

"Don't let me hold y—" she started to say, but as she spoke, the ground beneath them began to shake violently.

Clayton grabbed his mother's arm, and searched her features to ensure she wasn't scared. When she returned his glance, she didn't look afraid at all. She held her chin up, confident. "Funny how another tremor happened right after that conversation." She smirked. "Probably just a coincidence."

31

Alyssa

The hospital was already buzzing when Alyssa walked through the double doors with her usual Styrofoam cup in one hand and her canvas tote bag in the other. The adrenaline began pumping through her veins from the moment the sounds reached her eardrums, before she'd even had a chance to sip her latte. It was a double edged sword. By the end of each day she was covered in superficial slices from all the burdens she bore throughout her shift. But, if she didn't have her work, the abrasions felt more like one deeply penetrating stab through the chest.

Everyone here knew Alyssa, even if she didn't know them. Though not many doctors bothered, she made it a point to learn as many names as she could. "Good morning, Dr. Hart!" she heard Susan, her favorite nurse, call out.

"Hey Ms. A, how's Mr. Mayfair looking today?" She cut right to the chase, eager for updates. She was so passionate about every surgery she performed that spending time away, even just the few hours a night used to sleep and refuel, was often torturous for her. Being with Jackson made it less so, but still,

215

she thought of her patients often. Whenever she walked back into her second home, it was all she could do not to burst open with questions of their progress. Just a few months ago, she may have considered the hospital her *first* home, but her life was incredibly different now.

As Susan filled her in on the recovery details of last night's hernia repair, she walked behind the desk to perform her usual morning task. She grabbed the red felt-tipped marker from the top left drawer and lifted her hand to the calendar. As she assessed the days, she realized she'd "X'd" out the last day in October already. It was November? She double checked her phone. It was November.

She flipped the page so the proper month was showing, and marked the date as the first. She stared at the picture: newly fallen snow covering orange and brown leaves. Her thoughts drifted to the last time she saw this image - studying, the USMLE, preparing for Thanksgiving... and the computer store. Almost a year ago, she had trudged her way through the snow praying her paper wouldn't be lost, and she'd met Jackson.

How could one person's world switch to revolving around a completely new sun in just one year? That's what it felt like, anyway. Well, it wasn't so much a new sun as a new style of orbit. She was still roving through space circling her purpose, her happiness, but she'd added a few detours along the way. She could move more slowly some days, taking time to laugh and lie in bed with her love and read and listen to Jackson try to learn the piano and just breathe. She didn't need to race... after all, Earth keeps it's pace around the sun only to end up in the exact same place again. For the first time, she wondered, "what's the rush?"

Jackson didn't replace her sun, but he joined it in the center of her universe. She thought of him as much as she did the insides of the walls that surrounded her now. She used to dream of surgery when she was home, but now she had flashes of Jackson while she was in the OR.

November. One year. The best year of her life.

She must have been smiling because Susan peered over at her and conjectured, "Yeah, it is nice, isn't it? He'll be outta here in two days!"

Oh right. The hernia repair. "Super nice! Okay Ms. A, I'll see you later for afternoon rounds." She raised her hand in a little wave as she walked away, and then yelled back over her shoulder, "Oh, and we should see if they have any more cake we can steal from Plastics! You in?"

"You know it!" the nurse hollered back with a chuckle. Moments like this just added to Alyssa's love of this place.

There was a bond formed between soldiers fighting in the same war, one no one else could relate to no matter how sincerely they tried. Again, her mind wandered to Jackson. He wasn't a fellow warrior. He couldn't understand. But she didn't need him to. She had enough comrades-in-arms. What she'd been missing was that person who took her mind off of the war. The sweetheart back home who writes her love letters having nothing to do with the fighting, instead reminding her of what she is fighting for.

Her face must have had a mind of its own again, because someone else picked up on her giddiness. "Ally!" Will's voice was deep and full of joy, like a gospel song. "I've got a bone to pick with you!" He was clearly joking, but she didn't have any idea about what.

"I heard you and Rina ransacked Plastics and stole their cake, and you didn't invite me?" He put his hand over his heart, "crushed." He was a lot like Alyssa in many ways, including the dramatics, which is likely why they got along so well. He was probably her best surgeon friend at work. He was in General, too. A fellow soldier.

Will's efforts didn't make her feel the least bit guilty. First of all, she knew he was only teasing, but second of all, he was possibly given just as many surgeries as she was, so there would have been no time to grab him even if she'd wanted to, and he was well aware of that.

"We didn't steal it, they generously gifted us their leftovers," she told him as she pulled off her jeans and shimmied into her blue scrub pants. For a surgeon, privacy was non-existent. No one had a second thought before stripping down with someone else in the room. They showed each other their rashes and strange lumps on a weekly basis, which was much more disturbing. And besides, the human anatomy was nothing new to any of them.

"But if it makes you feel any worse," she reworded the old expression, "Ms. A was there too." Will's jaw dropped, and Alyssa shrugged, emphasizing her pretend nonchalant cruelness.

"You, Rina, *and* Susan were out eating cake while I was in the OR working on Mr. Riley's cyst removal for *three* hours?"

He'd over exaggerated the "three," which only gave Alyssa more fuel for her fire. "It took you three hours to remove a little cyst? Sounds like you don't deserve any cake."

He laughed a long, genuine, belly-laugh at her comeback. "Hey, it was right near his lungs, okay? We had to be super careful!"

"Eh, I reckon I could've done it in two."

"You know what, Hart?" Something about the way his voice

218

slowed and his head fell from the weight of his smile changed the mood of the conversation. "I reckon you could have."

He held her gaze for a beat too long, and she held it back simply because it caught her off guard. Then, as if he understood he'd challenged their unspoken "just friends" dynamic, he transferred his tone back to casual. The topic, however, remained complimentary. "No doubt in my mind, actually. Alright, well I gotta go prep Ms. Lang. I'll see ya later. Hopefully with cake!"

Alyssa was horrible at recognizing when people were flirting with her. At least, that's what everyone always told her... particularly Bella. As Alyssa drove home after her shift, she couldn't help but replay the interaction in her mind. *No, he was just being friendly.* Guys were just nice to Alyssa because she was nice to them.

People of the opposite sex can be sweet to each other and goof around and have inside jokes and be completely platonic. Why did people always assume there had to be a "burning passion" for each other just because they got along well in the workplace? At least, that's what Susan had called it over their chocolate ice cream cake date that afternoon. Apparently an intern had been in the locker room with them, overheard the conversation, and fed the already-established rumor that the two had a thing for each other.

She twisted the dial on her stereo to drown out all her thoughts from the day. The Taylor Swift album she'd listened to dozens of times was spinning in the player, resuming where she'd left off when she'd parked earlier that morning, and she turned the volume up even louder. She'd thought she'd lost the CD last year, but a couple days ago discovered that Bella had "borrowed" it and accidentally left it in the trunk of her car

219

until yesterday, when she apologetically returned it.

Alyssa's favorite artist was singing about a boy who was able to unnumb the heart of a not-so-cautious man's cautious daughter. She'd always loved the song, but never could relate to it. She used to think no one would be able to chip away as the ice her father left her submerged in.

Now, she almost instantly felt tears building in her eyes while she soaked up the lyrics like rays of sunshine after a swim in the ocean. The singer went on to tell the tale of the couple moving in together, and inevitably facing the numerous struggles that come along with that step.

Sleeping fear awoke in her heart. She'd been trying to keep it buried, but it was there. It had been there since the first thought of wanting to live with Jackson had entered her mind. It was the fear of building a life with someone, believing them, relying on them in many senses, and then watching them leave. She'd always thought it foolish to give a man that power. *Why do girls always insist on building a life* with *someone instead of building one for themselves?* That's what she'd always wondered. Why share the responsibility with someone else when you know you can do a better job all on your own, like a "straight A" student doing a project with their "C's get degrees" friend instead of creating the presentation alone.

She finally understood why. It wasn't about whether or not the outcome would be more successful, or the grade would be higher; it was about having the time of your life with your favorite person - the person who, when the teacher says you'll be able to pick your partner, you immediately look over at each other because you know you always choose each other. And Alyssa always wanted to choose Jackson. Always.

She rolled down the windows and blasted the speakers even

louder knowing the bridge of the song was approaching. She tipped her head back to feel the wind on her skin and she sang along as the girl on the disc described how she'd expected her love to leave after a big argument. Then, remembering the next verse, her singing turned to screaming, because he didn't leave. He said he would never leave her. And now, this was Alyssa's favorite song.

After replaying the track a total of three times on the way home, and another time as she sat idly in the parking spot, she ran up the steps and knocked on the apartment door. She had a key, but it was their little tradition for her to knock so Jackson could run to the door to greet her by scooping her up into a straddling hug. A horrible tradition really, as Jackson almost always had his volume up so high that it took several rounds of knocking for him to hear her, but it was theirs.

One knock.

She waited.

Two.

Nothing.

Should I just use the key?

She checked the time. He should be working. No excuse not to hear her. Where was he?

32

Bianca

This second pregnancy was the happiest chapter of Bianca's life. There was a time during her depression when she didn't think she'd ever recover from the loss of her first baby, but while she still grieved him every day (they'd never found out the gender, but she just knew he'd been a little boy), she'd come back from that experience stronger in every way.

She was more grateful this time around. She'd always just assumed she'd get married and start a family, that it would be easy, but seeing how quickly dreams can be stripped away forced her to spread those wings Derek always told her she had and get a new perspective.

When she flew up above her life and looked down, she saw how lucky she truly was. She'd been taking for granted the experiences in her life that some people never got to have.

She'd been overjoyed when she'd found out about her first pregnancy, but it was the type of joy a kid gets when they open a Christmas present they already knew their parents bought for them. Still thrilled to have it, but a totally different exhilaration than what she felt now. Now, she was a kid who was told her parents couldn't afford a gift, who'd never had a gift like this before, who'd accepted that she would probably never get this gift... and then she got it.

"Perspective, little bird."

With her newfound appreciation for her blessings, mourning her first baby didn't stop her from being the most cheerful, content, blossoming version of herself. She did everything she never got to do the last time, whether that was big events like hosting a gender reveal for her friends and family and having a "Baby Bash Baby Shower Extravaganza," or simply wearing overalls over her baby bump while repainting the walls of the nursery like she'd always seen pregnant women doing in movies and TV shows and seen herself doing in her dreams.

Though the new walls were blush pink and the new blankets had clouds instead of stars, she'd kept the little bird she'd gotten from Derek. The bird was a reminder of the beautiful baby boy she'd never gotten to meet. The bird was Derek's heart on display. The bird was her, learning to fly again after falling from the nest. And the bird would be her little girl, who she hoped would be brave and adventurous and unafraid of soaring from treetop to treetop, viewing the world from every possible angle.

Bee was all of that, and so much more.

As Bee grew, so did Derek and Bianca's relationship. She'd heard that mothers don't love anyone as much as their children, and while she would die for Bee, she would sacrifice herself for Derek, too. Seeing him as a father was *everything*, yet, somehow, knowing what he'd done for her to get to this point was *more*.

He'd loved her since she walked into that restaurant for their first date. He'd come to every soccer game, baked cookies for every ridiculously unnecessary event her small town decided to have. He'd celebrated her pregnancy, and patched her from the loss a million times more than any doctor or psychologist ever had. Considering the dark, hormonal, postpartum state she'd been in, Derek very well may be the only reason she was even still here. Here, helping her five year-old - *How is she five already!* - hang her kindergarten art piece on the refrigerator.

Five years old, and forever changing. First is was the color purple, then dinosaurs, then a brief stunt with princesses, and back to dinosaurs - but herbivores this time, she was very specific about that, then she was a daddy's girl, then she loved Grandma, then Mom was her favorite again, and now her kindergarten teacher. No matter how much her interests shifted and evolved, there was one constant that always, *always* stayed attached to her hip: Birdie.

That stuffed bird went everywhere with Bee, never leaving her side. Bee fell asleep with Birdie in her arms every night. Birdie traveled with them to the store, to Mommy's soccer games, even to school, sitting next to her on the bus the entire way.

It was never, "Mommy, can I have cereal please?" It was, "Mommy, Birdie wants cereal." "Birdie wants to watch cartoons." "Birdie says I can have one more strawberry." She loved that little bird just about as much as Bianca and Derek loved her, as much as they loved each other. As much as they still loved the baby they'd lost.

Bianca didn't know what she'd do if anything happened to Birdie. They didn't sell birds that looked like this one anymore, she and Derek had looked online and even went back to the original shop he'd bought it from to check, and even if they did, Birdie was so "well-loved" that Bee would instantly know if he'd been switched out. Birdie was irreplaceable.

33

Clayton

Clayton had gone to ask Dr. Barnes if he would be the face for the investors... a mission which had completely failed, of course. Dr. Barnes argued that Clayton needed to be the one to do it. He was the CEO, the founder, the inventor, the persuasive speaker... It only made sense for him to present himself as the face of the company.

Clayton admitted to the doctor that he'd been spending too much time in Salvation, and his body wasn't in great shape. Dr. Barnes hadn't cared, stressing that Clayton had to be the one to speak with them. He was the only man who could explain Salvation to people and get them to actually listen long enough to figure out what a genius idea it was.

If anyone else tried to pitch the Program, it sounded horrifying. The eyes held wide open, the bodies held down with restraints with IVs coming out of them, pale and limp. More intimidating men than Clayton would have shivered at the thought of it. He could see why; it sounded practically sickening when that was all a person would bear to listen to.

But Clayton had a way of getting listeners past those beginning rituals, and into the actual "meat and potatoes" of the whole thing. Except when it came to Courtney, of course. Then again, she'd always been his exception.

With Dr. Barnes' refusal to be the spokesperson for the investors, and both of them agreeing Gordon wouldn't be the right choice either, Clayton was forced to oblige. To take better care of his body over the next two weeks so he would be fit to see the investors at BrightView.

And on the subject of Brightview, Clayton knew he'd have to spruce up the patients there, as well. Most of them had done an okay job of taking care of themselves, thanks to Clayton's threats of getting them out the "hard way," so they wouldn't be a huge issue. Clayton and his mother, however, were some pretty tough cases.

Since Clayton was the boss over everyone, there was no one brave enough to make him leave the simulation himself. And even after promising Dr. Barnes he would log out more, he just… didn't. And who could blame him?

He was so productive inside Salvation. Something about looking and feeling his best made him want to do his best work. Not to mention, he had endless supplies, and a beautifully equipped office… with a three-hundred-sixty degree view of palm trees and poolsides.

Then, when he was done working, he drove his perfect car back to his perfect home and made love to his perfect wife who had a perfect meal prepared for him waiting on the kitchen table. He was in no hurry to spend more time in Chicago. Therefore, he was still in no shape to meet the investors.

Luckily for him, though it was unlucky for most people, three days before he was supposed to meet with them, COVID-19 flooded the United States.

***

Their meeting was postponed as the world tried to navigate the pandemic. Businesses closed, workers lost their jobs, and everyone was scared and struggling to survive in this new world. Everyone, that is, except for the residents of Salvation.

Contrary to everywhere else, Salvation was thriving. Clayton grew more and more confident in his new world as the old world seemed to be crumbling all around them. COVID reminded the users of the Program just how fragile the human body really is. "This is why we're all here, right?" Clayton had preached, "To create a new world where nothing is holding us back from our true potential. Why be limited by the weakness of our physical bodies when we could be the best, strongest versions of ourselves here, within this community? While the rest of the world falls apart, we are here, uniting together!" Everyone who'd gathered around him had cheered, realizing more than ever the power of Salvation.

And not to mention, the pandemic gave the founders an even better shot at making a fortune with the Program. If Salvation really took off, and they were all starting to become sure that it would, they could hire tons of employees and be the heroes that started hiring people again when every other business continued letting more and more employees go. While those other companies were losing business, Clayton saw this as an opportunity to *gain* business. *Supply and demand, baby.* Everyone was about to beg to be a part of a world that only became even more relevant when disease plagued the earth.

Social distancing was hard for the people of the real world, but Clayton's Program thrived, unaffected by this new set of rules. The coronavirus was like a gift dropped down from

Heaven for the members of Salvation. They were convinced it was going to be the start of their unmatched success.

People of the real world now had time on their hands. They were depressed. They couldn't do what they used to do. Their bodies were failing.

And why limit users to *just* patients who couldn't walk? Especially with Clayton's new additions, he was really beginning to cling to the idea of changing the purpose of the Salvation Program all together.

"Look at what the world is coming to," Clayton announced one day when they were all gathered in his yard for a barbeque. He showed them a compilation of the outside world: people wearing hazmat suits to run errands, hospital patients lying on the ground because all the beds were full, newspaper headlines with the number of fatalities increasing daily... Salvation users were in shock. They'd been going to Chicago enough to eat, drink, bathe, and maybe exercise, and that was it. They hadn't been prioritizing turning on the news.

Fear is the number one method of control, and Clayton wanted to seize every last drop of power he could get.

"This place isn't like that. Salvation is safe and protected." Heads nodded vigorously, but a voice cried out from inside the house.

"No it's not!"

Every head turned to see a frightened Courtney screaming out of the open window. He'd forgotten to lock it. She wasn't supposed to see any of this.

The videos from the outside world had jolted something awake in her.

In seconds Clayton was across the lawn, yanking the window closed with more force than intended. *Stay cool. Show them you're in control. They shouldn't be worried.* He rotated the latch to lock it from the outside.

"Dr. Barnes, why don't you come in here and take a look at her with me. Don't worry, folks, we'll make sure she's okay." Dr. Barnes jumped up and rushed over to join Clayton by the window. They started walking around to the front door.

"Hey!" one of the patients yelled in their direction. "We need answers! Is that going to happen to us? You never said anything to us about memory loss, or whatever that was." A couple of the others nodded in agreement.

"Is there a problem with the medications? I thought you said they were safe!" another member called out, anger and fear burning through every word.

The patients of Salvation were worried. Dr. Barnes shuffled nervously, while Gordon's frown lines were inquisitive, like he was trying to put the pieces of the puzzle together. Mayhem was ensuing. Lately it seemed like chaos was all-encompassing. He couldn't escape it. Not here, and certainly not in the real world. There had to be a way to stop it. To regain order.

Dr. Barnes stepped in. He whispered to Clayton, "Listen. You're the persuasive speaker here. You go run the party and keep them calm. I'll take care of your 'wife.'" When he said the word "wife," Clayton noticed him cringe a little. He really did know more than he let on.

"I gave her a 20% increase of ketamine and a 45% increase of clonazepam eight hours ago," Clayton muttered discreetly, then smeared a grin more sickly sweet than frosting on his face, clapped his hands together, and headed back towards the sea of frowns and whispers. Out of the corner of his eye, he could see that Dr. Barnes understood, wearing a grim expression as he stepped swiftly towards the door.

"Mayhem," Clayton thought out loud, "is our enemy." He assumed the position at the head of the lawn, and peered pensively towards his guests. "What we're creating here, this place, will be a world where we don't have to deal with these scary feelings that accompany disorder. How many of you feel a little scared right now?"

Multiple members of the group slowly raised their hands. "Yes," he nodded. "That was scary. And do you know why that scared us?" He waited, though it was obvious he was going to answer his own question. "Because chaos makes us feel vulnerable. It makes us question what's next, what's coming. Could something bad and unpredictable happen to us, too? And will it come without warning? Right?" Several people returned his nods. "We need order. Organization. Structure. And I'm here to give you those things."

He was winning them over. "One week from today, we're going to get all the money we need to eliminate mayhem. I guarantee it." He was eating up the excited smiles on everyone's faces. "As soon as that happens, we are going to build a world so structured, so safe, so orderly, that nothing scary can ever happen to us again. I give you my word on that."

"Let me finish showing you the outside world." He'd found the remote by now, and pressed play on his compilation. Sick children coughing up blood, hospitals so full that patients with colds were boarded next to those in the psych unit - losing their sanity along with the mentally unstable, men screaming at each other in the grocery store over the last roll of toilet paper while wearing odd concoctions of socks and t-shirts as makeshift masks… It wasn't a world any of them had ever known. Most of them were older and had lived through the Great Depression and World War II, but even then, humans at least kept their

231

decency. The world might have been against them, but they never resorted to turning on each other like this.

Clayton put on the performance of his life. He frowned at the screen, careful to look appalled, ashamed of his fellow man. He clucked his tongue three times. "All of this, because no one out there cares for one another. Out there, it's a dog eat dog world, every man for himself. But here, in Salvation," the eyes in the crowd locked in on his pacing frame like spectators at a tennis match following the green nylon ball as it pings and pongs from one side of the court to the other. "We are a team. A community. A family."

The breaths held by each member of the crowd were released one at a time. He knew what people needed to hear. "We don't have to be scared here. We love each other. That's why Doctor Barnes is making sure Courtney gets the best possible care she can, far better than she would get out *there*." He pointed at the screen again, spitting out the last word like a bite he'd discovered was covered in mold once it touched his lips. "You see, this is the care she deserves. This is the only place we can live the type of life we deserve. And we are damn lucky! It's more than I can say for most people."

One more nod to the screen for good measure, this time with his inner eyebrows lifted up in staged gratitude.

By this point, the patients of Salvation were not only letting out their breath, but using it to pray or laugh or whatever it was they needed to do to voice their relief that the situation wasn't one to be frightened of, after all. Clayton had done his job.

"Now," he smiled, every emotion he'd previously acted out gone from his face, "Let's enjoy it a little, shall we?" He grabbed the nearest red Solo cup and lifted it into the air. "To family."

"To family!" was echoed back to him as if he'd yelled it into the Grand Canyon itself. No time to celebrate, he'd leave that up to his party-goers. He needed to check on Courtney.

34

Alyssa

Alyssa's knuckles were sore when she rapped on the door for the third time, and she was beginning to seriously question his little "let me answer the door" tradition. Luckily, mid pattern, the wood was moved away from her fist and a smiling Jackson was standing there with open arms. "We need a song," she announced into his shoulder as they wrapped each other up, completely forgetting his prolonged response to her knocks.

"I missed you too!" He squeezed her tighter.

Oops. She'd forgotten that part. "Sorry! I missed you so much today!"

"You love me?"

Another tradition, and she answered, as was her custom, "More than anything."

They kissed a bit, until Jackson brought them back to the original topic. "Don't we already have a song? I thought you liked that Ed Sheeran one for us."

It was cute that he remembered that. "Ugh I love that one too, but now I've moved on to Taylor Swift."

They moved towards the kitchen as they talked. Alyssa's stomach growled; it had been a long shift as usual and she was starving. The scent of marinara sauce drifted past her nostrils, and she got excited.

"You girls and your T-Swift, why do you always—"

"Did you make dinner?" The question sounded more hopeful than she'd meant for it to; her grumbling tummy was speaking for her.

Jackson's sparkling eyes dulled. "Alyssa, you know I work until you get home."

She shouldn't have assumed. "No I know, I know, it's just that I thought I smelled something cooking, that's all."

"That's probably my lunch. I just heated up some SpaghettiOs real quick." He motioned to the saucy dish in the sink, waiting to be rinsed. "Anyway, if you already have another song for us, why'd you come in here insisting we need one?"

She was distracted by the charm of the upturned corners of his mouth. When he caught her daze, the corners rose even higher, which only stole her focus more. She dug her nails into her thigh, as she often had to do with him, to remind her brain to calm down and concentrate on her words.

"Because, those songs were written about someone else, and we just *relate* them to us. We need a song that was made *about* us. Don't you think?"

Rather than answering with words, Jackson wandered over to his keyboard bench and began plucking at the keys. "I'm still learning!" He reminded her, "But let's see what we can come up with, huh?"

No amount of nail marks in her leg could bring Alyssa out of her trance as her boyfriend played, and messed up, and apologized, and played some more. They came up with a string

235

of notes they thought sounded beautiful. Two fast, then one slow, lower note, then a couple pairs of quick partner notes and another long, and on and on it went. Then they needed words.

"Honey, I," for the first three notes, then "love you oh so much."

"It's too generic," Alyssa interjected. "Every couple loves each other, what's something specific to us? What do you love about me?"

"Everything," Jackson answered quickly. Easily. Even though Alyssa secretly liked this answer, she rolled her eyes and told him that wasn't helpful.

"Fine, then what would you want to change about our relationship? Like, what do you wish we could have, if you could dream of our perfect world, what would you want?"

As effortlessly as he'd purred his earlier answer, he belted out, "I'd never want you to leave. I just wanna be always by your side." He smiled like he was thinking back on something. "And I know you feel the same way. Here, I'll be you:" He dramatically hit the notes and put on his best "Alyssa voice" as he sang, "I'd die to be always by your side."

He wasn't being serious, but somehow it actually sounded really good… minus the theatrics and the high pitched attempt at sounding like a girl. "Wait, I love that, keep going!" As he slowly played for her, she proudly added, "it's so clear, far or near, I'm always by your side."

There was talk of what was too much repetition, what should stay and what shouldn't, and after half an hour they'd come up with: "Honey, I'm always by your side. It's so clear, far or near, I'm always by your side." They giggled and kissed as they created more lyrics, and thought a song about being together all the time felt very fitting to be the first music to be played in their very own apartment together.

236

Eventually Jackson stopped playing so he could take her hand and lead her to the dance floor, aka the living room, so he could spin her all around as they both sang to no music:

Honey, I'm always by your side.
  It's so clear, far or near,
  I'm always by your side.
  And honey, I can't believe you're mine,
  but at the sa-ame time,
  I deserve this love.
  Can't you see, I'd die to be
  always by your side.

You'll always be my heaven.
  I'm your double-oh-seven.
  Does that clock say five or eleven?
  I don't care.
  Ice cream in November,
  Galleries we'll always remember,
  Key ring in September,
  Laughter in the air.

And honey, it's,
  Always by our side.
  Don't you know,
  I'll go where you go?
  Always by your side.

She twirled and spun and fell down and he pulled her back up and this was their song.

***

They were living in a perpetual "honeymoon phase," but as with every couple, there's always a first fight - one small stick pulled out of the dam that protects their hope. One stick isn't enough to cause a foundation to crumble, but it's a test. Is the stick being pulled out so it can be replaced with a stronger, more suitable log? Or is it the first step of the fortress being stripped bare?

The first twig was lost when Alyssa decided to use the key one night. She knocked several times, but Jackson's headphones were drowning her out and she was too exhausted to wait for him. She walked towards the kitchen, stomach growling, and put a pot on to boil before even setting the keys on the counter. She was famished and Jackson was in his office as usual.

He was such a hard worker, and yet so considerate towards Alyssa. Instead of complaining about her unusual and inconsistent hours, he'd come up with the idea of forming his hours around hers to maximize their time together. He wouldn't start work until Alyssa left for the day, and he'd end it when she got home. It was a sacrifice she didn't take lightly. Without his efforts they might only get an hour or so together a day, but this way, he could turn every bit of *her* free time into *their* free time.

And not only was she thankful that he was courteous to her, she was also proud that he'd escalated his hours by so much. She knew he'd worked part time before they'd met, and now he was in his office ten, twelve, even fourteen hours a day sometimes. "What can I say? You've inspired me."

The least she could do was prepare them dinner when she got home. Sure, sometimes they cooked together, but Alyssa

238

typically took over the role to pay him back. It only seemed fair, with everything he was doing for her. Plus, he never knew exactly when she was going to be home, so he was often right in the middle of work when she knocked. He typically needed a few minutes to finish up, so she cooked.

Once the stove was on and all that was left to do was wait, she skipped over to Jackson's office to inform him she was making macaroni and cheese for them. On a normal day, she'd text him to ask what he wanted, but her growling belly had no patience tonight. She needed something fast, filling, and cheesy. Well, okay, she didn't *need* cheesy, but her want was so strong it felt like a need. So mac and cheese it was going to be.

Not energized enough to set the table, she decided she'd take the bowl directly to his office.

Jackson's voice was loud as she approached the door. "He's on your left! Your other left! Go, go, go…. Nooo! Bro, what were you thinking? When you respawn I'll meet you over at the base."

This certainly didn't sound like work…

She entered the room without knocking. Jackson was far too immersed in his game to notice her presence behind him. She took the opportunity to look around, analyze his environment. She'd never come in here without Jackson's knowledge. In fact, now that she thought about it, she hadn't been in this room since she'd helped Jackson decorate it. There was no particular reason for her absence; Jackson had never asked her to stay away. She guessed she really just didn't have too much of an interest, especially after each long day at the hospital, the only rooms she cared about were the kitchen and the bedroom. Occasionally the living room, if they had time for a movie.

She saw bags of potato chips and energy drink cans skewed

about haphazardly, as if he'd dropped them in the most convenient location as soon as he'd consumed their contents. She was surprised at the mess, not because Jackson was an exceptionally neat person - he certainly wasn't, but because they'd never bought chips with their groceries, except for one singular time, when they'd decided to make nachos because Alyssa's coworker had seen an easy recipe online and shared it with her. And she hadn't even *seen* an energy drink can since high school, well over a decade ago.

As a doctor, she was disappointed in his snack choices. He was home all day, of course he'd want to go out to the store sometimes for a break, and he didn't get free hospital food for lunch like Alyssa did. But couldn't he have picked up some baby carrots if he wanted something to munch on? Or an apple?

Constantly she lectured him on having healthy habits. "I want you around for a long time!" That's why she insisted that he get an exercise tracking watch, and she was diligent about making sure he reached the daily goals it was set to remind him about. She didn't care about how he looked, but she also didn't want him to jeopardize his health sitting at his desk at home all day. Then again, she was the one boiling two boxes of Kraft macaroni with no vegetables or sides, so maybe she didn't have a right to give him a sermon.

She tapped his shoulder and he just about jumped out of his skin.

"I'm sorry, I didn't mean to startle you!" Normally this would be enough for a person to say when they've spooked someone, but Jackson was clasping his hand over his heart, and not in an overexaggerated type of way. His face didn't lighten up.

"You good?" She half laughed, but was genuinely concerned about him. "I knocked a few times, but you didn't answer."

Jackson's eyes moved from one corner of the room to the other, no doubt assessing exactly how much of a mess he hadn't been able to keep her from witnessing. He drew in a deep breath. Once he let that breath out, he sounded much more relaxed. Or, at least like he was *trying* to sound relaxed.

"Yeah of course, I'm just happy you're home!" He pushed his hair off his forehead, though some stuck a little from the forming moisture.

He jumped up to give her a hug, and his screen went black at the same time. It was an awkward hug, because the wires from his headset got in between them and there was still a tenseness in the room. It reminded Alyssa of when she and Bella had walked in on Bella's boyfriend-at-the-time with another girl. *Why do I have this feeling? This situation is nothing like that. Nothing.*

Jackson hastily pulled off his headphones and untangled himself from the cords in order to give her a proper welcome. "Sorry, I, uh… I finished early today and didn't think you'd be home for a while." Alyssa peeked over at the clock. 11:23. "Which was really lucky. I can never just be done with everything. But we uh, we hired this new guy, James, and he's shadowing me and stuff this week so, lucky me! My job is so much easier."

He was talking a lot. By the time he finished, the water was almost certainly boiling already. "And what was also lucky was that some of my friends online just so happened to be free tonight, too. Such a cool coincidence. So, obviously I had to play with them." His eyes finally met hers. "If I'd known you were going to be home, though, I would've made some dinner for us."

Alyssa had promised herself she wouldn't decode Jackson

like she did with her patients. Doing so with friends and relationships had always caused her trouble in the past, and she was trying to grow.

I mean, if people didn't lie to me, then reading their body language wouldn't be any reason for them to get upset. It was a true, but negative, thought. She shook it out of her head, disliking the tone of bitterness in her voice… even if the voice was only in her own mind.

So, she chose not to dive into the fact that Jackson had folded in his lips before making four of his eleven points. And she ignored her observation that he'd made six large and obvious gestures with his arms. Both of these, of course, being in the top five of "The Ten Signs of Deception in Medicine and Life," which was an article she'd studied and been tested on countless times over the course of her schooling.

Instead of going down a path she'd been down too many times before, she allotted, "That's great; you deserve to have a little fun! You don't need to explain yourself to me, baby."

Jackson's shoulders relaxed. She was proud of herself. Why pick a fight over video games? Did she really want to be the "nagging girlfriend" stereotype? *Definitely not.* "I'm making mac and cheese, is that cool with you?"

And then he made her forget all about their weird encounter by reminding her why she loved him so much. "Ah, mademoiselle," he'd put on a very thick and probably somewhat offensive French accent. "I did not know zee chef was making 'er… 'ow you say? Special-tee!" She wanted to roll her eyes at him but she snorted instead, unable to hold in her laughter. "Could zis really be true? The amazing, world renowned chef Ah-lees-uh iz preparing for us 'er secret recipe from monsieur Kraft?"

He moved over to smooch on her as he always did when he

made her laugh like this, but she pulled away, because there was a fight going on between her libido and her stomach, and the latter was winning. She did not attempt to sound French, but she did play along. "Yes, that's right, it's gonna be a real treat... if it doesn't burn! So let me go so I can make sure it's up to the very high standards of..." She looked around, wanting to think of a clever name for their "restaurant," "...Cafe de Bond." She'd caught a glimpse of the *From Russia with Love* poster hanging in the upper corner of the wall above his computer setup.

He let her go, and she ran over to the kitchen, the poster still on her mind. Jackson really was special - a thousand times better than her old, fictional crush.

Her memories spiraled to their first "I love you," and how many more there had been since. How she told him she loved him "more than anything," and she really meant it.

Jackson's suspicious behavior faded from her mind all together. Until, that is, she met up with Bella a week later for lunch.

35

Clayton

A royally pissed-off Dr. Barnes was waiting for Clayton as soon as he opened the door to the bedroom Courtney was stored in. "Jeremy, I—"

"I'm not angry that you drugged her. I mean, I am, but we're past that. I figured that out ages ago." Clayton almost froze, shocked by the doctor's calm exterior, but then thought better of it, not wanting his colleague to catch on to his surprise. So, he sat and folded his hands in his lap. If Dr. Barnes was calm in his anger, Clayton would be zen. Tranquil. Serene. "No, what I'm angry about is the fact that it's been this long and you still haven't been able to figure out how to do it properly."

Clayton's defensive brain wanted to deflect the words, a goalkeeper against a penalty shot. "Everything is under control!" was his first instinct. Then, "Get off my back! I have a million little fires to put out right now, and by little, I mean the size of the cremator at the morgue!" came to mind. But he was cunning enough to think before he spoke, and so his initial defenses were vetoed. Defense wouldn't be enough. And offense clearly hadn't been, either. He swallowed his pride, a pill that usually got stuck in his throat on the way down, but this time he forced it, ignoring the pain as it scratched his esophagus. He needed to listen to his own speech. He couldn't be a one-man operation anymore. He had to start being a *team* player. Which meant he needed help.

"I've upped the dosages of medicine by 3% every few days. I've designed uniquely specific audio tapes catered directly to her and her subconscious. I play them for her instead of the generic tapes we play for the other patients. It helped a lot, at first. She's usually just like the other willing participants, for a while. But with time, shorter and shorter durations, lately, it always seems to fade. I don't understand why. As you know, the dosages she's getting should be more than enough to fog her brain. Even for someone who was forc— someone under her circumstances, this shouldn't be happening."

He watched as the doctor jotted down notes vigorously on a small pad he'd pulled from his pocket. He could have chosen a worse teammate, he supposed.

"I'm telling you all of this so you can see what I've tried. Edison said he didn't fail ten thousand times, he just found ten thousand ways *not* to make a light bulb, right? Those are all the ways that I've learned do *not* subdue her. Maybe together, we can figure out a way that does."

Clayton had stopped speaking, but the pen continued to travel across the page, an explorer looking for treasure with an incomplete map. Clayton wasn't sure the doctor remembered he was still there, and after a while wondered if his pen would run out of ink. It hadn't yet, but it did stop abruptly, and Dr. Barnes asked if Clayton could tell him more about the tapes.

"I've never quite understood them," the doctor revealed. "In med school I came across many psychologists, none as talented as you, of course," the side of Clayton's mouth twitched upwards at the compliment, "and I've seen how they're treated. Scrutinized constantly, being told their work is a load of crock." A laugh escaped Clayton's lips. The doctor wasn't wrong; it was a well-known fact of his chosen field. "But you and I both know that's not true." Clayton nodded once at him, curtly. The Program was irrefutable proof of that.

"Seconds within hearing your voice on that tape, I'm here. And it's *real*. At least, the psychosis makes it feel that way. I mean, just look at this, I'm using my arms to talk with you right now." He was, indeed. "And I know, I mean I *know* for an absolute fact that my real body is lying perfectly still right now. But I cannot explain just how real this feels. My mind is completely tricked into believing I'm moving. That I'm here. *How?*"

Clayton had conditioned the few people he allowed to work on Salvation with him not to ask those sorts of questions. It was proprietary, information he'd worked to ensure he was the only person privy to. His royal flush. He thought about punishing Dr. Barnes for daring to ask, then remembered *he* was the one asking for help here. Solo wasn't working. He needed a teammate.

He sat down with his partner - *partner*, he thought, for the first time not coating it in sarcasm - and gave him an extremely condensed lesson on what had taken him years to put together, after which the doctor formed two sets of hypotheses. The first was that perhaps Courtney was spending too much time with her own thoughts. It made a lot of sense, actually. Salvation was all mental. Drugs could dull the senses, sure, but Dr. Barnes explained it using the example of anesthesia.

"We see it all the time. It's impossible to win the battle

against anesthesia, but people fight it a lot, some being more resistant than others. The most common reason, apart from genetics or increased metabolism, is anxiety. Patients often work themselves into a panic or a rage about their surgery, causing them to reduce blood volume and resist the effects for a bit. This is bad for several reasons: For one, they take longer to fall asleep. And for another, there's a larger probability of complications."

Clayton was following intently.

"With what you've just shown me, Courtney experiencing similar mental stress could absolutely disrupt the process. It's all in her head. She ultimately enters Salvation, but there's a much higher possibility of distress."

He never thought he'd be so interested in what someone other than himself had to say, especially Jeremy. But he was. He'd try anything to get the so-called "anesthesia" to work properly on her. But while the doctor was saying a lot, Clayton still didn't quite understand how he proposed to fix the problem.

"It's simple," Dr. Barnes told him. "With our panicky patients, we distract them. Especially when they're already slightly under, it's very easy to do."

"Distract them?" His curiosity was at an all-time high.

"Precisely. We typically ask them to count down from one hundred. Or we joke around with them. Bring them a little doll to play with. That sort of thing."

It seemed far too simple to be true. "And that works?"

"Absolutely." Dr. Barnes seemed pleased to have Clayton's undivided attention for once. "The reason they're panicked is because their brain has nothing else to think about besides fear. You know how people get when they're alone with their own thoughts." *You have no idea.* "They spiral. And I'd wager that's what's happening with Courtney. You abandon her all day with nothing to do but think about why she's here. You need to find her a distraction."

A distraction. Hmm. "What kind of distraction?"

"Oh, anything you like. Have her do more for you around the house. Let her go out to the pool every once in a while. And, my biggest suggestion, give the woman some friends."

"Friends?"

"Yes, Clayton, friends. I know that may be a foreign concept to you." He was getting bold, holding his own set of cards now, no longer inferior. They were in this together. "But friends can be a better cure than some medicines." *So annoying with the philosophical shit.* "Which brings me to my second hypothesis: She needs to see that she's not alone."

Clayton was sick of asking questions, not being in control didn't suit him. So he crossed his arms and waited for the doctor to elaborate.

"Clayton, other than your mother, she's the only woman here. Certainly the only young woman, though your mother seems to look younger and younger each day." *Ouch.* So he'd noticed that, too? *I suppose it would be rather difficult not to pick up on her excessive obsession with filtering her avatar.*

"It's a single's party, besides her. That's got to be confusing, wondering why she's a woman surrounded by men, locked away while the men get to go out and play. Especially since we have all the power, and she has absolutely none."

Clayton supposed it could be rather dystopian-looking, a world run and filled almost entirely with men. But how could he hire women to be part of this experiment? Salvation needed architects, engineers, professional coders… these were all men's professions. Of course, women were starting to get all "woke" and sometimes tried to make a statement by pretending they could do these jobs as well as men, but no one really took them seriously, did they?

Unsure of how Dr. Barnes felt about all this, he said instead, "I don't have the funds to hire anyone right now, but in a week when the investors come, I'll consider bringing in more women if you think it will help."

"The ideal situation would be having a woman as our equal, running Salvation with us." Clayton knew he'd caved and preached of being a team, but *come on*, did Dr. Barnes truly believe they were equals? Regardless, he'd have to be extraordinarily desperate to hire a woman and allow her to even have the appearance of being his equal in this world. In the real world, he was nothing. But here, he was a king. Courtney had proven she wasn't capable of being his queen, but he'd never intended for her to be. He wasn't willing to share the empire he'd built. With anyone.

"Like I said, I'll consider it," he lied through his teeth. "Now, if you'll excuse me, I have some audio tapes to readjust." He left Dr. Barnes behind, heading to headquarters where he could exit the simulation and work on his edits. Though he fought to keep them out, thoughts of "teamwork" kept infiltrating his brain like undercover agents, trying to fit in where they didn't belong. They must have been doing a pretty good job, because they convinced Clayton to yell a quick "Thank you!" over his shoulder before the doctor was out of earshot. He was glad he was too far away to see the satisfied smile he was sure was dripping down Jeremy's face.

He hummed as he drove his glossy, apple-red Mercedes towards the giant building. He was feeling positive. The doctor's ideas had given him hope. It was refreshing to hear a new perspective, rather than being stuck inside his own head, trapped alone with his problems like a maiden in a tower. When he arrived at headquarters, however, his whistling faded as he saw he wasn't alone. The exit portal was being blocked.

36

Alyssa

When Bella had taken her out to lunch, as girlfriends do, they'd gone over every detail of Alyssa's relationship. Whoever said a relationship should be kept between the two people in it clearly never had a friend like Bella.

While prying apart all of the good, and inevitably, the bad parts of Jackson, the night of gaming, potato chips, and energy drinks was brought up. When she'd assumed her boyfriend was working while she made him dinner, but he'd been playing video games with his friends, instead, claiming it was a "one time thing." A "coincidence."

"I've always had a bad feeling about him, Alyssa; I don't think he's trustworthy. He reminds me way too much of Clark." Alyssa went to interrupt her friend at that remark, but she didn't allow it. "I know, I know, you think he's so different. And you know what, I actually believe you. I'll even do you one better, I'll say, out loud, that I honestly think he's a lot better than Clark." Alyssa didn't even attempt to hide her surprise at this confession. "I do. He's proved that he genuinely cares about you. I believe that. And that's way more than I could ever say about my stupid ex."

Alyssa smiled a little at that, not knowing how exactly to react to Bella positively reassuring her while also negatively reflecting on her past.

"Don't get too excited, because he still has some of the same tendencies. I can see it in him. He's shady. He might not be cheating," observing the proud look on Alyssa's face, she emphasized, "*might* not," and then continued, "but he's just as spoiled as Clark, and that always leads to no good. Always."

Alyssa came to Jackson's defense. "He isn't spoiled. He just has a close relationship with his mother, which is a *good* thing."

"Has he ever washed a dish?" Bella's arms were already crossed, and she raised one eyebrow in a "mic drop" sort of look, waiting for Alyssa's response.

Alyssa was glad she could sincerely answer, "Actually, he helps me with the dishes all the time."

"*Helps* you. That's not what I'm talking about. I'm asking if he's ever, at any point in time, of his own volition, without being prompted, taken out a sponge and cleaned a plate."

Alyssa huffed. "No."

"Mm-hmm." Bella hummed shortly. She still wasn't satisfied, fishing for more. "A cup?" she pressed.

"No," Alyssa sighed, defeated.

"A fork?" Now she was just being cocky.

"I don't think so, okay, but he—"

"He what? Makes the bed? Does your laundry? Oh no, let me guess, he cleans the windows?"

Alyssa was growing frustrated. Another person who only saw relationships in black and white. "He's busy, and I've never asked him to do those things. That's just not how our dynamic is, it doesn't mean—"

Bella was one of those friends who loved to be right, who always had to say "I told you so," but Alyssa knew she never truly enjoyed it. She'd act like she did, her chin up in the air, but Alyssa knew she was secretly disappointed every time. She wanted to have a reason to have hope in people, but she couldn't, because she'd been burned too many times. And now, she wanted to stop her friend from meeting that same fate.

"So what *is* your dynamic, Alyssa? You do all the cooking and cleaning like some kind of stay at home wife? Except he hasn't even put a ring on your finger, and you have a more-than-full-time job on top of it all. Oh, and this isn't the fucking 1950's."

That should have been the concluding note - a very powerful one since Bella had never cursed at her before, ever. But when Alyssa didn't take her turn right away, Bella kept going. Albeit, in a much softer tone.

"Girl, look at yourself. You can't honestly say this is you. Remember when I was dating Tyler?"

Oh did Alyssa remember. They were in the seventh grade, and it was the first boyfriend either of them had ever had. She chuckled, "Of course I remember. That was the year you joined the cross country team because you had the biggest crush on him."

"Exactly!" Bella thrummed, delighted she'd jogged Alyssa's memory. "And I wore booty shorts, tied up t-shirts, and Adidas sneakers to school every single day. I mean my legs looked incredible, but it was a crime against fashion, it truly was."

Alyssa was in a better mood, but confused. "What's your point?"

"My point is, look at me." Alyssa did. They were out at a

253

very casual diner with outdoor patio seating, and Bella was in a pink mini skirt, a skin tight baby blue long-sleeved top, and Jimmy Choo pumps. Not to mention the nine piercings in her ears alone, and the 90's butterfly clips in her hair that were just beginning to come back into style. Bella had always been into fashion; she'd had a hard enough time accepting she'd have to wear scrubs every day if she wanted to be a doctor.

"I hated the sporty look. And I really hated running. Ugh." She shuddered, as if even the thought of exercise was horrific. A bit dramatic, but, who was Alyssa to judge her on that? "It wasn't me. But I did it anyway. And do you remember what you told me?"

Alyssa thought back. "Yes," it was resurfacing; she was back in the Willow Middle School cafeteria. "I said—"

"Isabella Leyra Chen, I cannot be your friend if I have to watch you change yourself for a boy!" Bella finished for her; apparently this pep talk had been memorable. Which was weird, since Alyssa distinctly remembered having to give it at least two more times as they reached high school and she met Ollie and Lincoln.

"That sounds like me." She couldn't deny it.

"Well, the shoe's on the other foot now, Alyssa. I can't hang around if you're going to let him control you like this."

"Oh my god he's not controlli—"

"You pinky swore."

Again, she couldn't deny it. She opened her mouth to argue, but then took a breath and considered her friend's point of view. Maybe she wasn't so far off... How *had* Alyssa fallen into her role of the subservient girlfriend? Who was she? Cooking dinner every night after three three-and-a-half-hour surgeries? And that was on a good day. She thought back to last week, when she'd done their laundry so Jackson could take a nap. And a few days before that, when she'd filled out and sent both of their rent checks because Jackson was just "no good at that sort of thing."

When she looked down on her life like this, through a bird's eye view, her forehead tightened with anger, and questions. It wasn't fair... but then why had she always thought it was? Everything Jackson did and said made her feel like *she* was the lucky one for everything he did for *her*.

Maybe love really could blind people.

She thought carefully before speaking. "I think... I think we might each be half right and half wrong here." Bella sat silently, open to the conversation. "Maybe you're right about me changing. I shouldn't be doing all the chores and stuff and letting him get away with less." Bella nodded once, firmly. *"But,"* and this was a big "but," "I think you're wrong about him being controlling. He's not doing it on purpose, we just sort of fell into this pattern without knowing it."

"Okay," Bella chewed on imaginary gum as she mulled Alyssa's words over. "Let's come to a compromise then." Alyssa was all ears. "I'll start to give Jackson the benefit of the doubt for now. Maybe we can even invite him to lunch with us next week." *Great!* "But..." *Of course.* Alyssa had gotten her "but" so it was only fair that Bella had her turn. "You have to stop giving him the benefit of the doubt for a while."

"What do you mean?"

"I mean, you need to see if it really was just a 'one time thing.' What if he's always up there playing his little video games pretending to be working just to get out of having to do anything around the house?"

"That's crazy!" Alyssa wanted to say. But she couldn't.

Because the thought had crossed her mind as well. So instead, she accepted the deal. "Fine. Now can we talk about something else?"

Bella lit up, and leaned in real close to Alyssa, noses practically touching above the table. "Yes!" She applauded, "Let's talk about sex!"

Alyssa choked on the sip of water she'd thought she was safe to take.

"Come on, I've been dying to know! You gonna change my mind about IT guys?" Her eyes were closing up from how big she was grinning, clearly having way too much fun with the topic.

"I'll put it to you this way:" Alyssa assured her, "My nickname for him is 'my little stress relief.'" Bella fake gagged, but Alyssa didn't care. "What? You brought it up, so now you can suffer the consequences of your own actions."

"Ugh, I regret everything!"

"And you know what else?" Now Alyssa was the one having too much fun. "I get stressed out a *looottt*." Both girls burst out in giggles.

"Well, dang, maybe I need to find myself an IT guy!" They laughed again. "So," Bella pried, "I assume that means he…. you know…. is selfless in that department?"

"Ummm…" Alyssa stalled, not wanting to fully get into it, but accepting that she had no choice because Bella would get it out of her sooner or later, "Not exactly…"

"WHAT?" Bella's voice cracked with shock. "That man should worship the ground you walk on! And besides, if you're washing *his* dishes, shouldn't he be washing yours?"

"Ew!" She didn't know what kind of euphemism that was supposed to be, but she found it unsettling… and, okay, a little funny. "The thing is, he wants to, but, I... I don't think he's had too much practice... you know... with women."

"Oh." Bella's face was dancing with disappointment, but not an ounce of surprise. "Well, why don't you teach him? You know all about anatomy, *Doctor* Hart."

The idea had crossed Alyssa's mind, but she'd never been able to bring herself to do it. "It's an awkward subject," she shrugged Bella off. "And he's great in other areas. You know, the kind you don't need to have much talent with if you happen to be... um... *genetically* blessed."

Bella threw her hands up. "Ah, okay okay, I've heard enough! Now I'd like the request to change the subject! Before I have to go plunge my ears with bleach to try to rid them of what they've heard here today!

Alyssa laughed as she took a bite of her garlic bread. "Hey, you asked."

***

Keeping Bella's warning in the back of her mind, Alyssa spent the next two weeks surveying Jackson in ways she never had before. Internally, she questioned him: his actions, his words. It was like she was wearing glasses that compelled her to peer through a lens of mistrust.

By the end of the third day, she felt so bad about her lack of faith that she almost quit her endeavor already. Until she unfortunately discovered Bella was right.

Each day when she arrived home, Alyssa had been sneaking into the apartment without knocking. She'd tiptoe to the door of Jackson's office and press her ear against it, listening.

For the first couple of nights, after hearing nothing but typing and what sounded like a work phone call for several minutes, she snuck back out and pounded her fist against the door until he'd very quickly answered. Much quicker than usual - each time right after the first knock. Looking back, he was probably on high alert after being caught the first time.

By the third day, however, he must have believed he was in the clear, because when Alyssa crept in to listen, she didn't need to get her ear up to the door in order to hear the commotion going on inside.

"Max! Was that you? Okay, okay, cool. No man, I wasn't sure… Yo, did you see that! What? How did you miss it? Tony and his buddy were right at the top of the big hill! Yes, I swear! We gotta move!"

Still, Alyssa didn't want to race to conclusions.

Three days later, she was sent home hours early due to a scheduling conflict. It was a slow day and she wasn't needed. Instead of texting Jackson to let him know, she pursued her detective work further. Sure enough, while it was only 2:00 in the afternoon, more shouting emitted from the office.

She stole back out the door, and took the rest of the day to herself: shopping, reading at Barnes and Noble, treating herself to a smoothie… She didn't want to act too quickly.

For the entire next week, she put him through more trials, and he failed a solid half of them. She couldn't stall anymore. It was time to confront him.

37

Clayton

Gordon and Mr. Whitmore were barricading the portal, their bodies acting as a two-person couch shoved against the only door leading back to the real world. If Clayton were a more compassionate man, he would've seen the parallel between himself being trapped by these two men and Courtney being trapped by himself. Of course, the irony was lost, and all that remained was confusion.

"Gentlemen," he nodded at them, remaining undisturbed - on the outside, anyway. He kept walking straight towards the men, praying one of them would move aside when they saw he was not intimidated. Gordon put his hand out and Clayton stopped just short of barreling into his palm.

The men exchanged glances, and Gordon initiated the intervention. "Clayton, we need to talk."

He played it off. "Oh no, are we breaking up? I didn't realize we were going steady."

The men looked at each other again, unamused by his humor.

"You can spare me the whole, 'it's not you, it's me' segment, okay? I'll be alright."

"It's about the glitches," Gordon ignored him. "We have theories on why they're happening. How to potentially stop them."

Clayton wasn't in the mood for this. "Listen, gentlemen, my head is full to the brim of theories right now. Dr. Barnes just gave me a couple of his own about a separate situation. This is all getting so... complicated. I'm stressed enough as it is, the investors—"

"That's exactly the problem," Gordon butted in. "Stress. I think it explains the earthquakes. This whole place is controlled by your brain. When your brain isn't in a good place, well, neither are we."

I told you I wasn't in the mood, leave me alone. His blood was simmering, and he needed to stop it before it reached a boil. *Relax. They're going to let you out.* "This conversation isn't exactly helping that, so if I could just be on my way, we could discuss this anoth—"

This time Mr. Whitmore interrupted. "And that's not all. The program is too full. It was too full even before you began stuffing it with french poodles and designer suits."

Clayton's mother had filled him in on their hypotheses already, so he really didn't have the patience to hear it again. He told them what he'd wanted to tell her: "Both Salvation and my head are as perfect as they can be while we're waiting for the investors to come. I won't be completely stress-free until I've thoroughly impressed them and secured their money in my pockets. And the simulation is bound to have a few glitches given the limited budget and staffing we have to run it. You should know that more than anyone, Barry."

Mr. Whitmore thought this over, then questioned, "If you're aware the system is already at capacity, then why even bother with the upgrades right now?" Clayton was about to answer, but wasn't given the chance. "I know, I know, you want to galvanize these investors. But I'd wager they won't be blown away if a tree falls on their heads while they're marveling at the two-story movie theater."

He was being dramatic. It's not like they would die. Even if a tree did fall, they'd simply be booted out of the server and forced to re-enter. Not a big deal.

"How about this. I promise to do some little breathing exercises and stay as stress-free as I can inside Salvation until we get the money to upgrade. Especially when the investors come. I'll get a massage, sniff some incense, clear my chakra... that sort of thing. Okay?"

Seeming to accept that this deal was the best they were going to get out of him, they agreed and stepped aside so he could head back to BrightView.

***

The stench hit his nose before he could open his eyes. The secret room at BrightView reeked even to Clayton, and he knew he was mostly immune to it in the same way a smoker doesn't notice the ashy smell that's been embedded over time into everything they own. If he could smell it, he didn't want to imagine how it was perceived by a virgin nose. It was only a matter of time before the other residents and staff would catch wind once it seeped through the cracks of the two layers of highly secured doors. He had his work cut out for him.

First, he flushed the contents of the bed pans and catheter bags down the toilet, resenting the women in his life for getting to stay inside of beautiful Salvation while he was subjected to this torture. After sanitizing the pans and reinserting the tubes, Clayton got out the materials needed for the sponge baths.

After working on Courtney, he was already exhausted, but even if his mother was willing to exit the simulation, she wasn't capable of helping him. She couldn't stand or wiggle her toes or use her arms to scrub, let alone hop in the shower and save him from his duties altogether.

He was overwhelmed. Why did he take on such a massive project? Everything was so much easier before, when other people took care of his mother for him. When he visited her and she didn't have bedsores and infections and an odor that made him want to vomit. When Courtney was bubbly and funny and supportive instead of another chore on his never-ending list.

Stress began weighing him down, a hundred little rocks tied to his ankles, pulling him to the bottom of the lake he used to be able to tread water in. When it was just five stones, or even twenty five, he could keep his head above water, but it seemed like new problems were being added constantly and his arms were only getting more and more worn out.

He squeezed his eyes shut and thought of all the conversations he'd had in the past few hours. He needed to reassure his current Salvation patients, begin recruiting more employees - including women, make new tapes for Courtney, hire someone to help upkeep his software, and... *What was the last thing again? Right, avoid stress. Uh oh.*

Wait... Technically that was only while he was inside Salvation. No one said he couldn't let it pull him under while he was in the real world. He thought about letting his arms rest, allowing the rocks to pull him down to the quiet bottom. But he knew he couldn't do that. If he let himself sink, he'd never make it

262

back up to the surface.

It's okay, he reassured himself. He just needed to get through one thing at a time. He finished cleaning up the girls, swiped deodorant under their arms, and spritzed them with a bit of perfume. *There.* Now at least the smell wasn't an issue. At least, not as much. *One thing at a time.*

He refilled the feeding tube he'd recently installed for Courtney, since she wouldn't be exiting Salvation anytime soon. That thought jerked his mind away from his current task. He'd forgotten to add something to his to-do list: Take care of Courtney's family and friends. Hesitantly, he flipped her phone off of airplane mode.

Texts and missed calls took over the screen. Her parents had teamed up with her sister, threatening to call the police if she didn't get back to them soon. Even her followers online were expressing concern. Apparently she'd never gone this long without uploading.

His fingers hovered over the letters, unsure of what to text. Eventually, he settled on, "**Having the time of my life on this trip, getting lots of good content to upload, and totally finding myself! But OMG am I sorry I've worried you! We're doing a self discovery thing, and cell phones just get in the way of that. Plus, there's not a lot of service anyway... I don't even have enough bars to call you right now. But we'll be done in like a week, and I'll call you then, okay? Love you!**"

He scoffed at his sloppy explanations. It wasn't perfect, but he had too many problems to exert extra time and effort on a single one of them. *One thing at a time.*

He'd been feeding his mother without a tube, but he figured it was time she got one. How long had it been since she'd exited last? Three days? Four? More than that? He couldn't remember. *Better safe than sorry*, he thought, as he inserted the tube. He was getting pretty good at this stuff. It wasn't that hard. Dr. Barnes thought he was so superior with his medical degree. *Ha.* Anyone could do this.

The girls were looking better, but there were more tubes and wires in them than ever. He'd even raided the supply closet just to see what else was in there, and he'd found some compression gear to place around their arms and legs - he read they can help prevent blood clots. His mother had never had them before, but when he'd asked Amber about it, she'd said they were more for people who weren't visited by nurses as often. People who weren't conscious. Since his mother *was*, she used to have so many nurses checking on her and adjusting her limbs often enough that she hadn't needed them. She needed them now.

He made a couple quick rounds through BrightView, figuring it was a good idea to show face and reassure everyone interested that his project was going swimmingly and that the investors finally rescheduled a date and they were very optimistic about that. He thought they'd stare at him, comment on his declining appearance and obvious lack of self-care, but he found they were so swamped with COVID that they barely paid any attention to him. They hadn't even seemed to notice he'd been gone a lot more than usual. *One thing at a time.*

As he walked the halls, a bright painting mounted to his left caught his eye. It didn't belong in this dull place, like a bright red poppy amidst a field of wheat. It was some sort of fancy California town, like Los Angeles or Santa Barbara. People tend to surround themselves with bright, sunny places when they're in dark, dreary ones themselves. Again, the irony was lost on him.

Finally, he was nearing the end of his list. Granted, there was still the matter of hiring more staff and enlisting future patrons, but that would have to wait until after next week. For now, the last thing he had to take care of was the audio tapes. He needed Courtney on her best behavior by next week.

"You love it here in Salvation. You are safe. There is nothing to be scared of here," he asserted again for good measure.

Then, he moved onto his personal agenda. "You enjoy taking care of the house. Dusting, scrubbing, fluffing, wiping… they give you purpose, because you know taking the burden off your husband allows him to run this town to the best of his abilities. He couldn't do any of this without you, so it's your personal mission to help him."

There was only so much for her to clean, especially when he wasn't home much lately, so he added, "You have hobbies, as well. Hobbies are good, they keep you busy. You like being busy. It's good. Very, very good." Overkill, maybe, but he had to make sure. What could he have her do? "Your hobbies include journaling, reading, and…" and what?

"Swimming!" Yes, Dr. Barnes had mentioned letting her go to the pool. *No*, delete. Re-record. He couldn't let her wander. Plus, the pool wasn't usable yet, he still needed someone to help with that. And there was no electricity. Half the town still wasn't functional. He took a deep breath in. As soon as he got his money, those issues could be remedied.

For now, though Salvation *looked* incredible, it was practically an Amish town disguised as Beverly Hills. "Painting!" he exploded, remembering the art he'd passed in the hallway. "You could paint all day. It's a way to express yourself."

That would have to do until he could find her some friends. She just needed to stay under control for one week. One week until he could bring people in to help him fix this place. To fix the glitches. To fix the storage. To fix her.

38

Alyssa

"I know you've been lying to me." Alyssa wasted no time with formalities. Once she'd made her mind up to tell Jackson his secrets had been exposed, she saw no point in delaying it further.

Jackson chose the most predictable response. Denial. He laughed her off, looking a little too casual as he averted, "You always do look adorable when you're fake angry, Alyssa," and turned back to his computer, unflinching. To an untrained, more trusting eye, he might appear calm. Unphased. But Alyssa was neither untrained nor trusting, anymore. She had let her guard down, and where had that gotten her? A reminder of why she had closed herself off in the first place.

She sensed the drop of worry in his eyes that he was trying so desperately to hide. That drop became a lake when she threatened, "This is your chance to talk about this with me before I go. If I walk out that door without answers, I won't come back."

She'd never had daggers in her eyes like this before. They should've been enough to drop him to his knees, an apology forced from his lips. Instead, he tried to placate her, feigning naivety. "Whoa, I don't know what you're talking about. Just calm down, okay? I bet there's a painless explanation for whatever you think happened."

If she hadn't been so furious, she would have been impressed that he was able to continue to oppose her with a nearly perfectly calm face. Nearly.

But Alyssa had pulled the truth from people with secrets far more sacred than Jackson's. What did he have on the line? Their relationship? That was nothing compared to the patients she'd had to interrogate over all the years, people who had Death written on their faces, and talked about him as if he were an enemy kept closer than a friend. People who had far more to lose than a girl. He was foolish to think she couldn't see right through him, even without the hard evidence he didn't know she had.

For some reason, though, she still wanted him. Them. She was far more honest with him than Bella would be accepting of, far more than she told herself she would be going into this. "Jackson," she steadied her voice, trying to save this, for the both of them. "Listen to me." He finally appeared to understand that she knew about his fake excuses, his "improved" work ethic that didn't fully exist to the extent he'd tried to convince everyone it did. He stopped trying to hide the shame, and let it spread across his face and fill the room with its uncomfortableness. He listened.

"Laziness and withholding of relatively harmless information is not enough to kill this relationship for me." She blinked, wanting to ensure the daggers were gone from her eyes and only truth remained. "But lying to my face is."

He was quiet for several seconds, and the sound of his swallow seemed so obvious it couldn't have been missed even if the room wasn't so silent. For the first time, he looked like he had dropped every mask. The Charmer, the Flirter, the Overly Confident Boy - all fallen on the ground.

Maybe this was good. Crazy as it sounded, perhaps difficult times did bring people together. Her mother and father had seemed to have none, and still, they'd drifted apart. Had they simply never built the proper foundation? Was it possible she could build something stronger than they ever did?

She stopped those thoughts. It was far too soon to let him start removing the bricks from the barrier she had so recently built back up. Back to the facts. "You don't work as much as you say you do."

She waited for his reaction, but got nothing. She supposed his face was already drooping as low as it was capable of. "I don't know exactly how much you really do work. But I know you stop much earlier than you say you do. You can't deny that, right?"

He shook his head. Good. She was getting at least some response from him. "Right. The thing is, I don't police what you do. I never have, have I?" Again, his head made tiny movements from left to right. "Exactly. I haven't. I don't care if you work as much as me. So if you're trying to impress me," she was trying to give him the benefit of the doubt, "that's not the kind of thing I'm impressed by."

Jackson lassoed his chance to speak, pulling it to him and pinning it down, not letting it get away this time. Whether he was telling the truth or merely using her words as inspiration, she wasn't sure, but she heard him out. Despite everything, the water now leaking from his eyes wasn't a lie. "I'm so sorry," his voice caught with every word. "I just always feel like I can never compare to you."

Even if it shouldn't have, this surprised Alyssa to hear. She never thought of herself as more special than anyone else... even if she'd heard it many times before. She always thought people were just trying to flatter her. Though she was an expert in decoding body language, she was struggling to figure out if that's what Jackson was trying to do.

Her head told her that he was just trying to butter her up, to get out of the corner he was backed into, to lead the conversation in this new direction so he wouldn't continue to be accused of playing games to get out of tasks around the house and breeze by in life. But her heart kept screaming to believe him. Her heart didn't want to lose him. Didn't want to lay in bed with Bella eating chocolates and pouring her heart out about how her friend had obviously been right when she said all men are deceiving, lazy, selfish pigs.

She didn't want to believe that about Jackson. So she chose instead to deem his explanation as honest. "You're absolutely incredible," he went on, still crying. "I never know why you're with me. You're stunningly gorgeous, incredibly smart, unbelievably strong... and you never turn it off. At first I couldn't understand how you do it." He'd been thinking about this for a while. "But then I realized it's because there's nothing to turn off. It's all really you. None of it's fake. None of it."

Part of her was scared of his stream of compliments. What if he was trying to distract her from her anger by boosting her ego? But she felt seen. More seen than she'd felt through all her years in this world. She wanted to hear more.

"You don't form bonds with your patients because you're really good at *pretending* to care about them. You just do. You're just good." He kept going. Alyssa sat motionless, soaking in

270

his words, forgetting that she was supposed to be mad at him. "And you're not sweet to me because you pity me; you really think I'm special, don't you?" He didn't wait for her answer. "You really see the best in people." His words puzzled her again. Pity him? Why would she pity him? She'd never known he had that insecurity. "You don't force jokes just to get a laugh from people. And, you don't laugh at jokes that you don't think are funny just to make people happy. Everything about you is honest. You laugh when you mean it, and you laugh a lot."

When I'm around you.

"You don't say 'it's fine' if it isn't. You make everyone around you feel important, and not because you want something from them. You believe they *are* important. Even when you're the brightest light in every room."

Barely conscious of her actions, Alyssa's mouth dropped open to say something, anything, but he wouldn't let her. "And there! You want to stop me from praising you, from telling you the truth, but not because you want me to think you're humble. You truly don't know how much you mean to me. To anyone you allow to get close to you."

Along with his words, Jackson moved closer to her. To her heart.

Though they had been closer than this many times, there had never been a greater intimacy between them.

"And you don't work hard just to make money. You love your job. You live for it." He sighed, knowing he needed to get back to the whole reason they were here. "I did take the promotion, which was a big deal for me." He was telling the truth. "But still, I can't compete with you."

What is he talking about? "It's not a competition." The happiest images came flooding in: their laughing faces, ice cream in the snow, sleeping bags on the wooden floor beneath them. "And if it was, you'd be winning."

More pictures filled her head: her ear against the door, SpaghettiOs in the sink, his socks on her feet when no one had done the laundry and she'd run out of her own.

"Okay," she amended," you'd be winning in *some* areas." He winced in preparation for what was coming. "In others... I'm sorry Jackson, but you're failing."

For a minute he'd made her forget that he'd messed up. Now she remembered, and change needed to happen. But she also remembered that she loved him... something she wasn't so sure about even just ten minutes ago. But he always found a way to remind her.

Change first. She needed to see it.

His face, which had been slowly morphing into a happier expression, reverted back into its original flatness. Then, switched to determination. "I'll make it up to you. I promise."

He held out his pinky, and she flushed. Another reminder. *No.* She wouldn't just take it. Walls. She needed to remember her walls.

It took all of her strength not to immediately reach for his finger. *Make him prove it.* "How?"

Without taking any time to think, he insisted, "I'll take over the housework, if that's what you want. You do work harder, and I need to step up."

She didn't know how to feel about his answer. It was a nice gesture, but she didn't want the scale to tip to the other end. She wanted equality. Teamwork.

"What if you took over dinners on my later nights - Mondays, Thursdays, and Saturdays."

She pushed her lips together hard, as she often did in

concentration. This was her chance to turn him into her partner. But part of her wasn't sure how much he was capable of. As much as she defended him to Bella, her friend was right about him being babied. Spoiled. And she'd been contributing to that.

She didn't want to overwhelm him with impossible tasks right away, though. Anything would be better than nothing. Would give him a chance to prove himself to her. And if not... She'd cross that bridge when - *if* she came to it.

"And laundry once a week. Washed, folded, and put away." Time for her non-negotiable: "And no more lying." She paused to let the severity of those last four words sink in. "Can you do that for me?"

He looked into her eyes more intensely than the occasion called for, and pushed his still-extended smallest finger towards her. "I'd do anything for you."

Don't melt, she told herself, though his dark latte eyes were enough to make her knees buckle. She gripped her pinky around his. "I'll believe it when I see it."

39

Clayton

oday was the day. The investors were set to meet Clayton at BrightView in ten minutes. He double and triple checked the room, making sure everything was in place.

He'd asked his mother to log out of Salvation earlier this morning, removed her Oc X's, wires, tubes, compresses, and restraints, and lifted her out of her bed himself so he could give her a proper shower. It wasn't an easy feat, seeing as his arms were growing weaker and weaker as he entered the real world less and less. His mother didn't weigh much anymore, so that helped.

Foolishly, he'd thought she might bestow sweet sentiments upon him. Words of encouragement for her son who provided her with a new life. "Don't mess this up," was all he'd gotten, and it only riddled him with more anxiety. Flashbacks of previous interactions floated through his head like a message in a bottle ready to be popped open.

"Dr. Avery thinks it has something to do with your brain. He says when you're stressed out, that's when they're the worst."

"Stress. I think it explains the earthquakes. This whole place is controlled by your brain. When your brain isn't in a good place, well, neither are we."

Breathe, he'd told himself. Though he'd given a sarcastic reply about cleansing his chakra to Gordon and Mr. Whitmore a week ago, he had taken their words into consideration. Whether they were right or wrong about his stress causing problems, it certainly wasn't solving any, and it couldn't hurt to try to slow his racing heartbeat.

It was a blessing his mother couldn't feel anything below her neck, because her bed sores were looking nastier, and he was sure the soapy water entering those wounds would've been enough to bring her to her knees, if she'd been capable of feeling the pain, or standing. At least they were on her back side, so he'd been able to arrange her in a pose that made her look pure and peaceful underneath the covers. He'd left her feeding tube out, the investors didn't need to know the extremity of some patients' conditions, and placed her in an adult diaper that was also hidden out of sight. It wasn't a long-term solution, but the men would only be visiting for an hour or so.

After she'd entered the simulation, he moved on to Courtney. Not being able to take her out of Salvation was a challenge, but he'd done his best with the situation at hand, working around the IV tubes as carefully as he could. He was thankful the day he'd knocked her out was long enough ago that her bruises had healed nicely, yet she hadn't been unconscious so long that she looked pale and emaciated like Georgie.

He didn't bother checking on the other couple of patients he worked with at BrightView. The investors didn't have enough time to check on everyone, nor did they care to. He'd show them the girls, and then take them to an uninhabited room he'd prepared so he could allow them to enter Salvation themselves. He'd gotten the nurse to place enough beds in there, and had spent most of the week setting up the tents and projectors for them, as well as working with Dr. Barnes to calculate their drug doses.

Two minutes.

He left his secret room, soon to be not-so-secret, and headed towards the front door in the lobby while practicing his speech. "Especially in this new world of COVID-19, Salvation is the only town that is thriving more than ever!" They didn't have to know that this wasn't completely true. It just had to look perfect for an hour. Maybe less. *Just breathe.*

A black Rolls-Royce rolled to a stop in front of the doors, and three men, all wearing suits, stepped out simultaneously. They were here.

"Welcome to BrightView!" he greeted them, firmly shaking each of their hands. "But this isn't the exciting place. Let me walk you through the process quickly so I can say, 'Welcome to Salvation,' huh?"

They eyed him up and down, and the plug was pulled out of his tub of security, draining him of it, leaving him empty. Exposed. Self-conscious.

He already hadn't been the most attractive man, but months of getting hardly any exercise or showers had been accentuating his worst features. He'd washed, shaved, and put on a decent suit to greet the men, but evidently it wasn't enough to hide his disregard for his health in the real world.

Just breathe. They weren't here for him. This version of him. He needed to get them to Salvation.

He led the men through the hallways, to his secret room. He'd taken a risk and left all of the locks on both doors unturned. He didn't want his project to seem shady. Suspicious. Dangerous. The men stayed quiet the whole route, except for the tallest, oldest member, who was constantly apologizing for the whooping cough he couldn't seem to control. "With the pandemic going around, people hear a cough and treat me like I've got the plague. Sore throat is all, from spending too much time talking with the wife and kids lately with the office being closed down."

It seemed his intensive cleaning efforts hadn't been as successful as he'd anticipated. All three sets of eyes widened in concern, then narrowed in disgust as they entered the room. It was like a smoker's house, the smell would never truly be gone. Just because he didn't smell it anymore, thought he'd gotten rid of it, didn't mean it wasn't still there. Virgin noses. They were clearly picking it up.

Clayton began his speech, preoccupying their minds with his rehearsed spiel. They didn't appear to be listening. One of them couldn't stop staring at his mother. *What is he seeing?* The bed sores were covered, tubes removed… She didn't look that bad… Did she?

He stole a glance himself. *Oof.* He'd have to use that to his advantage.

"Horrible, isn't it?" Clayton addressed the man's lingering stare, startling him, getting his attention. "The human body is so fragile. So weak. So… limiting." All three men had their eyes on him now. "It's not the Oc X's, as we call them, or the IV dripping in the arm that are alarming you, though I'm sure that's what your minds are trained to believe."

He could do this. Speaking was his wheelhouse. His talent. His stacked deck. He had all the advantages here, not them. He could still win them over.

"No, those aren't what scare you. It's the fact that their bodies are injured. Weak. Not living up to their potential. Here, people who are deeply sick or paralyzed are often capable of nothing. It's only in Salvation that they get to live the type of life they deserve. Let me show you."

The tall man's cough was a welcome distraction, and Clayton used it as an excuse to pull them all out of this contaminated room and into the fresh, unused, prepared one. "Previously you all provided us with urine samples, which we have used to determine just how much of a drip your IV's should have once injected. Not to worry," he clocked the looks on their faces, "there is no danger in these tubes at all. They merely allow you to relax so you can immerse yourself in the experience."

They still seemed hesitant, so he moved on to something a little more fun. "How 'bout we pick our avatars, shall we? Get a look at this: You can choose your race, height, hairstyle, and that's only the beginning. Would you prefer a Ferrari, or a Lamborghini?"

Their faces lit up for the first time. He knew the upgrades had been the golden ticket idea!

The oldest man coughed again. It was getting old. "Sir, would you care to go first?"

***

Somehow, he'd done it. He'd convinced all three men to join. They'd laid on the beds willingly, curiously put on the Oc X's, and allowed Clayton to inject them with the needles. The hard part was over. He couldn't believe it. He was in the clear. He'd done his job, gotten them to Salvation. The rest would be easy.

He joined the simulation himself, and had to refrain from fist pumping when he saw their previously pursed mouths agape with wonder. "There, you see? This is what you've been waiting for. Welcome to Salvation."

He felt powerful. Dramatic. Like John Hammond opening the gates of Jurassic Park.

From here, everything was planned. They hopped in the Ferrari the tall man had chosen, his cough miraculously gone, and headed to Georgie's house.

"Take a moment to appreciate how your body feels right now. No more throat discomfort, huh?" He playfully punched the driver on the shoulder. He was pretty sure it was the older man he'd hit, but it was difficult to tell since they'd all chosen young, unbelievably handsome avatars. The man smiled at him, shaking his head. *Yep, that must be him.*

"No back pain. No creaky joints. All the athleticism and grace we can only dream of having in the real world."

Everything was going according to plan.

"And look out the window as we approach our first stop. You'll notice our beautiful pool, residents out for their afternoon jogs, the always-in-bloom flowers looking gorgeous under the palm trees and sunny sky. Especially in this new world of COVID-19, Salvation is the only town that is thriving more than ever!" Just like he'd practiced.

No. Even better.

With Clayton's directions, the driver pulled up in front of his mother's house. "Remember that poor, wounded, crippled woman you saw only minutes ago?" he queried gleefully. "I present to you, my mother, Georgie Reeves." He held his hand out for the grand reveal, directing their attention to the front door, where his mother had practiced stepping out for her shining moment.

279

But while she was supposed to step out of the door, a major glitch must have occurred, because she walked straight though the side of the house, her hand gripped around a doorknob that wasn't there.

A bead of sweat rolled out of Clayton's hairline. There couldn't have been a worse possible time for his simulation to glitch. Reluctantly, he swiveled his neck to absorb the disappointment he was certain he'd catch a glimpse of when he looked at the investors. He forced himself to *just breathe*, though his lungs fought him when he first sucked in.

To his astonishment, the men began clapping. Either they thought it was a magic trick, or they were so flabbergasted by her transformation that they hadn't even registered the mistake. Overjoyed, Clayton joined them in their applause, and Georgie bowed and curtsied like a Broadway talent after her debut performance.

"Do a cartwheel," he mouthed to her, spinning his index finger around to mime his request. She obliged, and the men hooted and hollered. The shortest one even put two fingers in his mouth and whistled.

The group toured the town, and as Clayton had encouraged, the users were extravagantly dressed in expensive-looking suits, all conveniently out and about, socializing and waving at the Ferrari as the four men drove past. "We're all like brothers around here," Clayton boasted, aware that these types of men always belong to some sort of club or society where they sit around and discuss how much better they are than the rest of the world. Clayton often dreamed about being a member. And, lately, a leader.

In their last fifteen minutes, Clayton had planned another gathering in his yard. Not a barbeque this time, that wouldn't be classy enough. It was more of a "whiskey and caviar" type of event. Very prestigious.

Once everyone was present and had had a few minutes to socialize, Clayton tapped his fork to his glass. "Members of Salvation, generous investors, my lovely mother. "He gestured at each of these groups as he spoke. "I'd venture to say we are the luckiest sons of bitches to ever live, because unlike everyone else back there, in the world of viruses, chaos, and tragedy, we've been granted access to the only place in existence that allows us to truly live the life we desire. We are here because—"

BANG!

There wasn't a single soul who didn't jump at the sudden smack against Clayton's bedroom window. Every head turned, and what they saw was disturbing enough to make hands cover mouths, gasps and screams ring through the crowd, and worried mutters quickly circulate amongst them.

Courtney.

She'd slammed her head against the window. Hard. Intentionally, judging by the determined stare that never wavered or left the crowd, even as she pulled her head back and plunged forward again, harder this time. The glass cracked, and red was now visible on her forehead and the window.

When Clayton watched her next move, paralyzed by what felt like infinite emotions, he instantly regretted his latest edit of her audio tapes. Yes, he'd told her to paint, to use it as self-expression, but he never thought *this* would be the outcome.

Her gaze fixed on the crowd, Courtney swiped two fingers across her gash and used the blood to scrawl a message across the canvas:

HELP ME.

All thoughts of "just breathing" vanished from Clayton's head.

281

A red deeper than the liquid gushing from Courtney's head was all that remained inside him.

YOU COULDN'T HAVE BEHAVED FOR ONE HOUR?

Red, flashing red, like lightning if it were created by Aries instead of Zeus. He ran into the house, forgetting the investors, forgetting he once loved this stupid, stupid woman. He found her in the bedroom, reached his hands towards her throat.

Gordon must have followed him, because Clayton felt himself being pulled back by the man, and then shaken. "Clayton!" he yelled, "Stop!" Dr. Avery's usually-straight tie was disheveled; he was hysterical, as Clayton imagined he probably looked, himself. Maybe *was*, himself. "Calm down! Breathe, Clayton. Breathe."

It was too late. The ground began to buck, a bull set on expelling its rider.

People flew into the air, slammed against walls, ran for shelter.

Dr. Avery changed his course of action, apparently deeming his attempt of subduing Clayton futile. "You need to log out. Go! I'll help the investors leave once you're gone."

Clayton wanted to argue, but he didn't have a better suggestion. He sprinted to the dazzling red Italian sports car, since it was parked closest, and turned the key in the ignition.

"Coward!"

He jerked his head to see who'd screamed at him. The lead investor. The ground shook harder.

"No, I'm leaving to help you, you don't understand!" He *needed* to explain himself. To win them back. To prove to them that he wasn't a failure. They were wrong about him. Everyone was wrong. Everyone had always been wrong. If they could just see—

"Understand? I understand how to pull out of a project,

that's what I understand!" The wheels of the sleek vehicle were already beginning to roll away. It was the only way to save them.

Something few people cared to uncover about Clayton was that he often broke down in the real world. He hated his failures, hated the hand he was dealt, hated himself. But the tears that landed on the leather seat beneath him as he sped over the convulsing streets were the first he'd ever shed in Salvation. And he vowed they would be the last.

40

Derek

"Birdie needs a raincoat too!"

Bianca had made Bee put on her bright yellow rain jacket and polka-dotted rubber boots, but now their always-opinionated child was insisting her little bird needed his own shelter from the storm. Derek stepped in to help.

"I can put Birdie under my jacket and run to the car real fast," he offered. "Here, I'll take him right now."

"No!" Bee held her ground, holding Birdie closer as her father's hand plunged forward to grab him. "He'll suffocate in there!"

Derek's mouth dropped open; he was in total disbelief that his now six-year-old knew such a word. He looked over at his wife, who was already waiting to meet his gaze, stifling a laugh at their daughter's newfound vocabulary.

He should've laughed too, but still, after all these years of marriage, Bianca's perfection put him in a trance. He stared into her eyes for only about three seconds, but that's all the couple needed to communicate with each other. They'd learned to share secrets with glances, tell jokes through stolen looks, decipher messages through the glimmer in the other's eyes.

Looking at her, he told her she was beautiful. In three seconds, he said he couldn't believe she was his. His lover, his best friend, the mother of their never-boring, ever-growing little girl.

His wife translated the glimpse, and retold their love story with the smile she sent back. Then, she turned back to focus on their daughter, and still blushing from the interaction, she got down on her knees to look Bee in the eyes.

I love that I can still make her blush.

"Okay, Bee, how about this: I happen to remember that one of the dollies that grandma got you came with an umbrella." She winked at Derek, showing off her problem solving skills, making sure he noticed. He always noticed her. "Why don't you go look in your play bin and get it for Birdie to use, huh?"

"Yes, mama, that's perfect! Be right back!" The little one raced up the stairs, and the lovers were alone again for a minute. Probably more like twenty seconds, considering how fast Bee could be once she was on a mission.

"You," he started, as he gripped her by the waist and pulled her to him, "are an amazing mother. And an amazing, gorgeous woman. You know that?"

She matched his energy easily. The undeniable chemistry their friends were always jealous of. He'd slid her so close that her lips were mere centimeters from his. "Hmmm... I might need a reminder."

Derek didn't miss his cue. He kissed her softly, then pressed harder, amplifying the intensity. Their bodies were so close he wished they could morph into one. Just before the footsteps sounded at the top of the stairs, he stepped a few inches away, leaving her breathless. Giggling. He didn't need to hear Bee coming, his parental instincts had kicked in long ago. He

285

basically had a sixth sense for knowing when he was going to be interrupted by the most extraordinary little girl in the world.

"Alright Dad, go start the car, we'll meet you there."

It felt right when Bianca called him that in front of Bee. *Dad*. He loved the title, almost as much as he loved *husband*. It was a beautiful life with these girls. His little birds. Showing him how beautiful life could be, always giving him a new perspective. Like grabbing a doll's umbrella for a stuffed animal to walk ten steps to the car with. Because the bird was that valuable, that special. It needed to be protected.

As he drove, Bee sang to herself in the back seat and Bianca did her make-up in the passenger side mirror. Usually they played car games, or at least had conversations, but the rain was coming down hard, blurring the windshield, so Derek was focused on the road.

Not focused enough.

The ambulance arrived sixteen minutes and twenty-seven seconds after the crash. Great time, really, considering the small town. Bianca had told him once that her cousin crashed his motorcycle off Hillshire road and laid on the ground with a broken ankle for forty-five minutes until the paramedics got there. It was a miracle he didn't pass out in all that time. This time, the ambulance arrived in sixteen minutes and twenty-seven seconds.

Sixteen minutes and twenty-seven seconds is less time than it takes to read a chapter of a good book. It's less time than watching a sitcom - even the real short ones. It's less time than it takes to do a load of laundry or run the dishwasher through a full cycle or make small talk with a stranger on a bus but apparently it's enough time for a girl to die.

It's enough time for a woman to break.

It's enough time for the world to flip upside down.

Sixteen minutes and twenty-seven seconds is enough time to watch a survivor beg to take the place of a lost soul.

If Derek could read Bianca in three seconds, imagine what he saw as he watched her for sixteen minutes and twenty-seven seconds. He observed every ounce of light be extinguished from her, a hand reaching down her throat straight to her heart and pinching the flames with its fingers until all that was left was darkness. He saw a bird clip her own wings, spiraling towards the ground after her chick flew out of the nest - straight through a windshield.

He saw all of that within the first minute. There were still fifteen left.

Plus twenty-seven seconds.

Plus a lifetime.

41

Clayton

Courtney was the problem.

She was causing mayhem. Mayhem causes stress. Stress only leads to more mayhem. This problem had to be eradicated. Immediately.

Following a discreet meeting with Dr. Barnes, the two men determined their next course of action. They were going to try to *shock* the old memories out of Courtney's head.

Dr. Barnes hadn't wanted to share his research with Clayton, but men are much more forthcoming when they're threatened. Blackmailed. Held hostage. *Let's just say, I can be very convincing.*

"Electroconvulsive therapy passes a current through the patient's brain, purposefully triggering a short seizure. It's been known, in some cases, to reverse the symptoms of various mental health conditions. Clayton..." he'd warned, "This kind of operation involves multiple doctors, advanced equipment, and a precise diagnosis... and even then, it's risky."

The side eye Clayton had thrown his way had shut the doctor up quickly. Clayton wasn't interested in precautions. He'd wasted too much time with them already. His mind was made up.

He insisted Jeremy continued sharing. "It helps - *sometimes* - with severe depression, even depression that hasn't reacted to any other form of treatment. Mania, agitation, aggression in people with dementia…"

It was perfect. "We can do it at my house, that way we won't need to move her. I'll get her strapped down. Be there in thirty minutes. Tell no one."

"You don't understand." The doctor swallowed harder than usual. "It has to be in the real world. On her real body."

Shit. There was no turning back now. If he stopped to think about what that meant, it would only delay the inevitable. Only scare him. Clayton didn't like to be scared. He liked to do the scaring. Time to log out.

***

There was a fear in Courtney's eyes before the shock that was unlike anything Clayton had ever seen. She wasn't human, more like prey, struggling against two predators. Outnumbered. Outsmarted. But that wasn't Clayton's fault. He'd given her more than enough chances. He could've pounced at her from the bushes a hundred times before this, but he hadn't. He'd carried her to the watering hole time and time again.

Besides, sometimes a wounded animal needs to be put out of its misery. For its own good.

Dr. Barnes hesitated, screened Clayton's face for a change of heart, found none, and accepted his fate. The decision had been made for him. He held the two paddles, one in each hand, near her temples, closed his eyes in what Clayton assumed was a prayer, and pressed down.

Courtney's body rose and fell reminiscent of an exorcism, something Clayton had only witnessed on television when the hero uses the defibrillator pads to bring someone back to life.

Was he resurrecting her?

Or sentencing her to death?

She wasn't moving, still as Snow White after biting the apple.

All the men could do was wait. They decided to log back into Salvation and prepare for Courtney to wake up there, rather than stay in the stench-filled room at BrightView. They'd see the results either way, and they both preferred the beauty of the fake world over the mess of the real one.

They fidgeted with their watches, scuffed the heels of their shoes on the floor, adjusted their cuff buttons... anything but let themselves stay still long enough to think about what they'd done.

Clayton was running out of clothing items to rearrange when Dr. Barnes stammered, "She's awake."

Sure enough, her eyes were open, slowly moving from side to side. She was almost peaceful. Relaxed. The knot in Clayton's stomach loosened, and the long exhale coming from beside him hinted that Dr. Barnes felt the same way.

"Courtney... how are you feeling?" Clayton's question was little more than a whisper, though he hadn't meant for it to be.

"Pretty lights," was Courtney's only response, as her glazed-over eyes hyperfocused on the lamp they'd brought in and hooked to a generator, along with various pieces of medical equipment. Her cadence was slow. Drawled out. Loopy, almost.

He tried again. "Do you know where you are right now?" Dr. Barnes was pacing. They waited far too long for her answer that wasn't an answer at all, rather, another question.

"Do you have candy?"

Their fears about her being physically harmed from the shock were alleviated, but they'd surmised the biggest risk would be mental damage.

Clayton snapped at Jeremy. "I thought you knew how much of a shock to give her!"

"I told you, I don't know anything for sure, this isn't my area of—"

"Doctors have lollipops, right?" Her interrupting voice was like a child in a horror film: so innocent that it was freaking them out. "Yummy. I love lollipops."

If looks could kill, Jeremy Barnes would've dropped dead from Clayton's glare.

"Something is wrong with her! She sounds like she has the mental capacity of a six-year-old!" What he didn't say was that he'd known the risks. That he was as much at fault as his colleague, if not more. That he didn't want to direct his frustration - his *guilt* - at himself, so he was lashing out, instead.

The doctor let out everything Clayton knew he'd been too afraid to say. "I told you this could happen! I told you I wasn't trained to do this, that serious side effects could happen!"

Before Clayton matched Dr. Barnes' rage, he took a moment to breathe. His anger and stress had led him here, to this point, where he didn't want to be. He was doing this - endangering Courtney - to *eliminate* stress, not add more. If he didn't calm down, he could destroy everything he'd built. He'd already knocked down one domino, he didn't need to knock down any more.

Of course, once dominoes are set into motion, it's awfully difficult to stop them from tumbling. The first hits the second, and the second the third, and if he didn't act quickly, the whole row would be down and he'd have to start over from scratch.

291

He concentrated on his breathing, tried to think of the positives.

Courtney was alive. That was good... wasn't it? They weren't murderers, at least. Clayton had a rap sheet a mile long, but he had yet to add "Cold Blooded Killer" to it, and he'd like to keep it that way.

What else?

Dr. Barnes was still here. Yelling, sure, but he hadn't left. He'd never left, even after every questionable, experimental, or even illegal endeavor Clayton had put him through. And now he was in far too deep to ever abandon Clayton in the future. An Everest hiker buried by an avalanche, relying on his partner to uncover his mouth and expose it to the fresh air.

Jeremy needed Clayton. Needed him to keep quiet about the immoral choices he'd made. Needed him to never reveal what he'd done both in and out of Salvation.

The doctor was loyal. Whether it was by choice didn't matter anymore. Loyalty was something Clayton was going to need going forward. Those dimwitted investors didn't have an ounce of loyalty in their bodies. If they did, Clayton wouldn't have had to resort to torturing his girlfriend... *Wife?... Ex-girlfriend?* They were supposed to be a band of brothers. Dr. Barnes deserved to be rewarded for his allegiance.

"You did," was Clayton's reply. Dr. Barnes stopped in his tracks, holding in the big gulp of air he'd just inhaled and had undoubtedly been about to use to continue his chastisement. "You've questioned this process all along the way. And yet, you've continued to do as I've asked. I am lucky to have you by my side." Dr. Barnes' mouth was opening and closing, like a bass taken off the hook and dropped on the floor of the boat.

"In fact," Clayton continued, "I believe you should be compensated for your devotion. As soon as I get the means, and rest assured, I'll get them, you can be the first to have your house remodeled in Salvation. Before me, even. How's that sound?"

The newly created child in the room stopped Dr. Barnes from answering. "Can I have a blanket? I'm ready for a nap."

"Okay, here's the plan," Clayton assumed control. "Jeremy, you get her untethered, tuck her in for her nice little nap," he flashed Courtney a bright, reassuring smile, "and lock the door on the way out. We'll take turns checking on her for the next few days until we figure out what to do."

The doctor didn't object. Clearly he had no better ideas. "I'm going to log out and make sure her real body is doing okay. We can reconvene tomorrow." Dr. Barnes nodded, and began undoing the restraints around Courtney's wrists.

Clayton headed to headquarters to exit, proud of the perfectly motionless earth he observed outside on his way there.

42

Alyssa

Her fortress still standing strong, Alyssa twisted the key in the knob of the apartment door without knocking. She was intent on keeping her belief that actions speak louder than words. Jackson had told her a lot of things. How much was really true? She hoped most of it was, then she dug her nails into her palm to punish herself for being an optimist when she'd sworn to be a realist. Still… How could eyes like his be lying? Eyes that dripped adoration like an espresso machine filling a Styrofoam cup when he held her in his arms.

Snap out of it. She swung the door open, readying herself to tiptoe to his office, preparing for the sound of machine guns or race cars coming from his computer. She took one quiet step inside, and tripped when she saw Jackson, staring at her from the living room couch.

Had he been waiting for her?

He beamed as he rushed up to take the bag and water bottle from her arms. "Let me help you with that, my lady," he purred as he planted a kiss on her cheek and scurried off to put away her belongings. *What is going on?*

She was about to ask him, when the strong smell of garlic infiltrated her nostrils. Had he spilled the bottle? Alyssa sighed, moving towards the kitchen in search of the dustpan.

"Ah, looks like you're ready to eat!" Jackson had a strange look on his face... almost like pride but there was a fog of something else. A secret? She turned the corner to see what looked like Thanksgiving dinner spread across the table.

She saw sweet rolls in a basket, and carrots and onions in a small dish. In the middle of their table was a beautiful roast chicken - not quite as extravagant as a turkey, but it was only the two of them after all. There was another bowl full of mashed potatoes, which were Alyssa's favorite, and one little cup of brown gravy. Had she forgotten an anniversary? A birthday? Were his parents coming over for dinner or something?

She searched her mind for what she could've missed, but came up empty. Maybe she'd gotten the day wrong... She did that a lot, and everyone at work teased her since she was the girl who marked the calendar every day. "What day is it today?"

Jackson, who now had two sets of silverware in his hands, chuckled under his breath. The people at work were no longer the ones who knew her best. Even Bella didn't hold that title, anymore. Jackson knew her from the inside out, more thoroughly than a surgeon studying what lies under her skin. They might know where her heart rests, but he knew what was inside it. What made it smile. What made it glow. What made it break in two.

He'd witnessed her struggles remembering dates more than anyone. Since they'd moved in together, she'd gotten up and driven to work on three separate occasions to find the doors locked. They'd been Sundays. She didn't work on Sundays. Jackson laughed at her each time she came back home frazzled, asking her how she hadn't known, considering he usually woke up with her to give them more time together. She'd laughed along with him, explaining how she was so tired after the week she hadn't even noticed.

"It's Thursday," he informed her as he set the silverware down by their plates, though she hadn't meant which day of the week. "It's your late day. My turn to make dinner."

His words were completely matter-of-fact, like it was obvious he was going to follow through. Like it was crazy to doubt him. A pang of guilt constricted in her stomach. She'd expected him to forget their talk. Even worse, she'd anticipated he'd find some excuse to get out of it. How unfair that she thought so little of him. She was awful.

Her hungry eyes feasted on the spread covering the table again, and hunger mixed with the guilt in her gut.

Almost as if he could read her thoughts, Jackson finished straightening the fork he'd been fiddling with and walked over until the two of them were nearly forehead to forehead. "I took our talk yesterday *very* seriously."

How could she have questioned him? All he'd done was play some video games, and she'd painted him as the enemy. She'd believed the worst of him, assumed this was the beginning of the end for them. She'd been wrong, and she cursed her past for turning her so untrusting.

He wasn't like her father. He was the boy in her now *second* favorite song who didn't leave after the fight. Who wasn't going to abandon her. Maybe she should've been mad at herself as she let her armor drop to the ground like she'd promised she wouldn't allow to happen, but the only emotion flooding her was love.

The boy she loved interrupted her thoughts about him. "I'm

never going to come that close to losing you ever again, Alyssa."
She believed him.

"You've already made me so much better, even if I haven't always shown it. I feel like the best version of myself when I'm with you. For a minute, I got lazy, and I forgot myself. I forgot the man I want to be for you. But I am going to be that man. Nothing will get in my way now." She believed him.

"You say you love me more than anything, but I love you *more*. More than anything. More than *everything*." She believed him.

After that day, her armor stayed on the floor where she'd left it. She trusted him. Whether Bella thought that was wise, she didn't care. Whether she was going to get hurt in the end, she didn't care. And even though she gave him her trust without waiting for him to continue proving himself to her, prove himself he did.

***

On top of having someone who made her laugh, someone she could climb on top of after a long day, and someone who she could be anything other than "Doctor Hart" with, Alyssa now had a partner.

Jackson continued making dinners, and not just mac and cheese, which in Alyssa's mind would have happily sufficed, but elaborate, colorful meals with vegetables and meats and carbs all combined. "You talk about wanting us to be healthier," he'd reminded her. "Plus, my mom—"

He'd stopped abruptly. She'd wondered why, but then he'd coughed, saying he'd choked on his green beans and he guessed he shouldn't be eating and trying to tell a story at the same time. Then he'd finished, "My mom sends me some of her recipes to try. She knows I've been cooking more, and it's been a nice way to bond." *See, Bella. A good relationship with his mother is not a bad thing.*

And every Saturday night, Alyssa would open her drawers to find fresh socks and t-shirts folded neatly and put away - not always in the right spot, but he was trying. Trying - that's what Alyssa cared about more than anything.

Though she'd granted him her trust long ago, the first night he'd laid out the roast chicken, he continued to earn it back over and over and over again. He even started talking about work, sharing stories and prideful moments where he'd been able to fix a problem in record time. It sounded like the other company employees were really impressed by him, calling him the "Steve Jobs of the office." "I like that title, but I'd rather be James Bond to you over anything else."

Each week they grew closer. Him, filled with newfound pride and confidence, and her, completely open and vulnerable for the first time. They had their routine, and yet, the time they spent together somehow always felt exciting and new. This was love, Alyssa was sure of it. True, better than a storybook, richer than Porcelana chocolate, stronger than whiskey love.

Even though she'd proclaimed her love a million times, he kept their tradition of asking if she loved him and waiting for her to answer, "More than anything." She knew he didn't believe her, insisting that *his* love was ultimately greater, but he must have liked hearing her say it, because he never stopped her. And she said it all the time.

They liked to think their neighbors in the building across the street watched them fondly as they danced in front of the window to their song. Sometimes they sang together as Jackson twirled her in endless circles, and in others Jackson played along on the piano with his ever-improving musical abilities. He could sight read quite well now, and sometimes Alyssa would pull up the notes from her favorite artists on her phone and ask him to try and play it for her. But for *their* song, he didn't need the music. He knew every note, every word, by heart. *Don't you know I'll go where you go? Always by your side.*

The words rang true. He was always in her mind. Always with her. Always by her side, even when he wasn't. In conversations with co-workers, during phone calls with her mother, even in the middle of surgeries, Jackson was constantly there in the background. Nothing could wave away the misty thought bubble above her head she so carefully kept him in.

Nothing, until March. When word of a deadly virus began circulating around the hospital, and then around the world.

43

Clayton

He'd forgotten about the cell phone. And the threats to call the police. One hundred seventeen missed calls in the past week. Sixty-eight text messages. Fourteen voicemails. One more chance to provide answers before authorities got involved.

Clayton had a plan. He didn't know if it was the best plan, or even a decent one, but it was his last resort. He needed to make Courtney disappear. Not just on vacation. Not "off the grid." Gone. With no chance of coming back. No reason to keep contacting her. He was going to fake her death.

It couldn't be murder, or he'd be the number one suspect. It had to be natural, even though she was so young. *Thank you, COVID.* He couldn't lie, this virus had been so very convenient for him.

Forging the hospital records and death certificate was too easy for someone like Clayton. The internet was like a long-time lover to him. So familiar it was like he'd known her forever. Her strengths. Her weaknesses. How to manipulate her to get what he wanted.

The fact that he'd used the excuse that they were on a remote vacation worked even better. Foreign medical documents were easier to plagiarize. And as a bonus, he could choose a country with limited resources and poor health care, a place where it would surprise no one that she'd not only contracted the disease, but died from it due to lack of proper tools and treatment.

He placed her cell phone in a plastic bag to send to her family, happy to finally be rid of it. There wasn't an ocean near him he could chuck it in, and besides, why raise suspicion? He'd covered his tracks. He had nothing to hide.

Except her body.

Her family was going to want her body. *Think, Clayton, think. How can you get out of this?* Good thing he was getting better at managing his stress. He took a few breaths, closed his eyes, and tried to concentrate.

After two or three minutes of ransacking every corner of his brain for information that could help, he remembered an article he'd read while he was gathering gruesome images to show at his Salvation barbeque. He dashed over to one of the several computers he kept in his secret room in BrightView and searched for the headline.

There! "Burial traditions clash with coronavirus safety in Indonesia." The document proclaimed that the bodies of the dead had to be claimed within twenty-four hours for religious purposes. Courtney wasn't Hindu, but he could make this work. He'd tell them the hospitals were overwhelmed because of COVID and made him bury her quickly and he didn't have time to think, or that he was confused and thought he had to bury her within twenty-four hours or she'd be cremated. It didn't matter. They'd be so completely taken aback by the whole idea of Courtney being gone that they wouldn't question it.

He made one phone call, to Courtney's sister, from his own phone. Fortunately, he didn't need to conjure up real tears since she couldn't see his face; he just needed to sound like he was upset. Easy.

They'd gone on a spontaneous trip to Indonesia, where Courtney had contracted COVID and been admitted to the hospital. Sadly, they were in a poor town with limited health-care, riddled with coronavirus patients, and one thing quickly led to another. Clayton was absolutely devastated, so distraught that he couldn't call them for several days. But not to worry, he had the death certificate he could send them, along with the medical documents and her cell phone. Even her shoes, if they really wanted them. But she was already buried peacefully under the beautiful Indonesian soil. At least she'd gotten to travel before her tragic passing.

When he hung up, her sister was still crying. He knew she'd tell their mother, along with anyone else who needed to know. She hadn't asked many questions, considering she could barely speak through her sobs, let alone think straight. Much easier than expected. So easy that, specifically in this pandemic, anyone could do it.

Yes... *Anyone could do it.*

His vision slid from the cell phone to Courtney. She was a chore, but not an unmanageable one. Clean the bedpan every couple of days, refill the feeding tube and the IV, drip some water in her mouth, and that was pretty much it. Clayton had been able to manage it on his own with not only one, but two women, all while under immense pressure to complete the project of his lifetime. If he could undergo such a feat, without having any guidance or anyone to help him, surely other men

302

wouldn't have a problem if they followed his instructions.

Clayton could teach people to bring others to Salvation, even if they didn't, or *couldn't*, consent.

Over the years, he'd received dozens of letters from individuals asking if they could apply for family members or close friends instead of themselves.

"My father has been in a wheelchair for the past ten years and we've watched him slowly decline, but he would never sign up for something like this. You know how old people are, he doesn't trust technology. We are working on convincing him to try it. If we are ever successful, I hope you'll have a spot for him in Salvation!"

"Clayton, can you please talk to my brother? He won't listen to me when I tell him the Program is exactly what he needs, but maybe you could convince him. Please, he hasn't been himself lately. You're our only hope."

"Hello, I'm a healthcare professional over at The Hope Institution, and honestly, I'd say the vast majority of my patients would thrive in your world. The problem is, they are nonverbal and unresponsive to most questions so they are not able to consent. However, if we could just get them in Salvation for a few minutes, I know they'd be hooked! Is there any way that would be possible, or do you absolutely need to have their signature or verbal consent?"

Was this his solution to gaining more clients? Helping more people? He could teach their loved ones how to do exactly what he did, how to get them to Salvation even if they don't think it's a great idea, even if it's initially against their will, because he was sure they would love it and be forever grateful once they arrived.

And the extra money wouldn't hurt.

Courtney wasn't grateful, though, was she?

He could fix that. *One thing at a time.*

They could try the electroconvulsive therapy again, with a smaller shock this time. Courtney seemed happy now. Okay, so it had worked a little *too* well. But it had worked, hadn't it? She wasn't asking questions anymore. About Salvation, anyway.

Besides, Courtney had never been paralyzed or bedridden or had a miserable life. She wasn't Salvation's intended clientele. She was an accident. An accident he could learn from, perfect his methods for next time.

44

Jackson

He didn't want to sound like a jerk, but Jackson was convinced the spread of COVID-19 had come at a pretty ideal time for him.

He'd been working with his promotion for a few months before the virus hit, which typically consisted of thirty-five to forty hour work weeks. Sure, it was less than the sixty-plus hour work weeks he'd allowed Alyssa and his parents to believe he was working, but for him, it was still a lot more than he was used to.

So thankfully, coronavirus offered him a much needed two week vacation from work. Though he was sad that people were getting sick, and concerned about his mother given the secret they shared, all in all, he was in a great mood about the whole thing.

Since nearly everyone else at the college worked in person, all employees were awarded two weeks of paid time off. Jackson had no responsibilities; he could sleep, use his phone, or go online as much as he wanted during the day. And with Alyssa's hours being even longer than they were before, he had giant chunks of time where he was alone.

Actually, the part about having no responsibilities wasn't entirely true. He did promise Alyssa he would put in more effort, and part of that push meant preparing meals for them on certain nights. Well, the original agreement was three nights a week... but now that he was going to be off work for a couple weeks, was he supposed to make them dinner *every* night?

It did seem only fair. More than fair, he admitted to himself, but that still didn't make him want to roll out of bed and pick up a spatula.

Luckily, that was never part of his plan.

The plan he'd developed when he'd almost lost the best thing that ever happened to him.

The plan to have his mother make the dinners Alyssa had asked Jackson to make.

Alyssa's eyes usually reminded him of spring, when bright green starts to emerge and overtake all of the brown. But the day Alyssa found out he'd been keeping secrets from her, they'd been barren as the middle of winter. He could never make her look at him like that again.

He *wouldn't*.

And yet, here he was, with another secret.

He told himself this was different, this one wasn't hurting anyone. Alyssa didn't mind those kinds of secrets, she'd practically said so herself when she told him the video games weren't the problem and she wouldn't have broken up with him over them. No, she didn't mind that kind of secret. What had made her mad was the fact that she, in turn, had to do all the chores around the house when she thought he was busy. He'd learned his lesson: Don't tell secrets that hurt the person you love.

He concluded that secrets were sort of like lies. It's not okay to lie to your mom about borrowing money from her purse because a lie like that could come back and hurt her or someone else in the future. She might need the money for gas and get stuck, she may blame your father for taking it, or you could get into trouble with that money and she'd have to go out of her way to help you. However, it *is* okay to lie to your mom on Christmas morning when she asks you if you like the twelve pairs of Pokémon socks she got you in an advent calendar. That's what people call a white lie. It doesn't hurt anyone, and, in fact, it makes everybody happy.

That's what his plan was. A white secret.

Jackson told himself it was just a white lie, a white secret, as he ordered the chicken parmesan from Beth's diner, and kept telling himself that as he threw away the plastic containers in the dumpster in front of their complex after scooping the contents onto two of their plates in the kitchen.

First of all, he'd specifically noted that Alyssa technically asked him to "take over dinners" on certain nights. "Taking over" didn't necessarily mean "cooking." But even if it did... who was this hurting? Not him, he had the time to pick up the food and a little extra money to spend. And certainly not Alyssa, who loved chicken parm and still wouldn't have to make dinner. It was a win-win.

Before COVID, it had been a win-win-*win*, back when Jackson had gotten his mom to make the meals.

When Alyssa first gave him the assignment, he was happy to do it, if it meant keeping their relationship alive, but he didn't know where to start. He'd never been any good at cooking, even though his mom had offered to teach him time and time again. *Of course*, he'd thought. His mom could "help" him. It was the perfect plan. And if she wanted to use her own ingredients, or pick some up beforehand based on whatever lesson she had planned, who was he to stop her?

Cathy's teaching methods often shifted quickly from a mentorship to a do-it-yourself program… meaning she ended up doing it all herself. She meant well, and she did want him to learn, but she was so good at cooking and so used to not getting any help that she never really noticed if her "student" wasn't contributing. She was just happy to have the company and the conversation, which Jackson provided. His mother was excited they were spending more time together, Alyssa was thrilled with the beautiful meals and nights off from preparing them, and Jackson wasn't hating how impressed Alyssa was with him: Win-win-*win*.

But now with the virus spreading, he couldn't visit his mom. The food aspect wasn't so bad. He kept with his usual canned foods for lunch, and ordered dinners from various restaurants to keep up with his illusions. No big deal. A small price to pay for the adjournment from work.

The bigger price was his mother's health.

Jackson's mom had been diagnosed with systemic lupus erythematosus when he was twelve years old. She always told him not to worry, but he knew how dangerous SLE could be. As a kid who spent hours online, it took him all of about two minutes to figure out the sickness was a bigger deal than she wanted to make it seem. The most prominent threat: catching any sort of trivial illness.

Lupus is an autoimmune disease, which to a twelve-year-old basically meant his mom wasn't allowed near any person who was sick at all, even her own family. Even him.

Hospitals were her second home, especially during flu season.

"They just want to be extra careful, Jackie. It's nothing to worry about; I'll be home before you know it."

At first, he didn't believe her. He was afraid she would never check back out after being checked in - the white-sheeted bed like a glue-covered mousetrap, sticking its victims there and causing a slow, deteriorating death. He'd seen hundreds of examples in the articles and news reels online. Little children like himself losing their mothers as commonly as they lose teeth.

As he grew, his worries lessened. Because she always came back, sucking on her lollipop and joking about enjoying her time to herself away from her boys. Her nonchalant attitude allowed him to release some of the breath he felt he'd been holding in his chest forever.

But he always still held a little.

He could never breathe in completely deeply, and his breaths grew more and more shallow as the impact of coronavirus plagued the front page of every newspaper.

He wanted to tell Alyssa, but his mother had made him swear not to share her diagnosis with anyone outside of their own little family. She didn't even want her own mother, Jackson's grandmother, to know. When they had to cancel hosting Easter a few years ago because Cathy had gotten a cold, they had to tell his grandma that Jonathan's brother (who lived a few hours away) needed them urgently to help with a plumbing issue. And before that, they'd missed Jackson's cousin's graduation, using the excuse that their flight was canceled and there was no time to get a new one.

In a way, Jackson had always been around lies. Or as he would call them, white secrets. And while he wished he could share this part of himself with Alyssa - the anxieties, the fear, the breath stuck in his chest - he had made a pinky promise long before Alyssa had made one with Bella.

Keeping his vow, he didn't voice his concerns to Alyssa when she walked in the door. Instead, he swept her up in a storm of kisses, which she only escaped when she discovered the scent of the food coming from the reheated plates on the table. She marveled at the beautiful job "he'd" done, but then turned her attention to the new can of Chef Boyardee atop the mountain in the trash can.

"I swear, what would you do without me?" She flicked the lid of one of the cans to signal what she was talking about.

Did she realize the chicken was take-out? "What do you mean? Just look at this spread!" He tried to sound mellow, reading her expression. It seemed jovial... He was probably safe.

She confirmed his thoughts. "You're such a *guy*!" She hit him on the shoulder and he pulled her in for another kissing session. Jackson had been earning his nickname since the pandemic started. This was already shaping up to be a good couple of weeks.

"You know, like a stereotypical bachelor. It's like the classic trope in the old sitcom where the guy doesn't take care of anything unless there's a girl to motivate him. Like, you can make this gorgeous dinner when you know I'll be here, but you can barely even feed yourself when I'm away." She was rambling again. Babbling like an adorable, green-eyed brook. "Ugh, I shouldn't even be participating in those stereotypes. Guys can be all sorts of things—"

Jackson ran with that, ready to move the subject away from the microwaved dinner that she still believed was homemade. "I'll show you what guys can be!" He yanked her towards the bedroom, and she obliged happily. It must have been another

310

extra stressful day.

***

Those first two weeks had been the respite he'd been hoping for, but two weeks turned into four, then six - unpaid, then a phone call. "After great consideration, we have come to the conclusion that it isn't sustainable for us to keep our current number of staff under these unfortunate economical circumstances." They couldn't have at least bothered with a "sorry?"

Once the initial anger faded away, all that was left in its place was hopelessness. How was he going to get another job with his history? How was he going to tell Alyssa? What would she think? Would he still be the kind of guy she'd want to be with? He'd never seen a Bond film where double-oh-seven was eating potato chips on the couch, unable to provide for his girl.

Jackson had witnessed both thriving rainforests and decrepit wastelands in his lover's eyes, but when he'd wept into her chest that night, rivers running into her soul, he'd seen something new in them, a landscape he couldn't identify. Her eyes had been almost blue, as if they were absorbing his streams. At first he'd assumed it was the stormy sea of her giving up on him, overwhelmed and finally crushed by the last wave. But he'd traveled that land before, far too many times with far too many people. He'd recognize the terrain. Dare he believe this blue was the abundant ocean overflowing with unconditional love?

She'd stroked his hair as his head lay below her sternum, and he allowed the calming motion of her gentle tide rising and falling beneath him to appease his anxieties. "Don't worry, honey. You'll get another job in no time. Everything is going to be okay. And no matter what happens, I'll be here. Always by your side."

45

Clayton

Clayton clapped his hands together, glad to be done with Courtney's always-buzzing cell phone and the police threats from her family.

The faucet ran cold water onto his cloth, and he rang out some droplets into his mother's mouth. Was it just him, or was she looking worse than usual? He couldn't quite put his finger on it, but her breaths were concerningly shallow, and her skin was a shade of gray that reminded him of the clay he'd used to sculpt his first mock-up of the Oc X's. Food was probably a good idea.

Her tube refill was on the side table, but when he went to grab it, he heard "Logging out. Prepare to exit in five, four, three, two..." And then his mother was awake.

She began coughing profusely; the drips of water didn't do much for her throat. He hastily filled a new glass for her, placed a straw inside, and held it up to her lips. "Fancy seeing you here!" It was true. It'd been a while since he'd had the pleasure of talking to her in the real world. Though he typically preferred to be in Salvation, his mother was far too distracted there. Here, they could actually have a real conversation. Her attention could remain solely on him.

"Thank you, dear," she murmured, though the water didn't seem to have helped with her hacking at all. "You look awful."

Why exactly had he been hoping for her attention again? "It's been a long day. Hell, it's been a long..." He mulled over his words. *Week?* Not long enough. *Past few months?* Still not accurate. "While," he settled on.

She nodded slowly. "Yes. Your girlfriend put on quite a show the other day." Clayton didn't know how to respond. He wondered how much she knew about Courtney. How she'd gotten to Salvation. Why she was so unwell there. He'd figured she'd been far too engulfed in her own life there that she hadn't noticed. People were surprising him lately, though. Perhaps she knew more than he thought. "Anyway, I'm not here to talk about that."

Hallelujah. "Oh?" was all he could think to ask. Her coughing was distracting him.

"And don't curse. You know how I hate it."

What had he said? Oh, *hell.* He'd been away from her for too long. He'd lost the habit of watching his language extra carefully around her. He apologized and sat in awkward silence, waiting to hear what topic she had in mind.

"I just, well I..." She was struggling to form words. Was it the obvious discomfort in her throat, or was she about to say something difficult? She was going to yell at him, wasn't she? Tell him what a disgrace he was. How he'd ruined everything. Lost his chance with the investors, couldn't stop the constant chaos inside Salvation, was letting her body deteriorate in the real world. "I just wanted to tell you how very proud I am of you, Clayton."

"What?" He'd meant for the question to be only a silent thought inside his mind, but it echoed off the windowless walls and he knew the word had escaped his lips. He couldn't help it. For the first time in he didn't know how long, he was hit with a shock that was actually the good kind. He'd gotten so used to bad news and disappointment that he didn't know what to do with this information.

She gave him a big, not-so-bright smile - due to lack of teeth brushing - and an invisible string yanked the corners of his mouth into one as well. He'd seen her smile in Salvation a million times, but couldn't remember the last time she'd done it in real life. Without malice. Without a snarl behind it. Sincere.

"I said I'm proud of you. Immensely, incredibly, over-the-moon proud of you."

In theory, the words should have become less surprising the second time, but they didn't. When her avatar said them it was one thing, but coming out of her real, wrinkle-covered face... it felt like they were really coming from *her*. His mom.

She told him what he'd accomplished was amazing, and that he was the smartest boy she'd ever known. That she didn't like to coddle him, or raise his ego with compliments, but she'd always understood that he was special. "Destined for greatness," she'd said. He hugged her for what felt like an eternity, until her wheezing made him pull away. He stayed close to her face, though, and looked deeply into her eyes, savoring this moment for as long as he could.

"Do you remember when we used to play that simulator game?" Though her throat was rough and coarse, her eyes were smooth. Pure. Two puddles on the street that would soon be gone, but not before they brought joy to a child as he jumped in each one.

All at once he was infected with information he didn't want. He didn't ask for.

Somehow he just *knew*.

His mother was dying.

One millisecond ago he'd been blissfully naive. Wonderfully oblivious.

He pleaded with his own thoughts, begging them to forget the realization he'd come to, at least for a few more minutes. *Can't I have a few more minutes?*

His mother wiped away the droplets he hadn't felt forming and stopped most of them from falling down his cheeks.

Stop! Her cold hands on his wet skin made it real, and he didn't want it to be real. It couldn't be real.

"You're sick." This truth was taking up too much space in his head, suffocating him. He didn't want it to come out, but he would've broken otherwise. Saying the words out loud didn't help. His voice broke as they came out, but he was breaking more.

"You remember the one, don't you, honey? With the plane?" Georgie acted as if she hadn't heard her son. Maybe she hadn't. Maybe he was imagining things. Or maybe Time had granted his wish, turning back its hands for him, making a detour from its usual route so that he could steal a few more seconds. He'd stolen much in his life, but nothing this valuable. He didn't know what to do with it. It was so precious. Fragile. He was scared to do anything, lest it break, too.

Despite the malnutrition and the agonizing noise coming from her throat, his mother didn't look like she was in pain. She looked peaceful. She was a photo album, turning back her pages to remind him of their favorite memories. The ones with smiling faces. The only ones people place in photo albums. The only ones people think about when it's the end.

"We loved that little, blue plane. I think all those times playing with it may be my fondest memories with you. The best times we've had together. Wouldn't you agree?"

Her eyes were pleading with his to look into them, connect with them, but he couldn't. Even if he looked, the water in his would distort them anyway. He didn't want to remember them like that. "Yeah mom," he said to his fingers. "I agree."

They were both silent as he held Time in his hands. He had to accept that it wouldn't stay with him forever. He felt Time stretching in his palms, itching to catch up to where it was supposed to be. And it would catch up. He had to take advantage while he could. "Remember when you screamed the 'F' word every time we crashed the darn thing?"

"Clayton!" She looked like he'd just ratted her out for cheating on a test, or shoplifting from the grocery store. He let out a laugh, and, to his surprise, it was genuine. The sound lifted his chest and let it fall again, and repeated the process a few more times. He let it lift his mouth into the smile it was longing to form, and lift his eyes to finally meet hers. "You be quiet about that! You know it just slips out when we play those games... I don't know how it happens."

By the end of her explanation she was laughing, too. A new photo added to their album, filling the last empty slot.

His shoulders shook as he reveled in the duet they were making. He wished he could record it, put it on a CD and play it over and over and over again, forever. "Don't worry," he managed between breaths, "I won't tell anyone." Then, he couldn't resist, "Except maybe Pastor Burks. He'll want to know what a dirty mouth you've gained since you stopped going to church regularly."

She yelled at him and they joked back and forth and Time stayed in his hands for longer than he deserved but then she was gone.

He couldn't stay in the real world, the world that took her from him, the world that was plagued with a pandemi—

COVID. That cough. It was the same cough the old investor had, the one he swore was just a sore throat.

Clayton screamed into the air. Cursed at no one and everyone, and especially himself.

He shoved the Oc X's onto his face, prying his dripping eyes open, not caring that he was too forceful, that he was cutting his skin. He jabbed the IV into his arm, turned on the projector.

Gordon's annoyingly optimistic voice played in his ears. "You're allowing yourself to sink deeper and deeper into the world you want to be a part of. The world you know you deserve."

Deserve.

You know what? I do *deserve this.*

I'm owed *this.*

I've worked damn hard for this. Everything gets stripped away from me. Opportunities, chances, loved ones... they all get taken. Two can play at this game. It's my turn to take.

"Logging in in five, four, three, two..."

Fire. Smoke. Screams. The earth ripping in two. In three. In a million pieces beneath his feet.

He heard an engine failing and looked up into the sky. A blue plane. For a moment, life felt beautiful as he followed the trail of the plane. It soared against the baby-blue backdrop of a cloudless sky.

He saw himself holding the controller. His mother's laughter consumed his senses. Her face formed in the clouds. Then he

318

remembered this wasn't real.

She was dead.

The blue plane plummeted into the hillside, exploding upon impact.

His earpiece buzzed but he didn't answer it. He refused to accept reality. He wished he could live inside the daydream, in the sound of his mom's voice, even if it was all in his head.

"Clayton!" He whipped his head to see who dared interrupt his memories. It was Gordon. "What happened?"

Clayton couldn't answer. The psychologist couldn't wait. "You've got to get out of here, man. We can talk about it later. But... it's too dangerous for you to be here right now."

Dr. Avery's eyes were sad. He had the curse of those in his profession: He took on the emotions of others. He could see when they were hurt, and felt that pain right along with them. He could see through Clayton's anger, straight to the agony it was failing to mask.

"Go," he instructed, softly, and Clayton went.

Kicked out of one world, and unwilling to face the other, he was lost.

46

Jackson

He'd stupidly allowed himself to believe what Alyssa had said. That he'd be hired again in no time. That she'd be there for him. That everything would be okay.

She was a liar. At least, that's what Jackson thought as he sat at the hospital cafeteria table, waiting for his mother's dinner order to be prepared.

At first he'd tried to ignore the problems: Having to get dinner ready for Alyssa and himself every night, only spending limited time with her, even getting laid off from his job… Those were all doable. He could compartmentalize. He could force himself to share Alyssa's mantra that life would get better.

Who does she think she is? Life wasn't better. *Not even close.*

The anger seethed inside him as he watched a little girl with no hair lick an ice cream cone next to her smiling mom. *Ice cream isn't going to fix the fact that she has cancer, is it, Mom?* He wished he could send his thoughts directly to this woman. *Look where we are. This isn't Disney World, or the zoo.* How could she pretend life was happy? Especially when, most days, Jackson couldn't see the point in any of it.

Since he'd been fired, six months ago now, he'd spiraled into what he refused to admit was the beginning of a deep, dark depression. He had no control over anything anymore. He couldn't find a job, no matter how hard he tried- and he used to try a lot, but the search had slowly turned nonexistent over time.

He didn't recognize himself in the mirror, when he found the energy to get up, place his glasses on his face, and look into it. His hair was beginning to grow to a length that was too short to be trendy but too long to look intentional. Many of the barber shops were still closed, but it didn't matter anyway. He couldn't risk going to one and compromising his mom's health whenever he visited.

He hadn't loved taking showers even before his life went to hell, and he surely didn't have more motivation now than he did then, so there was a layer of grease in his hair that he became highly aware of when he saw an exceptionally attractive doctor sit down a few tables over with perfect hair, a perfect body, and perfect teeth to boot. And that jacket he wore over his scrubs... Something was familiar about it.

Jackson stared at the man and his mind wandered back to before he'd met Alyssa. He'd known he was never the most attractive guy in the room, but he'd always tried to have confidence. Every podcaster he listened to, and even his own father, preached the power of confidence. He used to be pretty good at pretending to be confident. And through the course of his relationship with Alyssa, he'd begun to not have to fake it anymore.

Watching this guy was like a spike to the heart of his confidence, killing it completely. Not only was this man handsome, but he looked happy too. Genuinely happy. *Jerk.* And he was obviously successful. He was a doctor for crying out loud, maybe even a surgeon, like Alyssa. He did have the same uniform.

Jackson bet this guy hadn't been slowly losing everything throughout this pandemic. Business was booming for him. He most assuredly wasn't running out of money. Unlike Jackson, *he* wasn't wondering how he was going to pay the rent next month. And he probably got to spend more time with Alyssa than Jackson did.

Alyssa. Alyssa was his lighthouse, and he needed her to lead him out of these thoughts, back to the shore.

Lately, her light had faded from a solid beam to a dwindling dot on the verge of going out completely.

She didn't run to Jackson when she got home like she used to. Before, her lips were like a magnet to his, and if they still were, it was a magnet flipped to the other side, repelled by his force. She made up every excuse in the book: She was tired, she didn't feel well, she'd had a twelve-hour surgery... He'd heard it all.

These days, when he reached out his hands to touch her, she shrugged them away, often using his mom as an excuse. "You're visiting her soon, and I've been around sick people all day. We shouldn't get too close."

She divulged her stress more than ever, but didn't want any relief. She just wanted to complain. And not in her unique, over-dramatic fashion that always used to make him laugh. She vented with exhaustion, as if the simple act of even discussing her day was a chore, too much for him to ask of her.

With all the tension, Jackson still hadn't found a way to confess his financial inadequacies to her. He'd had to fight off his demons for a bit so he would be able to talk to her tonight.

As much as he wanted to keep it a secret, this was much more than a white secret. This one was a bright, crimson red. And anyway, she was going to find out by tomorrow when she went to cash in their rent checks.

"Cathy Halloway, order 152?" He grabbed the tray with too much force, and the woman serving the meals stumbled in surprise. He had to get it together, for his chat with Alyssa tonight, and, more immediately, his visit with his mother right now. He took some deep breaths, but thinking of his mom drew his attention back to the very reason he was here: His life was falling apart. He'd lost his job, run out of money, his relationship was failing, a virus was keeping him trapped in his apartment, and to top it all off, his mother was in the hospital.

Stop it. His mom didn't need to see him like this. She just needed to get better. He approached her room and saw himself reflected in the window. He really should have showered before coming.

Sure enough, his hygiene was the first thing she noticed, as usual. "Jackson, I thought you were taking better care of yourself now that you're living with Alyssa." She gave him that look that mothers give: judgmental, yet loving at the same time.

He stuttered, because even though he'd expected this from his mother, known she would comment, it strangely still caught him off guard. Denial allows a person to believe two truths at the same time. In Jackson's case, he knew the weight he carried was heavier than the average sadness, but he also was sure it wasn't. "I– I am, well, I was, but, you know…"

"No, I don't know." Now that she'd had a chance to hear his shaky voice, see the despair he knew wasn't hidden on his face, she turned pale, more sick than he'd ever seen her. "Talk to me. What's going on."

Even with his mom, Jackson wasn't able to get out the whole truth. But he did let her know that he was worried. Worried about her, worried about work, and worried about his relationship.

He left out the parts about being worried for himself. His anger. His hopelessness.

She clucked her tongue at him, taking extra care to sound like he was being ridiculous. It was the same tone Alyssa used when she said everything was going to be okay. But Alyssa had been wrong. Everything was not okay. Not even close.

"First of all, you don't need to worry about me. You know how it goes; it's always just a precaution. They don't want a lawsuit on their hands, so they make me hunker down in here for a while. And I always come home feeling fit as a fiddle, don't I?"

He couldn't argue with that. "You always do. But this is scary, there are so many people dying, and—"

"What's scary is the thought of you losing Alyssa, honey." Her words startled him. So blatant. So blunt. "Everything else in life can be lost and then found again: jobs, apartments, money... all those material items. But love," she looked at him like he was a little boy again, "Love is not so easily salvaged. If that girl walks away from you, it's not a guarantee that you'll be able to get her to come back."

He was quiet for a few seconds. Hearing his greatest fear spoken, out loud, by someone other than himself... terrified him. And as scared as he was, his mom looked at least twice as worried. After the short silence, he finally dared to ask, "Do you really think she'd leave me?"

His mother's pause was even longer than his. "Honestly, I don't know, Jackie. But if she did..." Her voice cracked as she trailed off. Jackson thought this was odd. He knew she loved Alyssa, but not to this extent. "Well," she continued, after collecting herself, "we just need to make sure that doesn't happen, don't we?"

There was a poorly masked tone of desperation in her voice. What happened to "We don't force people to love us, honey?" What about "If she wants to go, let her go?"

She knew.

She knew what Jackson would never say out loud: He wouldn't survive without Alyssa.

He'd grown too attached. Dependent. She was everything to him, *did* everything *for* him. He couldn't even make dinner for them, for God's sake. And he wanted to. He'd really wanted to learn to cook for them, to be the man who could take care of them. So why hadn't he? As his mind wandered around, following this train of thought, he concluded that this was a pattern of his: constantly wanting to be better, but constantly failing.

The only times he was even half the man he wanted to be was when her love was the bait on the end of the hook dangling in front of him. If she reeled it away, he'd be left with nothing. No reason to try anymore.

But she hadn't reeled in her line... not yet. That worm was still squirming within his reach, and he needed to get it while he still had the opportunity. Before it was too late. He looked square into his mother's eyes, a flame forming in his that he hoped would spread like wildfire. "What do I need to do?"

Cathy smiled at her son, and it appeared that the fire had indeed made its way to her eyes, as well. "You need to tell her that it's not gonna be easy. It's gonna be really hard, and you're gonna have to work at it every day. But you wanna do that because you want her. You want all of her, forever. You and her. Every day."

There was no mistaking the infamous film, but he let her complete the dialogue even after he'd known the answer from the second line. He could breathe again, seeing his mom be his mom. Not the sick lady in the hospital bed, just his mom.

"*When Harry Met Sally?*" He smiled back at her, a real smile, waiting for her reaction, knowing he'd get one.

Her face dropped and she huffed, looking entirely too disappointed. "Are you serious? Oh, my gosh, Jackson, no, it's—"

"*The Notebook.* I know. I just wanted to see if I could get your heart rate high enough to make your monitor go crazy." It kept its steady beeping, with no fluctuation. "Guess I'll have to try harder next time!" There was some life coming back into his cheeks.

His mom punched his shoulder, like Alyssa used to do. What he'd make sure she'd do again.

"There's a reason why that movie's so popular. What Noah says is true: Relationships take work, every single day. Starting today. What time is Alyssa getting home?"

It was a Thursday, and all her shifts were impossibly long since COVID invaded. "Not 'til really, really late."

His mom mulled over that information briefly, then shrieked, "Oh! You should bring her some coffee!"

That wasn't as possible as his mom made it sound. He could never find Alyssa. He was here fairly often visiting his mother, and Alyssa was always in some surgery. "That won't really work, she's usually in the OR for hours."

Cathy wasn't giving up. "Then you'll wait hours! What else have you got to do?" She had a point. "Come on, Noah didn't say he wanted to work for Allie but only if it took twenty minutes.

326

He said he wanted to do it even when it's really hard. Every day. Right now, you have every day with her ahead of you. Don't let that go. If you have the chance to keep someone you love from leaving you, you need to take it, Jackie. We don't always get that chance." Her eyes were glistening, and there was a faraway look in them. It was like her body was in this moment, but her mind was in another. Then her pupils turned back to him, the fire already extinguished. "I'm sorry you won't get that chance."

Wow. She really wanted him and Alyssa to be together. "Okay okay mom, chill. I'll get her the coffee, alright?"

Whatever emotional tactic she was trying to use on him was working. *Geez, you'd think someone was dying the way she's talking.*

It kind of *was* like life or death, in a way. His life. Alyssa was his life. And he wasn't ready for it to be over.

47

Clayton

Grief had given Clayton time to think. Anger had shaped his new ideas. He was ready to get back into Salvation. But this time, he was going to do things his way.

Screw the old Salvation. Screw helping people like his mother. Look what his attempts had gotten her: buried six feet in the ground. People like her, weak people, damaged people, they were bound to live a short, miserable existence, and he should've left it that way.

But people like him, *they* were the ones who truly deserved to live. They were strong. They were ready. They had waited long enough.

The world takes everything from people like Clayton. He was bullied as a child. His father left, and his mother had never truly been there for him. She'd blamed him for her injuries. Insinuated he was stupid. She'd been so busy focusing on herself that she'd never stopped to wonder if he might have been hurting too.

People like Clayton were stomped on, by the Converse of the

cool boys and the high heels of the pretty, popular girls. No one ever offered them a hand. Not their parents, or their teachers, or the janitors, or the lunch ladies... No one. They'd always been alone. It was time to bring them together, and he was going to be the one to do it.

It was their turn. The world owed them for using them as its own personal punching bag all of these years.

Clayton thought back to all the opportunities he'd lost to the people the world smiled on. Claudia had won first place in the science fair because she was cute and didn't have to go to school wearing clothes from the Goodwill and her mom was on the school board. Henry had received the promotion at work because he wore Calvin Klein suits and knew how to use hair gel and went to a barber in the heart of the city who shaved his face with a razor and used hot towels. Leonardo had gotten every girl he'd ever had a crush on in school because he was six foot two by freshman year and his daddy bought him a sports car.

Clayton was done with the charity cases in the hospitals and senior homes. It was time for men like him to finally have the life they'd always wanted. The life they deserved.

And he knew just where to find these men.

He turned to the place where men like him tend to feel the most at home: The internet. Online chat rooms. Forums. Every corner he'd crawled to when *he* was bored. Lonely. Bitter.

Incels. Losers. Creeps. These were all names men like him had been given. But it's not who they really are. No one ever took the time to consider that. Clayton understood them. He was one of them.

Over time he'd learned to blend into society. He'd observed what sorts of clothes successful men tended to wear, the way they held their body when they walked into a room, and, most importantly, how they spoke.

In those early years directly following his mother's accident, she'd been getting paid enough by the state that Clayton's only job was being her full time caretaker. She hadn't wanted to talk, and she couldn't and wouldn't do much with him, so he'd spent those years watching people. Learning from them. The men on television taught him more than any college professor. And when he'd discovered the secret corners of the internet, a whole new world opened up for him.

YouTube tutorials showed him how to ace job interviews. Social media allowed him to practice his people skills again and again and again until he could predict their responses. Reddit was where he found his friends. Friends who were not quite as lucky as he was. Who never were able to shake away their awkwardness. Never able to live the life the less deserving men got to live.

Until now.

This should have been his mission all along. It made perfect sense. These types of men would form a line a mile long to be a part of his virtual world. They were already holed away, had already isolated themselves from the rest of the world. Wouldn't be missed. They wouldn't judge him for what he'd done to Courtney. In fact, they could do it too. They could bring whatever girl they wanted. The cute waitress who wouldn't give them the time of day. The ex who'd left too soon. A random sex worker they found on the street - what did he care?

More users equaled more money. More power. And he'd already been thinking about teaching people how to bring on other users even without their permission. It was all coming together.

The more he thought about it, the more perfect his new plan was. Dr. Barnes said Courtney needed to feel less alone. He could recruit these men to join him, to work for him, and they could each bring a woman with them. Plenty of friends to solve his Courtney problem.

He wouldn't have to hire female employees, to *pay* women to join, not when the men could take care of "recruiting" females for him... for free. Everybody wins.

That's what these men wanted, wasn't it? A world where they could have every desire they'd forever been denied handed to them on a silver platter? *Is sex not our greatest desire?*

And these kinds of men would make the perfect employees. Most of these sad, lonely men were exactly what he needed: coders who could help him fix the glitches in his world, graphic designers and construction workers who could build the utopia he'd envisioned, men who couldn't get jobs anywhere else because of their lack of social skills or their shady pasts or the pandemic.

Clayton could afford to hire them all, and pay them handsomely. Now that his mother was gone, he could take out all the money from the government in one lump sum - what he'd wanted to do from the very beginning. The money was in the millions. Enough to buy him a couple of years to build Salvation into the world of his dreams. A world investors would have bidding wars over. He could picture it now. The ugly, COVID-ridden, old, tall man would eat his words. He would have to live with the neverending regret until it killed him, just like he'd killed his mother.

His army of employees would work for him in the real world during the day, perfecting his empire, and in return, they would get to log into Salvation at night. They'd give him what he wanted, and he'd give them what they wanted: Sex. Money. A life of luxury. They'd live like kings.

***

After three notebooks had been filled to the brim, ideas written down and crossed out, then new ideas replacing the old, he'd come up with the new Salvation. A Salvation fit for his fellow "incels, losers, and creeps." They'd be transported to a world where perfect men had perfect women and perfect food and perfect homes and the world was the way it should be. A man's world.

No more feminist bullshit.

No more "equality."

No more "nice guys finish last."

This world would be straight out of an old sitcom, like *Father Knows Best*, or *I Love Lucy*. The women could have their fun, but they would stay in their lanes. Keep house. Serve their husbands.

The ideal, suburban family dynamic.

A life Clayton had only seen on TV. A life he'd always envied. A life he never thought he would have. A life all of these poor men never dreamed they could have.

Just call me the Sandman, because I'm about to grant them their wildest dreams.

It was genius, in his humble opinion. Just like the "good old days" that Clayton had never gotten to be a part of, men could have anything they dreamed of. And they would go to work, sure, but when they got home, they'd never have to lift a finger. Whatever they wanted, whatever they *deserved*, would be given to them.

The best part was that Clayton already knew this was possible. He'd thought Courtney had been a mistake, but perhaps she'd been the key to all of this. She'd opened his eyes to what this world could be, showed him that he could manipulate the audio tapes, make her act as he pleased. There were still some issues, but nothing his newfound millions of dollars couldn't sort out. Millions of dollars could buy him what he needed most: help. He could bring in people to fix his broken world. To fix girls like Courtney.

He pitched his new idea to Dr. Barnes first, who he'd known would say yes because he was loyal. He had come this far. He couldn't go back. The doctor's emotionless eyes, staring at nothing, told Clayton that he wished he could go back. That he didn't want to be here. But "want" wasn't a word in his vocabulary anymore. If he continued to be loyal, Clayton told him, he could gain that word back. Clayton could give him anything he wanted. When Clayton made this promise, however, he knew it was an empty one if the only thing the doctor really wanted was to turn back time. Time can be merciful, but not that merciful. Clayton had recently learned this lesson, and it was time Dr. Barnes did too.

***

Gordon wasn't on board, and Clayton still had nothing to hold over the psychologist's head.

"Absolutely not. I've gone along with your crazy antics because I believe in helping people, and I thought that's what we were doing, but this is crossing a line. Even more than perhaps we already have."

Dr. Avery's "we" sounded a lot like "you," and Clayton didn't appreciate it. "*We* weren't getting anywhere standing behind that line, so I suggest *we* learn how to cross it or *we* will be left behind."

Gordon reached out to touch Clayton's shoulder. *What kind of game is he playing?* Though a part of him wanted to swat the man's chubby fingers away, another part was curious to let the game continue. Clayton was especially good at games. He had nothing to lose.

"Look, man, I know you're going through a lot right now." *Who told him about Georgie?* "But I can't stand by you anymore. Things are getting out of control." Where was his loyalty? "I've been keeping my mouth shut, but I need answers, and I think you need somebody to talk to. I'll listen, I really will, but I can't continue helping you with this project."

No, no, no! Clayton needed Gordon to keep recording his tapes, otherwise he wouldn't be able to enter Salvation. It was impossible to put himself in. "I have no problem answering your questions. I have nothing to hide."

"What about your girlfriend?" Clayton had never heard Gordon raise his voice like this before. His adrenaline was clearly pumping, and Clayton's rose to match. "What was that sign supposed to mean? You've done something to her, haven't you?"

He'd dealt with chiming cell phones and spineless investors and disposing of the daily contents of two separate bedpans, but he was not about to put up with one of his own men turning against him. "She's fine! It was a slight mishap, that's all!"

"No," Gordon shook his head rapidly from side to side, "She's not fine. You've done something to her. I know you have. And if you don't want to talk to me about it, it must be pretty awful. I can't help you if you don't talk to me."

Clayton was done. "Take a break, Dr. Avery."

"Excuse me?"

"You heard me. Log out. Get out of here for a while. Clear your head. Think it through. And come back ready to work."

He tried to make it easy. He tried to be reasonable.

"No! That's not a solution, and I'm not going to change my mind. What you're doing is wrong, maybe even illegal, and I—"

"I said take a break!" Clayton's mouth was a matchbox, his words the matches, and his guilt was gasoline spilled on the ground. Once the words rubbed against his lips they caused a flame, which shot to the ground and there was an immediate explosion.

As he yelled, he lunged at Dr. Avery and shoved him into the glass dome that made up the top of headquarters, where they'd been standing. When Gordon hit the glass, it shattered from the force, and he tipped backwards, falling down, down, down to the pavement, along with the shards of glass. Clayton counted the seconds his mangled body laid in a disfigured heap, staining the concrete: One, two, three... poof. Gordon was gone, but the crimson pool remained. A warning. This was Clayton's world, and no one was going to tell him how to run it.

There was one, teeny tiny problem, however. The brain adjusts to repeated audio too quickly. Once the same hypnosis is repeated, it becomes ineffective. It's essential for the audio tapes to be updated regularly; otherwise they simply turn into white noise. In other words: without Gordon's voice, Clayton had no way to log back in.

48

Jackson

itting at the reception desk was a young, freckled nurse who seemed approachable. "Hello! All check-ins are virtual now, you can just fill out your information on that touch screen over there." She flashed him a perfectly white smile that made him wonder if she'd wanted to go into dentistry, originally, and gestured towards the kiosk.

"Oh, um, actually, I'm looking for a surgeon who works here. Her name is Alyssa Hart."

Like it was second nature, the girl responded, "Any information you want from your surgeon can be asked through one of our assistants. Fill out this card with your question and they'll get her answer to you just as soon as they can." *Guess they haven't gone completely virtual*, Jackson mused as she handed him a small, white slip of paper.

"Sorry," he corrected, "Alyssa Hart isn't my surgeon, she's uh, she's my girlfriend."

For some reason Jackson felt embarrassed again, like no one would believe this greasy-haired slob of a boy could possibly be dating someone like Alyssa. It must have been a combination of his recent insecurities mixed with the attractiveness of the nurse, and all the employees at this hospital, for that matter. He thought back to the muscular man who'd also had straight white teeth and tanned skin.

But the pretty girl didn't seem to judge him at all. In fact, she squealed, and some of the people waiting in the chairs looked up, amused. "Oh...em...gee!" She separated the letters so distinctly that they sounded like their own words. "You're Jackson?"

"In the flesh," he replied, feeling a bit more like he belonged, and sort of relieved that Alyssa mentioned him. *A lot*, apparently. Maybe things weren't as bad as he thought. Then he remembered his mission. "I want to bring her some coffee and say hi to her, if that's possible." He was staring down at his hands before, but the nurse's excitement helped him look up. "I can wait as long as it takes. Hours, even, if she's in surgery."

You'd think Jackson was the star of *The Notebook* the way the young girl looked at him now. "Oh my goodness, isn't that just the sweetest thing!" She placed her hand over her heart. "Why don't you have a seat right over there." She pointed to a newer, more comfortable-looking chair compared to the ones all the other waiters were plopped down in. "You just make yourself at home and I'll give you a nice little ten minute warning when she's close to being finished so you can get her coffee nice and fresh, how's that sound?"

It sounded wonderful, and Jackson told her so. He hadn't thought to bring a charger, so after a couple hours his phone was dead and he decided to lay his head back, close his eyes, and rest. The next thing he knew, the nurse was tapping his shoulder and giving him directions to the lounge Alyssa would soon be in.

He smoothed his hair back, thankful for the courage the

freckled girl's nonjudgmental smile had given him. He did need a shower, but now that he peered around the room, he looked better than most of the people in here. It was a hospital, not a nightclub, after all.

Satisfied with the way his hair laid, and the straightness of the lid on the coffee cup, he puffed out his chest and headed towards the lounge. *This is going to be great.* Alyssa would be as thrilled as the little nurse. Maybe even some of her colleagues would compliment his gesture just like the girl had, and it would already be the fresh start he needed in order to mend the unstable bridges he'd been slowly letting crumble and fall piece by piece into the water ever since he'd lost his job. Maybe even before that, if he was being honest with himself- which he rarely liked to be. But this could be it. The beginning of his "Notebook-style" redemption arc.

The room was within his view, and the bait was within his reach. There was Alyssa! Ridiculously perfect-looking after this many hours and not a splash of make-up. The hair that framed her face was sticking to her forehead, but she was smiling. He knew that smile: a little extra toothy, sending new shades of pink to her cheeks. He knew what that smile meant. She'd look at him, and—

She wasn't looking at him. She didn't even know he was here yet. So who was she...

The perfect-toothed nurse's male counterpart, with scrubs the color of Alyssa's. And a smile the size of hers, to match.

He wasn't smiling like that in the cafeteria.

In the few milliseconds Jackson dared peek at the doctor, he took off that familiar gray jacket he'd been wearing before - and placed it around Alyssa's shoulder's.

That's where he recognized it from! It all came back to him

338

now… this may have even been the same break room from the Facebook post. Back when he'd first looked up Alyssa, and seen that very same jacket, covering her as she slept. He'd barely known her then, and he'd still had to fight off the twinges of jealousy beginning to permeate his skin.

Those pricks of envy had stung even after he'd only met her one time, for less than ten minutes, and didn't know anything about her except that her laptop had died, she went to UMich, and he needed to know more. Goosebumps rose on his arm from the thousand needles stabbing him because now, he knew everything. *Loved* every part of her. More than anything. More than everything.

He knew her entire soul, from how she liked her coffee to her deepest fears and desires to the way her pajama top bunched up from sleep every night, revealing a pattern of moles on her ribcage that looked like a smiley face. He knew why she never mentioned her father and that she loved strawberry ice cream even in the middle of winter and that she was way too overworked lately but wouldn't cry on anyone's shoulder but his.

He knew that she played Tetris on her phone when she couldn't sleep, and that she once went on a first date where the guy sang to her in the restaurant, acapella, unironically, and that the restaurant was called Turned Tables, and she'd gone on two other first dates to the same restaurant before. And he knew how much she loved the movie quotes game he played with his mom, and how much she used to love life, but knowing her, he also knew she'd since lost some of that spark she'd had in the campus store.

At least… I thought I knew her. Knew everything about her. Maybe I was wrong.

He didn't know everything. For starters, he didn't know who this guy was, sharing a jacket with his girlfriend. He didn't know when he'd last seen Alyssa's smile that wide. And he didn't know what to say as Alyssa's eyes finally shifted and saw him standing there near the doorway.

The coffee slipped from his palm and hit the floor, the contents exploding a representation of his current state of mind. If everything hadn't already been building up, he might have been able to think more clearly, but it had, and he couldn't. He wanted to scream as his heart sank down like the Titanic, a ship which passengers had been guaranteed wouldn't sink, but it happened anyway.

Alyssa swore their foundation was secure, that no leaks would be able to get in. But Jackson had watched as their boat sailed recklessly forward these last several months when they both knew it wasn't strong enough to sail as fast as they had been going before. They were both too proud to acknowledge they needed to take a step back. And now they were about to slam into an iceberg.

Alyssa raced over to help him clean up the mess, unphased by him witnessing her interaction, and seeming excited to see him there. The iceberg flashed his pearly whites at Jackson, exclaiming that he'd heard "so much about him," and gripped his hand in a strong shake. Jackson eyed him for what seemed like the thousandth time. He should have been alleviated, as Alyssa had clearly told even Mr. Flirty here about his existence, and their status.

But he wasn't.

All he could see were the muscles and the two-hundred-dollar haircut. The tall stature and clean-shaven face. The smile creases at the sides of Mr. Perfect's mouth, cutting a sharp line in his cheeks, resembling a little too closely the ones worn by Sean Connery. He was everything Jackson wished he could be. Everything he didn't feel like he ever was, let alone now, in this moment - jobless, unkempt, kneeling over a puddle of brown liquid.

However, gut wrenching as it may be, "Will," as he introduced himself, wasn't the iceberg at all. Compared to what was happening down the hall, this Bond wanna-be was merely a tiny wave in their ocean, lifting their ship for a brief moment, causing no damage.

A nurse raced past them, headed towards the real glacial mass. Then another, her pager beeping wildly from the waistband of her scrubs. Will and Alyssa paid no mind to her, clearly used to this type of frenzy. But Jackson had a pit in his stomach deep enough to force him to forget about his girlfriend and her "work boyfriend" now beside him on the floor, and the spilled beverage which was the reason they were on their knees.

Like a sailor lured by a siren call, his body stood up and carried him out of the doorway of the lounge, through the labyrinth of hallways, towards his mother's room.

All the nurses made it impossible for him to walk inside, or to believe things would ever be the same. One look at the scene, and the siren whispered in his ear: *Your mother is dead.*

Later, an actual person would confirm the voice was right, but he didn't need the confirmation. The pit in his stomach hadn't been a pit at all - it was a hole. A puzzle with a missing piece. No, a stolen piece. It had been taken from him.

Mom was right. "If you have the chance to keep someone you love from leaving you, you need to take it, Jackie. We don't always get that chance. I'm sorry you won't get that chance."

She hadn't been talking about Alyssa, had she? She must have known.

Another liar.

She'd betrayed him just like Alyssa had. How could she not have warned her own son? She hadn't asked him to convince his dad to visit early or anything; he wasn't going to come until tomorrow because of work. Nothing made sense anymore. She didn't even let him say goodbye.

He scanned his mind for a movie quote, some way to pretend the world wasn't falling apart as quickly and furiously as the tears were falling down his face. What felt like moments ago, his mother's face was smiling up at him. Moments ago, he was thinking about how happy she would be when he and Alyssa told the story of how they rekindled their love over a cup of coffee because of her. Moments ago, the only scenes playing in his head were from *The Notebook*. He wanted an example with just as much of a happy ending, but the only film that came to his mind was *Blade Runner*: "All those moments will be lost in time, like tears in rain."

49

Clayton

There was no time to worry about Gordon. If he was going to contact the police, he would have done so by now. Clayton could only hope Dr. Avery was taking advantage of his forced logging out, using the time to come to the conclusion that Clayton's world was one he was lucky to be a part of. That he shouldn't concern himself with the morality of Clayton's methods, rather, he should be *grateful* for the privilege he was being offered. Because that's what Salvation was: a privilege. One Clayton was pretty sure the psychologist wouldn't be able to live without now that he'd grown accustomed to it. The man hid under the guise of wanting to "help people," but Clayton couldn't believe that was his only motivation. No one is that selfless. He'd be back.

Once Dr. Avery returned, Clayton would be able to log back in, be the most perfect version of himself again, and everything would return to the way it was supposed to be. In the meantime, Clayton had some recruiting to do.

He knew his target audience now: men who were reminiscent of himself, who were misunderstood, outcast, lonely, and desperate. Desperate was the most important quality. He couldn't risk any more mistakes. People wanting to leave. People thinking about tattling. No, he would be smarter this time. Desperation ensures loyalty. Desperation guarantees no one can rebel.

How could desperate souls be found? By their pleas. If he could get inside these men's minds, hear their inner thoughts, he could hand-pick employees who would be sure to pledge their loyalty to him. Some men pray on their knees to Jesus in the middle of the night, begging for their wishes to be granted. Others are willing to make deals with the Devil. Both vow to pledge their undying loyalty if their cries are heard and answered. Clayton could be their savior, bringing them Salvation from the cold world and gifting them a spot in heaven. He could also wield a pitchfork and watch the world burn... he wasn't picky. Either way, he was what they were looking for.

Time to call upon his old love, once again.

The internet was his solution.

She would be his guide. The portal through which he could peer into their minds and read their thoughts. After all, what reveals more about a man's deepest desires than his search history?

Though Clayton detested being stuck in the real world with his weakened body and worsened imperfections, he used the time to his advantage. After eighteen hours of energy drinks and bloodshot eyes focused on his many screens, he'd created a database.

Many years ago, he'd nearly been recruited by the FBI because of his abilities, but this was a much more lucrative use of his talents. His position would have been a technical analyst, which meant he'd have been asked to help the BAU find their suspects, using the world wide web instead of sirens and guns. While the rest of the agents would be out in the field, he would utilize a computer to search for the unsub.

With the FBI's database, he would have been able to seek out the culprit by narrowing down his options. For example, if he knew the unsub was a male who lived in Chicago, he could start there. However, he'd have over a million options. So, he'd need more information. Maybe he'd discovered the unsub had burn marks on his body, so he'd narrow his search to only men who had medical records indicating those types of burns, which would lessen his options to a dozen. He'd learn the man was heard speaking Russian by one of the witnesses, so he could search for someone who's parent's descended from Russia and voila! Only one remaining choice! That was their guy.

Clayton's database worked in a similar format. The system would first scan for men with the skills he needed: architects, engineers, coders… anyone who could help *fix* Salvation, build it into the world he envisioned. Once those men were found, he would use their search history to narrow his choices down to only men who seemed otherwise hopeless. *Desperate.*

Their despair called to him like a Siren, their keywords like morbid lyrics in a mermaid's disturbing song.

Their fingers were googling loneliness and grief, but they may as well have been playing notes on an enchanted piano. "How to get a girlfriend" was the hook, "How to get out of debt quick" was the chorus, and "How to get over depression" was the bridge that tied the melody together.

50

Derek

This was never going to change, was it? The sixteen minutes and twenty-seven seconds would never really end, would they? They'd be stuck inside of a never-moving clock. An hour glass that drips water instead of sand, except the bitter cold will keep the water frozen in place forever.

He thought the worst thing he'd ever have to experience was watching Bianca go through the miscarriage. Seeing the woman he loved refusing to eat. Staring at the wall. Losing herself. Giving up.

He was wrong.

If the miscarriage was an earthquake, the death of Bee was the whole world splitting in two, spilling its contents into space to be lost in the void until the end of time.

I'm never going to get her back, am I? It was a miracle he'd been able to fish her old self out of the murky, black lake already. What were the odds a second cast would reach her again?

As the days turned into weeks that rolled into months, Derek grew terrified. He threw his net out over and over again, every single day. It was all he did anymore, ignoring his aching arms and burning muscles, tossing it out again and again, searching for his Bianca. The light she'd lost. The will that went along with it. And nothing. He was panicked. Scared. He didn't have much strength left.

"I think it's time," he told her mother, reluctantly. Gravely. "I have to go back to work, and none of us can get her to eat enough as it is." He sighed, a shell of his former self, only holding his cracked pieces together for a woman who would probably never notice. Who'd likely never make room in her brain for anything other than sorrow. At least, that's how it was beginning to feel. "I've already been in contact with them. They can take her on Monday if that's what we decide."

Derek's mother-in-law had never looked more like Bianca than she did now. They'd both lost their daughters in that crash. "Whatever you think." She had a faraway look in her eyes. He recognized it easily. He saw it every day, every night before he closed his eyes to pretend to sleep. Unlike Bianca, however, her mother could still acknowledge reality every now and then. Still look people in the eye, occasionally, and she peered over at Derek's now. "I trust you. If you can't help her... I trust you."

Her eyes were so sad he found himself wishing that faraway look would come back. He almost missed it.

He dropped Bianca off at St. Mary's at exactly 7:00 in the morning, the moment they would accept her. They were his only hope. They had a great reputation. They could help her... couldn't they? They had to. He took a deep breath, and remembered his search:

Best trauma care centers near me

St. Mary's had been the very first place that popped up. They

had five star reviews. The internet was an interesting place...
the fate of his marriage, of a woman's mental state, dependent
on yellow filled in stars. Questionable as it was, this was the
only solution.

He'd done his fair share of research long before he'd gotten
to this point.

How to help my wife with depression?
    Can people ever get over trauma?
    What qualifications do you need for adoption?
    Is there a grief hotline I can call?
    What can I do for my wife who has postpartum?
    Does my wife still love me even if she can't show it?
    How often does the death of a child lead to divorce?
    How to get a depressed person to eat?
    **How to know when to submit someone to the psych
ward?**

All those questions, and St. Mary's had been the only answer
he'd been able to find. Until he was contacted by Clayton
Reeves.

51

Jackson

If losing his job had been the beginning stage of Jackson's now significant depression, losing his mom was the climax, and losing Alyssa could quite possibly be his final chapter. Though he couldn't fathom life without her, he also couldn't do anything to keep her from going. On a good day, he could microwave his own lunch and remember to eat it. And on a bad day... there was certainly not enough energy inside him to try and save his relationship.

Even if he could talk about it, his friends online wouldn't be any help with this sort of emotional trauma, his dad had left to go be with his mother's family in Ohio - not that he would have been any more help than twenty-something "gamer bros" anyway, and the only person he'd been close enough to discuss his love life with was... no longer available for him to confide in.

Sometimes he talked to her anyway, letting his voice float into the air, hoping a gust of wind would catch it and carry it into the heavens for him, but he never got a reply.

The one small spark of hope he still had was that, right now,

Alyssa didn't seem to care what he did. She told him not to worry about the rent, which they'd ultimately had to discuss in the midst of their grief since it had been due, and no longer held him to his promise of working around the house.

That's the interesting thing about pity: it gives you exactly what you wanted, but makes you feel like you don't want it anymore. Like asking a genie for a wish, and it's granted with a series of loopholes and tricks that make you wish you'd never made the wish in the first place. Or at least rephrased it.

He wasn't expected to do anything but mourn, and he took that job very seriously. Every day, he layed in bed, letting his head swirl with thoughts of misery and sorrow. He thought about how *everything sucks*, and everyone had lied to him and manipulated him. His boss and coworkers had all told him he was indispensable to the company. Alyssa said things would get better. His mom said she was fine.

But as much as he wanted to hate all of them, he couldn't. Two of the three being taken from him had taught him that *having* something, no matter how much anguish it may cause you, is always better than losing it.

***

No one has ever really been able to pinpoint exactly how long grief should last, or how much of a grace period should be allotted, but everyone seems to agree that it eventually has to end.

When you're a kid and your grandma dies, you might get a week out of school, and everyone is so kind, and tells you to "take as much time as you need," but they don't really mean that. At some point, whether you feel okay or not, you have to turn in your project about the tropical rainforests or the most recently extinct species of primate.

At first, Alyssa had encouraged him to, "just rest, you'll find another job, baby, right now your only job is to try and process everything and feel better." She swore he could take all the time he needed, that there was no rush.

Like those childhood teachers, she did, in time, decide that enough was enough. She'd run out of patience. It was time to submit his project.

She wouldn't say it, but Jackson was sure that by the six month mark, she thought he was milking the situation. And maybe, to some degree, he was. But it's hard to go back to school when your mother has let you stay home and eat ice cream for breakfast and take naps whenever you want because "sleep heals," and you get to watch Netflix in your pajamas all day... especially when you never liked going to school in the first place.

"I can't keep paying rent for both of us, baby, I... I just can't." She looked worse than he'd ever seen her. In her case, that was still more beautiful than most girls. But compared to their museum dates and James Bond marathon days, she was hardly recognizable.

Were the dark gray circles under her eyes his fault? What about the definition of her rib cage as she reached up to run her stressed hands through her uncombed hair? There used to be a healthy layer of fat where those bones stuck out, accentuating her womanhood and emphasizing her enjoyment in the indulgences of life.

She paced back and forth, her scrub pants sliding down her waist even though the strings were pulled tightly together in a bow. "I still have so many student loans to pay off, you knew this when we met."

Yes, he decided, this was all his fault. She was right; he did know that. They'd discussed financials at length when hunting for apartments together. Alyssa had been impressed that he'd had so much saved. Living at home and attending an online school had its perks. Still, he hadn't anticipated being out of work for this long, and the money had run dry ages ago.

He hung his head, ashamed. It was a feeling he knew all too well these days, an old friend, coming back to visit him again, threatening to move in permanently. "I know, you're right, I... I'm looking."

"Okay." Her eyes looked past him as she spoke, as if she didn't have the energy to choose where they landed, so she simply let her gaze fall wherever her face was pointed. "What did you find today?"

The pressure burned underneath Jackson like a flame below a pot of water. Bubbles began forming as he realized this was a pop quiz he hadn't prepared for... even though the teacher had reminded the class three times, scribbled it on the board, and asked that they write it down in their planners.

"Ummm... Well, today I haven't exactly... I'm still waiting to hear back from that company in San Diego."

Alyssa stirred his pot, its bubbles now bursting, even though it was empty of any other ingredients. "The one you applied to last month?"

He had nothing to add either, but he still tried. "Their website says the position is still open."

Even though Alyssa was adding fuel to the fire, she herself looked completely burnt out. There was no passion behind her words. Even when they'd had little fights in the past, at least she'd been passionate, feverish, emotional. He didn't think he'd miss that. Another example to tack onto his growing list of things he'd taken for granted before COVID, before the devil decided to use him as his own personal shooting target.

"That doesn't mean you can't apply for other things just in case." She sighed, for what felt like the millionth time. With how tired she looked, it was hard to believe she could stand up, let alone continue this sad attempt at an argument. She reminded him of his baby cousin, when her mom forced her to do "tummy time" and she struggled to use her neck muscles to keep her head up. "You should be doing it every day, not just once a month. That doesn't make any sense."

In a desperate attempt to stop the pot from spilling over, Jackson changed his tone completely. "You're right, I need to 'do it' every day." He winked at her, knowing they were both hyper-aware of the poor timing, but having no idea of what else he could try. "It probably has been about a month. That's not healthy for either of us." He stretched his fingers towards Alyssa's head to try to fix the knotted hair she'd run her own hands through earlier.

Rather than switching the tension from angry to sexual, all he did was hurt her as his finger got stuck in the strands.

"Ow!" She exclaimed, looking more alive than she had all night. Then, the understanding of his intention swept over her, and even more life came back to her, but like the genie and the wish, it wasn't the type of passion he'd been hoping for.

"Seriously?" She scanned him, as if to assess whether he really was serious or not. "That's the last thing that should be on your mind right now. It's the last thing on mine."

That stung, and Alyssa looked upset with herself. Even in a fight, she never wanted to hurt him. "I've been puked on by like three people today, you know? I just really need a shower."

Without asking if the conversation was over, she grabbed a towel out of the washing machine and headed towards the bathroom.

They had a system with laundry: Their dirty items went straight into the machine, and the clean ones were kept on top of the dryer. She'd had to grab from the washer directly, since neither of them had done laundry in a while. A damp, dirty towel. Jackson felt lower than even that used piece of cloth right now.

At least Alyssa *needed* the towel.

Who was this girl? She'd looked disgusted at his attempt to initiate intimacy, but she used to jump on him every chance she got. Sure, it might not have been the perfect time to make a sex joke, but Alyssa used to do that far more than him.

He remembered their date at the museum, and Alyssa calling herself "Ms. Anatomy Expert" while preaching about sexual stimulation, when all *he'd* been doing was reciting facts about the Egyptians. And that was only the first example of many. She'd never shied away from these jokes before.

Come to think of it, that wasn't the only part of Alyssa that had changed. She used to talk about surgery like it was her one true love. Not anymore. These days, she acted as if it was a toxic relationship she couldn't bring herself to leave even though it was obvious to everyone else she needed to get out.

This wasn't Alyssa. She wasn't happy. Some of it was his fault, he knew, but maybe not all of it. She was extremely overworked, and hadn't she lost someone she loved, too? Over time she'd become very close with Cathy. She was probably grieving as well. He'd never considered that until now.

The flames beneath him were settling down. As he heard the water running in the shower, he closed his eyes and imagined those droplets extinguishing all the hatred and bitterness he'd stored up since his mother passed. Once the ashes were cleared, he saw, for the first time, that he wasn't the only one hurting.

Alyssa hadn't had a chance to breathe since this whole pandemic started, his mom had known she'd been dying... It seemed they both had their own battles they'd been facing. They hadn't lied to him on purpose, perhaps their falsities were the only way they could cope. As if by convincing him they were okay, that everything would be okay, it would somehow become true. They were lying to themselves more than anything. He could understand that. Finally, he could understand.

The devil didn't have just one target, he had a whole shooting range in front of him and he was aiming at everything he could. Every*one* he could. And he had gotten Jackson's mom. But Jackson wouldn't let him win.

This didn't have to be *Blade Runner*; he refused to let those moments get washed away. If his mom had made one thing clear, it's that she wanted him to hold onto Alyssa. That's how her memory could live on. He'd been holding a grudge against his mother, against Alyssa, against everyone, but that's what this demon wanted. He wanted Jackson to give up, to let them go. Jackson had been so complacent before, crippled by his own sadness that he hadn't had the ability to fight. That was different now. He was ready to grab his sword and march into battle.

He ran to the bathroom to find Alyssa, suddenly filled with energy, but she wasn't there. *Huh, that was pretty short for a shower.*

A heat had come over him, and he thought a cold splash of water might help, but when he turned the faucet, nothing came out.

Crap. He'd known they'd been late on the electric bill in order to make rent, but he didn't know they were this late...

He changed his course and headed to their bedroom. The door was slightly ajar, and he skidded to a halt as he heard what sounded like crying coming from inside.

"No it's fine, I'm sure he went to his 'office' to cool off, and if he turned on a game he'll be in there forever." She was talking about him. But to whom? The room was a chilled quiet, waiting for the words on the other end of the phone to thaw the ice and release whatever thoughts were frozen inside.

Only Bella spit fire hot enough to evoke the reaction Alyssa provided. "Yep. I know. And maybe you were right. I love him, but—"

But?

But what? Whatever Bella was whispering in Alyssa's ear, Jackson telepathically pleaded with her to stop. He needed her to *shut up* so he could hear what the end of that sentence was going to be.

He manifested Alyssa's response. "*But* I just don't get enough time with him. *But* I miss his mother so much. *But* I don't tell him enough." He willed this to the end of her sentence, but he knew it wasn't. His telepathy hadn't worked.

"Exactly. Just remember, we *both* have to agree. That's how the promise works."

Seriously? That dumb vow they'd made basically giving Bella a say in the outcome of their relationship? Jackson knew girls could be crazy with their best friends, but this was on a whole other level. Bella was a psycho. Jackson bet she was in love with Alyssa, just like everyone else was. She probably wanted to control Alyssa, to get her to break up with every boyfriend she had. And it had worked up until this point, hadn't it?

It's not going to work this time, bitch.

Couldn't she see Alyssa loved him far more than the snobs of her past? He made her laugh... Well, he used to. He satisfied her... Well, he used to. He made her smile bigger and brighter than any other person she knew... Well... No.

No, no, no. This was all wrong.

Desire to snatch the phone away from her ear burned another hole into his already punctured torso, but the desire to hear her unedited response was like an incinerator.

"Trust me, I'm getting close. I keep thinking more and more about it every day. But it's just hard... He lost his *mom*, Bella."

The pity card. He'd take it over another condolence one.

"I know it was, but imagine if it was *your* mom, would you get over it that quickly?"

Each pause after Alyssa spoke was the top of a roller coaster for the opposite of a thrill seeker: regretting getting on the ride, horrified at what's about to come, a steel bar trapping you in agonizing anticipation, and nothing to do but wait for your downfall.

"No you're right, he should at least do that. You don't understand, he doesn't do *anything*. It's like I'm his maid - don't even start, okay, you were right about that too."

The roller coaster went up another painfully slow climb.

"Yeah. Look, I gotta go, I still have soap in my ears and I don't know how I'm gonna get it out. But I'll keep you posted. I'm gonna give him a little more time, for Cathy. But I don't know... Do you think Kayla wants to renew the lease, or can I move back in if I have to? Okay, thank you. I will. I will. Okay, love you, bye."

Knowing this was his cue, Jackson ran to his office and turned on the screen, unhappy to be perpetuating Alyssa's assumption that he'd already been in there playing games, but it was better than being caught eavesdropping on such a monumental conversation.

It didn't matter anyway, Alyssa didn't come looking for him. After thirty minutes, he found her asleep on the bed, still draped with the used towel. He marveled for the millionth time at her beautiful, beautiful face. The lips he'd fallen in love with before he'd ever touched his own to them. The same lips that hadn't met his in days. The lips that had just spoken of leaving him.

While staring at hers, his involuntarily parted and uttered, "No. You're not leaving me."

He backed out of the room, not recognizing the primal stance he was arched into. He went back to his lair, only lit by the artificial glow of his wall of computer screens, sat in his chair, and placed his fingers on the keys.

His cursor blinked in the blank bar of the search engine. Once he clicked, his previous history appeared like a frenemy ripping the t-shirt off your adolescent body at a pool party in the midst of puberty and telling you to join them in the pool. Exposed.

Easy recipes to impress girls
   Restaurants that deliver near me
   Best websites for finding jobs
   How to save a dying relationship?
   How to get over depression?
   How long does depression last?
   What to do if your girlfriend won't have sex with you?
   What happens if you don't pay rent on time?
   How to get out of debt?
   How to cut your own hair?
   Why is my girlfriend always stressed?

How to cope with stress?
How to deal with loss?
How to move on after loss of a parent?

Avoiding eye contact with this list, he began typing, adding to it, feeding it like the sun feeds a weed that should be cut.

How to stop your girlfriend from breaking up with you?

His right pinky pressed the "enter" key, and he devoured the content, ravenous as a bear after hibernation.

Meanwhile, two hundred miles away, another bear rose in his den, his screen blinking and beeping, awakening him and signaling the end of winter. When he crawled over to investigate, Clayton found the feast he'd been waiting for all this time, dreaming about. He didn't see Jackson as a bear. He saw a wounded elk, limping right in front of him, begging to be killed.

52

Clayton

For a dying animal, Jackson Halloway wasn't falling to the ground easily. He stupidly thought he could survive. Save himself. Save his relationship. Live his life in the forest.

But any life in the woods would be a half-life for Jackson, and it was only a matter of time before he realized that and came to Clayton, asking to be put out of his misery.

Clayton had sent Jackson his tester podcast, and Jackson hadn't responded at all, but he'd viewed it. And when Clayton sent a second one, the data showed Jackson had listened to it in its entirety, as well. He was interested, Clayton was certain, he just needed some time to come around. And to let Clayton's words work their way into his head. Once he'd absorbed enough of Clayton's material, he'd be awakened to how much he was missing out on. The life he could have, the life he was being offered. Until then, Clayton couldn't afford to wait around. He pulled out his to-do list.

The next three bullets were:

- *Work on updated tapes*
- *Manufacture at least a few home Set-ups for new members*
- *"How to Fake her Death" tutorial*

Ah yes, the tapes. He would need to adjust their focus and re-record a bunch of new material. Since he couldn't get back into Salvation, he had nothing better to do, so he got to work.

Honestly, he was excited to make the new tapes. He could be his true self on them. There was no longer a need to hold back, to pretend to care about those weak patients. He could rant to men like him, men who would agree, men who would one day chant his name and thank him for finally giving them a life.

Plus, the audio would be a great way to weed out the selection of potential men, just in case his database wasn't perfect. He could send the candidates some of his material to listen to before ever meeting them in person, just to see who was really serious about joining his cause. Who he could count on to be a part of the foundation of a whole new society alongside him. They would be bettering the world.

Clayton had the time of his life preaching into his recorder.

"Are you ready to finally have the type of life you deserve? For too long, others have looked at you as unworthy. They may have even poisoned your brain enough that you believed them. But not anymore.

"In Salvation, you will be nothing short of the very best version of yourself - as attractive as other people get to be just because the gods rolled a dice and decided they'd randomly be blessed. The world is unfair, but Salvation is our chance to right what we've been wronged. Here, we can be successful. Powerful. Victorious.

"The world is full of mayhem. Disorder. Anarchy. We are fed lies that only benefit other people. We work like dogs, and for what? To come home to a shitty, lonely apartment and eat SpaghettiOs from a can before we fall asleep in front of a computer screen, just to wake up and do it all over again? Enough of that. In Salvation, your life will be more. So. Much. More.

"In this new world, this better world, you will no longer be the dogs. The slaves. The welcome mat everyone else gets to wipe their feet on. You will be the leaders. The masters. The kings. Your queens will give you anything you ask of them. You won't have to worry about them saying "no." They will say "yes." To your deepest, darkest desires. Why should you be deprived, when, in Salvation, you are capable of reaching your full potential? Of stomping on anyone who has oppressed you. You don't have to be quiet anymore. Meek. Timid. Afraid to ask for what you actually want. You can be yourself. And have everything, *everything* you have ever wanted, and more."

Pleased with himself, he moved on to the second item on his list. With new users soon to join, they'd need to have Set-ups of their own. *There's no way in hell I'm housing any more people at BrightView.* This bullet was easy; he'd get Dr. Barnes to do it for him. It paid to have dirt on someone. He made the doctor do everything he didn't feel like doing himself. He made the call, and was assured that at least ten home Set-ups could be completed by next week. *Good enough for now.*

On to the next bullet. He opened his computer to a blank presentation, and began creating slides. Each slide was numbered, and described step-by-step what the men would need to do with the women. If they wanted a woman by their side, and he was sure they'd all want one, they had to follow these

362

steps, regardless of circumstance. Clayton didn't care if a man thought perhaps a woman might agree to willingly join him; it was too risky to involve anyone other than the men Clayton hand selected. No asking the women. No telling the women. Period.

1. Select your "wife." This will be your companion in Salvation. She will take care of you in any way you desire, ensuring your hard work ends the moment you clock out of work and clock in to Salvation. Your "wife" can be any woman, but it tends to be easier if the woman has limited friends/family. Remember, even if you already know and trust your future "wife," you may NOT tell her about Salvation. Doing so will result in immediate termination from the Salvation Program, and the consequences that come along with that.

2. Learn her schedule. You'll need to watch her for a period of time long enough to allow you to know key information including: When/where she is consistently alone, who would notice her absence, who is her main contact, and how soon would she be expected to be seen by someone (most likely work, if she has a job).

3. Collect a urine sample. We need this data to determine the proper supplements to place into her IV. She will be completely unharmed by the medicine, just as you will, but we wouldn't want her to become confused by remembering that she doesn't remember you, right? So we just need to make sure the happy new memories you'll be giving her won't be messed up by the pesky old ones.

4. Forge the documentation (help provided). While you're

waiting for the results of her urine sample, we will be in contact with you and work with you to get the death certificate, hospital records, and other paperwork made and printed out for your convenience.

5. Set up your Set-up. You'll need a space for your "wife" to lie down (in bed with you is ideal, so that you can share one tent), one white tent (provided), one projector (provided), two pairs of Oc X's (provided), restraints for protection (optional, provided), leg and arm compresses for her health (provided, sizes may vary), two IVs plus replacement bags (provided at the start, and refills will be provided each week along with your paycheck), one catheter for her (provided), one bedpan (provided), one cloth to ring water into her mouth, a place to dispose of the bedpan contents, and adult diapers for yourself for your allotted time in Salvation. Once we've received the sample and you've passed all the required assessments, you'll be ready to enter Salvation yourself first (directions in separate presentation).

6. Knock her out. Once you've acclimated to Salvation yourself, it's time to include your lucky gal. You've learned her schedule, so you must determine the best time to get her unconscious without anyone knowing. Remember, you'll need to get her back to your Set-up once she's out, so plan accordingly. We recommend using the syringe included in your welcome packet, so all you'll have to do is one quick poke! However, if you prefer to do it another way, be our guest.

7. Hook her up. Follow the same instructions you used in the "Logging in" document for yourself, plus read the extended pages at the bottom to learn how to insert her catheter and

secure her properly.

8. Reach out to her number one contact (help provided). You're almost there! Now that you're this close and she's been with you for an assumed several hours, it's time to inform people in her life that she will be going on a vacation. Using her cell phone, we will work with you to send messages about her spontaneous trip until it is time to declare her dead.

9. Log in with your "wife!" You've been lonely long enough. It's time you both get to live the lives you deserve. This is the moment you've been waiting for! Don't worry, a team will be waiting for her arrival, and will assist you in getting her acclimated to the system.

10. Send the documents (help provided). You've been loving your new life and don't want to give the outside world another thought, we know, but it's time to make it official. We will work with you to provide her contact(s) with the documentation and explanation of her untimely death. And that's it, she's officially yours! Everyone is safe, everyone is happy, and you're doing both yourself and your "wife" a huge favor. No matter how she may look inside the Set-up, especially over time, just remember that you are following the regular maintenance checklist and she is perfectly fine. In fact, she's amazing, and it's all because of you!

Upon finishing his work, he figured he might as well grab a snack. The sensation of eating in the real world was one he missed. The food in Salvation, while beautiful, didn't do real food justice.

Shall I go out and get something really delicious? A steak would be heaven right about now. Just as he reached for his phone to search up his options, his headset began furiously beeping. He put the headphones over his ears. "Login available. Login available. Login available." The alarm was playing on a loop. Gordon had finally come around.

53

Jackson

I *can't do this to her. She has friends. She has a job. She has a life. What am I thinking?*

"If you are questioning whether this is the right thing for the lovely lady you wish to make your wife, let me stop you right there. The life these women are currently living is an egregious one. The twenty-first century is not conducive to the type of life they truly deserve. Working themselves into the ground, splitting the bills or even covering them all themselves, and, in today's world, wearing masks as they run to the grocery store... Is this the kind of life little girls dream of? I don't think so. They don't deserve to be scared. Exhausted. Mentally and physically ill. No. That's where us men come in. They need us to take care of them. They *want* to be spoiled. Pampered. The stress graciously taken away from them. Do not be worried about the life you are quote-on-quote "taking from them." Be proud of the life you are *giving* them.

What if something goes wrong? What if she finds out? What if her memory comes back to her? I can't go through with this. She'd hate me forever.

"If you're thinking, 'Should I be worried? Is it possible something bad could happen?' let me just stop you right there! Both our team and technology are elite. The best of the best. Miles ahead of our peers, our competition. You've been selected to be a part of this team because I see potential in you. Potential perhaps you don't even acknowledge within yourself. This is not the outcast lunch table we've all been forced to grace at one point or another. You're not banished to Salvation, you were *chosen* for Salvation. Everyone here is at the top of their craft, and will ensure your safety. Since you are among the first founders, there may be minor bugs, as is custom for new programs, but nothing serious can go wrong. I promise you that.

Any question Jackson had, the podcast was able to answer. His headphones funneled in Clayton's words hour after hour, day after day, until he couldn't decipher between his own thoughts and Clayton's.

Cults recruit members through three initial steps. Social isolation. Jackson was already there before he'd even heard of Salvation. Promised rewards. The thought of the life he could have in Clayton's world was more than enticing. And phobia indoctrination. New fears were invading Jackson's head every day.

If I don't do this, I'll lose her. I'll be alone. My mom will look down on me and be disappointed.

The world gets more dangerous by the day. The pandemic. Greed. Poverty. Global warming. I can't stay here.

What if I never get an opportunity like this again and I regret not taking it for the rest of my life? What if I die a loser? A coward? All my potential would be wasted.

So should I be worried? The only thing I should be worried about is letting this chance slip through my fingers.

54

Clayton

"I've had time to reflect... to think things over," were the first words out of Gordon's mouth when Clayton logged back into Salvation. *Great*. This is exactly what Clayton predicted would happen. Gordon couldn't live without this world. No one could, once they got a taste of it. Oh how Clayton loved watching his minions come crawling back to him.

The psychologist looked miserable. Clayton would be too if he had to make his way back with his tail between his legs.

"And I just wanted to let you know that if you don't shut this down, I have no choice but to contact the authorities."

What? He couldn't possibly be serious. Did no one have a sense of loyalty anymore?

"You know I can't do that." Clayton remained cool and collected, hoping his tranquil voice and demeanor would trick his mind into calming down, too. An earthquake right now wouldn't be ideal. "I've— *we've* worked far too hard to make an irrational decision like that. Use your head, Dr. Avery."

Gordon was shaking. "I figured you'd say that. I only have one other alternative, if you're willing to negotiate."

Not a chance. "Of course. What is it you propose?"

"I need to have final approval over everything. That's the only way I could possibly feel comfortable letting this continue. No more surprises." He gulped, as if confronting Clayton was something that made him nervous. *Good.* Clayton liked it that way.

Even though the psychologist was bartering for more control, Clayton was the only one who truly held all the power around here. Which is why he felt confident enough to agree. To placate the man until he could be subdued. "Sounds good to me." Gordon's eyes grew wide with astonishment. "Here, I'll show you the latest development."

For some reason, perhaps because Gordon's trembling hands made him seem afraid of Clayton, or maybe he just didn't feel threatened by anyone anymore or value their opinions, Clayton showed Gordon the tutorial he'd created.

Even as Dr. Avery's eyes widened yet again, this time with horror, Clayton found he didn't have to work at calming his breathing anymore. He wasn't stressed. The worst had already happened. Courtney, his mother... So what if someone else had to get hurt at this point? In fact, imagining what he might have to do to the psychologist gave Clayton a sense of exhilaration. A new body to practice on. Maybe he'd get it right this time.

He'd had the needle in his hand just in case. When he saw the green-ish color Gordon's face was turning after reading the slides, he knew what had to be done. The man was never going to be okay with this. He was a problem. A threat. A cockroach that came back after being stomped on.

Clayton wondered amusedly if anyone had ever tried to *shock* a cockroach.

***

Dr. Barnes had used a lower dose this time, but it was still an experiment, and like most experiments do on their first few attempts, it failed again.

"One, two, three, four, five, six, seven, eight, nine, ten." Gordon was amazed by his hands, his face pinched in concentration. "I have ten fingers! Wow!"

Yep. Too much of a shock again. Oh well. He could stay in the bedroom with Courtney. To anyone on the outside looking in, the room was a prison cell. The inmates were on death row. It was unlikely the captives would ever leave, and definitive that they'd never have a life again.

While it had to be done, it wasn't the best solution, because now Clayton was forced to log out again, and there was no one capable of getting him back in.

He got to work scouring the internet for another psychologist, motivational speaker, or anyone else whose words could potentially be his portal into Salvation.

It was tricky, because he was picky. He could see through people's bullshit, which unfortunately meant not many people were able to actually get through to the part of his brain that they needed to in order for the entry process to work.

It was during times like this he wished he could talk to his mom again. She was always a sounding board, someone he could bounce ideas off of. She'd often come up with suggestions he would've never thought of himself.

His mind wandered away from the task as he continued thinking about Georgie. He couldn't help it. He tried to suppress her memory as often as possible in order to focus on his work, make her proud, but he wasn't perfect, and so the

372

memories flooded in.

For several minutes, he thought only of the good times. The flight simulator, her first visit to Salvation, her bragging about him in the letters to her friends.

Those letters were always his secret indulgences, his guilty pleasures. He'd sneak a peek at them after she'd fallen asleep, and bask in the light of the kind words that she never said to his face. Sometimes he thought she just made her enthusiasm about him up in order to impress the other mothers, but he always squeezed those thoughts out as soon as he caught himself thinking them. It was much more fun to believe she actually meant the boasting words.

The sentences in those letters were far kinder than the ones she'd criticized him with on a daily basis. He was always "too far behind the others," "too lazy," "too undisciplined." That's why she'd sent him to Vanessa's Ranch.

The ranch was a place where young men went to "reflect, repent, respect, and reform," as they so inaccurately phrased it. Four better-fitting words would be, "torture, brainwash, degrade, convert." When explaining it to Courtney years later, the only places Clayton could compare the ranch to were the old fashioned conversion therapy camps where sick minds used twisted methods to try to "reshape" someone's sexuality.

It was awful, and even the memories made Clayton shudder. He'd been sent there due to some bad decisions and even worse friendships he'd made when he was younger. His mother wanted to change him into a "good boy." Someone who followed orders. And it worked.

Clayton left that ranch a changed kid. But though his life had been full of bullies and gangsters and liars and traitors, Ms. Vanessa was the number one person he never wanted to see again.

Which was exactly why he decided to knock on her door.

A light bulb had lit up above Clayton's head. Cruel as she was, Ms. Vanessa was the only person who'd truly been able to influence Clayton. He listened to her. He hated her, but he respected her. She'd made sure of that. She could put him back in.

***

The ranch looked exactly how he remembered it, except for one, major detail: There were no boys.

Teenage girls marched like soldiers in training. Left, right, left-right-left. Clayton had to stifle a laugh, though, because their faces were hard and their bodies rigid... yet they were in ballet outfits. It was hard to take the teenagers seriously in their pink skirts and cream slippers.

Vanessa led the girls in their march, but she broke stride when she saw Clayton waving at her from across the field. "At ease!" she called sternly, and the girls relaxed their arms and chattered with each other quietly.

"Clayton Reeves. I never thought I'd live to see the day where you'd willingly come back to see me." She reconsidered her words for a moment. "It *is* by your own will, I assume?" she teased him. He'd never seen her be so friendly.

Out of nowhere, one of the girls slapped another across the face.

"My office. Now."

Vanessa's voice was so quiet it was almost inaudible, but it was still the most frightening sentence Clayton had heard in years. Clearly the girl thought so too, because she began apologizing

374

profusely, trying to explain what the other girl had done to provoke her.

The dictator wasn't having it. She simply lifted her finger and pointed towards her office. The girl was too terrified to argue any more, so she hung her head, saluted, and turned on her heel to head to the far building. This was the Vanessa he remembered.

She looked back to Clayton and raised an eyebrow, still expecting him to answer her question as though nothing had happened. "Um…" Clayton sputtered, trying to collect himself from the flashbacks he was having. "Yes," he pulled himself together, "I came to offer you a job."

"I already have a job." Vanessa gestured towards the group of girls, who were now silent, probably imagining the punishment in store for their friend. "One I'm good at, if you remember."

Clayton shivered again. "I can pay you double whatever you're making here at this little juvenile detention center." He immediately regretted the way he'd said it, belittling the camp, but he'd wanted to come across as confident. Powerful. No longer scared.

The woman cocked her head, letting his words sink in, rolling them over in her mind to see them from every angle. "Girls," she barked abruptly, "class is canceled today. Go take an hour of free time in your cabin. And tell Rami I'll speak to her later. I trust you'll all be on your best behavior while I'm out speaking with my old friend?"

"Yes ma'am!" the girls answered in unison as they exchanged shocked expressions. They quickly saluted, and ran back towards their bunk before Vanessa could change her mind.

"Okay," Vanessa crossed her arms and gave him her full attention, "Let's talk. What exactly did you have in mind?"

55

Vanessa

"Logging Clayton into Salvation in five, four, three two... One of the biggest atrocities in this world is wasted potential." The IV drained more liquid into Clayton's arm. His pupils dilated. It was working. Obviously it was working. Vanessa got what she wanted. Vanessa wasn't like Clayton. Vanessa didn't fail time and time again before finally getting it right.

Vanessa was a lioness, motionless in the bushes. She wasn't anything like the males: too lazy to hunt enough, too flashy to camouflage themselves effectively, too quick to rush into a kill so they missed the majority of the time, too proud to work in groups. No. Vanessa was motivated, never resting her eyes for more seconds than absolutely necessary. She was humble, allowing everyone to underestimate her so she could wander unnoticed until she was ready to pounce. She was meticulous and patient, waiting on the sidelines as she watched others fall, making the mistakes first so she could get it right when it was her turn. And she could be a team player, or at least pretend to be, until that time came. The time for her to strike, instantly killing her prey.

"You have so much potential, Clayton, and there is a place where you can unleash it. A place where everything you want can be yours. Breathe in for me, and allow yourself to float into that version of yourself. The one you long to be. The one no one can stop you from being anymore."

Vanessa rolled her eyes as she saw the consciousness slip away from the weak person that laid before her. She couldn't even bring herself to call him a man. He was still the same undisciplined, selfish, irrational boy who'd come to her camp all those summers ago. Except now, he was an undisciplined, selfish, irrational boy with a billion dollar idea. And she was going to take it from him.

It would be all too easy. Play along for as long as she needed to, pretend to be the nice "wife" Clayton wanted her to be, and all the while, learn the lay of the land. She would study Salvation. Study the men. Study the women. Study Clayton until she'd watched him enough to know when to make her move.

It was ironic, really. She'd stalk him and take him out just like he planned to teach all the men to do to their women. The teacher wasn't paying enough attention to his own lectures. She'd counted on that.

He was so excited to bring her in as a partner that he didn't consider for one second that she could be his enemy. She stifled back a laugh as she kept speaking and watched his helpless little face go limp.

He was such a sexist pig that he couldn't fathom working with a woman until he'd found her. He'd told her his entire plan, including all his screw-ups up until this point. Idiot.

He'd said she was perfect, because of the whole Courtney situation. He didn't know how to control the women, and luckily, that was her specialty. He thought he was so smart, so smooth, but he couldn't even take command over one small woman. He wouldn't get anywhere without her. That was something else she counted on.

Clayton had told Vanessa she'd be killing two of his birds with one stone: She could put him in the simulation, *and* she could be in charge of the girls. She wished other people could have seen the look on his face when he'd realized she was an integral part of his plan, like a kindergartner showing his mom his hideous finger painting. So proud of himself. Ridiculous. But he was right. She was exactly what he needed. She could be the disciplinarian he was looking for, as well as the "example" for the other women, playing the role of the obedient wife so that they'd all fall in line and follow her lead.

Vanessa knew how to get people to listen, especially girls. Girls need order. Patterns. Symmetry. Routine. That's why she made all the girls at her camp take ballet, gymnastics, synchronized swimming, and marching band. They needed repetition. Sequence. Structure. Harmony.

Her specialty was getting women to follow her beliefs by whatever means necessary: "There is honor in structure. There is elegance in repetition."

She would get them to listen. She'd solve his small problems of rebellion and confusion. That wouldn't be an issue. Like she kept saying, she could make anyone listen to her.

Even herself.

Little did Clayton know that, unlike him, Vanessa didn't need anyone else to put her into Salvation. Clayton was aware that he was full of crap. So untrustworthy he couldn't even convince himself to join his world. He had to rely on other people. Better people. *Ha.*

This was a secret Vanessa planned on keeping in the bushes with her, holding onto it patiently, only revealing it after she'd crushed his neck, paralyzing him like the pitiful antelope he was. Or like his former Salvation clientele. She couldn't choose which analogy was more fitting.

She could throw the audio tape he'd just recorded for her earlier that morning in the trash, but then he'd know she didn't need it. So she put it in, laughed for a few minutes at his amateur rantings, and then hit fast forward so it appeared she'd absorbed the whole thing. Then, she switched the tape to the one she'd recorded in secret for herself.

There were many moving parts to Vanessa's grand plan to take over the company for herself, but she didn't mind. She wasn't Clayton; she could multitask. Clayton had been too careless too many times. That's why he'd failed so much. Simple mistakes, really. Careless. But Vanessa was careful. Meticulous. Detail oriented. She wouldn't forget to log out before Clayton and switch the tapes back. She would remember to pre-record her own tapes in advance. Those tasks were easy.

There were harder tasks ahead of her. But that didn't scare her. First, she needed to earn Clayton's trust. She'd help take care of Courtney and Gordon, and he'd be grateful to her for solving his problems. Next, she'd create a program for the women. A regiment that would make them move in unison, and follow orders. She'd condition them to both fear and respect her. Two tasks that were more difficult, but she had no doubt she could handle them.

The third task, however, was the most important. Vital to her plan. If only she knew how to accomplish it.

It was only her first day logging into Salvation; she cut herself a little slack. There would be plenty of time to figure that out later. For now, she could log in and begin the first two.

She turned on the projector, and immediately noted another problem with Clayton's invention. *A pendulum? Really?* No wonder he hadn't been able to subdue his victims, especially the female ones. They needed more stimulation than that to distract their brains. An idea popped into her head, and she knew what to do with Courtney.

She settled into the sound of her own voice, feeling the cold liquid in the IV pump through her veins. Her first time logging into Salvation. Time to put her plan into action.

She walked around headquarters searching for Clayton, quite enjoying the sleek little body she'd put herself into. While she was still strong in the real world, there was no doubt she was aging, and she'd noticed the tiniest bit of lost respect as her hair grayed and her back arched. Of course, she'd whipped anyone into shape who'd ever questioned her authority, and quickly showed them that aging didn't make her weak. Still, it was fun restoring herself to her prime in this world. She was beginning to understand the attraction to this place.

"Ah, there you are, Ms. Vanessa. Wow... you look exactly like you did thirty years ago. It's frightening."

Just the introduction she was hoping for. "I barely recognized you, yourself. You really do look like a leader. It suits you." Clayton blushed at her comment. She knew she'd have to butter him up. She was initiating phase one: earn his trust. "Do you happen to have a mirror around here?"

Clayton's eyebrows moved towards the center of his face, confused, but he quickly led her into the hallway where he'd placed one of the many mirrors in this world. People liked to look at themselves here.

Vanessa stood in front of the mirror, and then gently put her hand on Clayton's arm. His new look made it much easier to play this role. She lightly tugged him into the frame with her, and looked into the mirror once more, signaling him to follow suit. Still confused, he obeyed.

"And *we*," his lips twitched as she said the word, "*We* look like a team, don't you think?" The gulp that got stuck in his throat answered her question. "And you'd better just call me Vanessa." She feigned a bashful smile. "For appearances."

Seducing Clayton wasn't necessarily one of the steps, but he clearly hadn't been touched by a woman in a long time, judging from the goosebumps she'd caught forming when her hand rested on his arm. *God, men make things too easy.*

Though she suspected he was taken by her beauty, he had more restraint than she thought, and didn't show it. Instead, he cleared his throat. "That's good. We need the women to see us as a happy couple so they'll believe they should be happy too." Practical. She forgot he was just as power hungry as she was. Success was still his number one priority.

"Now," he walked away from the mirror, this time signaling her to follow him, "Let's not waste time. I'm ready for you to earn your very generous paycheck. How are we going to do this?"

She'd been prepared for this question. He was a damsel in distress, after all. She was the strong knight who was supposed to swoop in and solve all his problems. And she would do just that. This world would be hers someday, so it worked in her favor as much as his to help him fix it.

"Okay, listen up. You have three main problems: One - the earthquakes and glitches. Two - Courtney and Gordon. Three - controlling the women, a.k.a., the main reason I'm here." She counted each of them off on her fingers as she spoke.

Clayton had to argue, as usual. "We're already working on eliminating the earthquakes. We've discovered the source of the problems, and are taking the steps to eradicate them."

Vanessa rolled her eyes, not caring if Clayton saw this time. "Sure, you're attempting, but we've seen how well your attempts have been working out for you. Face it, the earthquakes are going to keep happening."

Clayton was getting frustrated. His feathers ruffled far too often for her liking. "That's not your concern, your job is to focus on the women."

He really was stupid. "Precisely. That's why I bring it up. Because, since we both know you aren't going to completely stop the rumblings any time soon, I just wonder what the women who are supposed to feel like "everything is wonderful" are going to think when they're cooking breakfast and the whole world begins to shake."

It was apparent Clayton hadn't considered this. She didn't wait for him to admit that. "If you learn to let me speak, you'll see I have a lot to offer you. For example, I already know how to handle this problem."

Too eager to hear her idea to continue being upset, Clayton waited excitedly to hear her out. He was practically drooling, a puppy watching the stick in his owner's hand, ready for it to be thrown.

"We've already decided the women can't know what the men really do for a living - that they work for you, building the simulated world they are trapped in." Clayton gave her a "duh" expression. Of course this was true.

"So we tell them the men are doing something secret, something important, something they can't know much about." Clayton nodded, invested. "We could insinuate they're literally building a whole new world. A new community, away from the rest of civilization. It would tie up a bunch of our loose ends."

His loose ends, but she chose her words carefully.

"Don't you think the women will question why they're here, in one singular, tiny neighborhood, unable to visit family or old friends?" Vanessa knew the answer, which was yes, the women would question why they're here. More importantly, Clayton knew the answer too. And he wanted it to change.

"My job is to stop them from asking too many questions, which I can do, but I can't stop them from asking any questions at all. That's why we answer some questions for them.

We say the earthquakes are from huge power tools, tools the men are using to build this sanctuary. We say we can't tell them much, but that this is a very important project that will better the world. That's why they need to support their husbands. That's why they had to move out here. That's why everything is so secretive. Because," and this was the key, "because it's dangerous."

At last, Clayton was catching on, and he decided to chime in. "Fear is the best way to control." Vanessa pointed at him, encouraging his thought process, assuring him he was right. "If we say it's dangerous for them to stray away from their homes, they'll stay put. Safe inside this town. Their salvation."

"Exactly," Vanessa agreed. "We move headquarters far away, so they'll be sure not to find it. We move the pool to the center. Give them shopping centers, friends… little bits of freedom. We let them take a bus around town. They won't have cars, but they won't need them. They won't question us because we will let them do whatever they want… except leave. The only thing we will ask of them is that they stay in town, where it's safe. We give them the illusion of knowledge, the illusion of freedom, so they obey."

Clayton's grin dulled just a bit. "The men who have access to Salvation aren't going to want to have those jobs, though. Bus drivers, mall workers, lifeguards... it just won't work. They'll be working for me during the day anyway, and when they do get to log in... I just don't see where we'll find the people to run such operations."

Finally. Vanessa had been waiting for him to put the pieces together. "That's where people like Courtney and Gordon come in."

56

Clayton

Waiting is an enemy disguised as a mentor.

Everyone tells us that patience is a virtue, that we are better people if we learn to wait. That it teaches us something. That it's smart to be cautious. That there is some perfect plan already laid out for us, and we are just supposed to sit back and watch it unfold.

This is a lie.

Waiting allows someone else to get to the finish line first. By holding back, windows of opportunity close on us and they don't reopen. Adrenaline is lost in waiting. That's why it's easier to run and jump into a cold lake rather than wading in slowly. Wait too long, and we suddenly decide we don't want to do it anymore. We feel every inch of the cold, torturing us with its slow, agonizing climb. Anxiety builds a fortress around us, thinking it's being protective when in reality, it's paralyzing. We question our choices, turn back and see the comfort of the sun-warmed dock and wonder if it's worth it. The person who ran and jumped has already made it to the other side.

Clayton was tired of waiting for Jackson. He was losing time.

Was Jackson the best coder and candidate for his number one "tech man" that Clayton's machine had found? By a mile. But was he the only technical engineer out there? Definitely not. And he certainly wasn't the only desperate man, longing for love, broken by bad fortune. The closest second was Rick Fletcher.

Rick was fifty-six, five foot five, and about one hundred twenty pounds of leathery skin and brittle bones. He was like one of those rich men who live in Florida, lay out in the sun way too often, and look for sugar babies to spend their time with... minus the rich part.

His chosen "wife" was a twenty-two-year-old lifeguard who apparently had no family and had just moved to Miami, so she had no friends yet, though she still managed to reject Rick in the most brutal fashion.

"So I smacked her ass as she was walking past me," Rick recounted to Clayton, "and I says, 'damn, all that swimmin' really pays off!' Then she tells me not to touch her, and I says to her, I go, 'Sweetheart, you don't wear a piece of dental floss for a bathing suit if you don't want male attention,' I mean come on, it's just basic facts. These Miami beach girls are all askin' for it, and then they try and act all high and mighty when you give it to 'em. So she asks me who do I think I am and I says, 'There it is!' 'Cause she wants to get to know me, so I tell her, 'I can show ya who I am, just take me up to the lifeguard stand with ya and give me a half an hour and you'll know exactly who I am.'"

Clayton was fascinated by Rick's story. It plagued him with a flurry of emotions. He felt sorry for the man, clearly lacking social etiquette and therefore he'd likely experienced many hardships over the years, particularly with women. He felt sad for Rick, imagining him living a life on a beach where so many men were far younger and more attractive than him, with their sandy hair and surfboards and their toned stomachs that the women on the beach probably drooled over.

But Clayton also admired Rick, how he still had the confidence to go after what he wanted even after being turned down time and time again. He didn't sit around waiting. That impressed Clayton.

"So anyways, long story short, she ends up telling me I'm disgusting and that I need to get a life, and then wouldn't you believe it, I come home to a message from you!" The little man said this all as if it were fate, as if he'd won the lottery right after buying his first ticket. "The timing was crazy. And anyway, I like a girl who's a little feisty." Clayton could relate to that. All too often, he found himself missing Courtney. The challenges she presented him. The flames in her eyes. They kept things interesting.

After Rick finished his psychological evaluation, chose his avatar, and completed all of his basic training, Clayton was ready to see if the man could help him with the glitches in his world.

"Strange things happen," Clayton told him, praying Rick would know what this meant, and, more importantly, how to fix it. "It's like a video game that takes a second too long to load sometimes. Or that just jumps, glitches. For example," he explained, tired of repeating himself, hoping he wouldn't have to address this again after Rick began working, "the door will be where it's supposed to be, but then the next second, it's suddenly moved two feet to the left and a member ends up walking through the wall instead. Or, on occasion, someone bumps into the wall and stumbles backwards."

Rick's listening face was making Clayton nervous. It wasn't

an expression filled with confidence, like there would be an easy solution. He kept going, wanting the engineer to have as much information as possible. "Other times, a user will open the refrigerator to pull out a block of cheese and set it on the table, but once they've turned around to close the fridge and swiveled back, the cheese is gone, returned back into the fridge. Or the freezer, from time to time."

Clayton recounted every example he could think of, and Rick said he'd see what he could do.

Though the lack of a definite, "Yeah, I can fix that!" worried Clayton, he had to admit, Rick was amazing on the engineering end. He was able to transform a world that used to simply *look* functional into one that actually *was* functional.

Users could now officially swim in the pool. They could turn on all the lights in their houses, enter every room, and even watch TV! Clayton was able to enjoy luxuries like hot baths and car radios and even the food ended up having a bit of taste thanks to Rick. These were all factors that, for all intents and purposes, were completely unnecessary to the people living in Salvation, but Salvation wasn't about necessity. It was about having a second chance at life when the first one was crap, and Clayton wanted this life to be as realistic as possible. Even down to eating food and taking baths.

Rick was extraordinary with everything he set his mind to, apart from the glitches. He had gotten them to dull a bit, but they still happened from time to time, and Rick's only answer was that they were "inevitable." To that, Clayton sucked in a deep breath and refused to agree. Rick just couldn't deal with the fact that he wasn't the best of the best. This problem was solvable, just not by him, apparently. Clayton still needed someone better. He still needed Jackson.

57

Vanessa

While Clayton was worried about Jackson and the glitching, Vanessa had her own concerns.

Clayton didn't like many people, Vanessa knew that, but he liked her. She'd already begun earning his respect, because unlike everyone else Clayton worked with, she never came to him and dumped problems in his lap without offering solutions.

She told him that the swinging pendulum wouldn't be enough for the women of Salvation. Vanessa controlled women through routines. Dance, order, synchronization. Every part of the women needed to be fully immersed in routine at all times, including their subconscious. That's where the dancing girls came in.

Clayton's women would need patterns. Repetition. Consistency. That had always been a part of Vanessa's course, and Salvation was no different. The women would stare at the projection on the ceiling, but it wouldn't be a swinging pendulum or ticking metronome. No. It would be Courtney. Courtney, along with several other electroshocked girls.

Vanessa would choreograph the shocked girls to always be in sync. That's what Clayton's women needed to see. Over and over and over again. Happy, smiling girls, perfectly in unison. Always the same movements, the same tasks, the same answers.

Clayton wouldn't need to pay people for these menial tasks. Not when there were people who could do it for free. People who weren't capable of doing anything else. People like Courtney. Brain dead.

Courtney and other shocked girls could dance from the screen straight into the womens' minds, sending subliminal messages of symmetry and control. Courtney and other girls could work at the shopping centers, modeling outfits and encouraging the women that all is normal. All is good. Courtney and other girls could fill in the empty spaces: attending parties, hanging at the pool, talking about how great Clayton is… They could be everywhere.

Vanessa knew exactly where to find those "other girls." Her ranch was full of delinquents, and not just the teenagers who attended the summer program. Most of the girls were homeless. Girls who sold their bodies on the street. Girls who stole and got into fights and dealt drugs. Girls who would never truly be rehabilitated. They contributed nothing to society. At least in Salvation, they could be useful. They could have purpose.

Clayton was completely on board, and they transformed Salvation together. While Clayton began to interview and hire more candidates his machine had found, Vanessa worked on bringing in the background workers. Dr. Barnes teamed up with her to shock them all, erasing their memories, and training them from scratch. Their own personal slaves.

Vanessa referred to them as the "NPCs." The term is often used in video games, short for "Non-Player Characters." In games, NPCs are the random characters in the background who perform the same actions over and over again, like the lady selling jewelry at a stand or the train conductor driving in circles. The abbreviation gained such popularity that it's become well known as a metaphor for a person who cannot think for themselves, and blindly follows instructions.

Vanessa's NPCs had a few phrases and actions they could perform, but that was about it. They were incapable of thinking for themselves, or straying from their programming.

Vanessa convinced the few brain cells that were left inside their heads that working for Salvation was the best. She taught them how to dance and showed them where they were allowed to go and what they were allowed to say and they never questioned a thing.

As a bonus for Dr. Barnes, he was able to experiment with the electroconvulsive therapy. They needed it as a back-up plan. If any of the "wives" did get out of line for some reason, Dr. Barnes wanted to be able to shock them to the point of forgetting, but not forgetting so much that they became as loopy as the NPCs. He actually said he'd made progress on some of the girls from the ranch. A few of them had positive results, and could actually function like normal after just a small amount of electricity. They forgot what they were meant to forget, and that was it. Dr. Barnes was thrilled, but per Vanessa's request, after taking notes on them and the dosages that seemed to work, he would add the much larger shock.

Clayton was thrilled with her progress. He'd already been recruiting new members. Aside from Rick the engineer, he'd found a few other men who were also stellar employees. Salvation was improving little by little. Vanessa wouldn't go so far as to say they were stellar (or even decent) human beings... They were kidnapping women from coffee shops and bus stations. *Disgusting*. But they'd be easy to control when she took charge.

Besides, she was plotting a murder herself, so really she wasn't in the position to question their morality.

Clayton did express one concern. "We still don't know what to do with Gordon. He's not exactly built to be a dancer, although I suppose we could give him a new avatar..."

"We need someone to drive the bus still, don't we? His brain is pretty fried, but I think he could handle that." Clayton had no complaints, and so Vanessa trained Gordon to do one task: drive the bus in a loop.

"This is your route." She told him, seriously. This is where you go. You need to only stay here, in town, where it's safe."

"I stay here where it's safe," he repeated.

"Good," she flashed him a bright smile. "But Gordon, what if some lady asks you to go somewhere else?"

Gordon couldn't seem to comprehend this. He began to almost malfunction. "Somewhere else? I can't go anywhere else... it's not safe. I don't know how to drive anywhere else, I only know my route... I don't go anywhere else, I don't know what to do!"

The electroshock therapy was such a blessing.

"That's right, Gordon. Don't you worry, you don't need to go anywhere else. You just stick to what you know, right here, okay? You're just so good at following your route. You do such a good job driving this bus."

Gordon beamed with pride. Ah, to have such a simple mind. She was almost envious. His life would be so uncomplicated.

Clayton said his machine was nearly done scanning, and soon there would be potential new hires. Vanessa had a few more strategies she wanted to implement in her - *their* world before they officially brought members in.

"You should find some men to serve as guards. Just like my women, look for people who are a waste to the world. Bad men who are strong but incapable of making the right choices. We can have Dr. Barnes shock them and we'll train them up to watch the 'wives,' as a precaution."

Clayton jotted this suggestion down. *He'll do it.* He knew enough of these types of men. Where to find them. How to fake their deaths... if they even had anyone who would care or come looking for them. He'd helped Vanessa do the same with her NPCs.

"Also, our voices should be everywhere. I know I'll have classes with the women every day when they come for gymnastics and ballet and their other lessons, but your voice should be more prominent as well. I suggest you implement radios all around, and speak through them all. The car radio, the TV, a speaker in the kitchen... things like that."

He scrawled messy notes hastily on his paper. "Anything else?"

"Nope. I think we're almost ready. We're in the final stages now." Their relationship continued to be extremely professional, all talk about business. But Vanessa still threw in subtle bouts of flirtation every once in a while. Never a bad "plan B" to have on the back burner, should she need it. He did seem awfully excited about the idea of kissing her in front of the new members to make it seem like they really were husband and wife. He'd mentioned it three times already. He was as desperate as his clients, even if he believed he was more advanced.

"By the way, great hire with that engineer. What was his name again, Rick?" Clayton gave a proud nod. "It's wonderful to have running water and electricity. I know we don't need it here, but still. He did a good job. Let me know when you hire an architect. I'm ready for a home makeover."

He said he would, and went away to implement her suggestions. It was really happening. Salvation was coming together. People were being hired. The glitches were lessening, and hopefully once they found a better coder, the mistakes would cease completely. They were going to be rich!

Ugh, "they." She grinded her teeth together every time she had to say that word. Clayton had been useful in getting this place started, but it wouldn't be "theirs" forever. One day, this would all be hers.

Which meant that while Clayton was busy addressing the final details, Vanessa had to get to work on her third task. The most challenging item on her to-do list, but the one that would ensure her ultimate success. She had to rewrite the code. Change it, so that when men died in the simulation, they wouldn't simply "respawn" - they'd die in real life.

58

Clayton

He wasn't angry at Vanessa for giving him so much work to do. Quite the contrary, he was grateful that she'd shared her insight with him on how to make his world the best it could be.

Clearly, on his own, he'd missed some vital signs. Left cracks in the concrete base he'd poured a little too quickly. Maybe there was some merit to being patient. She'd helped him see that. She balanced him out. Dare he say, they were a good match.

As a team, and nothing more. Clayton couldn't afford to let his guard down. He had to see the big picture. He needed to focus on creating a whole world that fulfilled his desires long term, not just fulfilling them in the short term. But Vanessa was breathtaking in here. She looked nothing like Courtney, and that's what Clayton wanted most right now. To forget. To let go of his past mistakes, and see the good right in front of him. The beauty.

Which was Salvation. Not Vanessa. *Not Vanessa.* Not right now. Play the long game. Implement her suggestions, and keep hiring, and focus, and make sure it's flawless, and focus, and build a strong team, which means finding an architect, and getting Jackson Halloway to join, and focusing.

Ding ding ding, Ding ding ding. Well, this was a good start. His computer had found an architect.

Derek Thomas. Thirty-five. Married. A good-looking guy, and successful in his field... Why had the machine chosen a man like him?

One look at Derek's search history answered Clayton's question. He was, perhaps, the most desperate of anyone Clayton had seen so far. Two children lost, a wife with severe depression, gave up his job trying to take care of her, ended up throwing her in a mental hospital... This was pure gold.

Clayton sent Derek the podcast, and within two days, he'd listened to the entire series and was reaching out to Clayton wanting to pursue the next steps. After passing every phase of his testing, Clayton set up a date for the final interview, sooner rather than later.

Every time he messaged Derek, Clayton also checked his mailbox for word from Jackson, but it remained empty. This only made Clayton want Jackson more.

People always want what they can't have, don't they? That's what Salvation relied on, after all. Rick wanted the hot young lifeguard, Derek wanted to bring his children back. Usually, all people do is *want*. They wish and they hope and they pray but they never actually get a shot at the life they dream of. Clayton had built a place so magical, so extraordinary, so unthinkable that it actually granted people their wishes.

Clayton was a genie, and he'd thrown his lamp at these pathetic men, tempted them to rub it by promising to share with them the magic that lied within. He would bring all their wildest fantasies to life. And for a moment, he felt guilty, because in every genie story, the wishes are always a trick. Not what the wisher thought they would be. Not what they'd envisioned.

If someone wishes to be younger, the genie might turn them into an infant. If they wish for a million dollars to be transferred into their bank account, the genie won't tell them that it's being wired illegally and they'll be arrested the next day. If they wish for fame, the genie isn't obligated to make it positive fame… Hitler was famous, after all. And if someone wishes for the life they've always desired, one where they have a stunning wife and a giant house and flawless skin and loads of friends and a multi-course dinner prepared for them every night, Clayton doesn't mention the nightmares. Or how it feels to see a woman's eyes staring, always staring, never blinking, for hours and hours and hours with no life left inside of them. Or the smell that starts about two weeks in and never goes away. Never. No matter how hard you scrub and spray and wash and rinse and sanitize and scrub and scrub and scrub. He doesn't tell them that.

And for a moment - one, brief moment, he felt guilty about his tricks. His deception. Making the men sign a contract without understanding what it truly means. Letting them dig their own graves, and encouraging them to bring a partner and dig her grave right next to theirs.

It wasn't fair. But then he remembered being punched in the fourth grade because his clothes stunk and getting turned down by every girl he asked out because he didn't make enough money or he wasn't attractive enough or he was too weird, and the investor pulling out but not before coughing, coughing all over his mother and his mother, his mother getting taken away from him and he remembered that life isn't fair.

He was granting their wishes. No one forced them to rub the

lamp. Life would never be perfect, but he was offering them the next best thing. They could either take it or leave it. But if they decided to take it, they weren't allowed to turn back. You can't undo a wish once it's made. He guessed that's why the saying goes the way it does: "Be careful what you wish for."

And that's why Clayton was grateful for Vanessa. She taught him that sometimes it pays to be cautious. That maybe patience really is a virtue. That rushing into things is dangerous.

If only she had taught him sooner. He wished he would have reunited with her just a little bit sooner.

There he went again, wishing. He was no better than the men he was recruiting.

59

Derek

"You're sure you'll be okay on your own here?"

Bianca reassured him that she would be, but Derek still felt uneasy about leaving her. He hadn't left her side since she'd gotten home from St. Mary's. Turns out, five yellow filled in stars really can help a person make the right decision. Bianca had gone for two weeks, and come back alive again. Not vivacious, by any means, nor vibrant, but she was speaking to him now. Microwaving meals for herself. Taking showers. That was something. Not enough to stop Derek from meeting with Clayton today, but something.

He shuffled uncomfortably. "I just don't want you to forget to take your pills." Bianca stiffened at the sound of the word. She didn't like acknowledging the situation any more than he did. Talking about the pills was a reminder that she'd been to a trauma center, because she'd been through a trauma, they both had been. Bee was gone. And no matter how many times she said she'd be okay, she might never really be okay. He may not be able to save her. But he had to try. Starting with the pills. And then meeting with Clayton.

He told his wife he was going to a job interview, which wasn't really a lie. If he did decide to join Salvation for them, for *her*, he would be working for Clayton. Getting paid double what he used to make. But he didn't care about the money. He just wanted Bianca to be happy again. To forget. Clayton said he could make her forget.

Clayton had said a lot of things in the few weeks they'd been talking. A lot of it scared Derek. He'd wanted to back out on more than one occasion. He continued telling himself he was doing this for *her*. He had to think of Bianca.

"I won't," were his wife's only words, and for a second, Derek was elated by them. *She's speaking again! This is great! She's making progress! Maybe we don't need Clayton's help after all!*

Then came the bitterness. Sour over the fact that he could be thankful for two words out of an inexpressive face. They used to be madly in love. Now he was celebrating over two words? St. Mary's might have moved them an inch, but Salvation could move them a mile. A marathon. Across the whole country. The universe.

He put on his best face, so tired of pretending to be alright. "Great, well in that case, I'd better scurry! But I'm so proud of you, and I'll see you around six, okay? I love you!"

He didn't wait for her to say it back. She hadn't since the accident. But as he grabbed his water bottle and ran out the door, he thought he heard the three words echoed back to him softly. Too soft... It was probably just his imagination. He found himself zoning out a lot, drifting off to happier worlds where she loved him again. He'd be there soon.

***

400

722 Sherman Ave was not at all what he'd expected. It was the middle of the day, and yet the abandoned alleyway was still the most uninviting place he'd ever seen. Two men in hooded sweatshirts exchanged items that Derek couldn't see and didn't want to, for fear of being a witness to whatever illegal action he assumed was occurring in front of him. There was trash littering the ground, and some sort of liquid that he prayed was water even though it hadn't rained in days.

I'm doing this for Bianca. I'm doing this for Bianca.

Turns out, he wasn't meeting with Clayton at all. It was all a test, to see if he'd really show up. Alone. Unarmed. To see if he was loyal. At least, that's how Dr. Barnes explained it to him. But not in person, no, the doctor was speaking to Derek through an intercom on the wall. His voice had scared the daylights out of Derek when he'd first crept in and hesitantly glanced around.

I'm doing this for Bianca. She needs me. This isn't wrong. I'm helping her.

Dr. Barnes proceeded to ask Derek a series of questions.

"Do you understand you will be held responsible for the body of your chosen 'wife?'"

Derek was sweating. "Yes."

"Are you able to assemble one of our home Set-ups in your current residence?"

He wiped his forehead with the back of his wrist. "Yes."

"Do you consent to the Salvation Program creating her death certificate?"

Sweating. Dripping. Burning. "Yes."

"Do you agree to memorize and recite the story of her 'death' to any friends or family who may ask questions?"

Burning. Itching. Her mother. Windpipe closing. Shirt

401

suddenly too tight. Her mother thinking she was gone. Too many buttons on this shirt. "Y- yes."

"Do you pledge your allegiance to the project for at least a two-year membership? For clarification, this means you will report every day to work for The Program, and only log in for your allotted evening hours. You may not have any other jobs during this time. You may not tell anyone else about the Salvation Program, to recruit them or for any other purposes. Do you understand and agree to these terms?"

Suffocating. Her limbs would be useless after two years. Gasping for air. Choking on nothing. Her family would already believe her to be dead, two years was a guise, two years really meant forever. He'd be insane to believe he could change his mind after he started. Gasping at dirty air, stench-filled air, tainted and polluted air.

How did I get to this point? They'd made their way inside his head somehow. Convinced him this was what he wanted. But this was crazy… wasn't it?

"Mr. Thomas?"

He didn't know what to do. Salvation was the only place she could forget about what happened to Bee. To their first angel baby. To them. He couldn't give her that relief in the real world. And Salvation was the only place she would be herself again. Would love him.

I love you.

He heard the soft words again. They replayed in his mind. He squeezed his eyes shut, trying to remember. Was it really just a daydream, or had she said it to him? Maybe there was hope. Maybe she could get better. Maybe forgetting Bee wasn't the answer. He didn't want to forget her, no matter how much pain it caused him to think of her. Maybe Bianca didn't want to forget either. Maybe they could still get through this. Together.

"No." The word plowed out of his mouth like a bull when the gates are lifted. American bull riding has been called "the most dangerous eight seconds in sports," and Derek was about to find out why.

"I'm sorry, did you say 'no?'" Dr. Barnes seemed genuinely confused. Derek suspected most people who made it this far didn't tend to change their minds.

He gulped down, closing the gate, but the bull had already been released. "I... Well, I just..."

"I'm sorry to tell you, Mr. Thomas, but 'no' isn't an answer I can accept at this point." The doctor wasn't disoriented anymore. He was threatening. "Clayton is adamant about making you a part of the team. Today was simply the final formality. You'll start Monday. 8:00 sharp."

Derek tried to argue, to fight back, to tell Dr. Barnes that this was absurd, he couldn't force him to do this. The doctor retorted that he couldn't force Derek to bring Bianca in and enter Salvation, this is true, but he could force Derek to work for them. Clayton needed an architect. By whatever means necessary.

"Need I remind you, Mr. Thomas, that Clayton has already entrusted you with mounds of confidential information. And that," the doctor paused, adjusted his voice to sound even more menacing, "he knows information about you. And your wife. He wouldn't want to hurt either of you, but he *could*, is all I'm saying. He certainly could."

All at once, the doctor's evil voice didn't sound so evil anymore. It sounded sad. Sorry. "Do you understand, Mr. Thomas?"

Derek swallowed, hard. What had he gotten them into? He'd

just wanted to help Bianca, and now… now she was in more danger than before. "I understand."

"Good… good. Well then," the voice was sad. Oh so sad. "I guess we'll see you on Monday. 8:00." The intercom clicked off.

60

Vanessa

Children are fleas. Barnacles. Tapeworms. Pregnancy is like sticking your arm into a parasite's habitat and inviting it to latch on. Vanessa had never understood the fascination. Why would someone want to voluntarily allow another creature to weaken their body? To suck the life, time, and finances out of them?

Parasites are the most vile of creatures. A lion is much more kind. Lions might kill their prey, but at least they make it quick. They don't force the animal to suffer, selfishly relying on their host for weeks or years or their entire lifetime for food and warmth and safety. As if it's the host's responsibility to provide for the unwanted hitchhiker just because it was able to jump in the back of their car without them knowing.

No dog would choose to get fleas, no fish wants barnacles to spread over its scales, and no person in their right mind invites an infection from a tapeworm, but for some reason, women *try* to get pregnant. On purpose. Vanessa found it baffling.

Looking around Salvation, all she saw these days were pregnant bellies. Granted, given the unique circumstances, it wasn't exactly a decision made of sound mind or free will by these women, so they weren't to blame. The desire for children was fed to them psychologically, ever since the Salvation founders came to the unanimous decision that children were a welcome distraction to the women, and would likely be a huge help in stopping the "wives" from thinking too hard and remembering the outside world.

Clayton had discovered early on that the women needed a diversion, that too much free time led to unwanted curiosity, but the buffoon hadn't been able to find a distraction that worked. Unless you call Courtney painting in her own blood and scaring away the investors "working." He really was completely incompetent without her.

It had been Vanessa's suggestion to give the women parasites. Allow the blood suckers to inhabit their bodies and minds, leaving no room for old memories to invade. So whenever a "wife" began to question Salvation, Dr. Barnes would throw a kid in there and all was well again. *What would these men do without me?*

Technically, the women didn't even need to be pregnant at all; the "husband" could design a "baby" avatar and insert it into the game - for an extra fee, of course. However, the process typically went smoother if the women were pregnant for at least a day or two first. Made it seem more real.

If only the "wives" could be created in the same way as the babies. It sure would save the trouble of all the kidnapping and taking care of bodies. *What a nuisance.* Unfortunately, creating a suitable adult companion for the men from scratch wasn't possible.

While the men inserted IVs to dull their senses, the women's medications were much stronger. They were drugged to the point where they wouldn't realize the difference between a fake child and a real one. The men who were paying for the experience, however, would not be content with a newly created "wife." Not only were the men more cognisant of what was real, but adults were also much more difficult to replicate than children.

Kids play and ride their bikes and read bedtime stories and fall asleep and the women are content. Adults are much more complex. The men needed partners to talk to about their day. To validate their emotions. To match their flirtation and fire back banter. As of right now, that kind of intelligence couldn't be replicated without using a real, human woman as the base.

Vanessa peered over the balcony. The town, at this point, was a regular suburban utopia. There were still some glitches that needed to be addressed, but, thanks to her contributions, the world was running smoothly. No one questioned any more, and happy couples with little babies lived quiet lives in their picture perfect homes where the sun always shone gleefully upon them.

"Breathtaking, isn't it?" Clayton boasted, taking full credit for the undeniably incredible view. She didn't mind; men were much easier to overthrow when they were too busy patting themselves on the back to notice the knife about to stab them in it.

"It really is. Magnificent. Especially your house." The woman knew how to flatter Salvation's creator. He was obsessed with that immoderate mansion. It was the first request he'd asked of Derek, the architect, as soon as he'd hired him. And now, Derek was his favorite little pet, even if the man refused to actually visit Salvation for fun. He was the only one.

Clayton tilted his chin higher from her compliment. "Yes.

It's all turned out so well." Though his words were positive, they were coated in a much-too-obvious negative tone, begging Vanessa to ask him what was wrong without actually asking her to ask him. *What a sad excuse for a man.*

Still, it was in her best interest to humor him. "That's great, isn't it? Why do you seem upset?" She even added a hand-on-shoulder touch for good measure. Clayton's cheeks turned beet red before he revealed, "It's turned out a little *too* well. I'm running into the same issue I encountered once already, before you arrived: Users are unwilling to log out as much as they're supposed to."

Vanessa was well aware of his lack of control, both past and present. *He has absolutely no power here. No dominance over his so-called "subordinates." Useless.* "I heard something about that... Didn't you kill people to log them out?"

A grinch-like smile twisted its way up Clayton's face. "Yep." Then, he elaborated, "Just in the simulation, of course. Their real bodies weren't harmed. I made sure of that."

That same grinch-like smile welled up in Vanessa's chest, but she was smart enough to keep it there, not let it reach her cheeks. *Keep it hidden.* "Of course, of course." She played with her fingernails as nonchalantly as possible. "Well... sounds like you'll have to try that again. Make an example out of someone so they'll listen."

Clayton nodded, but Vanessa was too excited to pay attention to him. While he'd been busy ordering Derek to give him a bigger swimming pool and a grand piano, the lioness had been working silently behind the bushes. She'd done it. She'd re-strung the simulation's DNA. Designed it so that when a man was killed in the game, he wouldn't die *only* inside the game.

At least, she thought she had. The formula had yet to be tested.

But by the sound of it, that was going to happen very, very soon.

61

Bianca

They say Time heals all, but Bianca had learned firsthand just how misleading that saying really is.

Time is a constant. The independent variable in the equation. It doesn't change from one person to the next. Whether someone breaks up with their boyfriend or moves away from home or loses their child in a car accident, Time keeps on moving just the same. It passes equally as slowly or quickly for all of them. A minute is always a minute, an hour is always an hour, a year is always a year, regardless of who the person is or how they choose to spend it.

How they choose to spend it, though, is the dependent variable. Dependent on actions. Dependent on other people. Dependent on her.

If she would've stayed in bed, shutting out the world, wishing Time away, Time would've obliged her wishes and left her there in the process. Not healed. No better than before. And it wouldn't have cared. Time doesn't care whether you get better or not. That's not its job. It's hers.

She'd had to go to St. Mary's. She'd had to put in the work.

She'd had to eat, no matter how much she wanted to wither away. She'd had to talk to Derek even when she'd been ashamed and scared of what he would say, what *she* would say back. She'd had to stand up, move her feet and force her body forward even when the fear of walking too far ahead, walking away from the memories of Bee and forgetting her daughter's laugh and smile and touch had filled her head.

She'd gotten out of bed every day. She'd showered and dressed herself and gone to therapy and let herself cry and picked herself back up each time she'd fallen backwards. She'd done that, not Time.

Time watched her go into a depression and didn't offer a hand. Time didn't ask if she was okay or tuck her into a pile of warm blankets or kiss her on the forehead or make her bowl after bowl of French onion soup until she slowly started to get better. Derek did that. And her mother. And the children of the community. And her soccer players. And her coworkers and girlfriends and even her neighbors, but not Time. Time didn't heal her. Yet, Time was passing, and she was healing. So she understood the misconception.

She was still broken, but working on welding herself back together. She still didn't know how to live in a world without Bee, but she knew she had to try.

She couldn't fathom how Derek could still love her after all the worst sides of her had been exposed, but she saw that he did, and she was grateful for him every single second that passed because Time was constant and it would keep passing, and even if Time hadn't helped her, she owed Time everything because it kept giving her more of it than she deserved.

There was a moment, after Bee's death, when she'd screamed at Time, told it she didn't want any more of it. She challenged it to reach the number twelve and just stop, at least for her. But it never did. Thankfully, Time knew better than she did in that moment. And so, for all she hated Time, and what it had taken from her, she was finally in a place where she was happy to have more of it.

More time to look into Derek's eyes, as he sat across from her on the couch. More time to talk with him, fall more in love with him, tell him how special he was to her. Time didn't give her the chance to tell Bee she loved her as much as she'd wanted to. She wasn't going to make the same mistake with Derek.

"I love you so much, my sweet, sweet darling." She slipped her fingers through the gaps between his as she spoke. "We've been through more than we could've ever planned for, more than the 'in sickness and in health' could've prepared us for. At the most, I thought maybe one of us would catch the flu, or break an ankle playing soccer. I never imagined you'd have to see me like…. You'd have to get me through something like… I just… I'm so lucky to have you."

Derek closed his hand around hers. "My love," she still giggled internally when he called her that, just like her soccer players blushed and swung their legs when talking about the boys they had crushes on. "I would face *any* storm hand in hand with you. Any storm. You have no idea. *No* idea how happy I am that you're okay. I can't even begin to tell you…"

The way he stroked the stubble on his chin and studied the paint on the wall clued her in to just how serious he was. She knew him well enough to spot his "tells." And anyway, she didn't need physical motions to understand what he'd gone through over the last couple of years with her. To understand how it'd changed him. Made him love her even more.

"I know. You had to make so many difficult decisions." Her

husband had to arrange the burial of their six-year-old daughter without her. He'd had to consult his mother-in-law about placing his wife in a trauma center. It doesn't get more difficult than that.

Something was off about his eyes. They were withdrawn, like they had secrets they didn't want. But Bianca knew Derek. He didn't have any secrets. He'd never cheat. Or spend their money without a discussion. Heck, he wouldn't even say "yes" to a dinner invitation from their close friends without checking with her first. So why did she have the feeling he was keeping something from her?

He fed her suspicions with his response. He sort of laughed to himself and continued counting the cracks in the paint as he muttered, "You have no idea. No idea..."

After a second he seemed to realize he'd said that out loud and apologized. "It's just... There's so much more to the story than you know. And I... I'm torn because I don't want to scare you or have you look at me differently... but... I've also never kept anything from you before, and it doesn't feel right."

I'll be damned. He did have a secret.

She needed to know. "After everything I've put you through, everything we've been through together, I swear on everything I own I will never look at you with anything other than love." He didn't look convinced. "Darling, I promise." She used their virtual telepathy to send him her thoughts, begging him to see just how honest she was being.

He must have been able to sense her sincerity, because it all came pouring out of him. The secrets released like a firework - slowly at first, building up, and then *BANG!* He told her about Salvation and Clayton and what he really did for a job now and what he'd nearly done to her. How he seriously considered faking her death, knocking her out, and brainwashing her just so she could forget. So she could be better.

The room was bursting with sparks and color and overwhelming noise and she didn't know what to think. Above it all, she knew she would keep her promise. She wouldn't judge him. Not after he hadn't judged her. She owed him that much.

But *my lord*... he'd gone from never keeping a secret to the craziest most deepest secret she could have dreamt up. No, she could never have predicted something like this; it was more elaborate and unbelievable than any dream she'd conjured before.

Derek was still talking, but she'd mostly tuned him out as her brain was fighting to process this new, inconceivable information, until she heard him say, "And to think, that was even *before* we knew about the children."

Children?

Bianca was a puppy who'd just heard the word "fetch." Her back straightened, head lifted, eyes on him faster than she could snap her fingers. "Children?" She was a little embarrassed of the speed at which the word raced out of her mouth. She was surprised she hadn't drooled as she'd said it, making it somehow even more obvious that she had a one-track mind. That she still craved a family over everything, no matter how much she said she was grateful for what she had. She was lying even to herself about that.

Derek's eyebrows came together quickly, confused, probably because after all he'd admitted to, he likely envisioned a thousand responses from her, and she wouldn't put money on *this* being one of them.

"Uh... yeah." He cleared his nervous throat. "We, uh, well Vanessa really, she... Well, she came up with the idea of giving many of the women children. You know, to, uh…" He kept pausing. Ashamed. Hesitant to reveal more about this awful world. But he didn't have to be. He could just tell her. Spit it out. She wanted to know.

"To distract them." *Ah*. That's where the shame came from. Salvation really did sound like a misogynist kingdom the more she heard. But she didn't care. A misogynist kingdom with children still sounded better than her current world without them.

Until, she gasped in horror as she put together what that meant. "Wait… so he's kidnapping children?"

"No, no, not at all, it's not like that!" Derek fumbled to assure her. "No, the children are completely fake. A part of the simulation. You can design them however you like. Make the avatar look however you want, act how you want, age as fast or slow as you want… They're just a part of the 'game,' basically."

With that statement, Bianca's mind was made up.

"So… I could make Bee?"

Derek thought about it for a second, not connecting the dots, not seeing that she actually wanted this. "Yeah, sure. It'd be pretty easy. In fact—" He halted, eyes widening, finally understanding.

"She wouldn't be real, sweetheart. It's all pretend." He was urgent, trying to stop her brain from solidifying a decision that had already been sealed in cement. "Besides, you wouldn't even remember it was her. The whole reason I ended up changing my mind is because I don't want you to forget Bee. Forgetting isn't the answer. We can remember her, and get through this together, just like we have been. We can do this."

And his biggest worry was that she'd be scared of him after he told her about Salvation. He should have been worried she'd

415

convince him to join.

"Don't you see?" she insisted. "I don't have to forget." She thought back to what he'd explained to her minutes ago, to the fireworks. "Didn't you say the reason the women get more drugs than the men is because they aren't going in willingly?" She didn't wait for his answer. "But I'm *choosing* this. I wouldn't have to have my memory wiped or my thoughts scrambled. I don't need the drugs. I'll enter all on my own!"

Derek didn't look as excited as she'd hoped. "Bianca," he was stern, trying to shut her down. "The men aren't allowed to tell the women. You're not supposed to know. It's against the rules."

He might have imagined that would put an end to things, but she wasn't deterred at all.

"So I'll pretend!" She was sitting up on her knees on the couch now, his hands in hers, willing him to listen to her. "We won't tell anyone that I know!"

She swore she could see Derek's hair graying with stress as the conversation continued. He regretted telling her about this. But she didn't. She was practically foaming at the mouth. Bouncing up and down with even just the prospect of entering this world.

He slipped one hand out of hers and ran it through his newly white locks. "I suppose it is possible..." His eyes shifted back and forth as he ran through the probabilities of this plan working. "But—"

"No buts!" She stopped him before he could get started listing all the reasons she knew this was a bad idea. She didn't care about any of those. "Please," she softened her voice, turning his head gently with her hand to face her again. "The whole reason you thought about doing this the first time was for me, right?" She knew the answer was "yes." "You *will* be doing this for me.

416

I want you to do this for me. For us. *Please*. Will you do this for us?"

He pondered her words like a rich parent ponders their child's Christmas list - already accepting they'll be purchasing every single item. Spoiling their child out of love. Whether it's good for the kid or not, they can't say no.

He told her exactly what she wanted to hear. "I'll talk to Clayton tomorrow. Tell him I've changed my mind. I can't guarantee that he'll let me—"

Derek kept speaking, but Bianca was already dreaming of hugging her daughter. Recreating Bee's room to look exactly like it did, just the way she liked it. Making a new Birdie inside of Salvation for the little girl to play with.

Maybe she could even design Billy, the baby she'd never had the chance to meet. She'd drawn his face a million times in her imagination, enough to know exactly how she could create him to look in the simulat— in their new home.

Bee would get the older brother she was always meant to have. Derek would get the wife and mother he'd expected when he'd said his vows to her. She would get the life she'd always pictured. The life she deserved.

62

Jackson

Apart from being overgrown and covered in a layer of grease, Jackson's hair had a crease from where his headphones had been resting the majority of the day. He'd been listening to Clayton's podcast.

At first he'd been afraid. Afraid of Clayton's world. Afraid of hurting Alyssa. Afraid of himself and what he was capable of. But Clayton's sermons had been seeping into his brain like fire melting through iron. Iron is supposed to be immune to the flames, but if they get hot enough, and the iron is exposed long enough, fire can melt its way through the pot and burn the contents inside.

The fire convinced him he had nothing to be afraid of. It whispered into his ear, told him he was doing this *for* Alyssa. It insisted that he look at her, *really* look at her, and when he did, he saw the severity of her situation.

The bags under her eyes were a shade of purple that was so far beyond "unhealthy" he didn't know if any amount of sleep could ever restore her to her original bright, energetic state. She didn't want to do anything except sleep for the few hours she was home, if she got a few hours at all. Well, sleep and sigh at Jackson. Make him feel like he was a waste of space. Like he was pathetic for not getting a job or providing for her or pleasing her in the ways he wished he could.

But this wasn't her.

It was the exhaustion, the fire told him, *Clayton* told him. The outside influences of the sad world we live in, fueled by the biased decisions of people who think they're more important, more worthy.

But Clayton saw Jackson's potential. Because of Clayton, Jackson could give Alyssa the life he knew she longed for, even if she'd never admit it. If he accepted Clayton's offer, he could provide for her, take care of her, please her more than he ever had, even during the best parts of their relationship. He could make her happy again. Make her laugh again. And she would be free. Free to enjoy the simple pleasures of life, rather than devoting her time and energy to patients who weren't even grateful, who didn't appreciate her, who took her away from him.

I know what she wants, even if she doesn't right now. What she needs.

He'd made up his mind. He was going to do this. For Alyssa, but also for himself. He deserved to be seen. To have the life other men got to have but he never could. To feel like James Bond for once, not just watch him on TV.

And he was doing it for his mother. Their last conversation had been about Alyssa. It was so clear now. His mother had known she was sick, and she'd done everything to save Jackson and Alyssa's relationship so he would have Alyssa when his mother was gone. His mom loved Alyssa, and believed they should be together. She would approve of this, approve of

Alyssa being his wife.

It's what she would've wanted.

So, Jackson reached out to Clayton, who was much more enthusiastic about Jackson joining him than any employer had ever been before. Clayton was practically a god, the ruler of a new nation, and he was not only giving Jackson the time of day, but thanking him personally for joining his team? That would never happen in the real world. No one as powerful as Clayton had ever noticed Jackson, never appreciated his talents and grasped the impressiveness of his skills.

The real world had forced Jackson to live like a hermit crab in a shell. Tucking himself away, protecting himself from the harsh environment, blending in with the rocks around him so no one would tease him or hurt him or make him a target. But Clayton was the first person to pick him up, paint his shell, and put him on display in his very own tank. Protected. Seen. Admired. Cared for. Shown off like he was special.

Clayton let him choose his own paint, giving him freedom over the colors and design of the shell he no longer needed. The options were endless. He could thicken and color his hair, and style it in a way where it always looked effortless, like Superman with one perfect curl falling flawlessly over his forehead. He could smooth out his skin and define his muscles and whiten his teeth so they looked more sparkly than even Alyssa's Facebook boy from the hospital.

Apart from looks, he could enhance his coordination and athleticism, fill his closet with a wardrobe he'd never been able to afford, even give himself the ability to speak another language if he wanted.

No more glasses. No more unmanageable scruff. No more imperfections.

420

He scrolled and scrolled through all the options, keeping Alyssa in the back of his mind throughout the process. He wanted to be her knight in shining armor. Her Prince Charming. He looked up, stretching, and noticed the poster on his wall. *From Russia with Love.*

He would be the James Bond she'd always dreamed of. Easy. With one click of a button, he was British. Charming. Beautiful.

After all the fun stuff, it was time to meet Clayton at an address just a few hours away. He told Alyssa he had a job interview, and she was thrilled. He was finally making her happy again. And this was just the beginning. She had no idea what was in store for her.

On his way out the door, he let out a low growl as his eyes met the white paper taped to the back of it: an eviction notice. And it wasn't the first. He'd been hiding them from Alyssa, and he did the same with this one, crumpling it up and stuffing it into his pocket to discard later. She didn't need to know. He would soon be making enough money to convince the landlord to let them stay.

The notice fanned the flames that were already in his eyes, and he stalked to his car to make the long drive to the undisclosed location from his latest email.

Turns out, it was all a test designed by Clayton to see if he'd really show up. If he was loyal. He beamed to himself, proud that he'd passed. He would show Clayton just how loyal he could be. How thankful he was for this opportunity. Prove that Clayton hadn't made a mistake in choosing him.

He spoke to someone named Jeremy Barnes over an intercom to answer one final set of questions and sign the documentation.

"Do you understand you will be held responsible for the body of your chosen 'wife?'"

"Yes." He wouldn't flinch. This was all part of Clayton's test. One last trial to gauge if Jackson was scared. If he'd back out.

He wouldn't.

"Are you able to assemble one of our home Set-ups in your current residence?"

He planted his feet firmly in place. "Yes."

"Do you consent to the Salvation Program creating her death certificate?"

He stood perfectly still. They wouldn't make him nervous. He wouldn't show fear. "Yes."

"Do you agree to memorize and recite the story of her 'death' to any friends or family who may ask questions?"

He thought for a moment of Alyssa's mom. Of Bella. He hesitated, then cursed himself for letting them get to him. "Yes."

"Do you pledge your allegiance to the project for at least a two-year membership? For clarification, this means you will report every day to work for The Program, and only log in for your allotted evening hours. You may not have any other jobs during this time. You may not tell anyone else about the Salvation Program, to recruit them or for any other purposes. Do you understand and agree to these terms?"

Their fear tactics were working. He started to change his mind. Two years really meant forever, right? Why even bother with the technicality? Once he went through with this, faked her death and everything, there was no going back. He couldn't just tell Alyssa's mom, "Just kidding! She's totally alive and I faked the whole thing!"

He couldn't do this. What was he thinking? He couldn't take a daughter away from her mother. He couldn't leave Bella without a best friend.

...Why not?

Alyssa's mom only ever hurt her. She'd married a man who she'd known was bad - who she should have known would damage Alyssa, but she'd selfishly chosen to do it anyway. And then she'd let him leave.

And she always made Alyssa feel like crap. Alyssa was the most incredible person Jackson had ever known, she was a freaking *surgeon* for crying out loud, and it was never good enough for her stuck up mother. Every time Alyssa got a ninety-eight, her mother was disappointed because it wasn't a one hundred. She didn't love Alyssa. She just wanted someone to brag about in her letters to her friends so they wouldn't see that she was really just a sad, bitter, washed up, divorced old lady who could never amount to anything herself so she placed all her expectations on her daughter.

And Bella? *Please.* All Bella ever did was remind Alyssa of their stupid pinky promise, trying to convince her to leave him. She wanted Alyssa all to herself. If she'd known about Salvation, she would've knocked out Alyssa in a heartbeat and taken her there herself. Jackson was merely beating her to it. It was kill or be killed, and Jackson wasn't about to let Bella take him down.

"Yes."

"Great," Jeremy Barnes seemed relieved, almost surprised that the initiation had gone so smoothly. "Welcome to the team."

63

Alyssa

Alyssa had traveled a lot as a child.

Her mother suddenly gained an interest in seeing the world after her father left. At first Alyssa assumed the trips were for her, an unsuccessful attempt at cheering her up, filling the hole in her heart where her dad used to be.

The thing about the hole in her heart was, it wasn't a pit or a crater. Those can be filled if enough is poured into them. Her heart wasn't just dented, it was pierced all the way through. Whatever she tried to pour in simply spilled right back out the other side. It might fall into her stomach, so she could feel full for a little while. Or it may fill her lungs, making it difficult to breathe, threatening her not to try that again. Either way, the effect was always temporary, and she'd feel the air breezing through the wound again eventually.

But her mother hadn't actually been thinking of Alyssa at all. She was on some *Eat, Pray, Love* journey, and Alyssa was just more luggage she'd brought along with her.

Whenever they'd buckled their seat belts and placed their phones on airplane mode, the flight attendants always gave the same speech: Don't block the emergency exits, make sure all carry-on luggage is stowed away safely for the duration of the flight, and, in case of an emergency, always be sure to put on your own oxygen mask before you try to help anyone else put theirs on.

Alyssa hadn't given much thought to that last part. Until today.

Today, Alyssa placed an oxygen mask over her mouth and nose, secured the straps, and breathed herself back to life.

Sleeping until noon was like puffing air through an inhaler into her struggling lungs. Taking a long, finally warm shower was the equivalent of sucking in a giant gulp of salty sea air after a wave had kept her under the water a few seconds too long. Dancing around the apartment and writing in her journal and painting her nails a happy bubblegum pink were all EMTs giving her CPR until her heart started beating again, despite the hole that would always be in it.

It was her first day off since COVID, since Cathy left them, since she and Jackson started falling apart, and she spent the day breathing.

Once her lungs expanded, she saw everything more clearly. Taking time away from the chaos of the hospital and using it to find herself again opened her eyes to what that safety spiel really meant.

She hadn't been able to help Jackson, as much as she'd let herself believe she'd been trying, because she hadn't put on her own mask first. How could she possibly help him if she couldn't even help herself?

Her stomach dropped as she realized how she'd acted all these months. Angry, bitter, frustrated, irritable... just to name a few. Because, while Jackson was grieving, while he needed her to charge his depleted battery, she had been expecting him to charge hers.

How selfish had she been? Thinking of breaking up with him because he wasn't doing "enough" for her? Because he wasn't helping around the house after his *mom died?* Because he was too busy battling his depression to get a job right away?

Video games were one of the few pleasures he had left, and she'd judged him for that. Chastised him for not folding her precious clothes or preparing adequate dinners for her poor, spoiled self. How could she have been so blind? So harsh?

It's okay, she soothed herself. *I feel like myself again, which means I can begin to help him feel like himself again, too. He has a job interview today for something he called a "really exciting opportunity." An opportunity I was too selfish to care about a few hours ago...*

Stop it. Give yourself grace. Just because his problems were bigger doesn't mean you weren't dealing with your own. But life is good, ultimately. Jackson's amazing. We're going to get through this.

She felt like a whole new woman. Refreshed, rejuvenated, and optimistic about life again. Mask secured.

Jackson was, and is, the best thing that had ever happened to her. She thought about how lucky she was to have him, and how they were just about to get over this hump and be the best possible versions of themselves.

Sure her job was tough, but she got to help people. Save people. And the pay didn't hurt!

She'd barely gotten to see any of that money because, for years, every extra cent she earned was going towards student loans. Loans that were about to be paid off. Within the next year she'd be debt-free, and they'd be living a more luxurious life than they'd ever known. No more water going out, no more cold showers or dollar store mac and cheese for dinner... Well, that probably wouldn't change, because it was honestly pretty delicious.

So their monetary situation was about to improve, and so was Alyssa's work life. They'd hired more staff at the hospital, and today was just the first of the regular "at least one day a week off's" she was going to get. She'd made it through the most challenging time of her life, and with her help, Jackson would make it out of the toughest time of his, too.

She was good. She could breathe. Now she could help him. *We're really going to be okay.*

In fact, he'd already seemed better this morning. He'd even told her he was going to come home with a special surprise for her.

She pulled out her phone to FaceTime Bella. Alyssa had been avoiding her friend for a while now, afraid the truth about her relationship would be reflected back at her when she dared view the shine in Bella's eyes. But she could face her now, could tell her that Jackson was good, that they'd be okay. And it'd actually be the truth.

Alyssa dialed the number, excited to rub her good spirits in Bella's face. *See? Things are finally looking up! My life is so good. So beautiful. Jackson doesn't hold me back, he—*

A sound at the door stalled her boasting thoughts. Bella would have to wait. Jackson was home.

She skipped to open the door, feeling prettier than she had in weeks with her extra long shower, face mask, at-home-blow-out, pink mani-pedi combination. But it wasn't just the clean skin and shiny toes - it was her rediscovered positivity. Her confidence in herself, her life, and their future. The fresh air she'd finally inhaled.

She grinned from ear to ear as she opened the door. When she saw the flowers in his hand, she could've sworn her smile doubled, though that wasn't physically possible.

Beautiful flowers. Beautiful life. Beautiful boy with the beautiful smi—

He wasn't smiling.

She'd never been scared of Jackson before, but her body was screaming that something was wrong.

She opened her mouth to ask Jackson what it was, or to scream, or maybe call for help, but before any noise could escape her lips and come back with a solution or an answer or someone to save her, he pulled something sharp out of the bouquet and then the world went black.

64

Bianca

"Well I don't know, Doctor, I've just been feeling a little confused ever since I got here."

Bianca blinked her doe eyes innocently at Dr. Barnes.

He jotted some notes down on a clipboard. "That's perfectly normal. But you just remember what I said, okay? Salvation is safe, as long—"

"As long as we stay in town," she finished for him, playing the role of the dazed but obedient housewife, just like she and Derek had practiced.

Dr. Barnes looked satisfied. "Very good. And if you would like to travel somewhere, you can always—"

"Take the Salvation bus. We can go to the pool, the shopping center, the ballet studio, the grocery store, the coffee shop, the diner, the library, and... hmm... I can't seem to remember the last one."

"The theater," Dr. Barnes reminded her, even though she knew perfectly well what the last location was. Derek had explained every privilege the women were allowed to have.

She just didn't want to come off as seeming too adjusted too quickly. She prayed the doctor was oblivious to the fact that Derek hadn't given her any of the extra drugs he was supposed to put in her IV. The ones that sedate the women. The ones that make them forget. Together, they'd flushed them down the toilet.

"And if you're ever ill, or just feeling like something's not quite right, you can always call me."

Is he done yet? Bianca was anxious to go. Yes, she was nervous about messing up her character, and worried about getting caught, but there was a more pressing reason she wanted to leave.

"Thank you so much, Doctor, really. I'm excited to be here. I just wonder if, um..." she was touching each one of her fingers to her thumb, starting with the pinky, then the ring finger, the middle and pointer finger, and back again. She didn't want to come off as too anxious to see Billy and Bee... But how could she not be? "I'm just curious if my children have finished their exams yet."

The real question, beneath the secrets that weren't really secrets but she had to pretend were secrets, was: "Have the avatars my husband and I custom designed together been created in this fake world that I know is a fake world but I can't say I know is a fake world yet?"

"Indeed they have." Bianca hadn't been aware she'd been holding her breath, but then it all came rushing out of her. This was really happening. She was about to see her babies. "They're at the house with your husband now. We gave him the day off since it's your first day here, so feel free to spend it as a family. And if you have any more questions, I'm sure Derek will be able to answer them."

She thought she said thank you and maybe she opened the door and it was possible that she ran all the way home but she really couldn't say because it was all such a blur and somehow she ended up in front of the door to her new house standing there with her hand just an inch away from the doorknob bracing herself to pull it open and finally see what awaited her inside.

The turning in her stomach told her to wait. She wasn't sure if she was savoring the moment or if she was afraid of disappointment or if it was regret or a combination of all three, but as she was standing with her arm outstretched, the sound of screaming pulled her away.

There was a commotion happening just a couple houses down. She couldn't see from where she was standing, so she jogged quietly over to find out what was going on.

A man she immediately pegged as Clayton was standing over the body of another man, one she didn't recognize. There was a woman she believed to be Vanessa, judging by Derek's description, standing a few feet away, with the head of who Bianca assumed was the unknown man's "wife" nestled in her shoulder as she heaved uncontrollably. Despite the clear distress from the "wife," Vanessa seemed completely calm. *Good at handling a crisis, I guess.*

None of them had noticed Bianca yet, so she kept watching, curious as to what was wrong with the man. She didn't have to wonder long, because Clayton started speaking frantically into some sort of earpiece while pacing, and when he moved away from blocking her view of the anonymous man's body, Bianca could see clearly that the man was dead.

And Vanessa… She wasn't sure, but it looked like Vanessa… was *smiling*.

She didn't have much time to take it all in, because just then, a swarm of four men who looked like some sort of security guards or police officers raced up to the man's body, picked it up, and ran off, carrying away all of the evidence.

Two more men grabbed the "wife" tenderly by the hands and led her away. What were they going to do to her? They seemed friendly, but was it all a front? An act to get her away easily before they killed her too?

Bianca wasn't naive. Without a husband to take care of the "wife," she was nothing but a burden to them. She couldn't imagine Clayton would be willing to send someone to wherever this woman lived, or was being kept against her will, and drip water into her mouth every day like she knew Derek was doing for her. He wasn't going to waste resources cleaning her bedpan, for crying out loud.

Concern for the woman only stayed in her head briefly, because Clayton's face caught her attention. He was squeezing his eyes shut, rubbing his temples, exaggerating his breathing. It was like he was trying to calm himself down, but before she could gaze at his odd expression long enough to decipher *why*, the ground beneath her feet began to tremble.

Houses were shaking violently, and Bianca was sure she was about to die just like the man she didn't know, that she never got a chance to meet.

Her thoughts quickly shifted back to the dead man. How had he died? Derek had told her everything about Salvation, and he'd clearly said this wasn't supposed to happen. That it would never happen. That it was impossible. She had to go tell him.

And she realized, surprised, that she could, because the ground had stopped moving and the houses quit rattling. She refocused her energy back to Clayton, and saw that he was smiling, like somehow he'd stopped the earthquake, even though he hadn't done anything, as far as she could tell. His grinning face lifted to look around, assess the situation, and that's when Bianca remembered that she was supposed to be hiding, but it was too late. Clayton looked right into her eyes.

And the lamppost next to him exploded.

And the tree beside Bianca snapped in half.

And she ran.

She sprinted back to her house, needing to get away from Clayton, needing to get into some sort of shelter, needing to explain to Derek everything she'd seen.

She got to the door and she didn't hesitate this time, she yanked it open and even though she was out of breath she opened her mouth to call for her husband, to tell him about all of it, to ask him what it meant... but it wasn't Derek standing in the living room.

It was Bee.

And then none of it mattered.

Bianca scooped her daughter who wasn't really her daughter but was close enough to her daughter and she would pretend it was her daughter because it was the closest she'd ever get to her daughter into her arms and squeezed the little girl so tight she thought she might break her in half. And Derek came out and said he'd just gotten off the phone with Clayton who said he'd send pills for Bianca so she'd forget but they got flushed down the toilet just like everything else he was supposed to give her and then she saw Billy.

Billy who wasn't really Billy but she'd never gotten to meet Billy so it was even easier to pretend than it was with Bee, and she pulled him to her chest with her left arm without letting go of Bee with her right, and none of it mattered.

She'd made the right decision. She wasn't sure why Vanessa had smiled or why the lamppost exploded when Clayton noticed her watching him or what happened to the anonymous man or what they were going to do with his "wife," but she was sure she'd made the right decision.

65

Clayton

Life doesn't have to be complicated. We make it that way for some reason.

There are over eight billion people in the world, and we don't need to fall in love with any of them. At the most, we potentially need to reproduce, to continue on as a society, but that doesn't have to be complex, either. We don't need to fall hopelessly in love with someone to do that. But most of us choose to search for our one, true love. Seeking a needle in a haystack when no one told us we had to find the needle. There's no punishment if we don't. And there's no guarantee the needle hasn't already been taken by someone else, or that it was ever placed there at all.

Yet, we search. We spend years sifting through hay. We don't settle for an easy life, we want more.

No one forces us to go to college, spending thousands of dollars and years of our lives for just another possibility. Another hope with no guarantee. No assurance that it will lead to our dream job. No proof that it will pay off. There are millions of jobs which do not require any form of higher education. But we decide we aren't content with that life. It's not enough. We want more.

We read books knowing they'll make us cry and we get pets even though one day they'll die and we drink too much knowing it'll make us sick and we wear heels that will blister our feet and we ride roller coasters even if we're afraid and our stomachs will drop and we'll get to the top of the track and experience a moment of regret when it's too late and all of these actions have consequences but we bring them upon ourselves because we are always looking for something more. We get bored, and we want to believe there's always something more exciting, that "fine" is never the most we can have, that "astonishing" will always be an option.

Clayton was bored.

His world was thriving but he was bored.

He'd achieved his goals and now he was bored.

Accidentally killing someone had been a mistake that had unintentionally brought on temporary excitement, but that was over now. He'd fixed it.

He was learning to control his stress. The bodies had been taken care of. Derek's "wife" was given her pills. He had a solution for everything.

Vanessa was managing the women, so he had little concern with them anymore. Dr. Barnes was capable of handling user and "wife" needs. His security team eliminated any problems almost immediately after they happened. Ever since Jackson joined the team, glitches had been few and far between - though even Clayton's top recruit couldn't yet get rid of them completely. They had pills in case they needed them, and the electroconvulsive therapy was always a last resort option they had in their back pocket. Salvation was beginning to run smoothly.

He swiveled his chair around inside his office so he could watch his wall of monitors. He could see nearly every inch of Salvation through these cameras that no one else knew he had. The pool, the tennis court, people's driveways, the interior of their bedrooms... wherever he deemed necessary.

He turned from left to right, spending several seconds on each screen, yawning at the predictability of each location. Women moved in perfect synchronization inside Vanessa's ballet studio. A child rode his bike around the backyard of one house, and a woman was vacuuming inside another. All the men were working, getting Salvation ready for its grand opening in a couple of years. Though it would be a while before they could officially open to a larger population, better the world, and become rich in the process, they were currently on track and had a positive trajectory. This was it for the next couple of years. Mild issues to iron out, limited work left to be done, nothing new to see through the monitors.

There was one screen that piqued his interest, though, now that he watched more closely.

"Thanks for doing this, Jeremy. She was beginning to ask questions, and I know the other men have had great success with giving their 'wives' children. It'll keep her busy." Rick said this as casually as if he was talking about the weather.

"I have no doubt it'll subdue her just fine." The doctor was confident. "You're sure you don't want a baby?"

"Nah," Rick waved him off, "I don't want to risk her asking me to change a diaper or anything like that. And the crying is so annoying."

"Totally understandable," Dr. Barnes agreed, practicing his bedside manner. "Adoption it is, then. He'll be ready soon. Wait five minutes, then send her in."

Rick nodded and headed to the waiting room. Clayton was curious, so he too waited five minutes to see what would happen next.

Roberta grabbed Rick's hand and dragged him back into the office when the time was up. When she saw the boy, her face lit up and she cautiously approached him. "Hi, I'm Roberta, and if it's okay with you, I'd love to be your new mom." She looked nervously at Rick, and he nodded in assurance. "What's your name?"

"Georgie"

Someone ripped out Clayton's insides and twisted them in a knot.

They stole the breath from inside his lungs and held onto it for too many seconds before putting it back.

They placed a photo album inside his head and flipped the pages one by one, forcing him to think about his mother. To picture her face. To remember that it was his fault she was gone.

And then he broke his promise. The pledge that he would never shed another tear in this place. The drop left his eye, slid down his cheek, wet his chin, held on for a moment, and then fell.

At the exact same moment the tear dropped, a blue toy airplane appeared at the little boy's feet. Clayton's mind had always been a part of this place. His emotions caused the earthquakes and the explosions and the plane crashes, and now this.

"Is this for me?" Georgie exclaimed excitedly, picking up the plane and looking at it in awe, like it was the first thing he'd ever owned. Technically, Clayton supposed, it was.

Roberta didn't know what to say to his question, since she hadn't brought the plane at all. It had manifested from Clayton's memories. It didn't matter, though, because before she had time to come up with an answer the boy squealed, "I love it!" and wrapped his hands around her waist.

When he touched her, embraced her, flooded her with love, Roberta's face twisted into a painful expression. He couldn't be hurting her, so why did she look tortured?

The men joked about how she was a natural mother and it was a match made in Heaven but Roberta wasn't listening to them. She was staring at the boy, like he was a math equation she'd solved before but couldn't remember how she'd done it and the gears were turning in her head as she tried to recall.

And Clayton's insides twisted once again because he figured it out first. He'd seen her file before. He ran to the filing cabinet so quickly he nearly slipped. He pulled out her folder and turned to the page marked "history." And there it was. She had a son. In the real world.

This boy was supposed to be her distraction, but the opposite effect was happening. He wasn't pulling her away from her past, he was directing her straight back towards it, leading the way, full steam ahead. She was going to remember. Dr. Barnes had no idea what he'd just done. Rick was just as oblivious. But Clayton saw the pot stirring.

He saw the same look in her eyes that he'd seen in Courtney's so many times before. Roberta was a fighter. She was smart. Ambitious. Stubborn. Feisty.

And he could have told Dr. Barnes right then and there. He could have warned Rick what they'd done - that they'd awakened a beast bound to disturb their peaceful world. He could have fired Rick altogether, and kicked them both out of

Salvation. But he didn't. Because he was bored. And this was just oh so interesting.

66

Vanessa

Neuro is the term used when referring to the brain. Plasticity is the ability of an organism to adapt to its environment. Put them together, and one can conclude that neuroplasticity means the brain is constantly changing to suit the habitat we live in.

We modify. Alter. Adjust. Convert. Redesign. Reshape. Remodel. Transform.

Always. The world is always changing. Therefore, so is our brain. Which is why Clayton had needed to find Vanessa in the first place. He couldn't just use Gordon's old tapes. Once his brain adapted to them, they were no longer stimulating enough to transport his consciousness into the simulation.

It's the same reason Clayton had to constantly re-record the users' audios. The same reason he gave new speeches daily through the radios and television sets. The same reason Vanessa had to sneak out and replace the recordings Clayton had made for her with ones she'd made for herself. The same reason she had to keep choreographing new dances for the NPCs.

The "wives'" brains were continuing to adjust to the visuals projected onto the ceiling of their tents. Just like it was Clayton's job to record his speeches for the residents of Salvation, it was Vanessa's responsibility to design new dances to bring the women order. Unity.

It's why the women were mandated to attend dance class at least twice a week. And, it's why the NPCs were mandated to perform new dances as often as needed. When the women watched the NPCs move together in unison, it was a sort of hypnosis.

But hypnosis can fade. Vanessa had convinced Clayton to use the visual of dancers instead of a metronome because of the "wives'" neuroplasticity. A metronome is always the same. "Same" doesn't work on the human brain. It will eventually transform. It's inevitable. So Vanessa was tasked with keeping up with the brains of the women.

"Five, six, seven, eight!" The NPCs were pros at this point. Because of the electroconvulsive therapy, their old memories were mostly gone, so they could move forward focusing only on the tasks Vanessa gave them. No distractions. No arguments. Just obedience.

All they knew was what Vanessa taught them. They followed her orders without complaining. Without getting bored. They were simple creatures.

It was annoying to work with these half-minded people, and even more frustrating to have all of their bodies taken care of at the storage facility, but it would all be worth it once she overpowered Clayton.

His world was just as stupid as he was, but the bones of it were genius. The only decent thing he'd ever been able to contribute to society.

When Vanessa got her turn, she was going to go back to

442

those bones, that foundation, and modify it. Alter it. Adjust it. Convert it. Redesign it. Reshape it. Remodel it. Transform it.

She wouldn't waste her money or resources or especially not her valuable time keeping all these useless bodies alive. No one would need to be abducted. That was pointless and unnecessary. She could make Salvation successful without all of that. Only a *man* would think of such an idea. A man who was toxic enough to repulse most women, and who'd managed to kill or brain-damage the only two who had ever given him a chance.

And who was naive enough to believe anyone else ever would.

It was hilarious that he thought she might enjoy playing the role of his "wife." His "partner." As if he was her equal. This world would have burned to the ground without her presence, and he would've been the distracted, dimwitted fool who'd dropped the match onto the gasoline coated floor. And he thought he deserved her attention? Deserved her companionship? Deserved her love?

All she ever heard these men say was "Deserve," "Deserve," "Deserve."

It's funny, because whenever they want something, they convince themselves they *deserve* it. But whenever anything happens to them that they're not happy about, they curse their luck, and mutter about how they didn't *deserve* for it to happen. So which is it? Do you, or don't you, *deserve*?

Deserve contradicts itself. "Look at what she was wearing, she deserved it." But everyone deserves to be treated with respect, right?

The Bible says, "For all of us must appear before the judgment seat of the Messiah, so that each of us may receive what he deserves for what he has done in his body, whether good or worthless."

443

"What he deserves for what he has done *in his body*." Vanessa wondered what that meant for those of them who did things *out* of their body. In a virtual one.

67

Jackson

At what point does optimism go from being admirable to ignorant? Commendable to brainless? Praiseworthy to laughable?

Why do we always think the grass is finally going to be greener, when every time we water it, the blades only brighten for a moment before shriveling up. Brown. Lifeless.

It's good for businesses, that much is true. "Nothing's worked for me before, but I think this new product is finally the one!"

Corporations rely on optimism. Face wash brands need customers who have poor skin to keep on believing that one day someone is going to come up with a serum that works for them. Cancer treatment centers count on patients and families who don't want to listen to the odds, and think this time, *this time* this new treatment is going to cure them. And people like Clayton prey on desperate men who would give anything to find out there really was a world where they can have everything they ever wanted, what they've lost or never gotten to have, the type of life they feel they deserve.

What did I ever do to deserve this?

Jackson discarded another can of SpaghettiOs into the sink. Without his mom or Alyssa to make dinner for him, he was on his own.

Technically he could order food, but that would require using his cell phone, which he'd thrown away weeks ago. Clayton communicated with him through the console, a pager, and a special headset, and Clayton was the only person Jackson was willing to speak to when he was in the real world. Everyone else wouldn't shut up, wouldn't leave him alone, wouldn't stop reminding him of everything he'd lost, everything he'd done wrong.

They all wanted to say sorry about his mom, sorry about Alyssa. They kept calling and calling, checking on him, asking him if he was okay, trying to get him to go to therapy to talk about his feelings. They wanted his address so they could bring him goodie bags or muffins or pasta salad, "anything to help," they said, but he couldn't give them his address. No one was allowed to know about this room where he kept the body of the girl who wasn't actually dead. No one could come here.

And he could go out, but he hated leaving the apartment. Ever since enrolling in Salvation, his confidence had plummeted. Sure, he was more self-assured than he'd ever been when he was "British Jackson," "Handsome Jackson," "Perfect Jackson Inside the Simulation." But after getting used to seeing himself like that, to how nicely he was treated when he looked like that, to how good he felt in that body, he was repulsed by his real self.

He'd stopped taking care of himself a while ago. Who did he have to impress out here? He wasn't going to go out, even to the grocery store, unless he absolutely had to.

So he stayed inside, which was arguably worse. Here, he had

so many responsibilities. He had to check Alyssa's medicine levels, clean her up, give her water, wrap her limbs, and, worst of all, he had to look at her. It made him sick. It made him wonder what he'd done. He took it back. He did deserve this.

He deserved to work an unrealistically difficult job for an unbelievably tyrannical boss whose expectations were completely unreasonable. He deserved to get screamed at for not being able to get rid of all the glitches when, given the amount of data Clayton was trying to overload his program with, no coder would ever be able to eliminate, no matter how talented they were.

Clayton said Jackson was supposed to be the best at this sort of thing, and he didn't understand why Jackson couldn't just *fix* everything. But Clayton was loading too much too soon. It was like using a computer, but there were no software updates available and a hundred tabs open at once and he was still trying to play the newest game on it. It just wasn't going to happen yet. It would take time. Jackson was making progress, but Clayton didn't seem to care about that.

So he deserved to work far too many hours in a dark room staring at a computer screen, isolated from the world. His body was rotting away nearly as much as Alyssa's. The virtual world was destroying both of them in the real one.

He deserved the loneliness. His only "friends," the only people he talked to besides Alyssa, were all kidnappers. Creeps. Villains. He'd truly thought he was nothing like them, but each day, he was finding it more and more difficult not to see the resemblance.

But, whether it was admirable or ignorant, commendable or brainless, praiseworthy or laughable, he kept his optimism. He told himself he was different. Better. Alyssa really loved him.

He'd known her before; he didn't have to memorize fake stories about how they met, or what they loved about each other.

His life in the real world was miserable. It wasn't what he'd hoped for. What he'd wanted when he started all of this. But, life in Salvation was flawless. Everyone was happy there. He was happy. *Alyssa* was happy.

It was tough to believe that last part as he grimaced at her face, so white it was nearly translucent. He stroked her hair and tried to ignore the blank stare in her wide eyes. "Honey, I'm always by your side," he sang to her, his voice shaking.

Her lips were blue.

He loved her, and he'd done this to her.

Her wrists were bruised from the restraints.

He loved her, and he was killing her.

Her mouth was open but she couldn't speak.

He loved her, but he'd taken away her voice. He'd taken away her life.

No.

He'd *given* her a life. A *better* life. He closed his eyes to block out her sickly image, so he could really concentrate, really believe his own thoughts.

Yes. She was happy. He pictured last night, and the night before, and the one before that. She was smiling in every memory. She was beautiful. She had no more stress. She was excited to see him. She was laughing with her friends.

When was the last time he'd seen her laughing with friends before Salvation? He tried to remember, but quickly switched to thinking about a different memory, because he didn't like the answer. It entailed Will's perfect white teeth flashing in Alyssa's direction. Right before his mom— Yeah, it was time to think of a new memory. A happier one. Like Alyssa's first visit to

448

Salvation. The day that started it all. The beginning of their perfect life.

After her initial acclimation, Jackson had finally been allowed to see her. He'd looked at himself quickly in the bathroom of Dr. Barnes' office while he'd waited. He'd been thrilled with what he saw... and so had she.

She'd run into his arms. They'd kissed. She'd stared at his face, and he didn't look away.

He smiled, his fingers still tangled in her hair he'd just washed, as all the memories of that first day played in his mind.

Showing her their beautiful house. Joking as she prepared a four-course meal for the two of them. Slipping under the sheets afterwards. Pleasing her in every way. Introducing her as his wife. It was a glorious feeling. A prideful feeling.

"Hey Derek, come here, you've got to meet my wife, Alyssa!"

Derek had grabbed his "wife's" hand and met them in their lawn. Derek was their neighbor, and Jackson didn't know much about his "wife," but she must have been questioning things pretty badly, because she had two children, who were now hiding behind her, shy about meeting someone new.

Derek let out a long whistle of approval. Alyssa was beautiful. And she didn't even have the enhancements on. It was all her. He remembered wishing he could tell Derek that in that moment, but knowing he couldn't in front of the women.

"Nice to meet you, Alyssa! Jackson's told me a lot about you. We're so pleased you two are our neighbors. We should have dinner together this weekend! Wouldn't that be great, darling?" He'd looked over at his "wife," and upon seeing her, he'd quickly apologized. "Oh I'm sorry, I was so anxious to meet you I forgot to introduce my wife!"

The woman had stuck out her hand, beaming at Alyssa. Alyssa

had shaken it, beaming right back at her. Jackson should've known right there and then that the two of them would end up being best friends.

"Hey, I'm Alyssa." She'd looked so fresh. So carefree. So optimistic.

"Hi," her soon-to-be companion greeted her, "I'm Birdie."

THE END

Epilogue

In a sea of black, his darkness stands apart from it all. Like he swallowed a bottle of ink when everyone else downed a raspberry martini.

Everybody assumes it's because he's at his girlfriend's funeral. Makes sense, right? "Oh, poor little Jackie, just lost the love of his life, of course he looks dark. He's probably completely miserable. Poor thing."

God. If there was a font that conveyed how much I was rolling my eyes, y'all'd be reading it right now.

I've seen misery. I've seen it banging on the glass behind my best friend's tired eyes, trapped in there, fighting to get out, ever since she she started dating that spoiled, low life, good for nothing piece of—

Anyway, it doesn't matter how I feel about him. This journal isn't supposed to be biased. This is my detective notebook, and it will be used to display the facts. The cold, hard *facts*. The evidence that will be used to put Jackson Alexander Halloway - that's his full name, by the way - in prison for a long, long time.

So let me get back to the facts. Today is March 22, 2021, my name is Isabella Leyra Chen, and I am attending the funeral of Alyssa Gloria Hart.

I am wearing a super cute Ralph Lauren black knit sweater, a tight but modest floor length black skirt, and some black, platform loafers. All black suits me; I look amazing. And I'm single, so if there happens to be a hot police officer reading this, call me. My info is written on the envelope I'm including all of my notes in.

Oh sorry, I should probably explain. I'm not just crazy insensitive. I wouldn't normally be joking (well... half joking) about flirting with you guys while I'm sitting in a pew with my best friend's ashes twenty feet away from me. I'm only acting like this because I don't believe it for one second. *He's lying.* And if you could see the look on his face right now, the darkness, you wouldn't believe him either.

It's not misery. It's not grief. It's not loss. Ink that black only gets swallowed for one reason: guilt. Guilty, guilty, guilty. Jackson Halloway is GUILTY. He's done something to her. I don't know what, but he's done something.

How convenient that they happened to go on a spontaneous vacation right before her "death," and to some foreign country she's never talked about wanting to visit, where they buried the body without even asking her family. Alyssa doesn't go on vacations, she hasn't since she was a kid. And don't go chalking it up to "young love," either. Like she's the type of girl who would get a boyfriend and suddenly want to see the world. That's not her. Plus, even if she wanted to, she doesn't get that kind of time off.

And she didn't tell anyone at work, either. Didn't even *try* to request vacation time - again, she wouldn't have gotten it... but she didn't. Even. Try. Pretty irresponsible for a straight-A med student turned surgeon who's never once called out without following the proper precautions, and even then, only if it was an emergency. I've asked Susan Able, Kenneth Hirsch, Christian Loyacano, and William Cooper. They all work at the hospital, and are Alyssa's closest friends there. She didn't say a peep about a trip. And more importantly, she didn't tell me.

Do you honestly think she wouldn't have told her best friend in the whole world every detail of her supposed out of country vacation? Weird, right? And you don't know Alyssa like I do, but she tells me everything. We talk basically every day. Well... Okay, lately, we haven't been. But do you know why? It's because she was about to break up with Jackson.

That's right. It's getting juicy now, huh? Isn't that what you detective guys call, um, I don't know... MOTIVE? Yeah, they were in a really bad place. *Really* bad. Do you wanna know the last phone call she made to me? I'll tell you exactly what happened.

I said: I know it's hard, but I think it's finally time. You have to end it.

She said: Trust me, I'm getting close. I keep thinking more and more about it every day. But it's just hard... He lost his *mom*, Bella.

I said: I'm not denying that's rough, but that was months and months ago.

She said: I know it was, but imagine if it was *your* mom, would you get over it that quickly?

I said: No, of course not. I'm not saying he has to be over it. But he has to contribute in some kind of way. I mean, even if he doesn't go back full time, isn't his job flexible? He needs to help with utilities, at the bare minimum. Like, come on.

She said: No you're right, he should at least do that. You don't understand, he doesn't do *anything*. It's like I'm his maid - don't even start, okay, you were right about that too.

I said: Remember our pinky promise? You said if we both decided he was bad news, you'd end it. I know you're attached, but I've decided. And I think you have, too. You just don't want to admit it to yourself. You need to break up with him, and you know it. He's holding you back.

She said: Yeah. Look, I gotta go, I still have soap in my ears and I don't know how I'm gonna get it out. But I'll keep you posted. I'm gonna give him a little more time, for Cathy. But I don't know... Do you think Kayla wants to renew the lease, or can I move back in if I have to?

Then I told her she could definitely move back in, she thanked me, and that was the last time I talked to her.

She was asking if my roommate was going to renew the lease. Don't you *see*? She was done with him. I knew it, she knew it, and Jackson knew it.

MOTIVE.

I'm watching him right now. He didn't even shed a tear during his speech. What kind of psychopath doesn't cry at his girlfriend's funeral? He kept glaring at me, and Alyssa's mom. He's never liked us.

As a matter of fact, the only people he did like ended up "dead." Alyssa said she saw his mom's body at her funeral, I guess it was an open casket, but I wouldn't be surprised if he did something to her, too. Do you know he was the last person to visit her at the hospital just hours before she died? And he was still at the hospital when she passed. Apparently he was bringing coffee to Alyssa, but in all the time they'd dated, he'd *never* done that. Ever.

They're singing now so I'll end these notes here. But I will keep up my investigation, and report back. Until then, I just have one more vital piece of information for you:

Jackson Halloway is lazy. If you've been digging through his life, and I hope you have been, you'll have discovered that for yourselves already. Lazy. Unmotivated. Incompetent. A lazy person couldn't have covered this all up. There were documents. I'm sitting at a real funeral home. Everyone is convinced. That kind of convincing takes a lot of skill, and a lot of work. I'm telling you, there's no way he did this alone.

And P.S., if you're wondering where to start - I'd start with his computer.

About the Author

When Kally Hallett graduated *summa cum laude* from SUNY New Paltz with a degree in English education and a teaching certificate, she assumed she'd be teaching kids how to write, not penning a novel herself! But she's always loved reading and throwing herself into stories, so she's thrilled to be on the other side. In fact, she's so enamored with fantasy and storytelling that she moved from her hometown in Pennsylvania all the way to sunny Florida to work at Walt Disney World and Universal Orlando Resort for several years before settling down just a bit further south in Sebastian, where she devours fantasy series, listens to Taylor Swift on repeat, and posts bookish content for her cherished little online community.

Made in United States
Orlando, FL
30 November 2023

39807202R10278